W9-CRM-856

c. 1

Salter, James
   Light years.

WITHDRAWN

Light Years

JAMES SALTER

Light Years

RANDOM HOUSE NEW YORK

Copyright © 1975 by James Salter
All rights reserved under International and Pan-American
Copyright Conventions. Published in the United States by
Random House, Inc., New York, and simultaneously in Canada
by Random House of Canada Limited, Toronto.

Library of Congress Cataloging in Publication Data

Salter, James.
    Light years.

    I. Title.
PZ4.S177Li3   [PS3569.A4622]   813'.5'4   74-29594
ISBN 0-394-49433-4

Manufactured in the United States of America

2 3 4 5 6 7 8 9

First Edition

Light Years

I

WE DASH THE BLACK RIVER, ITS flats smooth as stone. Not a ship, not a dinghy, not one cry of white. The water lies broken, cracked from the wind. This great estuary is wide, endless. The river is brackish, blue with the cold. It passes beneath us blurring. The sea birds hang above it, they wheel, disappear. We flash the wide river, a dream of the past. The deeps fall behind, the bottom is paling the surface, we rush by the shallows, boats beached for winter, desolate piers. And on wings like the gulls, soar up, turn, look back.

The day is white as paper. The windows are chilled. The quarries lie empty, the silver mine drowned. The Hudson is vast here, vast and unmoving. A dark country, a country of sturgeon and carp. In the fall it was silver with shad. The geese flew overhead in their long, shifting V's. The tide flows in from the sea.

The Indians sought, they say, a river that "ran both ways." Here they found it. The salt wedge penetrates as far in as fifty miles; sometimes it reaches Poughkeepsie. There were huge beds of oysters here, seals in the harbor, in the woods inexhaustible game. This great glacial cut with its nuptial bays, the coves of wild celery and rice, this majestic river. The birds, like punctuation, are crossing in level flight. They seem to approach slowly, accelerate, pass overhead like arrows. The sky has no color. A feeling of rain.

All this was Dutch. Then, like so much else, it was English. The river is a reflection. It bears only silence, a glittering cold. The trees are naked. The eels sleep. The channel is deep enough for ocean liners; they could, if they wished, astonish the inner towns. There are turtles and crabs in the marshes, herons, Bonaparte gulls. The sewage pours from the cities further up. The river is filthy, but cleanses itself. The fish are numbed; they drift with the tide.

Along the banks there are houses of stone, no longer fashionable, and wooden houses, drafty and bare. There are still estates that exist, remnants of the great land parcels of the past. Near the water, a large Victorian, the brick painted white, trees high above it, a walled garden, a decaying greenhouse with ironwork along the roof. A house by the river, too low for the afternoon sun. It was flooded instead with the light of morning, with the eastern light. It was in glory at noon. There are spots where the paint has turned dark, bare spots. The gravel paths are dissolving; birds nest in the sheds.

We strolled in the garden, eating the small, bitter apples. The trees were dry and gnarled. The lights in the kitchen were on.

A car comes up the driveway, back from the city. The driver goes inside, only for a moment until he's heard the news: the pony has gotten loose.

4

He is furious. "Where is she? Who left the door unlatched?"

"Oh God, Viri. I don't know."

In a room with many plants, a kind of solarium, there is a lizard, a brown snake, a box turtle asleep. The entry step is deep, the turtle cannot leave. He sleeps on the gravel, his feet drawn up close. His nails are the color of ivory, they curl, they are long. The snake sleeps, the lizard sleeps.

Viri has his coat collar up and is trudging uphill. "Ursula!" he calls. He whistles.

The light has gone. The grass is dry; it creaks underfoot. There was no sun all day. Calling the pony's name, he advances toward the far corners, the road, the adjoining fields. A stillness everywhere. It begins to rain. He sees the one-eyed dog that belongs to a neighbor, a kind of husky, his muzzle gray. The eye is closed completely, sealed, covered with fur so long ago was it lost, as if it never existed.

"Ursula!" he cries.

"She's here," his wife says when he returns.

The pony is near the kitchen door, tranquil, dark, eating an apple. He touches her lips. She bites him absent-mindedly on the wrist. Her eyes are black, lustrous, with the long, crazy lashes of a drunken woman. Her coat is thick, her breath very sweet.

"Ursula," he says. Her ears turn slightly, then forget. "Where have you been? Who unlocked your stall?"

She has no interest in him.

"Have you learned to do that?" He touches an ear; it is warm, strong as a shoe. He leads her to the shed, whose door is ajar. Outside the kitchen he stamps dirt from his shoes.

The lights are on everywhere: a vast, illuminated house. Dead flies the size of beans lie behind the velvet curtains, the wallpaper has corner bulges, the window glass distorts. It is an aviary they live in, a honeycomb. The roofs are thick slate, the rooms are like shops. It gives off no sound, this house; in the darkness it is like a ship. Within, if one listens, there is everything: water, faint voices, the slow, measured rending of grain.

In the principal bath, with its stains, sponges, soaps the color of tea, books, water-curled copies of *Vogue*, he steams in peace. The water is above his knees; it penetrates to the bone. There is carpeting on the floor, a basket of smooth stones, an empty glass of the deepest blue.

"Papa," they call through the door.

"Yes." He is reading the *Times*.

"Where was Ursula?"

"Ursula?"

"Where was she?"

"I don't know," he says. "She went out for a walk."

They wait for something further. He is a storyteller, a man of wonders. They listen for sounds, expecting the door to open.

"But where was she?"

"Her legs were wet," he announces.

"Her legs?"

"I think she was swimming."

"No, Daddy, really."

"She was trying to get the onions on the bottom."

"There are no onions there."

"Oh, yes."

"There are?"

"That's where they grow."

They explain it to each other outside the door. It's true, they decide. They wait for him, two little girls squatting like beggars.

"Papa, come out," they say. "We want to talk to you."

He puts aside the paper and sinks one last time into the embrace of the bath.

"Papa?"

"Yes."

"Are you coming out?"

The pony fascinates them. It frightens them. They are ready to run if it makes an unexpected sound. Patient, silent, it stands

6

in its stall; a grazing animal, it eats for hours. Its muzzle has a nimbus of fine hair, its teeth are browned.

"Their teeth never stop growing," the man who sold her to them said. He was a drunkard, his clothes were torn. "They keep growing out and getting wore down."

"What would happen if she didn't eat?"

"If she didn't eat?"

"What would happen to her teeth?"

"Make sure she eats," he said.

They often watch her; they listen to her jaws. This mythical beast, fragrant in the darkness, is greater than they are, stronger, more clever. They long to approach her, to win her love.

2

IT WAS THE AUTUMN OF 1958. Their children were seven and five. On the river, the color of slate, the light poured down. A soft light, God's idleness. In the distance the new bridge gleamed like a statement, like a line in a letter which makes one stop.

Nedra was working in the kitchen, her rings set aside. She was tall, preoccupied; her neck was bare. When she paused to read a recipe, her head bent, she was stunning in her concentration, her air of obedience. She wore her wrist watch, her best shoes. Beneath the apron, she was dressed for the evening. People were coming for dinner.

She had trimmed the stems of flowers spread on the wood of the counter and begun to arrange them. Before her were scissors, paper-thin boxes of cheese, French knives. On her shoulders there was perfume. I am going to describe her life from the inside outward, from its core, the house as well, rooms

in which life was gathered, rooms in the morning sunlight, the
floors spread with Oriental rugs that had been her mother-in-
law's, apricot, rouge and tan, rugs which though worn seemed
to drink the sun, to collect its warmth; books, potpourris,
cushions in colors of Matisse, objects glistening like evidence,
many of which might, had they been possessed by ancient
peoples, have been placed in tombs for another life: clear
crystal dice, pieces of staghorn, amber beads, boxes, sculptures,
wooden balls, magazines in which were photographs of women
to whom she compared herself.

Who cleans this large house, who scrubs the floors? She does
everything, this woman, she does nothing. She is dressed in her
oat-colored sweater, slim as a pike, her long hair fastened, the
fire crackling. Her real concern is the heart of existence: meals,
bed linen, clothing. The rest means nothing; it is managed
somehow. She has a wide mouth, the mouth of an actress,
thrilling, bright. Dark smudges in her armpits, mint on her
breath. Her nature is extravagant. She buys on impulse, she
visits Bendel's as she would a friend's, gathering up five or six
dresses and entering a booth, not bothering to draw the curtain
fully, a glimpse of her undressing, lean arms, lean trunk, bikini
underpants. Yes, she scrubs floors, collects dirty clothes. She is
twenty-eight. Her dreams still cling to her, adorn her; she is
confident, composed, she is related to long-necked creatures,
ruminants, abandoned saints. She is careful, hard to approach.
Her life is concealed. It is through the smoke and conversation
of many dinners that one sees her: country dinners, dinners at
the Russian Tea Room, the Café Chauveron with Viri's clients, the St. Regis, the Minotaur.

Guests were driving from the city, Peter Daro and his wife.

"What time are they coming?"

"About seven," Viri said.

"Have you opened the wine?"

"Not yet."

The water was running, her hands were wet.

8

"Here, take this tray," she said. "The children want to eat by the fire. Tell them a story."

She stood for a moment surveying her preparations. She glanced at her watch.

The Daros arrived in darkness. The doors of their car slammed faintly. A few moments later they appeared at the entrance, their faces bright.

"Here's a small gift," Peter said.

"Viri, Peter's brought wine."

"Let me take your coats."

The evening was cold. In the rooms, the feel of autumn.

"That's a beautiful drive," Peter said, smoothing his clothes. "I love to take that drive. As soon as you cross the bridge, you're in trees, in darkness, the city is gone."

"It's almost primeval," Catherine said.

"And you're on your way to the beautiful house of the Berlands." He smiled. What confidence, what success there is in a man's face at thirty.

"You look wonderful, both of you," Viri told them.

"Catherine really loves this house."

"So do I." Nedra smiled.

November evening, immemorial, clear. Smoked brook trout, mutton, an endive salad, a Margaux open on the sideboard. The dinner was served beneath a print of Chagall, the mermaid over the bay of Nice. The signature was probably false, but as Peter had said before, what difference did it make, it was as good as Chagall's own, perhaps even better, with just the right degree of carelessness. And the poster, after all, was an issue of thousands, this angel afloat in pure night, the great majority of them not even distinguished by a signature of any kind, however fraudulent.

"Do you like trout?" Nedra asked, holding the dish.

"I don't know which I like more, catching or eating them."

"Do you really know how to catch them?"

"There are times I've wondered," he said. He was helping

9

himself generously. "You know, I've fished everywhere. The trout fisherman is a very special fellow, solitary, perverse. Nedra, this is delicious."

He had hair that was thinning, and a smooth, full face, the face of an heir, of someone who works in the trust department of a bank. He spent his days on his feet, however, fishing for Gauloises from a crumpled package. He had a gallery.

"That's how I won Catherine," he said. "I took her fishing. Actually, I took her reading; she sat on the bank with a book while I fished for trout. Did I ever tell you the story about fishing in England? I went to a little river, perfect. It wasn't the Test, that's the famous one presided over for so many years by a man named Lunn. Marvelous old man, typically English. There's a wonderful photograph of him with tweezers, sorting out insects. He's a legend.

"This was near an inn, one of the oldest in England. It's called the Old Bell. I came to this absolutely beautiful spot, and there were two men sitting on the bank, not too happy to have someone else appear, but of course, being English, they acted as if they hadn't even seen me."

"Peter, pardon me," Nedra said. "Have some more."

He served himself.

"Anyway, I said, 'How is it?' 'Lovely day,' one of them said. 'I mean, how is the fishing?' Long silence. Finally one of them said, 'Trout here.' More silence. 'One over by that rock,' he said. 'Really?' 'I saw him about an hour ago,' he said. Long silence again. 'Big bugger, too.' "

"Did you catch it?" she asked.

"Oh, no. This was a trout they knew. You know how it is; you've been to England."

"I've never been anywhere."

"Come on."

"But I've *done* everything," she said. "That's more important." A wide smile over her wineglass. "Oh, Viri," she said, "the wine is marvelous."

"It is good, isn't it? You know, there are some small shops —it's surprising—where you can get quite good wines, and not expensively."

"Where did you get this?" Peter asked.

"Well, you know Fifty-sixth Street . . ."

"Next to Carnegie Hall."

"That's it."

"On the corner there."

"They have some very good wines."

"Yes, I know. Who is the salesman again? There's one particular salesman . . ."

"Yes, he's bald."

"It's not only that he knows wines; he knows the poetry of them."

"He's terrific. His name is Jack."

"That's right," Peter said. "Nice man."

"Viri, tell that conversation you overheard," Nedra said.

"That wasn't in there."

"I know."

"It was in the bookstore."

"Come on, Viri," she said.

"It's just something I overheard," he explained. "I was looking for a book, and there were these two men. One said to the other," his imitation was lisping and perfect, " 'Sartre was right, you know.'

" 'Oh, yeah?' " He imitated the other. " 'About what?'

" 'Genet's a saint,' he said. 'The man's a *saint*.' "

Nedra laughed. She had a rich, naked laugh. "You do that so well," she told him.

"No," he protested vaguely.

"You do it perfectly," she said.

Country dinners, the table dense with glasses, flowers, all the food one can eat, dinners ending in tobacco smoke, a feeling of ease. Leisurely dinners. The conversation never lapses. Their life is special, devout, they prefer to spend time with their children, they have only a few friends.

"You know, I'm addicted to a number of things," Peter began.

"Such as?" Nedra said.

"Well, the lives of painters," he said. "I love to read them." He thought for a moment. "Women who drink."

"Really?"

"Irish women. I'm very fond of them."

"Do they drink?"

"Drink? All Irish drink. I've been to dinners with Catherine where great ladies of Ireland have pitched forward into their plates, dead drunk."

"Peter, I don't believe it."

"The butlers ignore them," he said. "It's known as the weakness. The Countess of—who was it, darling? The one we had such trouble with—drunk at ten in the morning. Rather a dark lady, suspiciously dark. A number of them are like that."

"What do you mean, dark complexion?"

"Black."

"How is that?" Nedra asked.

"Well, as a friend of mine would say, it's because the count has a big cock."

"You do know a lot about Ireland."

"I'd like to live there," Peter said.

A slight pause. "What do you like best of all?" she said.

"Best of all? Are you serious? I would rather spend a day fishing than anything in the world."

"I don't like getting up so early," Nedra said.

"You don't have to get up early."

"I thought you did."

"I promise you, no." ,

The bottles of wine were finished. The color of their emptiness was the color in cathedral naves.

"You have to wear boots and all that," she said.

12

"That's only for trout."

"They're always filling with water and drowning people."

"Occasionally," he said. "You don't know what you're missing."

She reached in back of her head, as if not listening, unfastened her hair and shook it behind her.

"I have a marvelous shampoo," she announced. "It comes from Sweden. I get it at Bonwit Teller's. It's really grand."

She was feeling the wine, the soft light. Her work was finished. The coffee and Grand Marnier she left to Viri.

They sat on the couches near the fire. Nedra went to the phonograph. "Listen to this," she said. "I'll tell you when it comes."

A record began of Greek songs. "It's the next one," she explained. They waited. The passionate, wailing music beat against them. "Listen. It's a song about a girl whose father wants her to marry one of her nice suitors . . ."

She moved her hips. She smiled. She slipped off her shoes and sat with her legs drawn up beneath her.

". . . but she doesn't want to. She wants to marry the town drunk because he will make marvelous love to her every night."

Peter watched her. There were moments when it seemed she revealed everything. In her chin was an indentation, clear, round as a shot. A mark of intelligence, of nakedness, which she wore like a jewel. He tried to imagine scenes that went on in this house, but was hindered by her laughter. It was a disclaimer, a garment she could leave behind, like empty stockings, like a bather's robe on the beach.

They sat in the soft cushions talking until midnight. Nedra drank freely, holding out her glass to have it refilled. She was carrying on a separate conversation with Peter, as if the two of them were closest, as if she understood him utterly. All the rooms and closures here were hers, the spoons, the fabrics, the floor beneath one's feet. It was her province, her serai where she could walk barelegged, where she was free to sleep, her

13

arms naked, her hair strewn about her. When she said good night her face seemed already washed, as if in preparation. The wine had made her sleepy.

"The next time you marry," Catherine said as she drove home with her husband, "you should marry someone like her."

"What do you mean by that?"

"Don't be frightened. I just mean it's obvious you'd like to go through all that . . ."

"Catherine, don't be foolish."

". . . and I think you should."

"She's a very generous woman, that's all."

"Generous?"

"I'm using it in the sense of abundant, rich."

"She's the most selfish woman on earth."

3

HE WAS A JEW, THE MOST ELEGANT Jew, the most romantic, a hint of weariness in his features, the intelligent features everyone envied, his hair dry, his clothes oddly threadbare—that is to say, not overly cared for, a button missing, the edge of a cuff stained, his breath faintly bad like the breath of an uncle who is no longer well. He was small. He had soft hands, and no sense of money, almost none at all. He was an albino in that, a freak. A Jew without money is like a dog without teeth. The urgency of it, yes, he often knew that but its presence was all accident, like rain, it came or it did not. He was innocent of any real instinct.

His friends were Arnaud, Peter, Larry Vern. All friends are friends in a different way. Arnaud was his closest friend; Peter, his oldest.

14

He lingered before the counter, his eye passing over colored bolts of cloth.

"Have we made shirts for you before, sir?" a voice asked, an assured voice, immensely wise.

"Are you Mr. . . .?"

"Conrad."

"Mr. Daro gave me your name," Viri said.

"How is Mr. Daro?"

"He recommended you very highly."

The salesman nodded. He smiled at Viri, the smile of a colleague.

Three in the afternoon. The tables in the restaurants have emptied, the day has begun to fade. A few women loitering among the distant displays of the store, otherwise everything quiet. Conrad had a slight accent, difficult at first to place. It seemed not so much alien as a little special, a mark of perfect manners. It was, in fact, Viennese. There was a profound wisdom in it, the wisdom of a man who could be discreet, who dined sensibly, even frugally, alone, who read the newspaper page by page. His fingernails were cared for, his chin well-shaved.

"Mr. Daro is a very engaging man," he said as he accepted Viri's coat, hanging it near the mirror with care. "He has one unusual feature. His neck is seventeen and a half."

"Is that large?"

"From the shoulders up, he could easily be a prizefighter."

"His nose is too fine."

"From the shoulders up and the chin down," Conrad said. He was measuring Viri with the care and delicacy of a woman, the length of each arm, the chest, waist, the circumference of his wrists. Each figure he noted down on a large, printed card, a card which he explained would exist always. "I have customers from before the war," he said. "They still come to me. On Tuesdays and Thursdays; those are the only days I am here."

15

He laid his sample books on the counter, opening them as one unfolds a napkin. "Now, look through these," he said. "These are not everything, but they are the best things."

The pages had squares of fabric, lemon, magenta, cocoa, gray. There were stripes, batiks, Egyptian cottons light enough to read through.

"Here is a good one. No, not quite right," Conrad decided.

"What about this?" Viri said. He was holding a piece of cloth. "Would that be too much, a whole shirt of it?"

"It would be better than half a shirt," Conrad said. "No, truthfully . . ." He reflected. "It would be fabulous."

"Or this," Viri said.

"I can see already—I have known you only a few minutes, but I can see you are a man of definite tastes and opinions. Yes, I mean there is no question."

They were like old friends; a vast understanding had risen between them. The lines in Conrad's face were those of a widower, a man who had earned his knowledge. His style was respectful but confident.

"Try these collars," he said. "I am going to make you some wonderful shirts."

Viri stood before the mirror inspecting himself in various collars, long, pointed, collars with rounded tips.

"Not bad."

"Not quite high enough for you," Conrad suggested. "You don't mind me saying this?"

"Not at all. There is one thing, though," Viri said, changing collars. "The sleeves. I noticed you put down thirty-three."

Conrad consulted the card. "Thirty-three," he agreed. "Correct. The tape does not err."

"I don't like them quite that long."

"That's not long. For you, thirty-four would be long."

"And thirty-two?"

"No, no. That would be witty," Conrad said, "but what is

16

there about sleeves that makes you incline toward the grotesque?"

"I like to see my knuckles," Viri said.

"Mr. Berland—"

"Believe me, thirty-three is too long."

Conrad reversed his pencil.

"I am committing a crime," he said, erasing half an inch.

"They won't be too short, I assure you. I don't like a long
sleeve."

"Mr. Berland, a shirt . . . no, I don't have to explain it to
you."

"Of course not."

"A bad shirt is like the story of a pretty girl who is single and
one day she finds herself pregnant. It's not the end of life, but
it's serious."

"What about the pocket? I like a fairly deep pocket."

Conrad looked pained. "A pocket," he said. "What earthly
use do you have for a pocket? It ruins the shirt."

"Not completely, does it?"

"When a shirt already has sleeves that are a little short, and
on top of that a pocket . . ."

"The pocket isn't really on top of the sleeves. I pictured it
more or less between them."

"What can I say to you? Why do you want a pocket?"

"I need to carry a pencil," Viri said.

"Not there. Now that," he said, referring to a collar Viri had
put on, "that is an extremely nice collar, do you agree?"

"It's not too high in the back?" He was turning his head to
one side to see better.

"No, I don't think so, but if you like we can make it a little
lower—a quarter of an inch, say."

"I'm not trying to be too demanding."

"No, no," Conrad assured him. "Not at all. I'll just make a
little note . . ." He wrote as he talked. "Details are everything.

17

I have had clients . . . I had a man from a famous family in the city, politically very important, he had two passions, dogs and watches. He owned large numbers of both. He used to write down the precise time at which he went to bed and got up every day. His left cuff was made half an inch bigger than the right, for his wrist watches, of course. They were mostly Vacheron Constantins. Actually, a quarter of an inch would have been enough. His wife, who was in every other respect a saint, called him Doggy. In his monograms was the profile of a schnauzer.

"I have also had customers of the type—I am not being specific—but of the Lepke-Buchalter type. You know who he was?"

"Yes."

"Gangsters. Well, you know that criminal fashions have often made the transition into chic, but the fact is, these men were marvelous customers."

"They spent a lot of money?"

"Oh, money . . . aside from money." Conrad gestured broadly. "Money was not a consideration. They were so pleased to have someone who paid attention to them, who tried to dress them properly. Pardon me, but what do you do?"

"Me?"

"Yes."

"I'm an architect." It seemed a bit weak after kings of crime.

"An architect," Conrad said. He paused as if to allow the thought to descend. "Have you done any buildings around here?"

"Not around here."

"Are you a good architect? Will you show me one of your buildings?"

"That depends, Mr. Conrad, on what the shirts are like."

Conrad uttered a little sound of appreciation and understanding.

"In that regard," he said, "I can assure you. I am thirty, no, thirty-one years at my business. I have made some very good shirts, I have made some bad shirts, but altogether I have not failed to learn my art completely. I can say to myself, Conrad, you lack, unfortunately, the proper schooling, your exchequer is a bit frail, but one thing is acknowledged: you know shirts. From cuff to cuff, if I may be permitted. Now, when am I here?"

"Tuesdays and Thursdays."

"I was just testing you," Conrad said.

They chose a cloth that was printed like feathers, feathers of dark green, black, permanganate, another the color of deer-skin, and a third the blue of police.

"You don't think the blue is too blue?"

"A blue cannot be too blue," Conrad said. "How many shall we make?"

"Well, one of each," Viri said.

"Three shirts?"

"You're disappointed."

"I shall only be disappointed if they are not among your favorite things," Conrad said. He sounded a bit resigned.

"I am going to send you many customers."

"I am sure of it."

"I'll give you the name of one right now. I don't know when he'll be in, but very soon."

"Tuesday or Thursday," Conrad warned.

"Naturally. His name is Arnaud Roth."

"Roth," Conrad said.

"Arnaud."

"Tell him I am looking forward eagerly."

"But you'll remember the name?"

"Please," Conrad protested. He was like a patient who has had too long a visit; he seemed somehow worn.

"You'll find him very amusing," Viri said.

"I am certain of it."

"When will these shirts be ready?" he said, putting on his coat.

"In four to six weeks, sir."

"That long?"

"When you see them, you will be astonished at how quickly they were made."

Viri smiled. "It was a great pleasure, Mr. Conrad," he said.

"The pleasure was mine."

The avenue was dense with people, the sunlight still brilliant; the first commuters, well-dressed, were heading for early trains. The turmoil of traffic was sweet to him as he walked in the flowing crowd. He knew in that moment what all these people were seeking. He understood the city, the teeming streets, autumn days flashing like knives in the highest windows, businessmen issuing from the revolving door of the Sherry-Netherland, the wind-swept park.

In a phone booth he composed a familiar number.

"Yes, hello," a voice said languidly.

"Arnaud . . ."

"Hello, Viri."

"Listen, what is today? Tuesday. On Thursday I want you to meet someone. You will thank me until the end of your life."

"Where are you, in a brothel?"

"What is that story about the twelve absolutely pure men whose existence is essential to the world?"

"Give me the punch line."

"No, this is a kind of Sholom Aleichem story. These twelve men—you must know it. They're scattered over the earth. No one knows who they are, but when one of them dies, he's immediately replaced. Without them, civilization would crumble, we would sink into chaos, crime, utter disillusion."

"That's probably what's happened; we're down to four or five."

"I've met one."

"So that's it."

"His name is Conrad."

"Conrad? Are you kidding? He's a crook."

"No, this is a different Conrad. You have to meet him."

"The last time you told me that, you know what happened?"

"I'm trying to recall."

"I ended up investing five hundred dollars in a film."

"Ah, I remember."

"Conrad, eh? What's he going to do for me?"

Viri was watching the traffic, the sounds of which came to him faintly, trembling the metal beneath his feet, his gaze drawn past by the gleaming cars.

"He's going to make you some shirts."

4

WINTER COMES. A BITTER COLD. The snow creaks underfoot with a rich, mournful sound. The house is surrounded by white. Hours of sleep, the air chill. The most delicious sleep, is death so warm, so easeful? He is barely awake; he emerges for a moment at first light as if by some instinct, buried, lost. His eyes open slightly, like an animal's. For a moment he slips from dreams, he sees the sky, the light, nothing is moving, nothing is heard. The hour that is the last hour, the children sleeping, the pony silent in her stall.

The river was frozen. They learned it by telephone.

"Is it really frozen?"

"Yes," he was assured. "They're skating."

"We'll go."

Down past the bridge there were great skirts of ice along the banks, and people already out, men in overcoats, women bundled against the cold. They skated in blinding sunshine, scarves about their necks, shouting to each other, the ankles of the smallest children folding like paper. Far out in the channel, the river was gray, the shade of shattered ice. A wind was blowing, a cold wind that burned the fingertips. The little girl with one leg was there. She was three, she had cancer, they had amputated her leg. Before that she had been invisible. Afterwards, on crutches, she became luminous; she took a long time to pass by on the sidewalk or sat in the car, unable to leave it, her small face in profile, unmoving. Her name was Monica. She had two brothers, small teeth, never a smile. She was the martyr of a desperate family; they hated themselves when they were impatient with her. They lived in an ugly house, a house the color of chilblains, brick, a few naked bushes at each end. In the stinging cold her father pulled her along the ice in a sort of curved, aluminum plate. She sat gravely, not speaking, her gloved hands holding the rim.

"Hello, Monica," they called to her. They circled her and waved. She seemed not to see; she was motionless, like an old woman who has lived too long.

"Hold on," they cried to her. "Hold tight."

Her father was bareheaded. Viri knew him only by sight. He worked for an insurance company, driving to the city every day. "Hold on, Moni," he told her. He began a sweeping turn. The plate swung around, tilting.

"Hold on," they cried.

The air was crossed with voices, shouts, the scrape of skates. It was possible to go further out than anyone could remember; the ice was thick for half a mile from shore. People had lit bonfires and stood around them on the bank, warming themselves, still in their skates. A few dogs tried to run on the ice.

Nedra had not gone with them. She was in the kitchen. A fire burned. She had poured a dish of warm milk, and the puppy was drinking with brief, clumsy laps, the milk flashing in his mouth. He was tan, the color of a fox, with white underneath. His movements were hopelessly crude.

"You like it, don't you?" she said. She touched his soft coat while he drank beneath her hand. "Hadji," she said. "You're going to be a big man. You're going to bark and bark."

Viri came in from skating, rubbing his hands. Close behind him, the children were taking off their coats in the hall.

"I've named him."

"Good. What?"

"Hadji," she said.

"Hadji."

"Doesn't it fit him?"

"Yes. What does it mean?"

"What does anything mean?"

Hadji was licking the empty dish. It clattered on the floor.

"We saw that little girl with one leg."

"Monica."

"Yes."

"That's so sad."

"I can't bear to look at her. It takes away my courage."

"It was freezing cold."

In the early afternoon they had chocolate and pears. The light had changed. The sun had gone behind some clouds; the day had no source. Viri played an Arab game of beans with them. In the end he let them win.

"Is there more hot chocolate?" he asked.

"I'll make some," Nedra said.

On the river the gulls seemed to be standing on the water. The ice was invisible. Their reflections were dark; one could see the black lines that were their legs. A canopy of music in the room, a tray with three cups, white cubes of sugar in a bowl, many books.

Their life is mysterious, it is like a forest; from far off it seems a unity, it can be comprehended, described, but closer it begins to separate, to break into light and shadow, the density blinds one. Within there is no form, only prodigious detail that reaches everywhere: exotic sounds, spills of sunlight, foliage, fallen trees, small beasts that flee at the sound of a twig-snap, insects, silence, flowers.

And all of this, dependent, closely woven, all of it is deceiving. There are really two kinds of life. There is, as Viri says, the one people believe you are living, and there is the other. It is this other which causes the trouble, this other we long to see.

"Come here, Hadji," he says.

The dog, all knowledge already within it, all courage, all love, looks alert but uncomprehending.

"Come here," Viri says. He reaches for it. It does not cower; it submits to being held.

"So you're a cattle dog, are you? Where's your tail? What happened to it? You don't even know what a tail is, do you? You think a tail is something that hangs at one end of a cow. Now listen, Hadji, the first thing we have to talk about is hygiene. Our bathroom is in the house, yours is outside. The trees—"

"He wouldn't know what to do with a tree, Viri."

"You wouldn't know what to do with a tree? The grass then, to start with. Afterwards small rocks, the corner of the building, steps, and then—then a tree. You're going to be a huge dog, Hadji. You're going to live with us. We're going to take you down to the river. We're going to take you to the sea. Oh, your teeth are sharp!"

He slept in a fruit basket, on his back like a bear. One morning there was great excitement. Franca saw it first. "His ear is up! His ear is up!" she cried.

They all ran to see it while he sat, unaware of his triumph. But it fell again in the afternoon.

He became intelligent, strong, he knew their voices. He was stoic, he was shrewd. In his dark eye one could see a phylum of creatures—horses, mice, cattle, deer. Frogboy, they called him. He lay on the floor with his legs stretched out behind. He watched them, his face resting on his paws.

24

5

LIFE IS WEATHER. LIFE IS MEALS. Lunches on a blue checked cloth on which salt has spilled. The smell of tobacco. Brie, yellow apples, wood-handled knives.

It is trips to the city, daily trips. She is like a farm woman who goes to the market. She drove to the city for everything, its streets excited her, winter streets leaking smoke. She drove along Broadway. The sidewalks were white with stains. There were only certain places where she bought food; she was loyal to them, demanding. She parked her car wherever it was convenient, in bus stops, prohibited zones; the urgency of her errands protected her. The car was a little convertible, foreign, green and, unlike other things, neglected.

January. She drove to the city early, a cold day, the pavements were frozen, the pigeons huddled in the R's of a FURNITURE sign. The city is a cathedral of possessions; its scent is dreams. Even those who have been rejected by it cannot leave. An ancient woman was sitting on a doorstep, her face coursed by years, her hair disarranged, a hideous woman with her teeth gone. She had an animal in her lap, its eyes running, its muzzle gray. She lowered her head and sat, her cheek against the little dog's, silent, abandoned. In the next block was a derelict walking on his knees, his face so filthy, so red it seemed covered with wounds. His clothes were rags stained with vomit. He struggled, looking down into his pants as if for blood, oblivious to those who passed. In the theater lobbies were dwarfs, fat men, financial wizards with sullen faces, women in black stockings, furs. There were rings on their aging fingers, gold in their teeth.

She went to the museum, to her husband's office, to a shop on Lexington where she stood among the art books, tall, pensive, a woman with long legs, a graceful neck, on her forehead the faintest creases of the decade to come. In a nondescript restaurant she sat down to have a sandwich. She took off her coat. Beneath was an Irish sweater, ordinary, white, hung with necklaces of amber and colored seeds. Men alone at their tables looked at her. She ate calmly. Her mouth was wide and intelligent. She left a tip. She disappeared.

In the early winter evening she passes Columbia. The traffic is thick but moving. The food stores are crowded, the flashes of the railway above her make blue images lit like executions in the dusk. Home on the long, curving stretches, borne by other cars. By the time she had crossed the river the trees were black. She flew along, in the left lane only, above the limit, tired, happy, filled with plans. Her eyes were burning. On the seat behind her were white and orange bags from Zabar's, on the floor were gas slips, parking tickets, mail that had never been opened, bills. The road runs along the great cliffs of the west bank; for most of the way there is not a house visible, not a store, nothing except the long galaxy of towns across the river, beginning to shine in the dark.

She turns from the highway and enters the backwaters, the pools of small life, houses she knows intimately without any idea of who is in them, parked cars she recognizes, a corner post office, a grocery that sells the city papers, the wooden fence of neighbors, the lights of home.

"What are the children doing, Alma?" she asks. The dog is leaping about at her feet. "Hello, Hadji. Be quiet."

Drawing pictures upstairs, the Jamaica woman says. She has read to them; she has taken them on a walk.

"He is some dog," she says. "A fine dog."

"He is, isn't he?"

"Oh, he like to bark."

Her daughters are coming down the stairs. Mama, they cry.

"I brought something for you," she says, kneeling in her coat.

26

"What is it?" they say. "Your face is so cold."

"Yours is warm. What have you been doing?"

"We're making something," the younger says. "What did you bring?"

She names a French biscuit they love, LU's.

"Oh, good!"

"What are you making?"

"We're making an Egyptian temple," Franca says. "Come and see."

"But we have no more gold," her sister cries. They call her Danny. Her name is Diane.

"Can you bring it down?" Nedra asks them. "Bring it to the kitchen. I'm going to have some tea."

6

 "BRUCE ETTINGER IS BEAUTIFUL," Nedra whispered.

"Which one is he?"

"He's there in the corner. He's very tall."

Viri looked over.

"You think *he*'s good-looking?"

"Wait till he smiles."

The rooms were crowded. There were people they knew, people they might have known. Beautiful women, audacious clothes.

"He has a smile like a gangster," Nedra said.

Eve was across the room in a thin, burgundy dress that showed the faint outline of her stomach. She was pale, elegant, slutty. Her eyes were bad; she could hardly see who she was talking to. She wore contact lenses, but not at a party. The man she was facing was shorter than she was. Behind them was a painting that seemed to be of a primitive jungle: blue, violet, sea-green.

"It matches your shirt," Nedra said.

"Even Bruce Ettinger doesn't have a shirt like this."

"Oh, you have the best shirt. You have absolutely the best shirt."

"I think so."

"But he has the best smile."

"I'll get you something to drink," he offered.

"Nothing too strong."

She made her way slowly across the room, her face less animated than other women's faces. She passed behind people, around them, nodded, smiled. She was that woman the first glimpse of whom changes everything.

"Saul Bellow is here," Eve told her.

"Where? What does he look like?"

"He was in the hallway just a minute ago."

They could not find him.

"I don't think I've read anything he's written."

"Arthur Kopit is here," Eve said.

"Well, he can't even write."

"He's very funny."

"Bruce Ettinger is here," Nedra said.

"Who?"

"He's a man who doesn't have very nice shirts."

"Shirts. Have you seen the shirts Arnaud had made?"

"Viri sent him."

"Did he?"

"Are they nice?"

"He even sleeps in them."

Arnaud was coming toward them at that moment, warm, unperturbed, his shoulders flecked with what looked like talcum powder. In each hand was a glass.

"Hello, Nedra," he said. He leaned to kiss her. "Here you are, darling," he said to Eve. "Where's Viri?"

"He's here."

"Where?"

"You'll recognize him," Nedra said. "He's wearing the exact same shirt."

"Ah, you're jealous."

"Of course not," Nedra said. "I think you deserve to have beautiful things . . ."

"You know, I've always adored you."

"I mean, after all, you already have us." She smiled at him, knowing, direct, her white teeth showing.

"You're right," he said. "Here's Viri."

"They had no Cinzano. I got you a sweet vermouth—" he didn't finish; Arnaud was embracing him. "Wait, wait, you're spilling my drink! You're going to wrinkle my shirt!" he cried.

"You know, you're strong," he said when he was released.

"He's strong as a bull," Eve said.

Arnaud was strong in the manner of men who surprise you —math teachers, dentists. He was past his real strength, thirty-four, a pot-bellied figure already dark with cigar smoke. He was vague, cunning, clumsy. He could do fantastic tricks with cards.

"I used to wrestle," he said. "I fought some big men . . ."

"Where, in college?"

". . . some of them eight feet tall. The only trouble with it is that everyone smells so bad."

He was drinking. He smiled when he drank; it didn't affect him. It made him another man, a man who could not be offended, who swam in the warmth of life. Around him were women in gold dresses, women who once were models. They were the caryatids of a certain fashionable layer of New York. Arnaud, with his gray complexion, the dandruff on his collar, was their favorite. He was fond, irreverent, he loved to tell tales.

"You're coming to the film?" the host asked them.

"Is there going to be a film?" Nedra said.

29

"In a couple of hours," deBeque said. "It's a film we're distributing; it hasn't been shown."

"Do you know Eve Caunt?" Viri offered.

"Eve? Of course I know Eve. Everyone knows Eve." His eyes were as pale as a glass of water. His stare was scalding.

"I don't know half the people here," he confessed to Viri. "Well, the women; I know all the women." He lowered his voice. "There are some fantastic women here, believe me."

He took Viri by the arm and led him off. "I want to talk to you," he explained. "Wait, here's someone you should meet." He reached for a bare arm. "This is Faye Massey."

The bad complexion of a girl of good family. A low-cut dress on which the watery stare lingered. "You're looking very well, Faye," he said.

"Is the film as bad as I hear?"

"Bad? It's a ravishing film."

"That's not what I hear," she said.

"Faye is a very interesting girl," deBeque said, glancing down again into her dress. "A lot of people say so."

"Stop it," she said.

"I think this evening belongs to the women," deBeque decided.

"What do you mean by that?"

"You're all so good-looking."

Beyond them Viri could see a girl sitting on the edge of a couch.

"Why are you always talking in the plural?"

"It's natural for a man."

"What's natural and what's not natural?" she asked. "We're so far from being natural . . . that's the whole trouble."

Viri was waiting to excuse himself. "Do you think of yourself as natural?" she asked him.

"We all do, don't we?" he said. "More or less."

"You can think anything you like," she said. "Just name me one."

30

"Do you know Arnaud Roth?"

"Who?" Suddenly she smiled, a warm, unexpected smile. "Arnaud. You're right. I love him," she said. "I've known him for years."

In the woman who overwhelms us there must be nothing familiar. Faye was telling a story about Arnaud buying an airplane; it wouldn't fly, she said, wasn't that typical? It was parked near a pond. The girl on the couch had risen and was talking to someone. Viri tried not to stare. He was helpless at gatherings like this where the conversation was rapid and cynical, the encounters remote as at dancing class. He found refuge, usually, with someone grotesque, out of competition. He resisted handsome faces, he had learned not to look at them, but she was that unknown creature to whom he was dazedly vulnerable, slim, with full breasts as if she were burdened by them. Even her thumbs were bony.

He could not keep sight of her. He could not, even for a moment, imagine her life. If she had turned to him, he would have been speechless or worse, saying inane things he instantly regretted, illustrating for her a certain kind of pathetic, ordinary man fit only to be what he was: a commuter, the head of a family. But that's not what I am, he wanted to say, that's not what I am at all. Anyway, she was gone. She was someone's girl friend, obviously; a girl like that was never alone.

"Where have you been?" Nedra asked.

They drank; they ate dinner with plates on their knees. A waiter was serving champagne. Someone was playing the piano, barely audible over the din. Gerald deBeque was sitting with a Japanese girl. His wife, who had a splitting headache, began to tell people it was time to go to the film.

They went down in a crowded elevator and walked three blocks to the theater in shattering cold, walked and half ran, stood in the entrance waiting for deBeque to arrive and instruct the manager to let them in. Several people had managed to get in anyway.

31

"Come on, Viri," Nedra complained, "tell him that we're from the party."

"Everybody's standing around waiting."

"Oh balls, the waiting."

She was talking to the manager herself when at last deBeque appeared. "Gerald, your film's half over," she said.

"Let them in," he called to the manager. "Everybody can go in."

Viri hung back. He touched deBeque on the elbow.

"Gerald . . ." he said.

"Yes?"

"The girl standing by the sign, the sort of thin girl . . ."

"What about her?"

"She's wearing a leather coat."

"Yes, with a belt."

"Who is she? Do you know?" he said casually.

"She came with George Clutha. Her name is Kaya something . . . I forget."

"Kaya . . ."

"He tells me she's better than she looks."

They were calling him; they were already partway down the aisle.

"She's looking for a job," deBeque remembered.

"Yes, thanks."

"Viri." He would not let him go. "You can do better than that."

"It's just that I thought I'd met her somewhere."

Arnaud was standing at their seats, beckoning to him. It was a small theater, once respectable. They kept their coats on.

"I was trying to find out a little about the film," Viri said. "It's about a young woman's sexual awakening."

"I might have known," Nedra said.

Arnaud yawned. "Gerald probably stars in it."

The lights stayed on for a long time. There began to be whistles and claps. Viri looked back, as if to see if anyone else were entering. He seemed calm and at ease. He was doomed as a dog that chases cars.

"I have a feeling I'm going to go to sleep even before it begins," Arnaud murmured.

Finally it grew dark and the film started. The many shots of a young girl with her blouse open loitering along roads and through fields or working in the kitchen in this improbable attire were not enough to rivet the viewers.

"This isn't very interesting," Nedra whispered.

Arnaud was asleep. Viri sat silent, made unhappy by the vague connection between the heroine and the girl who sat hidden somewhere in the bored, coughing audience. If only out of the corner of his eye he could see her a row or two ahead. He wanted to stare at her unnoticed. There are faces that subjugate one, that are turned away from with a feeling like that of giving up breath itself. In the morning I will have forgotten it, he thought; in the morning everything is different, things are real.

There was a crowd waiting on the street as they went out, people who had come for the first public screening at midnight. Arnaud had his coat turned up like an opera star or gambler.

"The book was better," he commented as he passed through them.

"Oh, yeah? What book?"

"Save your money," he said.

They came home after midnight, the long, flowing drive in darkness, snow on the edge of the road. The sitter had crumpled on the couch; she was soft-faced and bewildered as Viri took her home.

They went to bed in the large, cool room, their clothes scattered, the window admitting just a blade of icy air.

"Gerald deBeque is a dissolute man," Nedra said. "And that movie was absolutely awful. There wasn't anybody there I was interested in. Still, I had a good time. Isn't that strange?"

He did not answer. He was asleep.

7

IT WAS A DAY OF COLD SUNLIGHT, the day on which, six years before, his parents had died. He sat at his desk. His two draftsmen were at work, the flats of their tables before them. The room was silent, that was what set him thinking; it was suddenly calm. His father and mother were lying beneath the earth, brown as the relics of saints, their funeral clothes rotting. He was thirty-two, alone in the world. Dreams and work.

Have I said he was a man of minor talent? He was born after one war and before another—in 1928, in fact, a year of crisis, a year on the path of the century. He was born in disregard of the times, like everyone; the hospital is there no longer, the doctor retired, gone south.

He believed in greatness. He believed in it as if it were a virtue, as if it could be his own. He was sensitive to lives that had, beneath their surface, like a huge rock or shadow, a glory that would be discovered, that would rise one day to the light. He was clear-eyed and exact about the value of other people's work. Toward his own he maintained a mild respect. In his faith, at the heart of his illusions, was the structure that would appear in photographs of his time, the famous building he had created and that nothing—no criticism, no envy, not even demolition—could alter.

He spoke of it to no one, of course, except Nedra. It grew more and more invisible year by year. It vanished from his conversation, though not from his life. It would be there always, until the last, like a great ship rotting in the ways.

He was well-liked. He would have preferred being hated. I am too mild, he said.

34

"It's your way," Nedra told him, "you must use it."

He respected her ideas. Yes, he thought, I must go on. I must make one building, even if it's small, that everyone will notice. Then a bigger one. I must ascend by steps.

A perfect day begins in death, in the semblance of death, in deep surrender. The body is soft, the soul has gone forth, all strength, even breath. There is no power for good or evil, the luminous surface of another world is near, enfolding, the branches of the trees tremble outside. Morning, he wakes slowly, as if touched by sun across the legs. He is alone. There is the smell of coffee. The tan coat of his dog drinks the burning light.

For the day to unfold it must in its blueness, its immensity hide the conspiracy he lived on, hide but enclose it, invisible, like stars in the daytime sky.

He wanted one thing, the possibility of one thing: to be famous. He wanted to be central to the human family, what else is there to long for, to hope? Already he walked modestly along the streets, as if certain of what was coming. He had nothing. He had only the carefully laid out luggage of bourgeois life, his scalp beginning to show beneath the hair, his immaculate hands. And the knowledge; yes, he had knowledge. The Sagrada Familia was as familiar to him as a barn to a farmer, the "new towns" of France and England, cathedrals, voussoirs, cornices, quoins. He knew the life of Alberti, of Christopher Wren. He knew that Sullivan was the son of a dancing master, Breuer a doctor in Hungary. But knowledge does not protect one. Life is contemptuous of knowledge; it forces it to sit in the anterooms, to wait outside. Passion, energy, lies: these are what life admires. Still, anything can be endured if all humanity is watching. The martyrs prove it. We live in the attention of others. We turn to it as flowers to the sun.

There is no complete life. There are only fragments. We are born to have nothing, to have it pour through our hands. And yet, this pouring, this flood of encounters, struggles, dreams

. . . one must be unthinking, like a tortoise. One must be resolute, blind. For whatever we do, even whatever we do not do prevents us from doing the opposite. Acts demolish their alternatives, that is the paradox. So that life is a matter of choices, each one final and of little consequence, like dropping stones into the sea. We had children, he thought; we can never be childless. We were moderate, we will never know what it is to spill out our lives . . .

He was not himself somehow. The faint sound of the radio playing near the draftsmen's tables was a strange distraction. He could not think, he was vague, adrift.

Arnaud came by in the late afternoon. He sat with his coat belted. He looked like a vintner, a man who owns land.

"What's wrong?"

"I was just thinking," Viri murmured.

"I had lunch today at the Toque."

"Was it good?"

"I'm getting so fat," Arnaud moaned. "Lunch is not a meal; it's a profession. It takes your whole life. I had lunch with a very nice girl. You don't know her."

"Who?"

"She was so . . . everything she said was so unexpected. She went to school in a convent. The mattresses were made of straw."

"Is that unexpected?"

"You know, there's a kind of education, a kind of upbringing which is ruinous, and yet if you survive it, it's the best thing in the world. It's like having been a heroin addict or a thief. We try to save too many people, that's the trouble. You save them, but what have you got?"

"Tell me more of what she said."

"It wasn't only what she said. She ate, that was the thing I liked about her, she ate as much as I did. We were like two peasants striking a bargain. Bread, fish, wine, everything. I began looking at her as something that was going to be served

36

next. And she's one of these girls who fill their clothes completely. She was—you know how they make those veal and ham pies in England?—she was *en croûte.* And the most interesting thing: she's lame."

"Lame?"

"She can't walk very well. She limps. You don't find that often. A lame woman . . . Louise de La Vallière was lame. Louise de Vilmorin, too. She had tuberculosis of the hip."

"Did she?"

"I think so. Something else very nice is a woman with slightly crossed eyes."

"Crossed eyes?"

"Just a little. And teeth. Bad teeth."

"You like all three?"

"No, no, of course not," Arnaud said. "Not in the same woman. You can't have everything."

There was something hidden in his expression, the smile of someone who should not reveal it. "It's terrible," he sighed.

"What?"

"I can't do this to Eve. I can't be unfaithful for a . . ."

"A bad leg."

"It just isn't right," Arnaud said. "I mean, she cooks meals for me. She has a wonderful sense of humor."

"And her teeth aren't that good."

"They're passable. They're not really bad."

He shifted in the chair slightly, and found a new position. His clothing was somewhat tight on him.

"It's so easy to be distracted," he said. "Eve is good for me."

"She loves you."

"Yes."

"And you?"

"Me?" He looked about as if for something to involve him. "I love everyone. It's your daughters I love, Viri. I'm serious."

"Well, it's reciprocated."

"I'm jealous of them. I'm jealous of your life. It's a sensible

37

life. It's harmonious, that's what I'm trying to say, and most important, it's intimately connected with the future because of your children. I mean, I'm sure you realize it, but what moment that gives to each day."

"Why don't you have children?"

"Yes. Well, first, I would say, I need a wife. And unfortunately, you also have the wife I like. Nedra doesn't have a sister, does she?"

"No."

"That's too bad. I'd like to marry her sister. It would really be an act of adultery." There was no insult in his voice. "No, you're very fortunate," he said. "But you know that. Well, if anything should happen . . ."

Viri smiled.

"No, I mean it. If anything happened to you . . . your wife, your children, I would take care of them. I would continue your love."

"I don't think anything's going to happen."

"Well, you never know," Arnaud said cheerfully.

"Listen," Viri said, "why don't you come out this weekend and have dinner?"

"Wonderful."

"You and Eve."

"I forgot something," Arnaud said suddenly. He was searching in his pocket. "I have a present for Franca. I bought it at Azuma, it's a frog ring."

"Why don't you give it to her?"

"No, take it with you. I want her to have it tonight."

"I'll tell her it's from you."

"Tell her it's from Yassir Rashid, the king of the desert. Tell her if she is ever in danger to show it and she will be safe in the heart of the tribes."

"Listen, Yassir, what would you think of a little Scotch before you disappear?"

"There are three things in the desert which cannot be hid-

38

den," Arnaud said. "A camel, smoke and . . . you know something? We see too many movies."

"On the rocks?" Viri asked.

"They kill the imagination. You've heard of blind storytellers. It's in darkness that myths are born. The cinema can't do that. Did I tell you about the girl I took to lunch? She was really okay. You know, in a sense it's that way with her. She can never dance. That's why the real grace, the real music is in her."

Evening had appeared. The light was gone. The street outside trembled with buses, with enormous, fleeing cars. Along the river was stretched an endless procession which Viri would join. He would move with it, his legs weary though he had not walked, his neck aching slightly, borne alone homeward, listening to the endlessly repeated news.

8

NEDRA ROSE LATE IN SUMMER AND winter, whenever she could. Her real self lay in bed until nine, stirred, stretched, breathed the new air. Long sleepers are usually nonconformists; they are pensive and somewhat withdrawn. Her hair was rich and clung to her. She bound it in various styles. She bathed it, she wore it damp. One thinks of the ten, the twenty gleaming years of her ascendance. She is a woman whose cool remark forms the mood of a dinner; the man seated next to her smiles. She knows what she is doing, that is the core of it; still, how could she know? Her acts are unrepeated. She does not perform. Her face is a face that electrifies—that sudden, exploding smile—and yet, she somehow gives nothing.

Her hair smells of flowers. The day is calm. The sun is still forming, the river is spilling light.

39

She has no friends, she says. Rae and Larry. Eve. It's very difficult for her to make friends. She has no time for friendship, she is quickly disappointed. It is the shopkeepers who love her, the people on the street who see her passing, wrapped in herself, staring in the windows of bookstores at the beautiful, heavy volumes of painters, the Italian edition of *Vogue*.

"Tell her how much we love her and miss her," the men who have the little shop for soap and perfumes near Bonwit's cry. "Where is she? We don't see her now that she lives in the country. Tell her to come by," they say. They love her height, her elegance, her hazel eyes.

She is interested in certain people. She admires certain lives. She is subtle, penetrating and sometimes mischievous, strongly inclined to love and not overdelicate in the ways that must be taken. All of this is written in her dream book. Of course she does not believe it, but it amuses her and parts of the book are very true. Eve, for instance, is exactly as described. It's also quite close to Viri.

One wants to enter the aura surrounding her, to be accepted, to see her smile, to have her exercise that deep, imputed tendency to love. Soon after they were married, perhaps an hour after, even Viri longed for this. His possession of her became sanctified; at the same time something in her changed. She became his closest relative. She committed herself to his interests and embarked on her own. The desperate, unbearable affection vanished, and in its place was a young woman of twenty condemned to live with him. He could not define it. She had escaped. Perhaps it was more; the mistake she knew she would have to make was made at last. Her face radiated knowledge. A colorless vein like a scar ran vertically down the center of her forehead. She had accepted the limitations of her life. It was this anguish, this contentment which created her grace.

In the summer they went to Amagansett. Wooden houses. Blue, blue days. Summer is the noontime of devoted families.

40

It is the hour of silence when the only sound is sea birds. The shutters are closed, the voices quiet. Occasionally the ring of a fork.

Pure, empty days. The sea is silver, rough as bark. Hadji has dug a hollow in which he lies, eyes narrowed, bits of sand stuck to his mouth. He always faces the sea. Franca has a black tank suit. Her limbs are shining and strong. She is afraid of the waves. Danny is more courageous. She goes out in the surf with her father; they scream and ride on their bellies. Franca joins them. The dog is barking on the shore.

That whistle of the sea in the long afternoon, the great beds of brown foam, of kelp brought up by the storms, the mussels, the whitened boards. To the west it is steaming, a long, brilliant stretch as if in rain. In the dunes Franca has found the dry husk of a beetle. She brings it, quivering in her hand, to Viri. It has a kind of single horn.

"Look, Papa."

"It's a rhinoceros beetle," he tells her.

"Mama!" she cries. "Look! A rhinoceros beetle!"

She is nine. Danny is seven. These years are endless, but they cannot be remembered.

Viri sleeps in the sun. He is tan, his fingernails are bleached. On Mondays he goes to the city on the train and returns on Thursday night. He is shuttling between one happiness and another. He has a new secretary. They work together in a kind of excitement, as if there were nothing else in their lives. The isolation and indifference of the city in summer, like a long vacation, like a voyage, casts its spell on them. He cannot get over her niceness, the beauty of her name: Kaya Doutreau.

Near him on the beach lie two young women on their stomachs. Beyond them, scattered, are families, clothing, men sitting alone. It's late. The sea is empty. Down near its dying edge walk a bearded young man in Levis, naked to the waist, and a girl in the slimmest of bathing suits. They are talking, heads down. The new freedom pours from them; their lives seem infinitely useful and sweet.

Sometimes at noon, reflected in shop windows, he sees himself and a child, sees them as if looking into the stream of life, among cakes and Bordeaux wine. For a moment they stand there, their backs to the street. They have almost finished their errands. Her face is against his arm. They are speechless, united. She has a straw hat. Her feet are bare. He is overwhelmed with a sense of contentment. The sun fills the summer town.

They return to the house. The faded sound of car doors closing. Danny is feeding the rabbit near the kitchen step, a black rabbit with two white paws and a spot on his chest; they call it his star. His mouth moves hastily as he eats. His ears lie flat.

In the brimming paper bags Viri finds a carrot. "Here," he says.

She slips it through the wire of the cage. The rabbit ingests it like a mechanical toy.

"He likes lunch," she says.

"What about breakfast?"

"He likes that, too."

"Does he wash his hands?"

The carrot greens are vanishing in little jerks.

"No," she says.

"Does he brush his teeth?"

"He can't," she says.

"Why not?"

"No sink."

Danny is less obedient; she has a stubborn quality. She is less beautiful. In the summer her leanness and tan skin conceal it. She goes out in the deep water in a rubber tube, daring, kicking like an insect. It is morning, the surf falling forward, its white

42

teeth hissing on the shore. Viri watches, sitting on the sand. She waves at him, her shouts carried off by the wind. He understands suddenly what love of a child is. It overwhelms him like the line from a song.

Morning; the sea sound faint on the wind. His sunburned daughters walk on creaking floors. They pass their life together, in a compact that will never end. They go to the circus, to stores, the market shed in Amagansett with its laden shelves and fruits, to picnics, pageants, concerts in wooden churches among the trees. They enter Philharmonic Hall. The audience is hushed. They are seated, the programs in their laps. To listen to a symphony is to open the book of faces. The maestro arrives. He collects himself, stands poised. The great, exotic opening chords of Chabrier. They go to perfomances of *Swan Lake*, their faces pale in the darkness of the Grand Tier. The vast curve of seats is lighted like the Ritz. A huge orchestra pit, big as a ship, a ceiling of gold, hung with bursts of light, with pendants that glitter like ice. The great Nureyev comes out after, bowing like an angel, like a prince. They beg each other for the glasses; his neck, his chest are gleaming with sweat, even the ends of his hair. His hands, like those of a child, play with the cape tassels. The end of performances, the end of Mozart, of Bach. The solo violinist stands with her face raised, utterly drained, the last chords still sounding, as if from a great love. The conductor applauds her, the audience, the beautiful women, their hands held high.

They pass their life together, they pass boys fishing, walking to the end of the pier with a small eel tied, doubled up, on the hook. The mute eye of the eel calls out, a black dot in his plain, silver face. They sit at the table where their grandfather eats, Nedra's father, a salesman, a man from small towns, his cough yellow, the Camel cigarettes always near his hand. His voice is out of focus, his eyes are filmed, he hardly seems to notice them. He brings death with him into the kitchen; a long, wasted life, the chrysalis of Nedra's, its dry covering, its forgotten source. He has cheap shoes, a suitcase filled with samples of aluminum window frames.

Their life is formed together, woven together, they are like actors, a group of devoted actors who know nothing beyond themselves, beyond the pile of roles from old, from immortal plays.

The summer ends. There are misty, chilly days, the sea is quiet and white. The waves break far out with a slow, majestic sound. The beach is deserted. Occasional strollers along the water's edge. The children lie on Viri's back like possums; the sand is warm beneath him.

Peter and Catherine join them, together with their little boy. The families sit separated, in the solitude and mist. Peter has a folding chair and wears a yachting cap and a shirt. Beside him is a bucket filled with ice, bottles of Dubonnet and rum. An eerie and beautiful day. The fine points of mist drift over them. August has passed.

At a pause in the conversation, Peter rises and walks slowly, without a word, into the sea, a solitary bather, swimming far out in his blue shirt. His strokes are powerful and even. He swims with assurance, strong as an iceman. Finally Viri joins him. The water is cool. There is mist all about them, the swelling rhythm of the waves. No one is in sight except their families sitting on shore.

"It's like swimming in the Irish Sea," Peter says. "Never any sun."

Franca and Danny come out to them.

"It's deep here," Viri warns.

Each of the men holds a child. They huddle close.

"The Irish sailors," Peter tells them, "never learn to swim. Not even a stroke. The sea is too strong."

"But what if the boat sinks?"

"They cross their hands on their chests and say a prayer,"

Peter says. He performs it. Like the carved lid of a coffin he sinks from sight.

"Is it true?" they ask Viri later.

"Yes."

"They drown?"

"They deliver themselves to God."

"How does he know that?"

"He knows."

"Peter is very strange," Franca says.

And he reads to them, as he does every night, as if watering them, as if turning the earth at their feet. There are stories he has never heard of, and others he has known as a child, these stepping stones that are there for everyone. What is the real meaning of these stories, he wonders, of creatures that no longer exist even in the imagination: princes, woodcutters, honest fishermen who live in hovels. He wants his children to have an old life and a new life, a life that is indivisible from all lives past, that grows from them, exceeds them, and another that is original, pure, free, that is beyond the prejudice which protects us, the habit which gives us shape. He wants them to know both degradation and sainthood, the one without humiliation, the other without ignorance. He is preparing them for this voyage. It is as if there is only a single hour, and in that hour all the provender must be gathered, all the advice offered. He longs for the one line to give them that they will always remember, that will embrace everything, that will point the way, but he cannot find the line, he cannot recognize it. It is more precious, he knows, than anything else they might own, but he does not have it. Instead, in his even, sensuous voice he laves them in the petty myths of Europe, of snowy Russia, the East. The best education comes from knowing only one book, he tells Nedra. Purity comes from that, and proportion, and the comfort of always having an example close at hand.

"Which book?" she says.

"There are a number of them."

"Viri," she says, "it's a charming idea."

9

IN THE RESTAURANT THEY WERE seated in the way he preferred, on adjoining sides of the table. The creases in the linen were fresh, the room filled with light.

"Would you like some wine?" he asked.

She was wearing a plum-colored dress, sleeveless—September is warm in New York—and a necklace of silver like foliage, like a swarm of *i*'s. He noticed everything, he fed on it: the ends of her teeth, her scent, her shoes. The room was crowded, brimming with talk.

He talked as well. He explained too much but he could not resist. One thing led to another, inspired it, the story of Stanford White, the city as it once had been, the churches of Wren. He invented nothing; it poured from him. She nodded and answered with silence, she drank the wine. She leaned with her elbows on the table; her glance made him weak. She was absorbed, hypnotized almost. She was intelligent, that was what made her extraordinary. She could learn, comprehend. Beneath her dress, he knew, she had nothing on; deBeque had told him that.

Her apartment belonged to a journalist who was away for a year. Books, sharpened pencils, wood piled neatly for the winter, everything one could need. There were copies of *Der Spiegel*, white Kneissl skis. She closed the door behind her and turned the lock. From that first moment, that cool and trivial act, it seemed a kind of movie started, silent, almost flickering,

46

a movie with foolish sections which nonetheless consumed them and became real.

There was one large room. Photos of friends on the wall, of boats, parties, afternoons at Puerto Marques. A plastic radio with the cities of Europe printed on its dial. *The Odyssey* by Kazantzakis. Red and blue edges of air-mail envelopes. Vailland's *Écrits Intimes*. In the sleeping alcove, a mirror set in hammered silver, carved birds, a hand-printed spread.

"It looks like Mexico," Viri said. His voice seemed to lurch from him, it had no tone. "Are those your skis?" he asked.

"No."

As if without reason then, she kissed him. He removed her shoes, one, then the other, they fell to the floor and rolled over. Her feet were aristocratic, well-formed. The faint sound of a zipper. She turned and raised her arms.

The wide afternoon bed, the dark of drawn curtains. He was escaping from his clothes, they fell in a heap. She lay there waiting. She seemed quiet, remote. He touched his forehead to her like a servant, like a believer in God. He could not speak. He embraced her knees.

It was an apartment in back facing courtyards with trees still in leaf. The sounds from the street had died. Her head was turned to one side, her throat bared. The newness of her drowned him. Somewhere near the bed the phone began to ring. Three rings, four. She did not hear it. It stopped at last.

They awoke much later, weak, reprieved. Her face was swollen from love. She spoke impassively.

"How do you like Mexico?"

He finally replied. "It's a nice town," he said.

He started her bath. In the dimness he saw his reflection like that of another man, a triumphant glimpse that held him as water crashed in the tub. His body was in shadow. It seemed strong, like a fighter's or jockey's. He was not a city man; suddenly he was primitive, firm as a bough. He had never been

47

so exhilarated after love. All the simple things had found their voice. It was as if he were backstage during a great overture, alone, in semi-darkness but able to hear it all.

She passed by him, naked, her skin grazing his. He was overwhelmed by this vision of her, he could not memorize it, he could not have enough. She was indifferent to his presence. Her nudity was dense, unchildish; her buttocks gleamed like a boy's.

She slipped into the water and bound up her hair. He was sitting outside, his knees drawn up, content.

"How is it?" he asked.

"It's like making love the second time."

His eyes moved around the well-arranged apartment. There are women who live carefully, who are cunning, who take a step only when the ground is firm beneath their feet. She was not one of these. There were her necklaces hung casually near the mirror, her scattered clothes, her cigarettes. He turned the television on without the sound. The set was foreign, the colors beautiful and deep. It seemed to him he was elsewhere, in a city in Europe, on a train. He had entered this room in which there was a woman who had been waiting for him, a clever woman who knew why he had come.

She stood against the doorway watching, whiteness encircling her haunches, the dark handful of hair. He longed to stare at her but was embarrassed. He was somehow dismayed that she should give herself to him. He knew he was eating her, like a fox.

"Do you think I should go back to the office?" she said.

"It might be better if we didn't go back at the same time." He picked up his watch. "My God," he murmured. "It's almost four. Why don't you come in about four-thirty? Say you've been to the dentist or something."

"Do you think they'll notice?"

"Will they notice?" he said. He had slowly begun to dress. "They probably already have."

48

He watched her comb her hair. She saw him in the mirror; she barely smiled. It was her silence, her submission which overwhelmed him. She wanted nothing, he felt; she would permit anything. He could not look at her without thinking of this, without filling with desire. It was as if she were lost. He was afraid to disturb her, to give her help. It was as if she had not really seen him yet. How long could it last? How long could it be before she recognized him, knew his thoughts? He was afraid of the sudden glint of a wrist watch, the flash of a smile, the sun on the hub cap of a car—any powerful male emission that might wake her. He wanted to continue to possess her even if he could not believe in it, to feel the confidence on which everything depended. He wanted to be invulnerable, even for an hour, to admire her as she lay face down, to talk to her softly as one talked to a child. He placed a pillow beneath her, doubling it with great care. They were swimming in slowness. It seemed five minutes were required to kneel between her legs. She lay stretched beneath him, his hand on her body to steady it . . .

He left her at the corner, near the museum. She stood waiting for the light. The buildings he passed seemed strangely dead, the street bare, even in sunlight. He turned to look once more. Suddenly, he did not know why—she was crossing the wide avenue alone—all his uncertainty fled. He began to run and caught up to her on the steps.

"I decided to go with you," he said. His voice was uneven; he managed to calm his breath. "There's a room of Egyptian jewelry, a beautiful room, I wanted to show it to you. Do you know who Isis is?"

"A goddess," she said.

"Yes. Another one."

She lowered her head in a gesture of profound contentment. She looked at him and smiled. "So she's one too, eh? You know them all."

He could feel her love plainly. She was his, he understood

49

it. He had never felt happier, more sure.

"There's a lot I want to show you."

She followed him into the great galleries. He guided her by the elbow, touching her often, her shoulder, the small of her back. In the end she would forget him; that was how she would win.

He drove home in a luminous twilight. The closing prices of shares were being given, the trees held the remnants of day.

Nedra was sitting at a table in the living room, notes spread around her. She was writing something.

"A story," she said. "Was the traffic bad?"

"Not very."

"You have to illustrate it for me." She had a certain, strange elation. Near her elbow was a San Raphael. She glanced up. "Would you like one?"

"I'll have a sip of yours. No, on second thought, I will have one."

She seemed calm, secure; she knew nothing, he was certain of it. She went to prepare the drink. He felt relief. He was like a hare, safe in his form at last. He had a glimpse of her crossing the hall and a feeling of great warmth came over him, affection for her hips, her hair, the bracelets on her wrist. In some way he was suddenly equal to her; his love did not depend on her alone, it was more vast, a love for women, largely ungratified, an unattainable love focused for him in this one wilful, mysterious creature, but not only this one. He had divided his agony; it was cleaved at last.

She returned with his drink and sat in a comfortable chair. "Did you work hard today?"

"Well, yes." He sipped the drink. "This is delicious. Thank you."

"And did it go well?"

"More or less."

"Um."

She knew nothing. She knew everything, the thought flashed, she was too wise to speak.

"What have you done today?" he asked.

"I've had a marvelous day, I really have. I'm writing the story of the eel for Franca and Danny. I don't like the books they give them in school. I want to do my own. Let me read it to you. I'll get it." She smiled at him before she rose, a wide, understanding smile.

"The eel . . ." he said.

"Yes. "

"That's very Freudian."

"I know, but Viri, I don't believe in all that. I think it's quite narrow."

"Narrow. Well, definitely narrow, but the symbolism is very clear."

"What symbolism?"

"I mean, it's clearly a cock," he said.

"I hate that word."

"It's inoffensive."

"No, it isn't."

"Well, I mean, there are worse."

"I just don't like it."

"What one do you like?"

"What word?"

"Yes."

"Inimitable," she said.

"Inimitable?"

"Yes." She began to laugh. "He had a big inimitable. Listen to what I've written."

She showed him a drawing she had done. It was just to give an idea; his would be better. "Oh, Nedra," he said, "it's beautiful."

A strange, snakelike creature of elegant lines lay adorned in flowers.

"What kind of pen did you do it with?" he said.

"A sensational pen. Look. I bought it."

He was examining it.

"You can use different points," she explained.

"It's a wonderful eel."

"For centuries, Viri," she said, "no one knew anything about them. They were an absolute mystery. Aristotle wrote that they had no sex, no eggs, no semen. He said they rose, already grown, from out of the sea. For thousands of years people believed that."

"But don't they lay eggs?"

"I'm going to tell you all that," she promised. "Today, all day, I was drawing this eel. Do you like the flowers?"

"Yes. Very much."

"You're much better than I am, yours will be fantastic. Besides, you're right, the eel is a male thing, but women understand it, too. It fascinates them."

"I've heard that," he murmured.

"Listen . . ."

He was empty, at peace. The darkened windows made the room seem bright. He had come in from the sea, from a thrilling voyage. He had straightened his clothes, brushed his hair. He was filled with secrets, deceptions that had made him whole.

"The eel is a fish," she read, "of the order *Apode*. It is brown and olive, its sides are yellow, its belly pale. The male lives in harbors and rivers. The female lives far from the sea. The life of the eel was always a mystery. No one knew where they came from, no one knew where they went."

"This is a book," he said.

"A book or a story. Just for us. I love the descriptions. They live in fresh water," she continued, "but once in their life, and once only, they go to the sea. They make the trip together, male and female. They never return."

"This is accurate, of course."

"The eel comes from an egg. Afterwards it is a larva. They

52

float on the ocean current, not a quarter of an inch long, transparent. They feed on algae. After a year or longer they finally reach the shore. Here they develop into true young eels, and here, at the river mouths, the females leave the males and travel upstream. Eels feed on everything: dead fish and animals, crayfish, shrimp. They hide in the mud by day and eat at night. In the winter they hibernate."

She sipped her drink and went on. "The female lives like this for years, in ponds and streams, and then, one day in autumn, she stops and eats nothing more. Her color changes to black or nearly black, her nose becomes sharper, her eyes large. Moving at night, resting by day, sometimes crossing meadows and fields, she travels downstream to the sea."

"And the male?"

"She meets the male who has spent all his life near the river mouth, and together, by hundreds of thousands, they return to the place where they were born, the sea of weeds, the Sargasso Sea. At depths of uncounted feet they mate and die."

"Nedra, it sounds like Wagner."

"There are common eels, pike eels, snake eels, sharp-tailed eels, every kind of eel. They are born in the sea, they live in fresh water and they go to the sea to spawn and die. Doesn't it move you?"

"Yes."

"I don't know how to end it."

"Perhaps with a beautiful drawing."

"Oh, there'll be drawings on every page," she said. "I want it filled with drawings."

His eyes felt tired.

"I want it to be on pale, gray paper," she said. "Here, draw one."

The children were coming downstairs.

"An eel?" he said.

"Here are a lot of pictures of them."

"Are they allowed to see what I'm doing?"

"No," she said. "No, it should be a surprise."

They ate in a Chinese restaurant that was crowded on weekends but this night rather empty. The menus were worn and coming apart at the fold. He had two vodkas and showed his children how to use chopsticks. The dishes were set on the table and uncovered: shrimp and peas, braised chicken, rice. Two lives are perfectly natural, he thought, as he picked up a water chestnut. Two lives are essential. Meanwhile he was talking about China: legends of emperors, the stone pleasure boats in Peiping. Nedra seemed watchful, quiet. He suddenly grew cautious and became almost silent, afraid of betraying himself. There was something he had overlooked, he tried to imagine what it was, something she had noticed by chance. The guilt of the inexperienced, like a false illness, bathed him. He tried to remain calm, realistic.

"Would you like some dessert?" he asked.

He called the waiter, who wore a name tag on his jacket.

"Kenneth?" Viri said in surprise.

"Kennif," the Chinese confirmed.

"Ah, yes. Kenneth, what is there for dessert? Do you have fortune cookies?"

"Oh yes, sah."

"Kumquats?"

"No kumquat," Kenneth said.

"No kumquat?"

"Jerro," he said appeasingly.

"Just the cookies, then," Viri said.

In clean pajamas he lay in bed waiting. His shoes were in the closet, his clothes put away. The coolness of the pillow beneath his head, the sense of weariness and well-being that filled him, he examined these things as if they were forewarnings. He lay resigned and cautious, ready for the blow.

Nedra took her place beside him. He lay there silent; he could not close his eyes. Her presence was the final pledge of sanctity and order, like those great commanders who were the last to sleep. The house was quiet, the windows dark, his daughters were in their beds. On Nedra's finger, somewhere near him, was a gold band of marriage, an ink-stained finger possibly, a finger that he longed to stroke, that he had not the nerve to touch.

They lay beside one another in the dark. In a drawer of the writing table, buried in back, was a letter composed of phrases clipped from magazines and papers, a pasted letter of love with jokes and passionate suggestions, a famous letter sent from Georgia before they were married when Viri was in the army, aching, alone. There were bees nesting in the greenhouse, erosion along the river shore. On a child's bureau, in a box with four small legs, were necklaces, rings, a starfish hard as wood. A house as rich as an aquarium, filled with the rhythm of sleep, limbs without strength, partly open mouths.

Nedra was awake. She suddenly rose on one elbow.

"What is that ungodly smell?" she said. "Hadji? Is that you?"

He was lying beneath the bed.

"Get out of there," she cried.

He would not move. She continued to command. At last, ears flat, he came forth.

"Viri," she sighed. "Open the window."

"Yes, what is it?"

"Your damned dog."

10

MARCEL-MAAS LIVED IN AN UNFIN-ished stone barn, much of it built with his own hands. He was a painter. He had a gallery that showed his work, but he was largely unknown. His daughter was seventeen. His wife—people found her strange—was in the last years of her youth. She was like a beautiful dinner left out overnight. She was sumptuous, but the guests were gone. Her cheeks had begun to quiver when she walked.

A thick beard, wartiness of nose, corduroy jacket, long silences: that was Marcel-Maas. His effort was all on canvas now; the window frames of the barn were flaking, the inside walls were stained. He repaired nothing, not even a leak; he seldom went out, he never drove a car. He hated travel, he said.

His wife was a mare alone in a field. She was waiting for madness, grazing her life away. She went to the city, to Bloomingdale's, the gynecologist, to art supply stores. Sometimes she would see a movie in the afternoon.

"Travel is nonsense," he announced. "The only thing you see is what's already inside you."

He was in his carpet slippers. His black hair lay loose on his head.

"I can't agree, somehow," Viri said.

"The ones who could gain something from travel, who have sensitivity, they have no need to travel."

"That's like saying those who could benefit from education have no need to be educated," Viri said.

Marcel-Maas was silent. "You're too literal," he said finally.

"I love to travel," his wife remarked.

Silence. Marcel-Maas ignored her. She was standing at the window, looking out at the day, drinking a glass of red wine. "Robert is the only one I've ever heard of who doesn't like to," she said. She continued to look out the window.

"Where have you ever traveled?" he said.

"That's a good question, isn't it?"

"You're talking about something you don't know anything about. You've read about it. You hear about these doctors and their wives who go to Europe. Bank clerks go to Europe. What is there in Europe?"

56

"What are you talking about?" she said.

Their daughter appeared in the doorway. She had lean arms, a lean body, small breasts. Her eyes were a riveting blue.

"Hello, Kate," Viri said.

She was engaged in biting her thumbnail. Her feet were bare.

"I'll tell you what Europe has," her father continued, "the detritus of failed civilizations. Night clubs. Fleas."

"Fleas?"

"Jivan's here," Kate said.

Nora Marcel-Maas pressed her face to the glass to see out. "Where?"

"He just drove up."

They heard the front door open. "Hello," a voice called.

"In here!" Marcel-Maas shouted.

They heard him come down the hall. The kitchen was the warmest room in the barn; the upper floors were not even heated.

Jivan was short. He was thin, like the boys one sees loitering in plazas of Mexico and countries further south. He was one of those boys, but with manners, with newly bought clothes.

"Hello," he said, entering. "Hello, Kate. You've gotten so beautiful. Let me see. Turn around." She did so without hesitation. He took her hand and kissed it like a bunch of flowers. "Robert, your daughter is fantastic. She has the heart of a courtesan."

"Don't worry. She's getting married."

"I thought it was just a trial," Jivan complained. "Isn't it?"

"More or less," she said.

"Viri," Jivan said, "I saw your car. That's what made me stop. How are you?"

"Are you driving your motorcycle?" Viri asked.

"Would you like another lesson?"

"I don't think so."

"That was nothing, that little accident."

"I'd like to try again," Viri said, "but my side still hurts."

Jivan accepted some wine. His hands were small, the nails well cared for, his face smooth, like a child's.

"Where have you been, in the city?" Marcel-Maas asked. "Where's Nora?"

"She was here a minute ago."

"Yes, I just came back," Jivan said. "I spent last night there. I went to a sort of reception . . . a Lebanese thing. It was late, so I stayed. They're very strange, American women," he said. He sat down and smiled politely. With him one was in cafés and drab restaurants warmed by the murmur of talk. He smiled again. His teeth were strong. He slept with a knife at the head of his bed.

"You know, I met this woman," he said. "She was the ex-wife of an ambassador or someone, blond, in her thirties. After the party we were near the place where I was going to stay. There was a bar, and I asked her, very matter-of-factly, if she'd like to stop there for a drink. You can't imagine what she said. She said, 'I can't. I have the curse.' "

"Haven't you had enough of them?" Marcel-Maas said.

"Enough? Can one have enough?"

"They're all like *lukoum* to you."

"*Locoum,*" Jivan corrected. "*Rahat locoum.* That's Turkish delight," he translated. "Very fattening. Robert likes the sound of it. Someday I'll bring you some *rahat locoum.* Then you'll see what it is."

"I know what it is," Marcel-Maas said. "I've had plenty of it."

"Not the real *rahat.*"

"Real."

Jivan was his friend, Marcel-Maas used to say. He had no other friends, not even his wife. He was going to divorce her anyway. She was neurotic. An artist should live with an uncomplicated woman, a woman like Bonnard's who would pose in only her shoes. The rest of it would follow. By the rest of it,

58

he meant a hot lunch every day, without which he could not work. He sat down to the table like an Irish laborer, hands stained, head down, potatoes, meat, thick slices of bread. He was silent, he had no jokes in him, he was waiting for things to resolve themselves while he ate, to form into something unexpected and interesting like the coat of fine bubbles on one's leg in the bath.

"So where's your mother, Kate?" he said. "Where'd she disappear to?"

Kate shrugged. She had the languor of a delivery boy, of someone who could not be hurt. She had lived through unheated bedrooms, unpaid bills, her father's abandoning them, his returns, beautiful birds he had carved out of applewood and painted and placed on her bed. He had spent a lot of time with her when she was a child. She remembered some of it. She had lived in the waves of color he had chosen, irradiated by them as by the sun. She had seen his torn sketchbooks on the floor with footprints across their pages, she had found him sprawled drunk in her room, his face on the thick spruce boards. She could never betray him; it was unthinkable. He asked nothing of her. All these years he had been beaten, as if in a street fight, before her eyes. He did not complain. He talked about painting sometimes, about pruning the trees. There was in him the saintliness of a man who never looked in the mirror, whose thoughts were dazzling but illiterate, whose dreams were immense. Every penny he had ever made he had given to them, and they had spent it.

Her boyfriend in California was a painter. They smoked, with music filling the air, for days at a time. They stayed out late, they slept half the day. Her father had taught her nothing, but the fabric of his life was the only one that felt good to her; she wore it as she wore his old shoes sometimes, his feet were very small.

"Well, where is she?" he asked. "You can't get rid of her when you work. Then when you want her, she leaves.

Why don't you go and tell her Jivan is here?"
"Oh, she knows," Kate replied.

11

JIVAN LOVED CHILDREN. THEY
showed him their games, they knew he would learn to play
them quickly. He did not descend to it; he became a child. He
had time for it. He embodied the simple virtues of a life lived
alone. He had time for everything—for cooking, for plants.

He lived in an empty store that had once been a pharmacy.
A long, serene room in front, the windows curtained with
bamboo and dense with plants. At night one could just barely
see in. It looked like a restaurant, the last patrons lingering. A
racing bicycle hung on the wall. A white Alsatian put his nose
silently, without barking, to the glass of the door.

He had birds in a cage and a gray parrot that spread its wings.
"Perruchio," he would say, "do the angel."
Nothing.
"The angel, the angel," he said. *"Fa l'angelone."*
Like a cat stretching its claws the parrot would slowly fan out
its wings and feathers. Its head turned in profile to one, black,
heartless eye.

"Why is he named Perruchio?" Danny asked. As she tried
to approach him, he moved sideways a step at a time.
"That was his name when I got him," Jivan said.

He played twenty questions. His education had been the
simplest possible: books. He read no fiction, only journals,
letters, the lives of the great.

"All right," he said. "Are you ready? I have one."
"A man," Danny said.
"Yes."

60

"Living."

"No."

A pause while they abandoned hope of its being easy.

"Did he have a beard?" Their questions were always oblique.

"Yes, a beard."

"Lincoln!" they cried.

"No."

"Did he have a big family?"

."Yes, big."

"Napoleon!"

"No, not Napoleon."

"How many questions is that?"

"I don't know—four, five," he said.

He brought them gifts, boxes in which expensive soap had come, miniature playing cards, Greek beads. He appeared for dinner in the October dusk, his feet crushing the cool gravel, a bottle of wine in his hand. Autumn was coming; it was in the air.

Hadji was lying on his side in the shadow of a shrub, the dark leaves touching him.

"Hello, Hadji. How are you?" He stopped to talk as if to a person. There was a faint movement near the dog's rump, a beat of the missing tail. "What are you, having a rest?"

He entered the house confident but correct, like a relative who knows his place. He respected Viri's knowledge, his background, the people he knew. He had dressed carefully, in the gray pants one finds in chain department stores, an ascot, a white shirt.

˙ "Hello, Franca," he said. He kissed her naturally. "Hello, Dan." He smiled as he extended his hand to Viri.

"Let me take the wine," Viri offered. He examined the label. "Mirassou. I don't know it."

"A friend of mine in California told me about it," Jivan said. "He has a restaurant. You know how the Lebanese are; when they come to a place, the first thing they do is find a good

61

restaurant, and then they always go there, they don't go any-where else. That's how I know him. I used to eat there. When I was in California, I was there every night."

"We're having lamb for dinner."

"It should be very good with lamb."

"Would you like a San Raphael?" Nedra asked.

"That would be nice," he said. He sat down. "Well," he said to Danny, "what have you been doing?" He was less at ease with them when their father was present.

"I want to show you something I'm making," she said.

"What is it?"

"It's a forest."

"What kind of forest?"

"I'll show you," she said, taking his hand.

"No," Viri said. "Bring it here."

They were almost the same size, the two men, the same age. Jivan had less assurance. They sat like the owner of a great house and his gardener. The one waited for the other to in-troduce a subject, to permit him to speak.

"It's getting cold," Viri remarked.

"Yes, the leaves are beginning to turn," Jivan agreed.

"It won't be long. I like the winter," Viri said. "I like the sense of its closing in on you."

"How is Perruchio?" Franca asked.

"I'm teaching him to hang upside down."

"How do you do that?"

"Like a bat," Jivan added.

"I'd like to see that."

"Well, when he learns."

Nedra brought his drink.

"Thank you," he said.

"Would you like more ice?"

"No, this is fine."

She was easily kind, Nedra, easily or not at all. Jivan sipped the drink. He wiped the bottom of the glass before setting it

62

down. He owned a moving and storage company, quite small. His truck was immaculate. The quilts were piled neatly, the fenders undented.

At noon, twice a week, sometimes more, she lay in his bed in the quiet room in back. On the table near her head were two empty glasses, her bracelets, her rings. She wore nothing; her hands were naked, her wrists.

"I love the taste of this," she said.

"Yes," Jivan said. "It's funny, no one else serves it."

"It's our favorite."

Noon, the sun beyond the ceiling, the doors closed tight. She was lost, she was weeping. He was doing it in the same, steady rhythm, like a monologue, like the creaking of oars. Her cries were unending, her breasts hard. She was flinging out the sounds of a mare, a dog, a woman fleeing for her life. Her hair was spilled about her. He did not alter his pace.

"Viri, light the fire, would you?"

"Let me do it," Jivan offered.

"I think there's some kindling in the basket," Viri said.

She saw him far above her. Her hands were clutching the sheets. In three, four, five vast strokes that rang along the great meridians of her body, he came in one huge splash, like a tumbler of water. They lay in silence. For a long time he remained without moving, as on a horse in the autumn, holding to her, exhausted, dreaming. They were together in a deep, limb-heavy sleep, sprawled in it. Her nipples were larger, more soft, as if she were pregnant.

The fire took hold, crackling, curling between the heavy pieces of wood, Jivan kneeling before it. Franca watched. She said nothing. She knew already, as a cat knows, as any beast; it was beating in her blood. Of course, she was still a child; her glances were brief, inconsequential. She had no power, only the buds of it, the vacancy where it would appear. She had already learned what it meant to say his name, artlessly pausing. Her mother was fond of him, she knew that, and she felt a warmth in him, not like her father's but less familiar, less bland. Even when he was doing something with Danny, as he was now, looking at the miniature landscape she had made of pine twigs and stones, his attention and thoughts were not far off, she was sure of it.

Nedra woke slowly to dreamlike, feathery touches. She struggled to come to the surface, to regain herself. It took half an hour. The afternoon sun was on the curtains, the voice of the day had changed. He held up an arm as if to the light. She held hers beside it. They stared at these arms with a vague, mutual interest.

"Your hand is smaller."

It moved closer to his, as if for comparison.

"You have better fingers," he said. They were pale, long, the bone within them showing. "Mine are square."

"Mine are square, too," she said.

"Mine are squarer."

Lunch, brandy, coffee. She loved the isolation, one side on a rising street, of this store that had been abandoned. She was filled with a sense of peace, of accomplishment. She had received goodness, now she radiated it, like a stone warmed for bed in the evening. She left by the side door. The ancient trees had burst the sidewalk, enormous trees, their trunks scarred like reptiles. Only a few leaves had fallen. It was still mild, the last hour of summer.

He was slight, Jivan, inconsequential. He was devoted to those American emblems of drab middle class, shoes, pastel sweaters, knit ties. She drove his car when her own was broken down. He scolded her for her carelessness with it, the papers it was strewn with, the dents that appeared in the side. She smiled at him, she apologized. She did as she pleased.

His ambition was to be a man of property. He had the cunning for it. He owned the storefront in which he lived, he was buying a house on ten acres near New City. He accumulated quietly, patiently, like a woman.

64

"I'm interested in your house," Nedra said.

"Yes, where is it, exactly?" Viri asked.

It was nothing, Jivan said, a very small house, but the land was nice. It was really a studio more than a house. There was a brook, though, with a ruined stone bridge.

They were eating dinner. They drank the Mirassou. Franca had half a glass. Her face seemed exceptionally wise in the soft light, her features indestructible.

"It's in your blood to have property, isn't it?" Nedra said.

"I think it's how you're brought up. But, in the blood . . . there could be something there, too. You know, I remember my father," he said. "He told me, 'Jivan, I want you to promise me three things.' I was just a little boy, and he said, 'Jivan, first of all, promise me you will never gamble. Never.' I mean, I was seven, eight years old. And he was saying, never gamble. 'If you must gamble,' he said, 'do it with the king of gamblers. You can find him in the streets, he is naked, he's lost everything, even his clothes.'

" 'Secondly'—I was still picturing this king, this beggar, but my father went on, 'Secondly, never visit whores.' Excuse me, Franca. I was eight years old, I didn't know what we were even talking about. 'Never,' he said, 'now promise me. If you do visit them, go only in the morning; that's when they have no paint, no powder, you can see what they are really like, do you understand?' 'Yes,' I said. 'Yes, Father.' 'Good,' he said, 'and the third thing, now listen: always paint a house before you sell it.' "

He was dark, he was filled with stories like the serpent in myths; each white tooth contained a story and each story a hundred others, they were all within him, intertwined, sleeping. The stranger, flashing with legends, he cannot be overcome. Once they have escaped him, these hymns, these jokes, these lies join with air, they are breathed, they cannot be filtered out. He is like the prow of a ship cutting through seas of sleep. Silence is mysterious, but stories fill us like the sun.

65

They are like fragments in which reflections lie like broken pieces; collect them and a greater shape begins to form, the story of stories appears.

"My father is dead," Jivan said, "but my mother is still alive. She's a wonderful woman, my mother. She knows everything. She has a house, a little garden, not far from the sea. Every morning she drinks a glass of wine. She's never left her town. She's like . . . who was it, Diogenes. In that little town with its trees in the square she's as happy as we are in the heart of the greatest city."

"Diogenes?" Viri said.

"Yes, isn't he the one that lived in the barrel?"

II

IN THE MORNING THE LIGHT came in silence. The house slept. The air overhead, glittering, infinite, the moist earth beneath—one could taste this earth, its richness, its density, bathe in the air like a stream. Not a sound. The rind of the cheese had dried like bread. The glasses held the stale aroma of vanished wine.

In the empty dining room hung the expulsion from Eden, a painting filled with beasts and a forest like Rousseau's from which two figures were emerging, the man still proud, the woman no less so. She was graceful, only half in shame; she was irreverent, her flesh gleamed. Even in the early light which deprived the marvelous serpent of his colors, the trees of their fruit, she was recognizable, at least to the painting's owner, her legs, the boldness of her body hair, its very life. It was Kaya.

He had noticed it only by chance. He had been drawn one day to its lambence, unthinking, as one is drawn to the worn spot on a relic, to a white face in a crowd. He had discovered it as if in confirmation, as if objects were proving his life.

On another wall was the famous photograph of Louis Sullivan in Mississippi, taken at Ocean Springs, his summer home. In white shirt and pants, a white cap, with a mustache and beard, he looked like a river captain or novelist. A large nose, delicate fingers, leaning almost daintily, posing, against a tree.

He could not be Sullivan, he could not be Gaudí. Well, perhaps Gaudí, who lived to that old age which is sainthood, an ascetic old age, frail, slight, wandering the streets of Barcelona, unknown to its many inhabitants. In the end he was struck by a streetcar and left unattended. In the bareness and odor of the charity ward amid the children and poor relations a single eccentric life was ending, a life that was more clamorous than the sea, an everlasting life, a life which was easy to abandon since it was only a husk; it had already metamorphosed, escaped into buildings, cathedrals, legend.

Morning. The earliest light. The sky is pale above the trees, pure, more mysterious than ever, a sky to dizzy the *fedayeen*, to end the astronomer's night. In it, dim as coins on a beach, fading, shine two last stars.

Autumn morning. The horses in nearby fields are standing motionless. The pony already has a heavier coat; it seems too soon. Her eye is dark and large, the lashes scanty. Walking close, one hears the steady sound of grass being eaten; the peace of the earth being milled.

His dreams are illicit; in them he sees a forbidden woman, encounters her in crowds with other men. In the next moment they are alone. She is loving, complaisant. Everything is incredibly real: the bed, the way she is arranged . . .

He wakes to find his wife lying on her stomach, the children on top of her, one on her back, the other on her buttocks. They are sleeping on her, clinging, head to foot. Their presence

68

absolves him, slowly he grows content. This world, its birds in their feathers, its sunlight . . . reason, at least for the moment. It consoles him. He is warm, potent, filled with impregnable joy.

What passes between them, this couple, in the endless hours of consort? What finds its way, what flows? Their bedroom was spacious, with a view of the river and waist-high windows, double-opening, the glass cut in diamonds, uneven, bowed outward, distorted as if by heat; here and there a sliver was missing, a lozenge escaped from its soft rim of lead. The walls were a faded turquoise, a curious color he no longer disliked. Beyond French doors was a white sunroom, white as linen, where, feet upward, on a wicker couch their dog was asleep.

Their life was two things: it was a life, more or less—at least it was the preparation for one—and it was an illustration of life for their children. They had never expressed this to one another, but they were agreed upon it, and these two versions were entwined somehow so that one being hidden, the other was revealed. They wanted their children, in those years, to have the impossible, not in the sense of the unachievable but in the sense of the pure.

Children are our crop, our fields, our earth. They are birds let loose into darkness. They are errors renewed. Still, they are the only source from which may be drawn a life more successful, more knowing than our own. Somehow they will do one thing, take one step further, they will see the summit. We believe in it, the radiance that streams from the future, from days we will not see. Children must live, must triumph. Children must die; that is an idea we cannot accept.

There is no happiness like this happiness: quiet mornings, light from the river, the weekend ahead. They lived a Russian life, a rich life, interwoven, in which the misfortune of one, a failure, illness, would stagger them all. It was like a garment, this life. Its beauty was outside, its warmth within.

*   *   *

69

For Franca's birthday there was a marvelous tablecloth Nedra had made, a jungle of flowers she had cut out of paper and then glued flat, piece by piece, the richest ferns and greens imaginable. She also made invitations, games, hats. There were chef's hats, opera hats, blue and gold conductor's hats with names painted on them. Over the table hung a great papier-mâché frog filled with gifts and chocolate coins. Viri played the piano for musical chairs, scrupulously careful not to look at the nervous marchers. Leslie Dahlander was there, Dana Paum whose father was an actor. There were nine little girls in all, no boys.

A cake with orange icing. Nedra had even made ice cream pungent with vanilla, so thick it stretched like taffy. The house was like a theater; there was the performance, in fact, of Punch and Judy to end the day, Viri and Jivan kneeling behind the stage, the script strewn between them, the limp forms of pup-pets arranged according to their appearance. The children sat on couches, screaming and clapping. They knew it by heart. In the midst of them was Franca. On this day of her birth she seemed more beautiful than ever before. Her face was filled with happiness, her white teeth shone. Viri had a glimpse of her through an opening at the edge of the stage. Her hands were in her lap. She sat attentive, hanging on every word.

"Where is the baby?"

"Why, didn't you catch him?"

"Catch him? What have you done?"

"Why, I threw him out the window, I thought you might be passing by."

Shouts of glee. Franca, radiant, was taller than the girls around her. She was clearly their star.

The automobiles turned slowly into the drive to pick up exhausted guests, the lights in the windows came on, a haze filled the evening. Hadji lay exhausted among the debris. At last there was quiet.

"Some of them are nice children," Nedra admitted. "I'm

very fond of Dana. But isn't it strange—do you suppose it's because they're ours—Franca and Danny are different. They have something very special I don't know how to describe."

"Jivan misread half the lines."

"Oh, the puppet show was marvelous."

"He stepped on Scaramouch—by mistake, of course."

"Which one is Scaramouch?"

"He's the one who says, *I'll make you pay for my head, sir.*"

"Oh, too bad."

"I can fix it," Viri conceded.

The room was silent, littered with bits of paper. The events of the day had already a kind of luminous outline. The frog, like a shipment of damaged goods, lay in pieces on the table, destroyed by countless blows.

She would make dinner after a while. They would dine together, something light: a boiled potato, cold meat, the remains of a bottle of wine. Their daughters would sit numbly, the dark of fatigue beneath their eyes. Nedra would take a bath. Like those who have given everything—performers, athletic champions—they would sink into that apathy which only completion yields.

2

 "ARE YOU HAPPY, VIRI?" SHE asked.

They were in traffic, driving across town at five in the afternoon. The great mechanical river of which they were part moved slowly at the intersections and then more freely on the long transverse blocks. Nedra was doing her nails. At each red light, without a word, she handed him the bottle and painted one nail.

Was he happy? The question was so ingenuous, so mild. There were things he dreamed of doing that he feared he never would. He often weighed his life. And yet, he was young still, the years stretched before him like endless plains.

Was he happy? He accepted the open bottle. She carefully dipped the brush, absorbed in her acts. Her instinct, he knew, was sharp. She had the even teeth of a sex that nips thread in two, teeth that cut as cleanly as a razor. All her power seemed concentrated in her ease, her questioning glance. He cleared his throat.

"Yes, I suppose I'm happy."

Silence. The traffic ahead had begun to move. She took the bottle to allow him to drive.

"But isn't it a stupid idea?" she asked. "If you really think about it?"

"Happiness?"

"Do you know what Krishnamurti says? Consciously or unconsciously, we are all completely selfish, and as long as we get what we want, we believe everything is all right."

"Getting what we want . . . but is that happiness?"

"I don't know. I know that not getting what you want is certainly unhappiness."

"I'd have to think about that," he said. "*Never* getting what you want, that could be unhappiness, but as long as there's a chance of getting it . . ."

They had only to reach Tenth Avenue and the street would be empty, open, as on a weekend; they would be free, speeding onto the highway, rushing north. The gray, exhausted crowds were trudging past newsstands, key shops, banks. They were slumped at tables in the Automat, eating in silence. There were one-legged pigeons, battered cars, the darkened windows of endless apartments, and above it all an autumn sky, smooth as a dome.

"It's difficult to think about," she said. "Especially when he says that thought can never bring you to truth."

72

"What can? That's the real question."

"Thought is always changing. It's like a stream, it moves around things, it's shifting. Thought is disorder, he says."

"But what is the alternative?"

"That's very complicated," she agreed. "It's a different way of seeing things. Do you ever feel you would like to find a new way of living?"

"It depends what you mean by a new way. Yes, sometimes I do."

It was the day Monica died, the little girl with one leg. The surgeons had not removed enough, there was no way to do it. She had begun to have pain again, invisible, as if it had all been for nothing. That pain was the knell. After it came fever and headaches. She swelled everywhere. She went into a coma. It took weeks, of course. Finally—it was in the evening, Viri was bringing in wood, bits of bark stuck to his sleeves, his arms filled, he was making a bank of cut ends, a parapet that would last through the winter when she died. Her father was still at work. Her mother was sitting there in a folding chair, and her child ceased to breathe. In an instant she was gone. She was lighter suddenly, much lighter, she lay with a kind of terrifying insignificance. Everything had left her—the innocence, the crying, the dutiful outings with her father, the life she had never lived. All these weigh something. They pass, dissolve, are scattered like dust.

The days had lost their warmth. Sometimes at noon, as if in farewell, there was an hour or two like summer, swiftly gone. On the stands in nearby orchards were hard, yellow apples filled with powerful juice. They exploded against the teeth, they spat white flecks like arguments. In the distant fields, seas of dank earth far from towns, there were still tomatoes clinging to the vines. At first glance it seemed only a few, but they were hidden, sheltered; that was how they had survived.

Nedra had a basket full of them. Viri had two. The weight

was astonishing. They were like wet clothes; they were heavy as oranges. A family of gleaners, their faces dirty, their hands dark with the stain of this last moist earth. It was a field near New City; the farmer was their friend.

"Pick the small ones," Viri told his daughters.

Their baskets were filled as well. They were putting the little ones in their pockets, those that were partly green. They moved down the endless rows, straying back and forth, tiring, learning to stoop, to work, to feel the naked fruit in their hands. They cried out to each other, sometimes they sat on the ground.

At last they reached the end. "Papa, we have so many!"

"Let me see."

They stood near the car, tomatoes piled around them, the dirt still clinging, the air turned chill. Nedra looked like a woman who had once been rich. She held her hands away from her. Her hair had come loose.

"What are we going to do with all these fucking tomatoes?" she laughed. Her marvelous laugh, in the fall, at the edge of the fields.

"Come on, Hadji," she called, "you filthy beast." His nose was caked with earth. "What a day you've had," she said.

Their fingernails were black, their shoes encrusted. They put the tomatoes in the unheated entry to the kitchen as Jivan drove up in the dusk.

3

"THERE ARE THINGS I LOVE ABOUT marriage. I love the familiarity of it," Nedra said. "It's like a tattoo. You wanted it at the time, you have it, it's implanted in your skin, you can't get rid of it. You're hardly even aware of it any more. I suppose I'm very conventional," she decided.

74

"In some ways . . ."

"If you asked people what they wanted, what would most of them say? I know what I'd say: money. I'd like a lot of money. That's the one thing I never have enough of."

Jivan said nothing.

"I'm not materialistic, you know that. Well, I am, I suppose; I like clothes and food, I don't like the bus or depressing places, but money is very nice. I should have married someone with money. Viri will never have any. Never. You know, it's terrible to be tied to someone who can't possibly give you what you want. I mean, the simplest thing. We really aren't meant to live together. And yet, you know, I look at him making puppets for them, they sit there with their heads close to his, absolutely absorbed by it."

"I know."

"He's doing the entire *Elephant's Child.*"

"Yes."

"The Kola-Kola bird, the crocodile, everything. You know, he is talented. He says, 'Franca . . .' and she says, 'Yes, Papa.' I can't explain it."

"Franca is very beautiful."

"This terrible dependency on others, this need to love."

"It isn't terrible."

"Oh, yes, because at the same time there is the *stupidity* of this kind of life, the boredom, the arguments."

He was placing a pillow. She raised herself without a word.

"With the milk goes the cow," he said. "With the cow goes the milk."

"The cow."

"You understand that."

"If you want milk you must accept a cow, a barn, fields, all that."

"That's it," he said.

He was moving unhurriedly, like a man setting a table plate by plate. There are times when one is important and others

75

when one almost does not exist. She felt him kneel. She could not see him. Her eyes were closed, her face pressed to the sheet.

"Karezza."

He was solemn, unhearing. "All right," he said.

He was slow, intent, like an illiterate trying to write. He was unaware of her; he was beginning the act as if it were a cure. The slowness, the deliberation struck her down like blows.

"Yes," he murmured. His hands were on her shoulders, on the swell of her buttocks with a force that made her helpless. The weight, the presumption of it was overwhelming. Her moans began to rise.

"Yes," he said, "cry out."

There was no movement, none at all except for a slow distending to which she reacted as if to pain. She was rolling, sobbing. Her shouts were muffled. He did nothing, then more of it and more.

Afterwards it was as if they had run for miles. They lay near each other, they could not speak. An empty day, the gulls on the river, blue and reflecting blue like layers of mica.

"When you do it," she said, "I sometimes have the feeling I'm going so far I won't be able to come back. I feel as if I'm . . ." she suddenly rose partway. "What's that?"

The door was rattling. He listened. "It's the cats."

Her head fell to the bed again.

"What do they want?"

"They want to come in," he said. "It's their one ambition."

The noise at the door continued.

"Let them in."

"Not now," he said.

She lay like a woman sleeping. Her back was bare, her arms above her head, her hair loose. He touched this back as if it were something purchased, as if he had discovered it for the first time.

She could never be without him, she had told him that. There were times she hated him because he was free in a

76

way she was not; he had no children, no wife.

"You're not going to get married, are you?" she said.

"Well, of course I think about it."

"It's not necessary for you. You already have the fruit of marriage."

"The fruit. The fruit is something else."

"You have plenty of time," she insisted. "I'm stupid. I've told you the thing I'm most afraid of."

"Don't be afraid."

"I can't help it. It's something I can't do anything about. I depend on you."

"Our lives are always in someone else's hands."

Her car was parked outside. It was afternoon, winter, the trees were bare. Her children were in class, writing in large letters, making silver and green maps of the states.

Viri came home in the darkness, headlights blazing his approach, illuminating the trees, the house, and ending like dying stars.

The door closed behind him. He came in from the evening air, cool and whitened, as if from the sea. His hair was even washed out of place. He had come from drawings, discussions with clients. He was tired, a little awry.

"Hello, Viri," she said.

A fire was burning. His children were laying out forks.

"Would you like a drink?" she asked.

"Yes." He kissed his daughters as each went by. He ate a small, green olive bitter as tea.

She prepared it. She liked her life this evening, he could tell. She was filled with contentment. It was on her mouth, in the shading of the corners.

"Franca," she said, "here, open the wine."

The radio was playing. The candles on the table were lit. The first nights of winter with their tidelike cold. From afar the house seems a ship, dark, unmoving, every window filled with light.

77

4

ROBERT CHAPTELLE WAS THIRTY.
His hair was thinning, his lips an unnatural red. Beneath his
eyes lay the faint blue of illness, asthma among other things,
the asthma of Proust. An intellectual face, the bone gleaming
in it. He was a friend of Eve's. He had met her at a dinner
during which he mainly sat alone. She tried to talk to him; he
had an accent.

"You're French."

"How could you guess?" he said.

"How long have you been here?"

He shrugged. "Yes, it's time to go," he agreed.

"I mean how long have you been in America?"

"The same," he said.

He was self-indulgent, a failure. He had not abandoned
failure; it was his address, his street, his one comfort. His life
was one of intimacy and betrayal. Of himself he wrote: extravagant, false. He was impractical, moody, a deviate. He suffered
and loved like a woman; he remembered the weather and the
menu in restaurants, hours that were like a broken necklace in
a drawer. He kept everything, he announced, he kept it here,
tapping his chest.

Chaptelle was a name that had originally been Russian. His
mother had come to Paris in the twenties, during the civil war.
He had met Beckett, Barrault, he had met everyone. There is
a kind of self-esteem which forces walls of ice. This is not to
say he wasn't remembered; his intensity, his dark eyes ringed
with shadows, the confidence he carried within him like a
tumor—these were not easily forgotten.

They talked about writers: Dinesen, Borges, Simone de Beauvoir.

"She is a dreary woman," he said. "Sartre, now Sartre has *esprit*."

"Do you know Sartre?"

"We have coffee in the same café," Chaptelle said. "My wife, my ex-wife, knows him better. She works in a bookshop."

"You've been married."

"We are very good friends," he said.

"What's her name?" Eve asked.

"Her name? Paule."

They had spent their marriage trip in all the little towns Colette had gone to in the years she was dancing in revues. They traveled like brother and sister. It was an *hommage*.

"Do you know what it is to be really intimate, to feel safe with someone who will never betray you, will never force you to act unlike yourself? That was what we had."

"But it didn't last," Eve said.

"There were other problems."

When Nedra met him, he was calm; he seemed bored. She noticed that his cuffs were dirty, his hands clean; she recognized him immediately. He was a Jew; she knew it the moment she saw him. They shared a secret. He was like her husband; in fact he seemed to be the man Viri was hiding, the negative image that had somehow escaped.

He drank a demitasse of coffee into which he stirred two spoons of sugar. He was an unmarried son come home in the morning, the son who has lost everything. He sniffed. He had nothing to say. He was as empty as one who has committed a crime of passion. He was his own corpse. One could see in him both the murderer and the half-nude woman crumpled on the floor.

"Your husband's an architect," he said finally.

"Yes."

He sniffed again. He touched his face with the napkin. He had forgotten Eve, that was obvious; one had only to look at them to see that.

"Is he talented?"

"Very," Nedra said. "You're a writer."

"I'm a playwright."

"Forgive me for not knowing, but have any of your plays been put on?"

"Put on? Produced, you mean?"

"Yes."

"Not yet," said Chaptelle calmly. It was his brevity which convinced one, his disdain. "Could I borrow one of your cigarettes?"

The desperation of certain people is such that even in inactivity, even in sleep, we understand that their lives are being spent. They are saving nothing for later. They have no need to save. Every hour is a kind of degradation, an attempt to throw away all.

He crushed the cigarette out after one or two puffs. "I'm writing plays, but not for the stage, not for the present stage," he said. "Do you know who Laurent Terzieff is? I'm writing a play for Laurent Terzieff. He's the greatest new actor to appear in twenty years."

"Terzieff . . ."

"I go to his rehearsals, no one knows I am there. I sit in the back row or over to the side. So far I have yet to detect a single failing in him, a single flaw."

He was eager to talk. For those we are born to speak to we need prepare nothing, the lines are ready, everything is there. He questioned her knowledge of the theater. He told her who the great writers were, he named the unknown masterpieces of the time.

*　　　*　　　*

80

"Viri," she said, "I've met the most marvelous man."

"Yes? Who?"

"You don't know him," she said. "He's a writer. He's French."

"French . . ."

An evening a week giving work as an excuse, sometimes twice a week, whenever he could, he stayed late in town. Slowly his life was being divided. It was true he seemed the same, precisely the same, but that is often all one sees. Collapse is hidden, it must reach a certain stage before it breaks the surface, the pillars begin to yield, façades pour down. His infatuation with Kaya was like a wound. He wanted to look at it every minute, to touch it. He wanted to speak to her, to fall on his knees before her, embrace her legs.

He sat by the fire. Two cast-iron Hessians held the burning logs, the glow of coals at their feet. Nedra was curled in a chair.

"Viri," she said, "you must read this book. When I'm finished, I'm going to give it to you."

A book with the edge of its pages dyed mauve, the title in worn letters. She began to read aloud to him, the wood erupting softly in the fireplace like shots.

"What is it called?" he said finally.

Earthly Paradise.

He felt weak. The words made him helpless; they seemed to describe the images that overwhelmed him, the silence of the borrowed apartment in which she slept, the width of the bed, her pure, lazy limbs.

In the morning he went early. The sun was white and glancing, the river pale. He drove in long, smooth curvings, straightaways, the fever of expectation making him blind. The great bridge gleamed in the morning light; beyond it lay the city, wide as the sea, its trains and markets, its newspapers, trees. He was composing lines, speaking to her, whispering into her ear,

*I love you as I love the earth, white buildings, photographs,
noons . . . I adore you,* he said. Cars drifted alongside him. He
looked at his face in the rear-view mirror; yes, it was good, it
was worthy.

He began to be silent. The city streets were bare. They gave
evidence in their stillness and desolation of the night that had
passed, they confessed to it like a weary face. He began to be
uneasy. It was like an anteroom that led to a place where
something terrible had happened; he could smell it as beasts
smell the killing house. Suddenly he became frightened. He
would find the apartment empty. It was as if he had caught
sight of her shoe outside a building; he could not bear to
imagine more.

A white, winter morning. The street was cold. He unlocked
the front door and ran up the stairs. At her apartment, not
knowing why, he knocked lightly.

"Kaya?"

Nothing. He knocked again, softly, repeatedly. Suddenly,
like a blow, he understood. It was true; she had spent the night
elsewhere.

"Kaya."

He unlocked the door and opened it. It stopped abruptly
against the night chain.

"Who is it?" she said.

He had a glimpse of her, nothing more. "Viri." There was
a silence. "Open the door," he said.

"No."

"What's wrong?"

"Someone's here."

For a moment he could not think what to do. It was early
morning. He was ill, he was dying. The walls, the carpets were
drinking his life.

"Kaya," he pleaded.

"I can't."

He was staggered because he was innocent. Everything was

82

the same, everything in the world was still in its place, and yet he could not recognize it, his existence had vanished. Her nakedness, late dinners, her voice on the phone—he was left with these, like scraps she had left behind. He started down the stairs. I am dying, he thought. I have no strength.

He sat in the car. I must see him, he decided, I must see who he is. A postal truck went down the street. People were going to work. He was too near the door. There was a place to park further on. He started the car and drove to it.

Suddenly someone came out, a round-faced man with an attaché case, wearing a loden coat. No, Viri thought, impossible. The next moment there were two more emerging—was it going to be a comedy?—and then, still another. He was fifty; he looked like a lawyer.

He sat in the office unable to think. His draftsmen were arriving. Are you all right, they asked. Yes. Their wide, flat tables were already spilling sunlight. They hung up their coats. It seemed that the white telephones, the chrome and leather chairs, the sharpened pencils, had lost their significance; they were like objects in a store that has closed. His gaze passed over them in ringing silence, a silence that could not be penetrated though he spoke in it, nodded, heard conversation.

At ten she came in. "Please, I can't talk," she said.

She wore a slim, ribbed sweater the color of shipping cartons; her face was white. As she walked through the room he was conscious of her legs, the sound of her heels on the floor, the bones of her wrists. He could not look at her, everything about her he had known, had access to, was fading.

He left before noon for a meeting. He called her as soon as he was outside. Pages were torn from the directory in the phone booth. The door would not close.

"Kaya," he said. "Please. What do you mean, you can't talk?"

She seemed helpless.

"I need you," he said. "I can't do anything without you. Oh,

God," he breathed. His eyes were filling with tears. He could not tell her what he felt. He was like a fugitive. "Oh, God, I know this girl . . ."

"Stop."

"I've gone to prison for her, my ribs are showing. I've given up my life . . ."

"How did I know you were coming?" she said. "Why didn't you call me?" She began to weep. "Don't you have any brains?" she cried.

He hung up. He knew perfectly well that talking was useless, that there had been a moment when he should have slapped her with all his strength. But he was not that sort of man. His hatred was weak, pallid, it could not even darken the blood.

Ten minutes later he excused himself from his client and rushed to call her again. He tried to be calm, unfrightened.

"Kaya."

"Yes."

"Meet me this evening."

"I can't."

"Tomorrow, then."

"Maybe tomorrow."

"Please, promise me."

She would not answer. He begged her.

"Yes, all right," she finally said.

He could not go back to work. He went instead to her apartment and rang the bell. No answer. He let himself in. A chill had come over him, a deep chill like the shock that follows an accident. The sun was shining. The radio gave the weather, the news.

The bed was unmade, he could not approach it. In the kitchen were dirty glasses, a tray of ice that now held only water. He went to the closet. Her things surrounded him, they seemed flimsy, without substance. His hand trembling, he somehow cut the heart out of a tumbling, dark dress, the most beautiful one she owned. He was afraid she might come back

84

as he was doing it; he had no explanation, no way to turn. Afterwards he sat by the window. His breath was shallow, like that of a newt. He sat motionless; the emptiness, the tranquillity of the rooms began to calm him. She lay in the gray light of morning, her back smooth and luminous, her legs weak. She was barelimbed, unthinking. He parted her knees. Never.

Nedra was happy that evening. She seemed pleased with herself.

"Are you all right?" she asked.

"What? Yes, it's been a long day."

"We're going to have our own eggs," she announced.

The children were ecstatic. "Come and see!" they cried.

They pulled him by the hand to the solarium with its floor of gravel. The chickens ran for the corners, then along the wall. Danny managed to catch one at last.

"Look at him, Papa, don't you love him?"

The hen sat panicked within her arms, its small eyes blinking.

"Her," Viri said.

"Do you want to know their names?" Franca asked.

He nodded vaguely.

"Papa?"

"Yes," he said. "Where did you get them?"

"That's Janet . . ."

"Janet."

"Dorothy."

"Yes."

"And that one is Madame Nicolai."

"That one . . ."

"She's older than the others," Franca explained.

He sat on the step. Already there was a slight, bitter smell in the room. A bit of feather floated mysteriously down. Madame Nicolai was sitting as if dumped in a great, warm pile of feathers, brown, beige, becoming paler as it descended to soft tan.

"She is wiser," he said.

"Oh, she's very wise."

"A sage among hens. When do they begin to lay eggs?"

"Right away."

"Aren't they a little young?" He sat idly on the step watching their careful, measured movements, the jerk of their heads. "Well, if they don't lay eggs, there are other things. Chicken Kiev . . ."

"Papa!"

"What?"

"You wouldn't do that."

"They'd understand."

"No, they wouldn't."

"Madame Nicolai would understand," he said.

She was standing now, apart from the others, looking at him. Her head was in profile, one unblinking eye black with an amber ring.

"She's a woman of the world," he said. "Look at her bosom, look at the expression on her beak."

"What expression?"

"She understands life," he said. "She knows what it is to be a chicken."

"Is she your favorite?"

He was trying to coax her to come to his half-closed hand.

"Papa?"

"I think so," he murmured. "Yes. She is a hen among hens. A hen's hen," he said.

They were clinging to his arms in happiness and affection. He sat there. The chickens were clucking, making little soft sounds like water boiling. He continued to extol her—she had now turned cautiously away—this adulterer, this helpless man.

86

5

FRANCA WAS TWELVE. IN THOSE slim dresses that fit a body still without hips one could not easily tell her age. She was perfectly formed, though without even the faint beginning of breasts. Her cheeks were cool. Her expression was that of a woman.

She made up stories and did drawings for them. *Margot was an elephant. Juan was a snail. Margot loved Juan very much, and Juan was mad about her. They used to sit and just look at each other. One day, she said to him, Juan.*

Yes, Margot.

Juan, you are not very intelligent.

I'm not?

You haven't seen the world.

No, Juan said, I don't have an airplane . . .

The writer as a child, solemn, serene. Viri took a photograph of her holding the rabbit in her arms, a white paw resting on her wrist.

"Don't move," he whispered.

He stepped nearer, focusing. The rabbit was calm, immobile. His eyes, black and gleaming, gave no sense of seeing; they were hypnotized, fixed. His ears lay along his back like wilted celery. Only his nose trembled with life. Slowly Franca put her face to him, her lips to his rich coat. Viri took the picture.

She was in touch with mystery, like her mother. She knew how to tell tales. The gift had appeared early. It was either a true talent or it was precocious and would fade. She was writing a story called *The Queen of Feathers*. She sat on the entry step observing the hens. The house was silent. They were aware of her and unable, at the same time, to maintain interest. Their

87

minds wandered, they searched for bits of grain as she patiently acquired their secrets. Suddenly their heads went up. They listened; someone was coming.

It was Danny. Hadji was with her. As soon as she opened the door he began to bark.

"Oh God, Danny."

"What are you doing?"

"Nothing. Get him out of here. He's scaring the chickens."

They both shouted at him. The chickens were huddled beneath an iron table filled with plants. The dog was in the doorway, barking. His ears went flat at each bark, his legs were planted firmly.

"He doesn't like them," Danny said.

"Make him stop."

"I can't. You know you can't make him stop."

"Well, take him away, then."

They flew at him with their hands, shooing him down the hallway. He gave ground unwillingly, barking at them, at the room, the unseen chickens.

"It's beginning to smell in there," Danny said.

As sisters they were not devoted. They complained about each other, they hated to share. Franca was more beautiful, more admired. Danny was slower to bloom.

Their opinion, however, when he came to dinner, of Robert Chaptelle was the same: he did not interest them.

He was nervous when he arrived. He had taken the train as far as Irvington, but it was as if he had made a journey of a thousand miles. He was undone. Viri attempted to put him at ease and even to discuss Valle-Inclan, whose plays he had been reading, but the reaction to this was as if Chaptelle did not hear a word. As soon as they entered the house, he said, "Do you have any music?"

"Yes, of course."

"Could we hear something?" Chaptelle said.

He waited, ignoring the children, while Viri selected some

records. The music began. It was like a powerful medicine. Chaptelle grew calm.

"Valle-Inclan had only one arm," he declared. "He cut the other off so he could be like Cervantes. Are you interested in Spanish writers?"

"I don't know very much about them."

"I see."

He ate with his head close to the plate like a man in the dining hall of an institution. He did not eat much. He wasn't hungry, he commented, he had eaten a sandwich on the train. As for wine, he had none. He was forbidden to drink any alcohol.

Afterwards they played Russian bank. Chaptelle, almost indifferent at first, became very animated.

"Ah," he said. "Yes, I have a talent for cards. When I was twenty I did almost nothing else. What is this? Is this the jack?"

"The king."

"Ah. *Le roi,*" he exclaimed. "Yes, I remember."

Viri drove him to the train. They stood on the long, deserted platform. Chaptelle peered down the empty tracks.

"It comes from the other way," Viri told him.

"Oh." He looked in that direction.

They entered a small waiting room where a stove was kept going. The benches were scarred with initials of travelers, the walls dense with certain primitive drawings.

"Can you lend me a few dollars for the taxi?" Chaptelle said unexpectedly.

"How much do you need?"

"I don't have any money with me. I have only a ticket. At least I can't be robbed."

Viri had withdrawn what money he had. He held out two dollars. "Is that enough?"

"Oh, yes," Chaptelle said grandly. "Here, a dollar is enough."

89

"You might need it."

"I never tip," Chaptelle explained. "You know, your wife is a very intelligent woman. More than intelligent."

"Yes," Viri agreed.

"*Du chien.* You know that expression?"

The floor beneath their feet had begun to tremble. The high, lighted windows of the train rushed by and abruptly slowed. Chaptelle did not move.

"I can't find my ticket," he announced.

Viri was holding the door. A few passengers had stepped down; the conductor was looking both ways.

"Why don't you get on and then look for it?"

"I had it in my *poche* . . . *Ah, merde!*" He began to mutter in French.

There was the piercing sound of a whistle. Chaptelle straightened up. "Ah, here," he said.

He hurried out and stood, indecisively, trying to see which doors were open. There was only one, in which the trainman stood.

"Where does one go up?" Chaptelle asked.

The trainman ignored him.

"There, where he is," Viri called.

"But that's two cars away. That's the only one they open?"

He began to walk toward it. Viri expected the first jerking movement of the wheels at any second. The trains were electric and accelerated quickly.

"Wait, here's a passenger!" he shouted. He detested himself.

Chaptelle was casually climbing the steps. The train began moving before he had taken a seat. He bent over slightly in the aisle to wave with an awkward motion, palm forward, like a departing aunt. Then he was gone.

"Did you get him aboard?" Nedra asked.

"He's one of a kind," Viri said. "I hope."

"He's invited me to come to France."

"It would be a trip you would never forget. What do you mean, he's invited you? Doesn't he know you're married? This evening, for instance, did he think it was just a coincidence we were here together?"

"It doesn't have anything to do with marriage. I mean, as a man he has no attraction for me. I wouldn't hide it."

She was lying in bed, white pillows behind her, a book in her hand. She seemed quite reasonable.

"We'd stay at his mother's," she said.

"Nedra, you don't even speak French."

"I know. That's why it would be so interesting." She could not keep from smiling. "His mother has an apartment on Place St. Sulpice. It's a beautiful square. You can walk out, he says, there's a balcony all around with an iron railing."

"Wonderful. A railing."

"Fireplaces in the bedrooms. It isn't dark, he says. It's on the uppermost floor."

"Linen is supplied, I presume."

"His mother *lives* there."

"Nedra, you really are extraordinary. You know I love you."

"Do you?"

"But as for going to France . . ."

"Just think about it, Viri," she said.

6

EVE WAS TALL. HER FACE HAD cheekbones. Her shoulders slumped when she walked. The shelves in her living room were bent beneath the books. She worked for a publisher; oh, you've never heard of him, she said.

Her life was one in which everything was left undone—

letters unanswered, bills on the floor, the butter sitting out all night. Perhaps that was why her husband had left her; he was even more helpless than she. At least she was gay. She stepped from her littered doorway in pretty clothes, like a woman who lives in the *barrio* walking to a limousine, stray dogs and dirt on the way.

Her ex-husband came to visit her. He sat hunched in a chair by the fireplace, an overnight bag near his feet. His suede jacket was stained, the pockets torn. He was only thirty-two; he had the face of a derelict. His eyes were spent, they had nothing in them. When he spoke, it was agony—enormous, long pauses. He was going to . . . build a model with his son, he said.

"Don't keep him up too late," Eve said. She was leaving in the morning for Connecticut, where they still owned an old house they used alternately.

"Listen, while I think of it . . ." he said.

Silence. Children were skating in the narrow, blind street. The afternoon was fading.

"The willow near the pond," he said. His voice was lost, wandering. "You should call Nelson, the guy who gardens, while you're there. It needs . . ." He stopped. "Something's wrong with it," he finally said.

"The one that's not growing?"

A pause.

"No, the one that is," he said.

He'd been living with a young woman. They ate in restaurants; they appeared at parties. When he stood up his pants were empty; they hung in the back like an old man's.

"He's so sad," Eve said.

"You're lucky he's gone," Nedra told her.

"She doesn't even keep his clothes clean."

"That's why he's sad."

Eve laughed. There was gold behind her teeth; it made them dark at the edges, a halo of bitumen, like a whore's. She was ready to laugh. She was funny. Her life had no foundation. She was only vaguely devoted to it, she could treat it lightly. It was this that made her irresistible—these smiles, this carefree air.

They were like sisters, the same long limbs, the same humor. It was easy for them to imagine themselves in each other's place.

"I'd like to go to Europe," Nedra told her.

"Wouldn't that be marvelous?"

"You've been to Italy."

"I have, haven't I?" Eve said.

"What was it like?"

Their words drifted off in the late afternoon. They were sitting in the worn love seats. Anthony was at a friend's. His schoolbooks were on the table, his bicycle in the kitchen. The untidiness of the apartment and its little garden were pleasing to Nedra; she could never live like that herself.

"Well, I was there with Arnaud," Eve said.

"Where did you stay? I'll bet Arnaud is great in Rome."

"He loves it. You know, he speaks Italian, talks to everyone. Long conversations."

"And what did you do?"

"Usually I kept on eating. You know, you sit in those restaurants for hours. He reads the menu, he reads everything on it. Then he discusses it with the waiter, he looks to see what people at the other tables are eating. If you're in a hurry, forget it. He says, no, no, wait a minute, let me see what he says about the . . . the *fagioli.*"

"The *fagioli* . . ."

"I forget, what are *fagioli?* I don't know. We were always eating them. He likes *bollito misto,* he likes *baccala.* We ate, we visited churches. He knows Italy."

"I'd love to go with Arnaud."

"He likes very small hotels. I mean, *minute.* He knows all of them. I learned a lot. There are certain kinds of bugs you can let live on your body, for instance."

"What?"

"Well, *I* never did, but that's what he claimed. He'll never marry," Eve said.

"Why do you say that?"

"I know it. He's selfish, but it isn't selfishness. He's not afraid of being alone."

"That's the whole thing, isn't it?"

"Yes. On the other hand, I am," Eve said.

"No, you're not."

"I'm terrified of it. I think I fear it more than anything. He knows how to face it. He likes people. He likes to eat, go to the theater."

"But eventually he's alone. He has to be."

"Well, I don't know. It doesn't bother him. He's content, he knows we're thinking of him."

She was terrific, Eve; that was what he said. She was generous in every way. She gave books, dresses, friends, she graced rooms with her hard, dissolute body, her wanton mouth. The kind of woman seen on the arm of a boxing champion, the kind who is not married, who appears one morning with blackened eyes.

They were thinking of him.

"Yes," Nedra agreed, "that is a difficulty. How is Arnaud?"

"It's his six-month birthday next week. I mean, it's halfway between."

"Do you celebrate that?"

"I sent him some handkerchiefs," Eve said. "He likes a certain kind of big workman's handkerchief, and I found some. I don't know, sometimes he drops out of sight for a week or two. Sometimes he even goes away. I wish I were a man."

7

CHRISTMAS. TOM, THE OLD SUPER, drinking as always. He had a lean face and an ulcerous ear. An honest man with bottles hidden in the basement behind the fuse boxes. He jumped back when Viri tried to hand him an envelope with some money in it.

"What's that?" he cried. "No, no."

"It's a little something for Christmas."

"Oh, no." He had not shaved. "Not for me. No, no." He seemed about to cry.

The draftsmen were bent over their tables in anticipation of their bonuses. The shops were glittering. It was dark before five.

Parked beneath a sign that prohibited it absolutely, Viri ran up the steps of the theater to buy tickets for *Nutcracker Suite*. It was a ritual; they saw it every year. Franca was taking ballet at Balanchine's school. She had the calm and grace to be a dancer, but not the resolution. She was the youngest in the class, their legs rose in unison to dry commands, it was above Broadway, over a melancholy Schrafft's.

Dusk in the city, the traffic, the buses pouring light, reflections in windows, optician's shops. It was cold, splintering, a world filled with crowds passing newsstands, cut-rate drugstores, girls in Rolls-Royces, their faces lit by the dash.

Parking by hydrants as Viri went in to buy a single bottle of wine and write a check for it, or flat, white wedges of Brie, soft as porridge—nothing in abundance, nothing stored up—they cruised along Broadway. It was their natural street, their boulevard, they were blind to its ugliness. They went to Zabar's, to the Maryland Market. They had certain places for everything, discovered in the days when they were first married and lived nearby.

The radio was playing, the parking lights were on. Nedra sat turned in her seat, talking to the children while in the store Viri was slowly moving to the head of the line. They could see his gestures through the window, could almost make out his words. The girl to whom he was speaking was sullen, rushed; she was picking up pastries with a square of waxed paper in her hand.

"You'll have to speak up," she said.

"Yes. What are those?"

"Apricot."

"Ah," he managed.

She had a wide, even mouth. She waited. He felt a sudden muteness, despair. Before him he was seeing a last image, as of a crude sister, of Kaya. Her breasts made him weak.

"Well?"

"Two of those, then," he said.

She did not look at him; she had no time. When he took the package she placed before him, she was already talking to someone else.

In the car it was warm, they were joking, it smelled of the perfume Nedra was letting them try. They drove through residential streets to miss the traffic, back streets, little used ways, to the bridge. And then in the winter evening, the children grown quiet, home.

Nedra made tea in the kitchen. The fire was burning, the dog laid his head on their feet.

She adored Christmas. She had a wonderful idea for cards: she would make paper roses, roses of every shade, and send them in individual boxes. She spread the tissue on the table— not this, not that, she said—to find pieces she liked, ah, here! There was an almost theatrical excitement in the house. For days now, spread on window sills and tables in the rooms she preferred were beads, colored paper, yarns, pine cones painted gold. It was like a studio; profusion bathed one, caught one's breath.

Viri was making an Advent calendar. He was late, as usual; a week of December had already passed. He had made a whole city, the sky dark as velvet cushions, stars cut with a razor blade, smoke rising from chimneys and vanishing in the night, a city that was a compendium of hidden courtyards, balconies, eaves. It was a city like Bath, like Prague, a city glimpsed through a keyhole, streets that had stairways, domes like the sun. Every window opened, so it seemed, and within was a picture. Nedra had given him an envelopeful, but there were others he had found himself. Some were actual rooms. There were animals sitting in chairs, birds, canal boats, moles and foxes, insects, Botticelli's. Each one was put carefully in place and in secret —the children were not allowed to come near—and the elaborate façade of the city glued over it. There were details that only Franca and Danny would recognize—the names on street signs, curtains within certain windows, the number on a house. It was their life he was constructing, with its unique carapace, its paths, delights, a life of muted colors, of logic, surprise. One entered it as one enters a foreign country; it was strange, bewildering, there were things one instantly loved.

"For God's sake, Viri, haven't you finished it yet?"

"Come and look," he insisted.

She stood at his shoulder. "Oh, it's absolutely fabulous. It's like a book, a fabulous book."

"Look at this."

"What is it? A palace."

"It's a section of the Opéra."

"In Paris."

"Yes."

"It's beautiful."

"See, the doors open."

"Open them. What's inside?"

"You'll never guess. The Titanic."

"No, really."

"Sinking."

"You're mad."

"The thing is, will they know what it is?"

"You don't have to know, you can see what it is," Nedra said. "What are the others?"

It was late. He was tired.

For Danny he had bought a bear, a huge bear on wheels with a collar and a little ring in his shoulder that, pulled, made him growl. What a face he had! He was all the Russian bears, circus bears, bears stealing honey from a tree. He was a present that rich children get and ignore the next day, the present one remembers always. He cost fifty dollars. Viri had brought him home in the trunk of the car.

On Christmas Eve it was cold and windy. The darkness came early, the cars were in endless lines on every road. Viri arrived late with the final packages, brandy, Nedra's cigars. The snow on the ground lit everything. Music was playing; Hadji ran barking from room to room.

"What's wrong with him?"

"He's excited," they said.

"I've been thinking about him. We don't have anything for him."

"I got him something," Nedra said.

"I think we should do a play about him."

"What?" they cried. "How?"

"About how he falls in love. With a toad."

"Oh, Papa!" Franca said.

"Oh, neat!"

In the driveway, Jivan, his arms filled with presents, was passing the lighted windows. A glimpse of white bookshelves, children whose voices he could not hear, Nedra smiling.

They sat by the fire as Viri read. *A Child's Christmas in*

Wales, a sea of words that wet his mouth, an unending sea. They were rapt, they were dazed by the very sounds. His calm, narrator's voice flowed on. The dog's head lay triangular, like a snake's, on his knee. The final sentence. In the silence that followed they dreamed, the wood dropping clots of white ember softly into the ashes, the cold at the windows, the house filled with brilliant surprises.

Jivan was quiet, he felt like a guest. His mistress was untouchable. She was in the midst of ritual and duty. He was jealous, but did not show it. They were precious to her, these things; they were her essence. It was because of them she was worthy of stealing.

There was no dinner; they were too busy with last-minute things. Viri and Nedra worked together, Jivan helping, and the girls wrapped presents in their rooms. The lights stayed on until after midnight. It was a great celebration, the greatest of the year.

Nedra had changed the sheets. They went to bed contented. Her sense of order was satisfied. She was tired, fulfilled.

"You read so beautifully tonight," she said.

"Do you think so?"

"Yes, I was watching their faces."

"They liked it, didn't they?"

"They loved it. Jivan, too."

"It was the first time he'd heard it," Viri said.

"Is that right?"

"He told me that. But you're right, he liked it. I think he liked it very much. You know, he reads quite a lot."

"I know."

"He's deeper than you think," Viri said. "That's what's interesting about him."

"How do you mean?"

"Well, I know him fairly well. He's really hiding something."

"What do you think it is?" Nedra asked.

"This word is so inclusive, it really doesn't express what I want to say, but I think he's hiding love. By that I mean a kind of sensitivity. He's a nomad, he's always had to struggle. You know, it doesn't seem we'd have anything in common, and yet in a strange way we do."

"I think you do."

"I'm sure of it," Viri said. "We're at different levels entirely, but there is something."

"It's so hard to really understand these things," she said.

They slept. The house was in darkness, its rooms ghostly. The fire had gone out, the dog slept, the cold fell on the roof in brittle white spots.

Christmas morning was clear, the wind was still blowing, the branches squeaked. Franca received a Polaroid camera with a shriek of pure joy as she unwrapped it; she almost wept. They took pictures of each other, of their rooms, of the tree. In the afternoon they had a party, just a small one, one guest each; Franca had a girl from school she had met, Danny had Leslie Dahlander. There was a treasure hunt, ice cream, lighting real candles on the tree, a huge tree standing near the window, thick as a bear's coat, birds in its branches, silver balls, mirrors, angels, a tree with a wooden village nestled beneath it and a ten-pointed star bought at Bonnier's on top.

The performance could not begin until all the presents had been seen, the chickens, the photographs, the Christmas eggs. Then Viri appeared as Professor Ganges in a mustache and an old set of tails. He was droning, inscrutable, he performed certain tricks. Nine magazines were placed on the floor, three in each row. He would leave the room, and on returning, tell them the one they had picked. Nedra was his confederate; she touched the magazines with a cane—Is it this one, she asked, is it this?

"Now I will tell you about a trick my master performs: he can stay under water for seven minutes, he can memorize a book at a glance. With an ordinary deck of cards, he invites you to think of one, merely *think*, and he throws the cards at the window. They scatter and fall, but one card sticks to the glass. It's the card you thought of. He says, Good, now go and remove it from the glass, and you go, and when you reach to take it, you discover it is on the *outside* of the glass! Would you like to see that?"

"Yes, yes!" they cried.

"Next year," he said; he was bowing in the manner of the East, backing from the room. "Show us!" they were crying. "Professor! Show us!"

What a party! There was a howling contest, a scissors game, dropping pennies into water and cards in a hat. When evening came, it was snowing. Snow coming down in the silent lumber-yards along the river, on the empty Christmas roads.

Besides the bear, Danny had gotten a radio, riding boots, a magnificent Larousse book of animal life. Franca received a guitar, a coat and an English paint box. In her diary she wrote: *The most beautiful Christmas ever. It even snowed. My presents were all a success. The party was fantastic. I really like Avril Coffman. She's very smart. She solved the magic square before anyone. Her hair is so terrific. Very long. Danny wouldn't go out and feed the pony, the pig (she is), so I did. I have the best mother in the entire world.*

8

HER FATHER WAS VISITING. HE WAS sixty-two. Teeth were missing. He had worn-out hair combed back over his head, hair cut by a provincial barber. He was garrulous, hard, with a solid cleft chin like a German postman. He smoked incessantly. His laugh was hoarse. He told many stories, he told the truth and he told lies. "I made it in seven hours," he said. "I never had it over sixty-five."

It was his birthday. He had come bringing two identical oversized dolls. The boxes were cheap, gray cardboard, open to view like a coffin, covered in cellophane. The two girls thanked him and stood not knowing what to do. "You're not too old for dolls?" he asked.

"Oh, no."

He began to cough in the midst of a long explanation of how to take care of an automobile. He had owned cars continuously since 1924. "People don't understand," he said. "You can tell them, but they still don't know."

In her oat-colored sweater Nedra was laying potatoes beside a leg of lamb. They were peeled and wet. She held them in her hand like marbles. She wore a dark, pleated skirt, knee-length socks, low heels.

"It's your oil," her father was saying. "You want to use nothing but top-grade, and change it—don't just add, *change* it—every thousand miles. I don't care what they tell you. Remember the Plymouth I had?"

"The Plymouth?"

"The '36 Plymouth," he said. "I drove it all through the war."

"Yes, of course I remember."

She was placing things on the table, cheese, hard Italian sausage, wine.

"Do you have any beer?" he asked. "I'll just have a glass of beer. Where's Viri?"

"He'll be home in a little while."

"He's the one who should be hearing this."

"I doubt it would do him much good."

That night he asked Jivan, "You have a car?"

"A car? Yes," Jivan said. He had been invited to come and play poker. They were all at the table, red and blue chips piled before them, the cards being shuffled. "I have a Fiat."

"Ante up five cents," Nedra's father said. He tapped the

table in front of him with an index finger solid as a peg. The Camels were near at hand. He dealt shakily. "A jack," he said. "A five. A seven. Another seven. A Fiat, eh? Why don't you get a Chevrolet?"

"Chevrolet is a good car," Jivan admitted.

"It sure is. It's a better car worn out than that one of yours is new."

"You think so?"

"I know so. It's your bet, Yvonne."

"Yes, let's play," Nedra said, "I feel lucky."

"She likes to win," her father said.

"I love to win," she smiled.

A friendly game in the warmth of the kitchen. How carefully she arranged things for him, how thoughtful she was. This coughing salesman who was her father, she accepted him wholeheartedly. He asked nothing of her other than an occasional welcome. He never outstayed it. He wrote no letters, his life was passed in an automobile going from customer to customer, in bars where women slurred their speech, in the house from which Nedra had escaped years before, a house in which one could not imagine her: ancient furniture, a shade on the back door. A house without books, without curtains, the basement smelling of coal dust. Here she grew, day by day, a child who even at sixteen gave no hint of what she was about to become, till suddenly in one summer she shed it all and disappeared. In her place was a young woman who had inherited nothing, in whom everything was unique, as if she were a message or the bearer of one, numinous, composed, not a blemish on her body, not a flaw.

"Is that really your father?" Jivan murmured.

She did not answer. Her forearms were on the floor, she was speechless, unseeing. The rug was biting her elbows, her bare knees. He was kneeling behind her. He did nothing. With a grave, an atrocious slowness he was waiting, like a functionary, like a man who will toll a bell. He listened to far-off traffic, she could sense his dedication, his calm.

"He isn't really?"

"Yes."

It touched her. The word was drowned by her breath. She wept. It was like a snake swallowing a frog, slowly, imperceptibly. Her life was ending without struggle, without movement, only rare, involuntary spasms like helpless sighs. His voice seemed to wash over her as if in a dream, "I find that incredible."

She said nothing. It was not finished, it was still being done. She was like a strangled woman. Her forehead was pressed to the rug.

"You're very devoted to him. Speak to me."

"Yes."

"I love to hear your voice."

She had to swallow first. "Yes."

She was wearing the bracelet he had given her of deep violet stones. She wore it amid three gold bands. One could hear it when she moved, a faint, a sensual sound that declared her as his possession, even as he sat with her husband and heard her in the kitchen or in his absence she turned the pages of a magazine.

"I found a recipe," he said. "Shall I read it to you?"

She could hear pages being turned.

"Rillettes d'Oie," he said. "Am I saying it right?"

She did not reply.

"Remove the skin from the goose and cut the meat away from the bones."

She was weak, fainting.

"Reserve some of the fat for the roasting pan." His mouth watered for her. He could taste her flesh.

They had begun the unending journey, forward a bit, then back. The book had dropped to the floor, he was seizing her

104

arms, her shoulders. She was moaning. She had forgotten him, her body was writhing, clenching like a fist.

In the stillness that followed, he said, "Nedra."

She did not answer. A long silence.

"Do you know the story of the Arendts?"

"The Arendts?"

"He owned this store. I bought it from him."

"The young man."

"He's an antique dealer."

"Oh, yes."

"His father was a sculptor."

"I didn't know that."

"I have some of his things. I found them in back."

They were two small pieces, one a horse, the metal etched like Assyrian mail.

"Do you like it?" he asked.

She was holding it in the air, over her face.

"This one too," he said.

Her hands were weak, she could hardly hold it.

"He had talent, didn't he?" Jivan asked. "His wife was a fabulous woman. Her name was Niiva."

"Niiva."

"It's beautiful, isn't it? They were famous, the two of them. She was very attractive, everyone liked her. She was passionate and strong, and he was very nice but something was missing. They had a house in France, in the South, beautiful books, they knew all the famous people of the thirties. But she was a mare, you see, and he was a goat—no, not a goat but a donkey, a nice, patient donkey.

"The result is the son. You've seen him; he's like his father, weak. He has some of the books, they're inscribed by the authors, and hundreds of clippings. The father finally left them and she began to drink. She didn't take care of the house. There were bottles piled everywhere. Finally she died."

"How?"

"She fell down the stairs. You know why I'm telling you this?"

"I'm not sure." She gazed again at the small bronze horse.

"You know. Look," he said suddenly, "I want to show you something. I'm a little tired at the moment, you understand that."

He picked up the telephone book. It was the county book, as thick as one's thumb. He took it in his teeth and, the muscles jumping in his neck and arm, began to tear it, slowly, steadily, between teeth and one hand, in two.

"You see?" he said.

"Yes. I know you're strong. I know," she said.

She received a letter from her father written on small sheets of lined paper. It thanked her for the three days he had spent there. He had caught a cold on the way home. He had made good time, though, even better than on the trip up. She was a good poker player; she must have inherited it. There are no real friends, he warned.

9

SUMMER AT AMAGANSETT. SHE was thirty-four. She lay in the dunes, in the dry grass. Her hand was marked in black, each finger divided in three parts, the thumb in two, the palm in quarters like a folded letter. At the base of her fingers she had circled the mounts, Jupiter, Saturn and Mercury, and colored the palm lines in red. She was deep in study, the chart beside her, entranced. Beneath, on the beach, her children played.

She was silent, an outcast, invisible except from the sea. Her body was dark brown. Her hidden breasts were pale, there was a thin band of white around her hips, a band no wider than a tie. Her eyes were clear, her mouth colorless; she was at peace. She had lost her desire to be the most beautiful woman at parties, to know celebrated people, to shock. The sun warmed her legs, her shoulders, her hair. She was not afraid of solitude; she was not afraid of growing old.

She stayed for hours. The sun reached its zenith, the cries of children faded, the sea became tin. The beach was never empty. It was wide, endless, there were always figures on it, distant, like nomads' camps. She saw wealth in her hand; she saw a prodigious final third of life. Three clear rings, of thirty years apiece, circled her wrist; she would live to be ninety. She had lost her interest in marriage. There was nothing else to say. It was a prison.

"No, I'll tell you what it is," she said, "I'm indifferent to it. I'm bored with happy couples. I don't believe in them. They're false. They're deceiving themselves.

"Viri and I are friends, good friends. I think we'll always be. But the rest, the rest is dead. We both know it. There's no use pretending. It's decorated like a corpse, but it's already rotten.

"When Viri and I are divorced . . ." she said.

Arnaud came that summer. His arrival was worthy of Chaplin. He drove up with Eve in a white convertible, giving little waves when the front wheels went up on a stump and lifted the nose of the car three feet in the air. He took over two rooms in the back of the house, a bedroom and sun porch overlooking the fields. He wore a white cap and a ribbed shirt, pants the color of tobacco or certain perfumes, and a scarf for a belt. He was outrageous, serene, sleek as a cavy. The first thing he did was to buy a hundred and fifty dollars' worth of liquor.

"A wonderful gift," Nedra recalled.

"Although," Viri said, "as a matter of fact . . ."

"He didn't drink it *all*."

"Well, not all."

And cigars. It was the summer of lunches and marvelous cigars. Every day, having finished lunch in the sun, Nedra would ask, "Arnaud, what are we going to smoke?"

"Let me see," he would say.

"A Coronita?"

"No, I don't . . . perhaps. What do you think of a Don Diego?" he would ask. "A Don Diego or a Palma."

"A Palma."

"That's it."

She wrote to Jivan: *You know how much I hated to think of being apart, even for a few weeks, but somehow I find it's not as difficult as I imagined. It isn't that I don't think of you. If anything, I think of you even more, but the summer seems like one long day after we've been together, I have time to reflect, to savor you again. It's like sleep, like bathing. We often talked about going to the sea together, and though I am here without you, I see it through your eyes and am content. I couldn't feel this if I didn't love you and feel your love strongly. We are so fortunate. There is that terrific electricity that goes back and forth between us. I kiss you many times. I kiss your hands. Franca speaks often of you. Even Viri does . . .*

There was a small drawing, done from memory, beside the signature.

She had mail from Robert Chaptelle, who was in Varenge-ville. His cards began without a salutation, his handwriting was illegible and dense.

My play is the first of its kind, running two hours and a half without intermission. It is called "Le Begaud." I am giving it its finishing touches.

"So he's back in France," Viri said.

"Yes."

"What a loss."

This is my schedule, and my aim is to follow it very closely. I will be at "Hôtel de la Terrasse" until the 15th of August. At

"L'Abbaye" in Viry-Chatillon until the 30th of August. At the
Wilbraham Hotel, Sloane Street, London, the whole month of
September.

A certain Ned Portman may call you. He is an American,
quite intelligent, I have come to know here. He has seen me at
work, and what he has to say about me may interest you.

She had nothing to say, but she managed to write a brief
reply. She was strangely elated by his addresses, their under-
lined words and stamps of Le Touquet and sculptured heads
of the thirties.

The children loved Arnaud. His curly hair was bleaching, it
was much too long. He had a big belly; it made their father
seem slender in comparison. Arnaud was a patriarch, an Alpha
man. He wore a straw hat, his toes moved contentedly as he
lay on the sand, a beachcomber with white teeth, white as
seashells, and pockets filled with crumpled money. He was a
book dealer. He had money because his business was well-run,
secure, and because he had no hesitation about asking the best
price. He could joke about money, he could waste it, it flowed
to him like water to a drain.

He ran with them on the beach. He was powerful in the
burning sunshine, his face shaded, his skin brown. Eve came
for the weekend. They moved to a motel.

"It's too quiet there," he complained the next day. He was
mixing drinks, rum with fresh fruit; it was the last of the fine
rum. Viri was gathering wood. The beach was almost deserted.
In the distance, half a mile away, one other group was bathing
in the sea.

While the ears of corn soaked in sea water were broiling,
they drank the icy rum.

"You've heard what happened?" Nedra said. "Our house
was robbed."

"Oh, God," Eve said. "When?"

"We just got a call this morning. They took the record
player, the television, they broke into everything."

"You must be just sick."

"I want to live in Europe," Nedra said.

"Europe?" Arnaud cried. "They're worse."

"Are they really?"

"They invented stealing," he said.

"What about England?"

"England? The worst of all. You know, I do some business there, I have friends in England. Their flats are broken into constantly. The police come, they look around, they dust for fingerprints. Well, we know who it is, they say. Wonderful, who? The same ones who did it last time, they say."

"Oh, but I love those pictures of England."

"The grass is quite good," he admitted.

Eve was drunk. "What grass?" she said.

"The English grass."

She was stroking his hair. "You really are beautiful," she said. "How can a woman hope to . . ."

"Hope to what?"

"Interest you," she murmured vaguely.

"There's surely some way."

She walked off a few feet, paused, and then in one motion turned and removed her dress. Underneath she was wearing nothing but a pair of white underpants.

"Are you hot, darling?" he asked.

"Yes."

"You're so impulsive about clothes."

"Let's swim," she said. Her arms were covering her breasts. The sea hissed behind her.

"The corn is almost ready," Arnaud complained.

"Darling." She reached out. "Don't make me swim alone."

"Never."

He carried her down to the water, soothing her as if she were a child. They could see her long legs dangling over his arm. The waves were silky. Hadji stood barking at the footsteps vanished into the sea.

Eve was no longer young, Nedra noticed. Her stomach was flat, but the skin had stretched. Her waist was thickening. Still one loved her for this, one loved her even more. Even the faint lines beginning to appear in her forehead seemed beautiful. When they came back, the ends of her hair were soaked, her body glistened, the womanly mons showed through her wet pants. She leaned against Arnaud in deep affection. She had put on his sweater; it came to her hips, she seemed naked beneath it. His arm was around her waist. "The trouble is," she said, "what can I do about it, I love Jews."

Summer. The foliage is thick. The leaves shimmer everywhere, like scales. In the morning, aroma of coffee, the whiteness of sunlight across the floor. The sound of Franca upstairs, of a young girl's steps as she made her bed, combed her hair, descended with the warm smile of youth. Her hair hung in a smooth column between her shoulder blades. When one touched it, she grew still, certain already, sure of her beauty.

Drives to the beach. The sand was hot. The sea thundered faintly, as if in a glass. Their limbs were tanned. Franca had the faint outlines of a woman, hips just beginning, long fine legs. Her father held them so that she could practice standing on her hands. She was in her black swimsuit. Her buttocks showed as she arched her body, her calfs, the small of her back.

"All right, let go!" she cried.

Wavering, unsteady, she took two or three brief steps with her hands and then fell. "How long was it?" she asked.

"Eight seconds."

"Again," she begged.

The wind was from the shore. The waves seemed to break in silence.

Days on the beach. They went home in the late afternoons, the great reaches glistening with sunlight no longer hot. Lunches that sheltered them like a tent. Beneath a wide umbrella Nedra spread chicken, eggs, endive, tomatoes, pâté, cheese, bread, cucumbers, butter and wine. Or they ate at a table in the garden, the sea distant, the trees green, the voices drifting from the house next-door. White sky, silence, the fragrant cigars.

She spoke of Europe often. "I need the kind of life you can live there," she said, "free of inhibitions."

"Inhibitions?" Arnaud asked. His eyes were half-closed in sleep. Viri had gone to the city. They were alone.

"I need a large house."

"I don't think you have many inhibitions."

"And a car."

"You're very uninhibited."

"Yes, well, it's other people's inhibitions I'm talking about."

"Ah, other people's. But you don't care about other people. You care less about other people than anyone I know."

She was silent. She was looking at her feet in which she noticed, as if for the first time, blue veins. The sun was at its apogee. She was conscious, as if it were a moment of weightlessness, that her life, too, was at its apex; it was sacred, floating, ready to change direction for the final time.

"You know, I think about divorce," she said, "and Viri is such a good father. He loves his children so, but that isn't what stops me. It isn't all the legal business and argument, the arrangements that have to be made. The really depressing thing is the absolute optimism of it all."

Arnaud smiled.

"I want to travel," she said. She was not thinking; the words came from somewhere within her and rose to her mouth. "I want to go to a pleasant room at the end of the day, unpack, bathe. I want to go downstairs for dinner. Sleep. Then, in the morning . . . the London *Times.*"

"With the room number on it in pencil."

"I want to be able to pay with a check and not even think about it."

112

"No matter what they say, that's the one great feeling, isn't it?"

"I'd like to buy all new clothes."

They sat beneath a dome of heat, of midday silence, in attitudes of languor, as if exhausted, as if somewhere in Sicily, exchanging secrets which encircled them like slow currents and were as sweet to confess as to hear.

"Arnaud, I'm very fond of you. You're really my favorite man, do you know that?"

"I'd hoped so."

"I mean it. You have a marvelous quality of understanding, of understanding and accepting."

"I seem to."

"You have a wonderful sense of humor."

"Unfortunately," he said. "Humor comes largely from not caring."

"Oh, I don't think so."

"Detachment is what brings forth humor. It's a paradox. We're the only creatures that laugh, they say, and the more we laugh, the less we care."

"I don't think that's true."

"Um," he reflected. "Perhaps. A lot of very clear insights that come in these hours of reflection, especially following lunch, later prove not quite so sound. This has been a lovely summer."

"I think that every day," she said.

Toward the end, in the last days of August, they lay on the lawn in the evening, Arnaud in shirt sleeves leaning on one elbow, posed like a Manet, Viri and Nedra sitting. The dinner cloth was spread before them on the grass. The great trees, rich in leaves, sighed in the wind. Viri's arms embraced his knees, his socks showed.

"A lovely summer," he said, "hasn't it been?"

They did not know what they were praising; the days, the

sense of contentment, of pagan joy. They were acclaiming the summer of their lives in which, far from danger, they rested. Their flesh was speaking, their well-being.

"I'm going to get the soup," Nedra said.

"What kind is it?" Viri asked.

She rose to her feet. "It's one of your favorites," she said. "Can't you smell it?"

The air was filled with the odor of grass, dry earth, the faint scent of flowers.

"No," he confessed.

"Your nose is your weakest part," she said. "It's *cresson.*"

"Did you really make that?"

She brushed her knees. "Just for you."

She went inside. Franca sat on the sofa, reading. The spoons were in the drawer. The pure light of evening filled the house.

"You're a lucky fellow," Arnaud was saying. From the house they seemed immobile, as if posed. The sheets of foliage drifted above them. The corner of the tablecloth blew gently back. "You've reached shore."

Viri did not reply. The vast, mild sway of summer moved the canopy of leaves, sifted through them, made them shimmer.

"You're responding to a greater reality than other men, Viri. I mean, I could give examples, but it's manifest. This is a kind of heaven."

"Yes, well, it isn't all me," Viri said.

"It's largely you."

"No, you brought the cigars." He paused. "The fact is, it's not what it appears. I'm too easy-going."

"What do you mean?"

"Women should be kept in cages. Otherwise . . ." He didn't finish. Finally he said, "Otherwise, I don't know."

114

10

THEIR FRIENDS THAT YEAR WERE Marina and Gerald Troy. She was an actress—she had played in Strindberg—her eyes were a piercing blue. She was rich. There was nothing recent in this wealth, it shone in everything: her skin, her fine smile. She went to the gymnasium three times a week, to an old Greek named Leon; his arms were still strong at eighty, his hair pure white.

Nedra began to go too. She had always been indifferent to sports, but from the first hours in the emptiness of the main room with its soiled windows above the traffic, the devoutness of the old man, the companionship, she felt she belonged to it. The showers were clean; the spareness, the green walls appealed to her. Her body awakened, she was suddenly aware that within it, as if existing by themselves, there were deep feelings of strength. When it was extended, hung upside down, when the muscles beneath were warmed and loose, when she felt like a young runner, she realized how much she could love this body, this vessel which would one day betray her—no, she did not believe that; the opposite, in fact. There were times she felt its immortality: on cool mornings, summer nights alone lying naked on top of the covers, in baths, while dressing, before love, in the sea, when limb-weary and ready to sleep.

She had lunch with Eve or Marina, sometimes with both. Noons when the restaurants filled with patrons, clamor, a perfect, calm light. In her handbag was a fresh letter from Europe which she had only glanced at, hastily scanned, the sight of the envelope was enough, the splash of its blue and red edge, the feverish handwriting. Robert had appeared sick and self-deluded, whining, sainted. He was being treated for his thyroid

115

condition in a clinic near Reims. *Two years from now I can hear people saying: Your play is extraordinary. And my answer: It took me ten years to perfect my craftsmanship. I am wrestling with giants here. Every morning I wake up in a sweat, ready for the struggle. The impact is great, but I am never defeated. It is the rehearsals I miss, to attend them and see the progress the actors make. My being there is an absolute necessity. My eye and ear criticize every move and every intonation. I listen to the "commas" of the play as if they were drops falling from a fountain. Dis moi comment vont tout tes affaires. I am alone.*

The room was nearly empty. It was that still, central hour of the day, slow, deliquescent, two-thirty or three, the invisible cigarette smoke mingled with the air, the peel of lemon beside the empty cups, the traffic on the avenue silent, floating past as if in death, women in their thirties, talking.

"Neil is sick. He has diabetes," Eve said.

"Diabetes?"

"That's what they say."

"Isn't that hereditary?"

They sat at a table near the front. The waiter was watching them from near the bar. He was in love with them, their leisure, low voices, the confidences which involved them so.

"I just hope my son doesn't get it," Eve said. "Neil is a mess. I'm surprised that's all he has."

"He's still living with whatever her name is?"

"As far as I know. She's so stupid she wouldn't know what to do for him anyway. She only has one . . . I don't know what to call it . . . quality."

"In bed, you mean?"

"She's twenty-two, that's her quality. Poor Neil, he's like a jellyfish. His teeth are rotting out."

"He looks terrible."

"I don't think he could even pick up a woman in a bar, in the dark. It serves him right, but it's awful for Anthony to see

116

him like that. It's so sad. And he likes his father, he always has. They've always been close."

"It's so much easier when there are two of you," Nedra said. "I couldn't have raised my children alone. Oh, of course, I could have, but I see in them qualities that aren't mine or a reaction against mine, that come from Viri. Anyway, I think girls need a male presence. It brings them to life in certain ways."

"Boys are the same."

"I suppose."

"Why don't you share Viri with me?" Eve asked. She laughed. "I'm not serious."

"Share him?" Nedra said. "Well, I don't know. I've never thought of it."

"I didn't really mean it."

"I don't think it would work, not with Viri. Now Arnaud . . ."

"You're right," Eve said.

"Oh, yes. As a matter of fact, I think he would be better with two women."

"But you're much neater than I am."

"I think you're more understanding."

"I don't think so."

"Yes," Nedra said. "And it's natural. I'm sure it would end with him loving you more. Yes, it's true."

They emerged from the narrow doorway unhurried, fond. On Lexington Avenue the traffic was endless, cars from the suburbs, taxis, dark limousines that floated over the ruts. They strolled. The streets were like rivers fed by tributaries along which they lingered, glancing at windows in which their reflections appeared. There were shops Nedra felt drawn toward, places where she had bought things, tablecloths, scent. Sometimes the stare of a salesgirl, idle, alone, met hers above displays of books, by stands of wine. She was not hurried; she did not smile. It was the intelligence in her face that struck them, the grace. It was someone whose face they had seen, someone who possessed everything—leisure, friends, the hours of a day were like a hand of cards. On these same avenues Viri walked alone. The rise of one is the fall of the other. His mind was filled with details, appointments; in the sunlight his skin looked dry.

She drove home in early traffic, between the cars of women returning from the doctor's and men whose work was ended. The trees were beginning to change.

Five in the afternoon. She arranged her hair before the mirror in her room, her hands were pale. She smoothed her cheeks, her mouth, as if pressing away traces of an event. There was no event, she was preparing for one: a telephone call, a piece of music, half an hour of reading.

It was the telephone. The voice of Mrs. Dahlander, wavering, composed.

"Could you come to the hospital?" she asked. "My husband's not here. Leslie fell from a horse."

It had happened an hour before. She was riding alone. No one saw the gallop, the stumble, the moment in which she sprawled through air in a position like a joke and then hit and lay still while her horse stopped and began to graze. The meadow was empty, invisible from the road.

At the hospital they pronounced it grave, a concussion. She was still unconscious. Her face was bruised. Her head had struck a rock. She was adopted, an only child. The doctor was explaining the urgency, the risk, to her stupefied parent. It was in the waiting room of the children's wing. Torn books were piled on the shelves, there were blocks on the floor. If the bleeding within the skull continued, it would exert fatal pressure on the brain.

"What can you do?"

"We'll have to operate."

The neurosurgeon was already visible in a green smock.

"We have to have your permission."

She turned to Nedra, begging. "What shall I do?"

They questioned the doctor again. Patiently he described it once more. It was dinnertime; the streets were becoming dark. The forgotten horse, still bridled, stood in the empty field. The grass was turning cold.

"I want to wait for my husband."

"We can't wait."

She turned to Nedra again. "I want to wait for him," she pleaded. "Don't you think I should wait?"

"I don't know if you can," Nedra said.

The barren woman nodded, gave up. She crumpled, yes, all right, save her. There was just a glimpse as the child rolled past, mortally still. She was gone for hours, she emerged like a broken doll, eyes closed, head in white bandages. That night she was placed in ice. The pressure within the shaved head continued to mount. The surgeon was called at midnight. He found her parents waiting.

"We'll know by morning," he told them.

A morning when Viri in the last of sleep saw a woman in a beautiful dress arrive at the elevator in a great hotel. It was Kaya. She did not see him. There were two men with her wearing dinner jackets. He did not want to be seen: his ordinary clothes, his teeth, his thinning hair. He saw them enter the elevator, ascend to a roof garden, a party, to an elegance he could not imagine, and suddenly he knew she was no longer the same; she was captured at last.

In the house on the river he dreamed in the early morning. Autumn, alone in his sleep, the rooms cool, deserted, winds from the Hudson washing him like a corpse.

11

THE FIRST SNOWS FELL. IT WAS like midwinter, the windows took on a chill. One could lie in bed in darkness and watch the coming of light.

On Thanksgiving Day there was a dazzling storm. Hadji was joyous. He leapt through the white like a porpoise, rolled on his back, ran wildly, bit at the snow. Danny could see him turn, far off, and look for her: black eyes, kohl eyes, tall alert ears.

"Here, Snowboy," she called. "Come here."

His ears lay back as he ran; he would not obey. She clapped her hands. He ran in great, drunken circles, sometimes pausing to lie in the snow and watch her with foxlike glances. She kept calling. He barked.

"You bastard," she cried.

All through December, it seemed, there were dinners. Discussions of the menu, the guests. Shrimp, Viri said, yes, all right, shrimp, but not gazpacho, he insisted. It was not the weather for gazpacho; it was too cold.

"Not by the fire," Nedra said.

"But there's no fire in the dining room," he cried.

She did not answer. She was hard at work. Who had she finally invited, he asked?

"The Ayashes," she said.

"The Ayashes!"

"Viri, we have to. I mean, I don't really care, but it's embarrassing."

"Who else?"

"Vera Cray."

"What is this? The county home for the aged?"

120

"She's a marvelous woman. She hasn't been out since her husband died."

"Yes, I believe that," he said. "But they're not going to mix. Mrs. Ayashe is an idiot. Vera is very intense."

"You'll be sitting between them."

"Not all night."

"Give them plenty to drink," she said. "Do you want to taste something?"

It was the *pâté maison.* "Oh!" he moaned.

"What?"

"It's brilliant!"

"Try it with mustard," she said.

They were having Meursault, *fromages,* pastries from Leonard's.

"It's going to be a wonderful dinner," he said. He thought for a moment. "Perhaps we won't have to talk."

Two weeks later they were having Viri's client who had bought some old brick houses and land near Croton and wanted to make them over into a compound. The original structures would be included in a larger, more elegant whole, much as ancient sculpture embedded in villa walls. His name was S. Michael Warner; he was also known as Queen Mab.

"He's bringing Bill Hale."

"Oh, shit," Nedra said.

"You don't even know him."

"You're right. And he couldn't be worse than Michael, could he?"

"Nedra, he's my client."

"Oh, you know I adore him."

An entire day was consecrated to preparations. She shopped for hours in her favorite stores.

By evening the house was ready. There were flowers beneath the lamps, the curtains were drawn, the fire crackled behind the Hessians' iron knees. Nedra wore a quilted dress of dark

121

blue and rose. Her belt was sewn with small, silver bells, her hair was drawn back, her neck bare.

Her face was cool and gleaming. Her laugh was gorgeous, it was like applause.

Michael Warner was immaculate, a man of forty-five with the ease and smile of someone who notices every mistake. He was charmed by Nedra. He recognized in her a woman who would not betray him. She would never be banal or foolish.

"This is Bill Hale."

"Hello, Bill," she said warmly.

A strange, winter party. Dr. Reinhart and his wife were late, but they arrived at just the right moment. They were like the last players for whom the game has waited. They seated themselves as if knowing exactly what was expected. Reinhart had wonderful manners. This wife was his third.

"You're a doctor of medicine?" Michael confirmed.

"Yes." He was in research, however, he explained. A form of research. In fact, he was writing.

"Like Chekhov," his wife said. She had a slight accent.

"Well, not exactly."

"Chekhov *was* a doctor, wasn't he?" Michael said.

"There have been a number—who have become writers, that is. Of course, I don't mean to include myself. I'm only writing a biography."

"Really?" Bill said. "I adore biography."

"Who is the subject of it?" Nedra asked.

"It's actually a . . . it's a multiple biography," Reinhart said. He accepted a drink gratefully. "Thank you. It's the lives of children of famous men."

"How interesting."

"Dickens, Mozart, Karl Marx." He sipped his drink as a patient might sip a glass of juice, an educated patient, frail, resigned. "Even their names are fascinating. Plorn, that was Dickens' last child. Stanwix, that was the son of Melville."

"And what becomes of them?" Nedra asked.

"Well, there isn't a fixed pattern. But perhaps it could be there are more misfortunes than with other children, more sorrows."

"Somerset Maugham was a doctor," his wife said. "Also Céline."

"Yes, my dear, that's right," Reinhart said.

"An awful man," Michael said.

"Nonetheless a great writer."

"Céline great? What do you mean by great?"

Reinhart hesitated. "I don't know. Greatness is something which can be regarded in a number of ways," he said. "It is, of course, the apotheosis, man raised to his highest powers, but it also can be, in a way, like insanity, a certain kind of imbalance, a flaw, in most cases a beneficial flaw, an anomaly, an accident."

"Well, many great men are eccentric," Viri said, "even narrow."

"Not necessarily narrow so much as impatient, intense."

"The thing I really would like to know is," Nedra said, "must fame be a part of greatness?"

"Well, that is a difficult question," Reinhart answered finally. "The answer is, possibly, no, but from a practical point of view there must be some consensus. Sooner or later it must be confirmed."

"There's something missing there," Nedra said.

"Perhaps," he admitted.

"I think Nedra means that greatness, like virtue, need not be spoken about in order to exist," Viri suggested.

"It would be nice to believe," Reinhart said.

It was Michael that his wife was watching. Suddenly she spoke. "You're right," she said abruptly. "Céline was an absolute bastard."

Nights of conversation that has faded, that rises to the ceiling and gathers like smoke. The pleasures of the table, the well-being of those around it. Here in a house in the country, comfortable, discreet, Viri suddenly knew as he poured the wine how foolish his statement had been, how wistful. Reinhart was right: fame was not only part of greatness, it was more. It was the evidence, the only proof. All the rest was nothing, in vain. He who is famous cannot fail; he has already succeeded.

Near the fire, Ada Reinhart was telling Michael where in Germany she came from. She had lived in Berlin. They were apart from the others. The white hair of her husband, his frail hand stirring the coffee, could be seen in the far room.

"I knew a lot then," she said.

"Did you? What do you mean?"

She did not answer immediately. She was much younger than her husband.

"Do you want me to tell you?" she said. "If I had only done what I thought I should do . . ."

"What you thought you should do?"

"Instead of what I did."

"That's true for everyone, isn't it?"

"When I fall in love, it's with a man's mind, his spiritual qualities."

"I feel exactly the same."

"Of course, one is attracted by a body or a look . . ."

Nedra could see them talking by the fire. At the table, Mrs. Reinhart had said almost nothing. Now she seemed passionately engaged.

"I'm not unattractive, am I?"

"Quite the opposite," Michael said.

"You don't find me unattractive?"

She hardly noticed the others entering the room. She continued to talk.

"What are you persuading Mr. Warner of?" Reinhart asked lightly.

"What? Nothing, darling," she said.

After the Reinharts had gone, Michael sat back and smiled.

124

"Fascinating. Do you know what she said?" he asked.

"Tell us," Bill said.

"There is something missing in her life."

"Is there?"

Michael paused. "Do you think I'm attractive?" he imitated huskily.

"My darling!"

"Oh, yes. And more. Do you think I should have taken her seriously?" he said.

"I'd love to have seen it."

Michael began to peel a piece of fruit, careful not to stain his fingers. The fire was dying among the ashes, cigarettes had lost their taste.

Nights of marriage, conjugal nights, the house still at last, the cushions indented where people had sat, the ashes warm. Nights that ended at two o'clock, the snow falling, the last guest gone. The dinner plates were left unwashed, the bed icy cold.

"Reinhart's a nice man."

"He has no pettiness," Viri said.

"I think his book will be interesting."

"What happens to children—yes, that's what one longs to know."

They lay in the dark like two victims. They had nothing to give one another, they were bound by a pure, inexplicable love.

He was asleep, she could tell without looking. He slept like a child, soundlessly, deep. His thinning hair was disheveled, his hand lay extended and soft. If they had been another couple she would have been attracted to them, she would have loved them, even—they were so miserable.

12

IN SIX YEARS SHE WOULD BE forty. She saw it from a distance, like a reef, the whitened glimpse of danger. She was frightened by the idea of age, she could too easily imagine it, she searched daily for its signs, first in the harsh light from the window, then, turning her head slightly to erase some of the severity, stepping back a little, saying to herself, this is as close as people come.

Her father in distant Pennsylvania towns already had within him the anarchy of cells that announced itself by a steady cough and a pain in his back. Three packs a day for thirty years; he coughed as he admitted it. He needed something, he decided.

"We'll take some x-rays," the doctor had said. "Just to see."

Neither of them was there when the negatives were thrown up before the wall of light, dealt into place as rippling sheets, and in the ghostly darkness the fatal mass could be seen, as astronomers see a comet.

The doctor was called in; it took only a glance. "That's it, all right," he said.

The usual prognosis was eighteen months, but with the new machines, three years, sometimes four. They did not tell him this, of course. His translucent destiny was clear on the wall as subsequent series were displayed, six radiographs in a group, the two specialists working on different cases, side by side, calm as pilots, dictating what they saw, stacks of battered envelopes near their elbows. Their language was handsome, exact. They recited, they discussed, they gave a continued verdict long after Lionel Carnes, sixty-four years old, had begun his visits to the treatment room. Their work never ended. Before them loomed skulls, viscera, galaxy breasts, fingers, hairline fractures, knees, appearing and disappearing in an eternal test, the two of them pouring out answers in a steady monotone.

Sarcoma, they are saying. Well, there are all kinds, there are sarcomas of the muscle, they do occur, even of the heart, but they are very rare, normally they are the result of metastasis. No one really knows why the heart is sacred and inviolable, they say.

The Beta machine made a terrifying whine. The patient lay alone, abandoned, the room sealed, air-conditioned because of the heat. The dose was determined by a distant computer taking into consideration height, weight and so forth. The Beta doesn't burn the skin like the lower-energy machines, they told him.

"No, just everything else," he said.

It hung there, dumb, enormous, shooting beams that crushed the honeycomb of tissue like eggshells. The patient lay beneath it, inert, arranged. With the scream of the invisible it began its work. It was either this or the most extreme surgery, radical and hopeless, blood running down from the black stitches, the doomed man served up like a pork roast.

The greatness of technology was focused on him for a moment, the nurses joked with him, the young doctors called him by his first name.

"Am I dying yet?" he asked them.

"Well, not at the moment," they said.

He was telling them about automobiles, about his three-legged cat.

"Only three legs, eh?"

"His name's Ernie," he said.

"Ernie, is that so?"

"Yeah, he's black. He gets a lot of fun out of life, old Ernie.

He climbs up trees and catches birds. Limps when he sees you," he said.

It was all in his cells, the stain of tobacco, the darkness. He had to give up smoking.

"Dying's nothing compared with that."

Easter Sunday. The morning was beautiful, the trees filled with sun. The Verns came out, Larry and Rae. They looked like a young working couple turning up the drive on their motorcycle. She was sitting behind him, her arms around his waist. He was wearing a white Irish sweater, the wind was scattering his hair. The children ran to meet them. They loved the machine, which was lacquered and gleaming. They liked his fine beard.

"You're just in time to help hide," Nedra told him.

"Good. Who's this?"

It was Viri in a hat with two ears sprouting from it, holding a basket of eggs. "Come inside and warm up," he said. "Are you cold?"

The table was laid in the kitchen: *Kulich*, a sweet, Russian cake, chunks of *feta*, dark bread and butter, fruit. Nedra poured tea. Her nature showed itself in the generosity of her table.

"Eve is coming," she said.

"Oh, nice," Rae said.

"And the Paums, do you know him?"

"I don't think so."

"He's an actor."

"Oh, yes, of course."

"Well, he may come, he may not."

"He drinks," Franca said.

"Ah."

"And I would think that on a morning like this," Nedra said, "he might have begun early."

"That's sad," Rae said.

"I understand it more and more."

128

Rae was dark, her face lean, intense. It was a face that appeared to have been in an accident; there was a certain contradiction between the halves. Her hair was cut short. She had an awkward smile.

They had no children, Rae and Larry. He worked for a toy company. His skin was white. He had the resignation of someone who has passed through many difficulties, the calm of an addict. He went off with Viri to hide the eggs.

"What have you been doing?" Nedra asked. She was warming her face on the cup.

"I don't know," Rae said. "You're so lucky you don't live in the city. I get up, I make breakfast, the window sills are covered with dirt, it must take me two hours a day just to keep things clean. Yesterday I wrote a letter to my mother. I suppose that took most of the day. I had to walk to the post office; I had no stamps. I went to the laundry. I didn't cook dinner. We went out for dinner. So what am I really doing?" She smiled helplessly, showing discolored teeth.

Outside they were hiding the eggs in the faded grass, beneath leaves, under stones.

"Don't make them too easy to find," Viri called.

"Do you put any up in the branches?"

"Oh, absolutely. There should be some they don't ever find."

"Your hat is beautiful," Larry said as they finished.

"Nedra made it."

"I took some pictures of you in it."

"Let me take yours."

"Later," Larry said. They had begun to walk back. "At the house."

It stood above them, bathed in the light, its gabled roof with chimneys at each end, the rain-washed gray of the slates. Like a huge barn it was stained by weather, like a ship that has crossed. Mice lived along its stone foundation, weeds grew at its ends.

The vastness of the day surrounded them. The ground was warm, the river glinting in the sun.

"It's a beautiful day," Larry said. He still had three or four small chocolate eggs. He turned his back to the house and gently scattered them.

"The dog will find them, don't worry," Viri said.

Eve had arrived. She was in the kitchen drinking a glass of wine. Her car, its fenders rusted, was parked along the edge of the driveway, wheels half in the drainage ditch.

"Hello, Viri," she smiled.

She looked older. In a single year she had abandoned her youth. Her eyes had lines around them, her skin showed tiny pores. Still, she could rise to occasions, there were times she was beautiful, even more, unforgettable, given the hour, the right room. And if she was fading, her son was coming into the light. Along the edge of his face, Anthony already gave a hint of the man he would be. He was very good-looking, but there was a risk of even more: a beauty made imminent by a deep, unfathomable silence. He stood near Franca. Larry took their picture, two young faces at once very different yet sharing the same sort of privilege.

"He'll be absolutely devastating," Nedra said.

Rae agreed. She watched him through the window, drawn to him. He was too old for her to imagine as a son, he was a youth already; the characteristics which would become pride, impatience, were seeded, germinating day by day.

Booth Paum arrived with his daughter. He had made entrances since the days of Maxwell Anderson. Like all actors he could unfurl long speeches, reciting with a kind of threatening intensity; he could mimic, he could dance.

"I hope we're not late," he said. He introduced the friend his daughter had brought.

Four girls and a boy, they were. Viri began explaining the rules. "There are three kinds of eggs," he said. "There are solid

130

colors, speckled, and there are also twelve gold bees. The bees are worth five, the speckled three, and the solid colors one."

He pointed out the boundaries.

"It's now eleven-thirty," he said. He told them how much time they had. "Are you ready?"

"Yes!"

"Begin."

They scattered across the sunny ground, Hadji dashing after them, barking. Soon they were far off, separate figures moving slowly, heads down among the trees.

"They're not all on the ground!" Viri called.

During the long hunt with its distant shouts and cries, the adults sat outside, the women on small, iron benches, the men on a bank. Paum had a glass of tea which he drank Russian style, a cube of sugar between his teeth. Actors were original, actors were vivid. He stood with the river behind him, a confident figure. It was as if all reports were unfounded; he refuted them with his ease, his well-combed hair.·

"I heard a funny story," he told them. "It seems there were two drunks in an elevator . . ."

The tea was brown in the glass, his fingernails were perfectly shaped, his shoes from Bally were shined.

Dana, his daughter, won the hunt. She found the most eggs, including four of the bees. The prize was a huge cardboard soldier filled with popcorn; second prize was a rosewood pen.

The women brought the food out and arranged a table. There was wine and a bottle of Moët and Chandon. The afternoon was mild, spacious. A slight breeze carried off voices so that twenty feet of separation were mysterious, one saw conversations, the words were lost.

"Danny will be beautiful," Larry said. He was watching as she sat with the others, a plate in her lap. "She's different from Franca," he said. "Franca was always beautiful, she simply grows like a cat. I mean, from the very first she had claws, a

131

tail, everything was there, but in Danny's case something more mysterious is happening. It will all come slowly. It will only appear at the end."

Beyond them was the sleeping grass, dry from the winter, warmed by the sun.

"She's like that in many ways," Viri said. "She has traits that are more or less awkward, even disturbing, but I have the feeling they'll make sense later."

"Your children give you something very special," Larry said. "Sheltering them, knowing them. But that's what it's all about, isn't it?"

Viri was silent. He knew their situation. Rae sat down beside them.

"Why don't you take some photos?" she asked.

"I'm out of film."

"Oh, you have film."

"No, I'm out."

"I told you to stop and get some," she said.

He was sipping the last of his champagne. "Yes, you did. You're always right, aren't you?"

She did not answer.

"I'm very lucky, you see," he said to Viri.

Her face seemed quite small as she sat there, knees drawn up beneath her skirt.

"Yes, very lucky. Rae is always right. She has to be right. Nothing can be her fault, can it?"

She said nothing. He did not continue. He lay there supported by his elbows, the glass in his hand. Their whole life was displayed in the image of them there, he motionless, chin on his chest, the glass empty; she, head lowered, barren, hands clasped about her legs. They had Siamese cats, they went to museums and openings, she surely was passionate, they lived in a large Village flat.

In the late afternoon they were all inside. Larry was drinking coffee, a scarf around his neck, preparing to drive home. The children were playing, their exhaustion had not yet touched them. They would fall asleep by the fire after dinner, their faces flushed, their hearts at peace. Rae said goodbye. She was cheerful. In her pocket she revealed a small grass nest, and in it four chocolate eggs. They were going to have an omelet on the way home, she said. She offered an affectionate smile, unhygienic, brief.

Nedra and Eve sat by the window. The sound of the motorcycle died away. Viri had gone for a walk. Nedra was needlepointing a pair of slippers. There was a sun god on each toe.

"She's very nice," Eve said.

"Yes, I like her."

"She talks a lot. I don't mean foolishly—she's interesting."

"That's true."

"He, on the other hand . . ."

"He talks very little."

"He hardly said a word."

"Larry is always silent," Nedra said.

"What hatred."

"Do you think so? You're very perceptive, Eve."

"I've lived through it."

Viri came in, the dog behind him, bits of grass stuck to his coat.

"Oh, you've been down to the river," Nedra said.

"He's had a day."

"You like Easter, don't you, Hadji? He's probably thirsty, Viri."

"He drank a lot of the river. Would you like some tea? I'll make it."

"That would be wonderful," Nedra said. After he had gone, she turned to Eve. "What do you think of Viri and me?"

Eve smiled.

"Can you see it in us?"

"You are absolutely . . . you're perfect for each other."

Nedra gave a slight sound as if finding a mistake in her work.

133

"It's impossible to live with him," she said finally.

"It isn't. That's plain."

"Impossible for me. No, you don't see it. I love him, he's a marvelous father, but it's terrible. I can't explain it. It's what turns you to powder, being ground between what you can't do and what you must do. You just turn to dust."

"I think you're just tired."

"Viri and I are like Richard Strauss and his wife. I'm as nasty as she was—the only thing is, Strauss was a genius. She was a singer, they had terrific arguments. She would shriek and throw the music at him. When she was nobody, I mean. They were rehearsing his opera. She ran off to her dressing room. He followed her and they kept right on fighting."

Viri returned with a tray and the tea.

"I'm telling about Strauss and his wife," Nedra said.

"He had absolutely beautiful handwriting," Viri commented.

"He was so talented."

"He could have been a draftsman."

"Well, anyway, the orchestra came and announced that they would not play any opera in which this woman had a role. And Strauss said, well, that's unfortunate, as Fraulein de Ahna and I have just become engaged. She was an absolute bitch, you can't believe it. He used to beg to get into her room. She told him when to work, when to stop work; she treated him like a dog."

Viri poured the tea. A perfume rose from the cups.

"Milk?" he asked Eve.

"Just black," she said.

Franca and Anthony came into the room.

"Would you like some tea?" he asked them. "Bring two cups."

He poured theirs; they sat on cushions on the floor.

"There's a certain kind of greatness," Viri said, "Strauss's,

134

for instance, which begins in the heavens. The artist doesn't ascend to glory, he appears in it, he already has it and the world is prepared to recognize him. Meteoric, like a comet—those are the phrases we apply, and it's true, it *is* a kind of burning. It makes them highly visible, and at the same time it consumes them, and it's only afterwards, when the brilliance is gone, when their bones are lying alongside those of lesser men, that one can really judge. I mean, there are famous works, renowned in antiquity, and today absolutely forgotten: books, buildings, works of art."

"But isn't it true," Nedra said, "that most great architects were accepted in their time?"

"Well, they had to be, or they wouldn't have built anything. There are many architects, though, who were very highly regarded and have passed into obscurity."

"But not the reverse."

"No," Viri admitted. "No one has yet gone the other way. Perhaps I'll be the first."

"You're not obscure, Papa," Franca protested.

"He obscure but he was honest," Viri said.

"What about Obscure, the Jude?" Nedra said.

"Ha, good, very good," he said. He felt a touch of bitterness at the jokes they were making.

When they began to prepare supper late in the day, he went upstairs. He looked at himself in the mirror, suddenly without illusion. He was in middle life; he could no longer recognize the young man he had been.

He sat in the bedroom drawing figures, words, embellishing them, making them into designs. *1928*, he wrote, and after it, *Born June 12 in Philadelphia, Pa. 1930 moves to Chicago, Ill.* He continued the entries, listing his life as if it were a painter's. *1941 Enters Phillips Exeter. 1945 Enters Yale. 1950 Travels in Europe. 1951 Marries Nedra Carnes.*

In the quiet the thoughts came streaming to him: days he

had nearly forgotten, failures, old names. *1960 The single most beautiful year of my life,* he wrote. And then, beneath, *Loses everything.*

He was interrupted by the calling of his wife: Arnaud was on the telephone. The chronology in his pocket, he came downstairs. The lights were on, evening had come. Eve, her knees bent to one side, her smooth, stockinged feet half out of her shoes, was talking on the phone.

"You know, I can't decide whether I wish I were there or you were here," she was saying. Arnaud had been visiting his mother, but now he longed to speak to his other family, the family of his heart. His affection was extravagant, he told funny stories, he begged for details of the day.

Viri took the phone. They were united, all of them, in the great, blue evening that reigned over the river and hills. They talked on and on.

Afterwards he sat with the paper, the Sunday edition, immense and sleek, which had lain unopened in the hall. In it were articles, interviews, everything fresh, unimagined; it was like a great ship, its decks filled with passengers, a directory in which was entered everything that had made any difference to the city, the world. A great vessel sailing each day, he longed to be on it, to enter its salons, to stand near the rail.

You are not obscure, they told him. You have friends. People admire your work. He was, after all, a good father—that is to say, an ineffective man. Real goodness was different, it was irresistible, murderous, it had victims like any other aggression; in short, it conquered. We must be vague, we must be gentle, we are killing people otherwise, whatever our intentions, we are crushing them beneath a vision of light. It is the idiot, the weakling, he thought, the son who has failed; once beyond that there is no virtue possible.

Night falls. The cold lies in the fields. The grass turns to stone.

In bed, he lay like a man in prison, dreaming of life.

136

"What was the joke Booth told that was so funny?" Nedra asked. She was brushing her hair.

"His smile is extraordinary," Viri said. "It's like an old politician's."

"Where was his wife?"

"She's learning to fly."

"Learning to fly?"

"So he says. Anyway, there were two drunks on an elevator. It was in some hotel . . ."

"This is the joke?"

"A woman got on—she was completely nude. They just stood there and didn't say anything. After she got off, one of them turned to the other: 'You know,' he said, 's'funny, my wife has an outfit exactly like that.' "

13

THE MORNINGS WERE WHITE, THE trees were still bare. The telephone rang. A soft vapor was rising from the roof of the Marcel-Maas barn. His wife was there alone.

"Come and see me," she begged Nedra.

"Well, I'm going into the city later. Perhaps on the way."

"I want to talk to you."

Nedra drove by at noon. The uncut grass was silent, the air cool. The stone walls of the barn shone in the clear April light. Still dry, still sleeping, the orchard sloped away.

"I'm having a *kir*," Nora said. "Would you like one? It's white wine and cassis."

"Yes, I'd love one."

She poured the wine. "Robert is living in New York," she said. "Here. Don't worry, I'm not going to tell you about it."

She sat down and sipped. "It should be colder," she said. She jumped up to get another bottle of wine.

"This is all right."

"No, I want you to have it exactly as it should be." She was filled with a pathetic energy. "You deserve it," she said.

Nedra sat calmly, but she was uncomfortable. She dreaded confidences, especially those of strangers.

"Here," Nora said again.

The glass was chilled. "Oh, it's good."

Calmly, like lovers raising their eyes, they exchanged unintentional glances.

"I'm glad you came. I just wanted to see you. You know, people around here are so boring."

"Yes," Nedra said, "why is that?"

"They're sunk in their lives. I don't know any of them anyway. We hardly ever entertained. Well, there is a girl named Julie," she said. "Do you know her? She sells cosmetics. She used to be a stripteaser. Do you like.the *kir?*"

"It's wonderful. What is it again?"

"Wine and cassis, very little cassis."

Nedra was inspecting the bottle in which it came.

"It's made from berries," Eve said.

"What kind of berries?"

"I don't know. French. I was telling you about Julie. She's had a fantastic life. Gangsters used to take her to the St. George Hotel. I mean, she can describe them. They sent her home with a bodyguard. Of course, you know what the bodyguard did. Now she's selling face cream. Would you like another one? You haven't finished."

"Not yet."

"Let's sit near the window. It's nicer there."

As they were moving the phone rang. Nora picked it up abruptly. "Hello," she said. She listened. "I'm sorry, Mr. Maas isn't here. Mr. Maas is in New York."

She listened again. "New York, New York," she said.

"One moment, please," the operator was saying. Then, "My party would like to speak to Miss Moss. Is Miss Moss there?"

"Miss Moss is in Los Angeles, California," Nora said. "Who is calling?"

Nedra sat in a comfortable chair, the sun on her knees. The window sill was dense with plants. The music from half-forgotten Broadway shows was playing. Nora came back, sat down and closed her eyes. She began to hum, to sing an occasional phrase, finally she was holding long, passionate notes with all her heart. Suddenly she got up and began to move from side to side, to dance. She shot out her hands in the style of hoofers. She laughed self-consciously, but she didn't stop. One saw the life in which she had bloomed, the gaiety, the foolishness leaking out like the stuffing from a doll.

"I used to know all the scores by heart," she confessed.

She could cook, her legs were good, what was she going to do, she asked, stay out here with the apple trees? Most of them were so old anyway that they never bore fruit.

"I like to read," she said, "but my God . . ."

She had good hands, she said. She looked at them, one side, then the other, a little worn, but they know things. Well, that was true of everything about her.

"The thing is, a man can go off with a younger woman, but it doesn't work the other way."

"Yes, it does," Nedra said.

"You think so?"

"Certainly."

"No, not for me," she decided. "You have to believe in it."

Here she sat, alone in the country. In the orchard were the trees; in the cupboard, clean glasses and plates. It was a house built of stone, a house that would stand for centuries, and within it were the books and clothes, the sunny rooms and tables necessary for life. And there was a woman as well, her eyes still clear, her breath sweet. Silence surrounded her, the air, the hush of the grass. She had no tasks.

"I'm not staying out here," she said abruptly.

Some of his clothes were hanging in the closets, his canvases were still in the studio above their heads. She could not stay. The ending of days was too long, the darkness came and crushed her, she could not move.

"It isn't fair," she said.

"No."

"What can I do?"

"You'll meet someone," Nedra said. How am I so different from this woman? she was thinking. Am I that much more sure of my life? "How old are you?" she asked.

"Thirty-nine."

"Thirty-nine," Nedra said.

"Katy's eighteen."

"It's been so long since I've seen her."

"I spent my life looking after him," Nora cried. "I can remember when I first met him. He was marvelous-looking, I'll show you some pictures."

"You're still young."

"Do we really only have one season? One summer," she said, "and it's over?"

14

IN THE MORNING, WITH THE FIRST light, a great wind—a wind that slammed doors and broke glass —devoured the silence in sudden, overwhelming claps. Hadji lay huddled in the blankets. The rabbit, his ears back, was crouched beside his box. There were periods of ominous calm and then, lasting sometimes for half a minute, the awful roar of air. The walls seemed to creak.

All day, though the sky was clear, even warm, the wind blew, tearing at the shutters, ravishing the trees. The vines stood erect in frenzy, shrieked and were pulled away. In the greenhouse there was a musical crash of panes. It was a wind that had no edge, a huge, open-mouthed wind which would not cease.

In the late afternoon there was a call. It was from another city, there was a strange, mechanical tone. "Mrs. Berland?" a man's voice asked.

"Yes."

"This is Dr. Burnett." He was calling from Altoona. "I thought I had better advise you," he said. "Your father is in the hospital. He's quite ill."

"What's wrong?"

"You're not familiar with his condition?"

"No, what is it?"

"Well, he's asked for you, and I think it might be a good thing if you could come."

"How long has he been there?"

"About five days," the doctor said.

She drove that night. She left an hour before the light began to go. Sibelius was thundering on the radio, the wind battered her car. She passed shipyards, refineries, throbbing, ugly neighborhoods she did not even glance at, the industry that supported her life. Cars streamed in both directions, their lights becoming brighter. Darkness fell.

She drove without stopping. The radio stations faded; corrupted by static, they began to devour each other. There were gusts of music, ghostly voices; it was like a vast, decaying canopy, like leaking roofs in a poverty-stricken town, a town awash in cheap advertisements, sentiment, mindless noise. The chaos filled her ears, oncoming headlights stung her eyes. The sky glowed with cities beyond the black trees.

She drove into darkness, the darkness of an old land, weary, close-held, sold and resold, and passed into the zone of deep night. The roads emptied. She was crossing the Susquehanna, still as a pond, when the first waves of sleepiness struck her. The drive became a dream. She thought of her father, of the past she was reentering. She knew the helplessness and despair of beginning again an endless journey, a journey that had been taken already, once and for all. The long white tunnel at Blue Mountain swept by like a hospital corridor. Then Tuscarora. The names had not changed. They were waiting for her, certain of her return.

Finally she slept for a few hours, the car solitary in a blue-lighted service area. When she woke, the sky to the east was faint. She was in country vaguely familiar to her: the slope of the hills, the dark trees. The road had become visible, smooth and pale, the woods as far as one could see were without a single house or light. She was thrilled; may it always be thus, she thought. The early day, like dawn at sea, stunned her and gave her new life.

Soon there were the first farms, barns beautiful in the silence, the radio giving prices, the number slaughtered of sheep and lambs. Old houses of faded brick that struck the heart, white pillars on the porches, the occupants still asleep. The sky grew more and more faint, as if washed away. Suddenly everything was colored, the fields turned green. Helplessly, she recognized her source, though far from it for years, the vacant, illiterate country, the hills that were long to walk up, the vulgar towns. She passed a single car, just as the cows were coming in, a lone Chevrolet, silent as a bird in flight. A boy and girl were in it, seated close together. They did not seem to see her. They drifted behind in the brimming light.

Small gardens, churches, hand-painted signs. She felt no warmth of recognition; it was desolation to her, ruin. What failure to someday crawl back; it would erase everything in a single day.

Morning in the heartland. Early workers driving. Near a farmhouse two ducks wandered dazedly in the road where, amid white feathers, a bloody third lay, killed by a car.

Greenhouses, ancient schools, factories with their windows broken out. Altoona. She was turning down streets she remembered as a girl.

The hospital was just awake. The newspapers of the day before were still in its vending machines, the schedules for surgery had not yet been typed.

She was quickly stopped. "I'm sorry, you're not allowed in," the receptionist said. "Visiting hours begin at eleven."

"I've driven all night."

"You can't visit now."

At eleven she returned. In a room with two beds she found her father near the window. He was asleep. His arms outside the covers seemed very frail.

She touched him. "Hello, Papa."

His eyes opened. Slowly, he turned his head.

"How are you?" she asked.

"All right, I guess."

She could see it plainly. His face seemed smaller, his nose large, his eyes worn.

"I've been in here a week now," he said.

There was nothing to show it. On the table were a waterglass and tray. There were no books, no letters, not even a watch. In the next bed lay an old man recovering from some sort of surgery.

"He never stops talking," her father said.

The old man could hear them. He smiled as if praised.

"Never shuts up," her father said. "Where are you staying?"

"At the house."

Outside was clear, sunny morning. The room seemed dark.

"Do you want a newspaper?" she asked.

"No."

"I'll read it to you, if you like."

He did not reply.

She stayed until two. They spoke very little. She sat reading. He seemed half asleep. The nurses declined to comment on his condition; he had a strong heart, they said.

The doctor spoke to her, finally, in the hall. "He's very weak," he said. "It's been a long struggle."

"His back hurts him terribly."

"Yes, well, it's spread."

"Everywhere?"

"Into the bone." He explained the loss of weight and strength, the inanition that was taking its course.

At the house she made herself some tea and rested. It was the house in which she had been brought up: papered rooms, the curtains gray. Near the back door the earth was packed hard, the grass never grew. She called Viri.

"How is he?"

"Very bad."

"Will he recover?"

"I don't think so," she said.

"Nedra, I'm so sorry."

"Well, what can we do?" she asked. "I'm staying at the house."

"Are you comfortable there?"

"It isn't that bad."

"How long do you suppose . . . What do they think?"

"He seems so weak, so far gone. This morning I was shocked at how far it had progressed."

"Do you want me to come down?"

"Oh, no, that really wouldn't do anything. It's very sweet of you, but I don't think so."

"Well, if you need me . . ."

"Viri, these hospitals are so awful. You ought to design a hospital, with sunlight and trees. If you're dying you should have one last look at the world—I mean, at least you should see the sky."

"It's all efficiency."

"Damn efficiency."

When she returned to the hospital her father was asleep

again. He woke as soon as she came near, wide-eyed suddenly, aware. She sat by his bed through the long afternoon. For dinner he took only a few sips of milk.

"Papa, you must eat."

"I can't."

The nurses came in occasionally. "How are you feeling, Mr. Carnes?"

"It won't be long," he murmured.

"Are you feeling better?" they asked.

He seemed not to hear them. He was being enclosed in an invisible shroud. His mouth was dry. When he talked it was barely a mumble, deep, almost unintelligible. Several times he asked what day it was.

That night, exhausted, she bathed and went to bed. She woke once during the night. The sky, the street outside, were absolutely silent. She was rested, calm, alone. The cat had entered the room and sat on the window sill, looking out.

By morning her father had gone into a coma. He lay helpless, breathing more evenly, more slowly, there were pads of moist gauze on his eyes. She called to him: nothing. He had said his last words.

Suddenly she was choked with sadness. Oh, peace to you, Papa, she thought. For hours she sat by the bed.

He was stubborn. He was strong. He could not hear her now, nothing could rouse him. His arms were folded weakly across his chest like featherless wings. She wiped his face, adjusted his pillow.

Viri called that evening. "Is there any change?"

"I'm going out for some dinner," she told him. She talked to the children. How was Grandpa, they asked. "He's very sick," she said.

They were polite. They didn't know what to reply.

It took a long time, it took forever; days and nights, the smell of antiseptic, the hush of rubber wheels. This frail engine, we think, and yet what murder is needed to take it down. The heart is in darkness, unknowing, like those animals in mines that have never seen the day. It has no loyalties, no hopes; it has its task.

The night nurse listened to him. It had begun.

Nedra leaned close. "Papa," she said, "can you hear me? Papa?"

His breaths came faster, as if he were fleeing. It was six in the evening. She sat all night as he lay there gasping, his body working with the habit of a lifetime. She was praying for him, she was praying against him and thinking to herself as she did, You're next, it's only a matter of time, a few swift years.

At three in the morning there was only the light at the nurse's desk, there was no doctor. The corridors were empty.

Below was the dark, impoverished town, its sidewalks crumbled, its houses so close there was not even space to walk between them. The ancient schools were silent, the theater, its windows covered with metal sheet, the veterans' halls. Through the center ran not a river, but a broad, silent bed of rails. The tracks were rusted, the great repair shops closed. She knew this steep town, she was friendless here, she had turned her back on it forever. In it, sleeping, were distant cousins, never to be claimed.

She listened to the terrible struggle that was going on upon the narrow bed. She took his hand. It was cool; there was no feeling in it, no response. She watched him. He was fighting far beyond her; his lungs were fighting, the chambers of his heart. And his mind, she thought, of what was that thinking, trapped within him, fated? Was it in harmony, his being, or in chaos, like the people of a falling city?

His throat began to fill. She called the nurse. "Come right away," she said.

His breath was frightening, his pulse weak. The nurse felt his wrist, then his elbow.

He did not die. He went on with the awful breathing. The effort of it made her weak. It seemed that if only he could rest

146

from it he would be all right. An hour passed. He did not know how he was exhausting himself. It was a kind of insanity, he was running on and on, had stumbled and gotten to his feet again a hundred times. Nothing could stand such punishment.

At a little past five, abruptly, he took his last breath. The nurse came in. It was done.

Nedra did not weep. She felt instead that she had seen him home. She suddenly knew the meaning of the words "at peace, at rest." His face was calm. It bore a gray ash of beard. She kissed his cheek, his bluish hand. It was still warm. The nurse was putting in his teeth.

Outside, the tears began to run down her cheeks. She walked dazedly. She made a single vow: not to forget him, to remember him always, as long as she lived.

The funeral was simple. She had requested no services. Near gravestones that said simply, *Father*, and crosses of stone carved to look like logs, amid tilted obelisks and markers for children—*Faye Milnor, Aug. 1930–Nov. 1931*, a small stone, a hard year—he was buried high on the hill, in a quiet section in back where the graves were slightly disordered. The town, dense with trees, seemed asleep in the afternoon, distant as a painting done by a primitive. She glanced at names as she walked. There were pigeons on the path. Miniature flags waved in brief ripples.

The gravedigger was a young man, naked to the waist, his long hair drawn back and tied.

He nodded politely and stopped working. His dog was lying in the grass beneath a tree.

"Go ahead," she said.

The lid of the vault was already in place.

"This is a really good spot," he told her. He had a narrow face. His front tooth was broken. "The next time you come, the grass will be up."

"So soon?"

"Well, you have to give it a couple of weeks."

"Yes," she said. "What's your name?"

"David."

He was Mexican, she realized. "David . . ."

"Yes, m'am."

He went back to work. His arms were lean, but he shoveled steadily. Far off was the dome of the cathedral, gray on the sky. She waited until the grave was half filled.

"Is that your dog?" she said.

It was a dog like a collie, with a long, narrow nose.

"Yeah, she's mine."

"What's her name?" Nedra asked.

"Anita."

She looked out once more at the town. "They'll take good care of it?"

"Oh yes, m'am," he said. "Don't worry."

She gave him ten dollars as she left.

"No," he said, "that's all right."

"Keep it," she told him and walked down. The path seemed steeper. In places the tall iron fence around the cemetery had collapsed. Overhead, quite abruptly, the sky had grown dark.

Her father's suits were laid on the bed to be taken by the Salvation Army, his shirts, his empty shoes. The earth had thudded down on the crypt in which he lay. All the ornaments, hats, belts, rings—how plain and cheap they seemed without him. They were like theatrical things—seen in the daylight very ordinary, even deceiving.

She kept a few of the photographs; the house and its furnishings she put up for sale. She was wiping out all traces, stepping back into a life unconnected to this, a life more brilliant, more free. She had waited here once for seventeen years, desperate years, the air filled with quiverings of the world beyond; would she ever be part of it, would she ever go forth?

Goodbye Altoona, roofs, churches, trees. The watershed where they had gone on many summer afternoons, the cool,

148

ferny ground, the abandoned ovens filled with butterflies and leaves. Broad Avenue with its houses, the neighborhoods of the unknown. In every dark parlor, it seemed, was a woman with swollen legs, or an old man, used, empty, stained. A town almost European in appearance, steep and spacious, shining in the sun of late afternoon. Like all such junctions it was a penal colony, pinned in the provinces by its rails.

She drove through the streets for the last time. Altoona was blue with morning, a city of trees. The cheap cafés were filled, the traffic passing. Poor food, plain people. All these meager lives were like mulch; they had made the trees of the town, its cornerstones, its endless solitude and calm. She thought of the snow falling in these same streets, of long winters, plays that had toured years before, of certain rich families whose homes were like another land, their daughters, their stores. She thought of her father, of men he once played cards with, his friends, their wives.

It was finished, done. Suddenly she felt it all through her like an omen. She was exposed. The way was clear for her own end.

15

ARNAUD WAS SITTING COMFORTABLY, veiled in the haze of cigar smoke, indolent, amused. The amusement was hidden; it was like coals beneath the ashes, it had to be uncovered to come to life. His hair seemed grayer, more tangled, his eyes more pale. There was the look of a marvelous derelict about him, a holy failure. He had full lips, stained teeth that were nonetheless strong, a face of the earth.

Nedra sat opposite him. "You must think of a question," she said.

"All right."

"And you must concentrate on it. I can't do this unless you're serious."

He was smoking a small cigar like a dark bit of wood. He nodded slightly. "I'm serious."

She began to look through the cards. He watched her. He was grave. It was as if they had entered a cathedral together. There fell about them a cool, a perceptible change of scale.

"I'm going to choose a card now," she said, "to represent you."

"How do you do that?"

"It depends on your characteristics, your age."

"And if you didn't know me, how would you do it?"

A swift smile. "How could I not know you?" she asked.

She laid down a card, a king who wore a yellow robe. His feet were hidden as well as the throne on which he sat, a Frankish king. "The King of Swords."

"Good."

It was winter. The days were deliciously aimless and long. She handed him the cards. "Shuffle them, and concentrate on the question."

He shuffled them slowly. "What is the origin of this?" he asked.

"The tarot deck?"

"Who invented it?"

"It wasn't invented," she said. "Are they well mixed? Cut them three times. You know, I'm not an expert, Arnaud," she said as she laid them out.

"No?"

"I don't know all there is," she apologized, "but I know quite a bit."

She placed the cards carefully, with a kind of ceremonial precision. She covered the king with a card. She put still another one crossways on it. Then, in the further form of a cross, she put single cards above, below, and to either side.

150

Strange cards, their illustrations like those in books. They left her fingers with a faint, crisp sound. To the side of the cross she placed four cards in a column, one after another. The next to last was Death. It seemed to spread darkness over the rest. It was as if, casually, they had begun to read someone else's letter in the middle of which suddenly was horrifying news.

"Well," Nedra said, "you have a marvelous card here." She was pointing to the last one. It was the Emperor.

"This is what is to come," she said. "It means reason, strength, greatness.

"The most important influence is here." She indicated the card on top of his. "This is a woman, a very good woman, a friend, loving, honorable. She is the key."

They were bound together by the fragrance of tobacco, by the cold that lay at the windows, by a winter sky white as a cup.

"I think that your question may even be answered by this woman. Am I right?" she said.

"You're too clever."

"She either has the answer or she is the answer."

"Well, the answer to my question is really a yes or a no."

"I don't think I can answer that yet."

"Neither can I," Arnaud said.

"Sometimes it's impossible to see things clearly in your own life. You have to rely on someone outside to show you."

"I'm willing to do that."

"We're talking about Eve, aren't we?"

"Of course."

"She's my closest friend."

"It's difficult, isn't it?"

"Well, you know you're the only man in her life. I mean, in her whole life the one true man."

"It's very difficult," Arnaud said. "I love her, I like Anthony, and yet there's something that keeps me from it."

"What?"

"I can't say."

151

"There probably has never been a marriage that hasn't been entered with some uncertainty."

"Were you uncertain?"

"It was just like going to be executed."

"Come on, Nedra."

"I suppose it wasn't quite."

"What else do you see for me?"

She looked at the cards. "I see another woman who is influencing you. I don't recognize this woman. She's dark, she has money, she's probably very confident, very secure. She is the obstacle, the opposing force. She has unusual tastes which perhaps are hidden."

"Have I met this woman yet?"

"I'm not sure."

"She doesn't sound like anyone I know."

"Well, it's here. You're covered by the Queen of Wands . . ."

"This one."

"Yes, and crossed by the Queen of Pentacles. That's very unusual. It shows that your true companions are women. Now, what has happened is that . . ." She paused. "Certain ideas, certain suggestions have been made. It's probably one principal proposition. You have a very hard struggle to face."

"Still?"

She was reading ahead, she did not seem to hear him. "I don't think I'm doing this well," she said suddenly.

"I think you're doing fantastically. I'd like to learn a bit about these unusual tastes."

"No. No, I'm wrong. There are things here that are confusing." She was vague, even a little nervous.

"Wait, I just want to know one thing." Death in black letters was astride a white horse. The banner he bore was Arab, stiff as wood. "What does this mean?" he asked.

"Well, it can mean a number of things . . ."

"For instance."

152

"Oh, anything. The loss of a benefactor, for example. Look, it's snowing," she said.

She took one of his cigars. Her long fingers held it at the end near her mouth. She leaned forward to accept a light.

Beyond the windows the snow was falling, more and more dense. Everything vanished in it.

"Let's find Viri," she cried.

He was out walking somewhere. They began to dress wildly in whatever was at hand. They bundled themselves like Russians in hats and scarfs and carried a coat for Viri.

"He's down by the river," Nedra guessed.

The snow was pouring down. It was covering their shoulders, brushing their eyes. They walked without speaking, as if in northern wastes. Their footsteps filled behind them. It was marvelous, strange. Then, racing toward them, his face white with snow, was Hadji. He barked, he dove at the soft drifts which were just forming, went sideways, rolled ecstatically, his legs in the air. Viri appeared behind him like a myth, a wanderer, his collar turned up, snow in his hair.

"We are your Eskimo guides," Arnaud said.

"What good luck." He was putting on the coat.

"This is Nushka, my woman," Arnaud said.

"Ah."

"Of course you know the Eskimo custom regarding wives."

"It is truly civilized," Viri agreed.

"Nushka, rub noses with our friend."

Nedra performed the act gravely, sensually.

"She is yours," Arnaud said.

"She doesn't speak?"

"Rarely. She who speaks does not nose," he said, "she who nose does not speak."

Hadji lay flat in the deepening snow, half buried: black eyes —mascaraed eyes, Danny said—tall, intelligent ears. He would not move when they called.

* * *

For dinner there arrived Jivan and, back from life with her boyfriend, Kate Marcel-Maas. Her face was sunburned, her arms lean.

"Do you know Kate?" Nedra asked.

"I don't think so," Arnaud said. He smiled. "Are you living in New York?"

"No, I'm just here for two weeks."

"Oh, really? Where have you come from?"

"Los Angeles."

"Where's that?" he murmured.

"Where's Los Angeles?" she said.

"I think I remember. What were you doing there?"

"We have a little house there, with a garden. Most of the time I was growing lettuce."

Jivan was in a cotton shirt open at the neck. He seemed filled with energy, almost impatience.

"Come, I want to show you something," he told her. He led her to the kitchen where, before the fascinated eyes of Franca and Danny, he had been carving the celery into birdlike shapes.

"Where did you learn that?" Kate said.

"Do you like it?"

"Fantastic."

"You should grow some celery," he said. "Here, now I'm going to make a swan. Will you have some wine?"

It was retsina. He poured her a little. She tasted it. When he was close to her, he seemed slightly shorter than she was. On his finger was a ring with a dark stone.

"It's bitter," she complained.

"You'll get used to it. Franca, would you like to try it?"

"Yes, I'd love some."

"You'll grow to like it," he told Kate. "In the end the things that were bitter are always the best."

"Oh, yeah?" she said.

Night had fallen. The house was illuminated as if for a ball, the lights on everywhere. Nedra was cooking. She was at her most beautiful: a slim, camel skirt, her sleeves pushed up, her wrists bare. Nearby stood a glass of wine she sometimes paused to sip.

Arnaud was talking to Viri. They were at ease amid the cushions of the largest couch. They laughed, their smiles appearing at the same time. They were like directors of a gallery seen through the clear, tinted glass of their window at the end of the day; they were like publishers, owners of shares.

Nedra brought them the St. Raphael. "What are they doing in the kitchen?" Viri asked.

"Jivan is trying to seduce her."

"Before dinner?"

"I think he's a little nervous," Nedra said. "He senses danger."

"Nedra, don't you think—I mean, in principle—that we have a certain responsibility to her parents?"

"What are you talking about, Viri? She's been married."

"That's not strictly true."

"It's the same thing."

"Isn't she a little young?" Arnaud asked.

"Ah, you forget," Nedra said.

The dinner, she announced when they were seated at the table, was Italian. *Petti di pollo.* Jivan poured the wine. This time Kate refused it.

"Have some," he urged.

"What is *petti di pollo?*" she asked.

"*Pollo* is chicken," Arnaud said.

"What's *petti?*"

"Breasts," he said. "You know what they say about chicken."

"No."

"Every part strengthens a part."

"I can use it," she said.

Arnaud was vague, amusing. He told stories of Italy, of towns on the sea that had no hotels and you went along the street knocking at doors to find a room, of Sicily burning in sunlight, of Ravenna and Rome. Franca sat beside him drinking wine.

He had an ear for language. He lapsed into Italian and wove in and out of it as if they all shared the power. "In Sicily everyone has a *lupara*—that's a shotgun. In the paper there was an article about a man who shot another man for making too much noise under his window. He went before the judge, he was furious at being brought there. 'You mean to say I can't shoot someone beneath my *own window?*' he asked."

"Is that true?" Franca asked.

"Everything is true."

"No, really."

"Either that," he said, "or it comes true later. I'll tell you another story. There was a father who gave his son a shotgun. It was very small. It was a *luparetta*. So the son went to school, and he met another boy with a wrist watch. It was a beautiful wrist watch, he fell in love with it. He wanted it, so he traded; he gave his *luparetta* to the boy and he got the watch."

"Is this a true story?"

"Who knows? When the son came home that afternoon, his father said, 'Where's your *luparetta—Dov'è la luparetta?*' And the son said, 'I traded it.' 'You traded it!' 'Yes,' he said, 'I traded it for this watch.' '*Fantastico,*' the father said, '*meraviglioso,* you traded it for a watch. Now when someone calls your sister a whore, what are you going to do, tell them the time?' "

They ate like a family, noisy, devoted, they passed plates freely. Kate was drinking from Arnaud's glass. Later, in the other room, she played the guitar. The table was left uncleared. Nedra lit the fire which had been carefully laid, dry pieces of kindling, paper beneath. It soared into life, blooming like those beneath martyrs. She sat beside Jivan. They were drinking pear brandy. Kate, the guitar across her lap, was singing for Arnaud in a faint, high voice.

"You'd better get her out of here," Nedra whispered.

"Don't worry."

"He's going to get her into bed, I can see it."

"She's had a little too much to drink," Jivan said.

"Yes, but nothing that you gave her."

"She told me she didn't like the wine."

"Why are you whispering, Nedra?" Viri called.

"It's fun," she said, smiling.

She poured more brandy. She was like a silver Christmas helix, a foil decoration turning slowly, the dazzle descending only to reappear time after time.

"You play beautifully," she said.

She excused herself to say good night to the children. Viri went up afterwards. He kissed his daughters. Sitting on their beds, he felt the warmth of their rooms, the chambers in which they slept and dreamed, were secure. Their books, their possessions filled him with a sense of accomplishment and peace. On the stairs he heard voices, the sensual chords from below. Kate was sitting near Arnaud. Her teeth had a bluish cast to them, the blue that flourishes on pure white, in diamonds. He had a moment of concern for her—no, not concern, he realized, but covetousness. He was like a sick man as he thought of her, stricken and unhappy. The pain he felt was a phantom pain, like that in the toes of a missing leg. It was only desire, which he hoped would leave him, which he prayed would not.

Nedra was talking to her. "I wish I'd had your courage when I was your age," she said.

Kate shrugged. "I don't really like California."

"At least you've lived there. You're seeing what it is."

"My mother doesn't like the idea. She'd like us to be married."

"Yours is a better way," Nedra said.

She poured them each a little more brandy. Jivan and Viri were listening to the music; Arnaud sat sprawled near the fire, his head back, his eyes closed. The snow was still falling, even the roads had disappeared.

The elegance of the evening, the dishes remaining on the

157

table, the ease with which Nedra and her husband treated each other, the understanding which seemed to stream from them, all of this filled Kate with a feverish happiness, that happiness which lies within the power of another to confer. She was drenched with love for these people who, though they had lived nearby all through her childhood, it seemed she was suddenly seeing for the first time, who were treating her as someone she longed at that moment to be: one of themselves.

"Can I come and see you while I'm here?" she asked.

"Of course."

"I mean, I really like to talk to you."

"I'd love to see you," Nedra said.

One afternoon, then. They would walk together or have tea. She had never set foot beyond the borders, this woman Kate suddenly loved, this woman with a knowing face, not at all sentimental, who leaned on her elbows and smoked small cigars. She had never traveled, not even to Montreal, and yet she knew so well what life should be. It was true. In her heart she carried an instinct like that of a migrant species. She would find the tundra, the deeps, she would journey home.

Arnaud's eyes were open. They were uninquisitive, calm, a signal that he was returning slowly. His face was soft, like a child's. "For some reason, I am being urged to sleep," he murmured. "Your house is so warm and good."

"You may do anything you like," Nedra said. "You should have anything you want."

There was a silence. "You told me that once before," he decided.

"And I've always practiced it."

"Anything I want . . . you've practiced that?"

"Absolutely."

"I'm waking up," he said.

He had not moved, but his eyes were alert. He was bearlike in his languor. One saw his innocence—that is to say, the

158

innocence of great actors—as he came awake. "You've stopped playing, Kate," he said.

She began again. She struck a few mournful chords, they fell slowly from her narrow fingers. In her thin girl's voice, her head down, she began to sing. She sang on and on. She knew endless words, they were her true eloquence, the poems she believed in. *The sheets, they were old, and the blankets were thin . . .*

"My first boyfriend used to sing that," Nedra said. "He took me for a weekend to his family's summer house. It was after the season, they were all gone."

"Who was that?" Viri said.

"He was older than I was," she said. "He was twenty-five."

"Who?"

"I had my first avocado there. I ate it, pit and all," she said.

III

 AT SIXTEEN, FRANCA CHANGED.
She began to fulfill her promise. As if in a day, the way leaves
appear, she suddenly had the power of self-possession. She
woke with it one morning, it was bestowed upon her. Her
breasts were new, her feet a little large. Her face was calm and
unfathomable.

They were close, mother and daughter. Nedra treated her
like a woman. They talked a great deal.

The world was changing, Nedra told her. "I don't mean
changes in fashion," she said. "Those aren't really changes. I
mean changes in the way one can live."

"For instance."

"I don't think I know. You'll feel it. You'll understand far more than I do. The truth is, I'm rather ignorant, but I am able to feel what's in the ground."

There is warmth in families but not often companionship. She loved talking to Franca, and about her as well. She felt that this was the woman that she herself had become, in the sense that the present represents the past. She wanted to discover life through her, to savor it for the second time.

There was a party at Dana's one evening during the holidays. Dana, whose face already had a curious dead expression, one almost of resentment, but after all, what can you expect, as Nedra said, the father a drunkard, the mother a fool. She was reading a book on Kandinsky that night, heavy, beautiful, the paper smooth. She had seen his exhibition at the Guggenheim, for the moment she was dazzled by him. In the silence of the evening, in that hour when all has been done, she opened it at last. He had come to painting late, she read; he was thirty-two at the time.

She called Eve. "I love this book," she said.

"I thought it looked good."

"I've just started reading it," Nedra said. "At the beginning of the first war he was living in Munich, and he went back to Russia. He left behind the woman—she was a painter, too—that he'd been living with for ten years. He saw her again just once—imagine this—at an exhibition in 1927."

The book was in her lap; she had read no further. The power to change one's life comes from a paragraph, a lone remark. The lines that penetrate us are slender, like the flukes that live in river water and enter the bodies of swimmers. She was excited, filled with strength. The polished sentences had arrived, it seemed, like so many other things, at just the right time. How can we imagine what our lives should be without the illumination of the lives of others?

She laid the book down open beside a few others. She wanted to think, to let it await her. She would go back to it, read again, read on, bathe in the richness of its plates.

Franca came home at eleven. From the instant the door closed, she sensed something wrong. "What is it?" she asked.

"What is what?"

"What happened?"

"Nothing. It was terrible."

"How?"

Her daughter was suddenly crying.

"Franca, what is it?"

"Look at me," she wept. She was wearing a suit with a little fur trim at the collar and hem of the skirt. "I look like some kind of doll you buy in a souvenir shop."

"No, you don't."

"I was the first one to leave," she said in desperation. "Everyone said, 'Where are you going?' "

"You didn't have to come home this early."

"Yes, I did."

Nedra was frightened. "What happened, was it the wrong kind of party?" she said.

"It was absolutely the right kind. I was wrong."

"What was everyone else wearing?"

"You always insist on my being different," Franca burst out. "I always wear different clothes, I can't go here or I can't go there. I don't want any more of that. I want to be like everyone else!" The tears were streaming down her face. "I don't want to be like you."

In one stroke she had established her own world.

Nedra said nothing. She was stunned. It was the beginning, she suddenly knew, of something she had thought would never happen. She went to bed troubled, torn by the urge to go to her daughter's room, and afraid, at the same time, of what would be said.

The next day it was all forgotten. Franca worked in the greenhouse. She painted. There was music in her room. Hadji lay on her bed, she was truly happy. It had passed.

*   *   *

A letter arrived from Robert Chaptelle, whose life had drifted downstream. It was difficult to remember him, his nervousness, his expensive tastes and impulses so like her own. He said nothing about the theater; it was all about some man who could save Europe.

. . . he is about five feet ten inches tall. He has the Kennedy appeal. His voice makes you tremble. It is an unforgettable voice. I have had the privilege of meeting him, hours in his company are minutes. His eyes! Finally I understand the nature of politics.

Cela tient du prodige.

She read it only hurriedly. He would write again soon, he said in this final letter. He was traveling for his health, vanished into the remote towns of France from the insurance agency where for a time he had tried to work. Gone, passed into silence.

She thought more than once of the woman Kandinsky had left behind. There are stories that win by their brevity. She had written the name on her calendar, above where the pages are turned: Gabriele Munter.

2

HE EARNED MONEY, HE WAS LIKED by his clients, he could draw beautifully. Ruskin said a true architect must first be a sculptor or painter. He was nearly that, and so absent-minded, so absorbed in work, that he once poured birdseed into his tea by mistake. He was talkative, witty; his handwriting was like print.

They went to dinner with Michael Warner and his friend. Nedra was their favorite, they adored her.

163

"Your daughter is so beautiful."

"I like her," Nedra admitted. "I find her a good friend."

"She's so inviolable. What will she do?" Michael asked.

"I want her to travel," Nedra said.

"But she'll go to school?"

"Oh, yes. Sometimes, though, I think the only real education comes from a single person. It's like being born—you receive everything from one perfect source."

"Well, she has that in you, doesn't she?" Michael said.

"Nedra, that's a very dangerous notion, really," Viri protested.

"A person whose life is so exceptional that it nourishes the life around it," she went on.

"Theoretically that might be possible," Viri said, "but a single relationship, basing everything on that, could be very dangerous. I mean, there is the chance of being imprinted with the ideas of a very strong individual, and even though they might be interesting ideas, they could be absolutely wrong for someone like Franca."

"Marina traveled for three years with Darin Henze when he was touring all over the world. It was a fantastic experience."

"Darin Henze?"

"The dancer."

"What do you mean by 'traveled'?"

"She was his mistress, of course. She was interested in his work. But it really doesn't matter what he did, he could have been an anthropologist. Specific knowledge is not education. What I mean by education," Nedra said, "is learning how to live and on what level. And you must learn that or everything else is useless."

Night in the city. They were at the bar of El Faro, packed among people waiting for a table. The noise of a crowded restaurant beat around them. In the back they were dragging in crates of food while customers wreathed in tobacco smoke shouted over drinks.

164

"You never know what's going to happen to people," Michael was saying. "I have a friend," he said, "she's very funny, very generous. She could have been an actress."

"Morgan," Bill said.

"You must meet her sometime."

Just then they were given a table. The waiter brought the menus.

"We're having the paella, aren't we?" Michael asked them.

"Yes." He ordered. "She lives on Fifth Avenue, just across from the Metropolitan. She got the apartment in their divorce. It's a fabulous apartment . . ."

In the small room, in darkness to which one's eyes must become accustomed, where even a face being searched for can be missed a few tables away, Viri suddenly saw someone. His heart staggered. It was Kaya Doutreau.

"One night she was coming home from the ballet . . ."

He was frightened; he was afraid she would see him. His wife was stunning, the company polished, and yet he was ashamed of his existence.

" . . . Swan Lake. Now say what you like, but there is my all-time favorite."

"So beautiful," Bill said.

"When she opened the door to the apartment she found her dog lying there . . ."

He did not hear, he was aware only of the clatter of utensils, of the sounds that underlay everything, as if listening to the mechanism which moved it all. It seemed terrible that he should be so stricken by her presence, by simple characteristics of which she was completely unaware—her ease, the way in which she sat, the weight of her breasts within the pale, ribbed shirt.

"Well, they don't know. They think someone pushed poison under the door. It was just awful. She didn't know what was wrong. She took him downstairs in her arms, he died in the taxi."

"Viri, are you feeling well?" Nedra asked.

"Yes."

"Are you sure?"

"Quite sure." He smiled briefly. He had forgotten how to eat, it seemed, as if it were a ceremony he had only memorized. His attention was directed toward the plate. He tried not to see beyond the table.

"I mean, here is the most interesting, warm person imaginable. She would never hurt anyone. An apartment filled with books. People are insane."

"It's an awful story," Nedra said.

"I hope I didn't upset you."

"It must be the season," Bill said. "February is like that. The only time in my life I've really been sick was in February. I was in the hospital for six weeks. On the death list for two. This is marvelous paella."

"What was wrong?"

"Oh, I had a bad infection. My family even bought a coffin for me. It wasn't even big enough. They didn't want to spend the money. They were going to bend my knees." He laughed.

"Viri, are you sure you're all right?"

"Oh, yes. Yes."

Throughout dinner he had glimpses of her. He could not evade them. She was alive; she was well. Suddenly she stood up. He felt a moment of utter panic, of physical fear. It was only that they were leaving. When she passed, making her way through the tables, he put his hand to his brow to conceal his face.

They drove home in a night that was cold and immensely clear. The blocks of apartments, great darkened hives, floated above them. In the distance the bridge was a line of light.

Across the river the road became empty. The moon was above it, the entire sky white. The car was filled with the faint aroma of tobacco, of perfume, like the compartment of a train. If one were standing in the darkness watching, they passed in an instant, the brilliant headlights pouring before them, a moment's glimpse of them, no more. In the cold the sound vanishes, then even the distant red of tail lights is gone. Silence. Overhead perhaps the faint noise, brushing the stars, of a plane.

That same night Arnaud was near the Chelsea in the studio of a friend. When he left it was after midnight. He walked east. They had talked for hours, the kind of evening he liked best, intimate, rich talk that flows unending and of which one is never exhausted. He was a Dickensian man; he ate, he drank, he held up the tip of his little finger to show how big someone's talent was, he swam in the teeming city. His overcoat collar was up. The sidewalks were empty, the stores dark behind their shutters of steel.

The traffic came up the avenue in isolated waves. The headlights of the cars rose and fell in ominous silence over the worn macadam. He looked for a taxi, but they drove with their signs reading OFF DUTY at this hour. The corner with its four bleak prospects was cold. He walked up the block. A cafeteria, the last lighted window, was closing. A wave of cars went by, most of them battered, driven by lone men, cars of the working class, every window up.

Around the corner, moving slowly, a motorcycle came. The rider was in black, plexiglass covered his face. A cab went by, Arnaud waved, it would not stop.

The cyclist had pulled to the curb a little way ahead, the engine was idling, he was looking down at his wheels. He had no face, only the curved, gleaming surface. Arnaud moved a few steps out in the street. He could see the lights of midtown, the great buildings. The cyclist had dismounted and was trying the doors of walk-ups, wrenching at the knobs. As he went from one to another he looked into empty stores, his hands pressed flat against the glass. Arnaud began to walk.

In the west Forties there were effeminate young men on

street corners, still waiting. There were men slumped in doorways with filthy hands, their drunken faces scalded by the cold. The taxis that fled along the great avenues were falling apart, their fenders rattling, trash on the floor.

He began to hold his ears. He couldn't walk from here; he lived on Sixty-eighth. He looked back toward the distant traffic, it seemed there were even fewer approaching cars. The tone of everything had changed, as when one listens too long to silence. His thoughts, which had been bundled about him like his coat, suddenly moved off, encompassed more: the dark, stained buildings, the cold legends of commerce written everywhere. He thought of going to the Chelsea; it was only three blocks away. Two men had turned the corner and were coming slowly toward him, one of them dancing a little from side to side, half-entering doorways.

"Hey, what time is it?" one of them asked. They were black.

"Twelve-thirty," Arnaud said.

"Where's your watch?"

Arnaud did not answer. They had stopped, the rhythm of their walking changed, they stood in his path.

"How you know the time with no watch? You unfriendly, man?"

Arnaud's heart was beating faster. "Never unfriendly," he said.

"You been to your girl friend? What's wrong, you too big to talk?" Their faces were identical, gleaming. "Yeah, pretty big. Got a hundred-fifty-dollar overcoat, so you're all right."

Arnaud felt the strength, the ability to move draining from him, as if he were stepping onstage without an idea, without a line. A group of cars was coming, they were five or six blocks away. He began to talk; he was like an informer.

"Listen, I can't stay, but I want to tell you something . . ."

"He can't stay," one of them said to the other.

"There was this deaf man . . ."

168

"What deaf man?"

The cars were coming closer. "He met a friend on the street . . ."

"Les see your watch. We played around enough."

"I want to ask you one question," Arnaud said quickly.

"Come on."

"A question only you can answer . . ."

He suddenly turned toward the approaching cars and ran a few steps in their direction, calling and waving his arms. There were no taxis among them. They were dark, sealed vessels swerving to avoid him. He was struck by something that stung in the cold. He fell to one knee as if pushed.

He tried to stand. Whatever they were hitting him with sounded like a wet rag. It was the beginning of one thing, the end of another. He was staggering forth, like a flagellant, from the ease of uninjured life. He held his arms about his head, crying out, "For God's sake!"

He stumbled, trying to grapple with the rain of grunting blows that was making him wet. He was trying to run. He was blinded, he could not see, lurching along the plank of legend, ridiculous to the end, calling out, his performance faltering in the icy cold, his legs crumbling.

On his knees in the street he offered them his money. They scattered the contents of his wallet as they left. His watch they did not even take. It was broken. It bore, like the instruments of a wrecked plane, the exact moment of disaster. He lay for more than an hour, the cars swerving past, never slowing.

Eve called in the morning. "Oh, God," she moaned.

"What's wrong?"

"You haven't heard?"

"Heard what?" Nedra said. Outside the window in sunlight her dog was walking on the frozen ground.

"Arnaud . . ." She began to weep. "They beat him. He's lost an eye."

"Beat him?"

"Yes. Somewhere downtown," she cried.

3

LIFE DIVIDES ITSELF WITH SCARS like the rings contained within a tree. How close together the early ones seem, time compacts them, twenty years become indistinguishable, one from another.

She had entered a new era. All that belonged to the old had to be buried, put away. The image of Arnaud with his thickly bandaged eye, the deep bruises, the slow speech like a record player losing speed—these injuries seemed like omens to her. They marked her first fears of life, of the malevolence which was part of its fluid, which had no explanation, no cure. She wanted to sell the house. Something was happening on every side of her existence, she began to see it in the streets, it was like the darkness, she was suddenly aware of it, when it comes, it comes everywhere.

In Jivan she noticed for the first time things which were small but clear, like the faint creases in his face which she knew would be furrows one day; they were the tracings of his character, his fate. The somewhat servile deference he paid to Viri, for example, she saw was not the result of a unique situation, it was his nature; there was something obsequious in him, he respected successful men too much. His assurance was physical, it did not go beyond that, like a young man practicing with weights in his room; he was strong, but his strength was childish. Things had somehow changed between them. She would always have affection for him, but the summer had passed.

170

"What is it?" he wanted to know.

She did not feel like explaining. "Love is movement," she answered. "It is changing."

"Yes, of course it's movement, but between two people. Nedra, something is bothering you, I know you too well."

"I just feel we need to breathe some new air."

"New air. You don't mean air."

"You know what I mean."

"Maybe I do. You know, you look wonderful. You look better than when I first met you. It's natural, but I'll tell you something you don't realize. You think when you have love that love is easy to find, that everyone has it. It's not true. It's very hard to find."

"I haven't been looking for it."

"It's like a tree," he told her, "it takes a long time to grow. It has roots very deep, and these roots stretch out a long way, farther than you know. You can't cut it, just like that. Besides, it's not your nature. You're not a child, you're not interested simply in sensation. I don't have another woman, I'm not married, I have no children."

"You can marry."

"You know I can't."

"Things will change."

"Nedra, you know I love Franca. I love Danny."

"I know you do."

"It isn't fair, what you're saying."

"I'm tired of looking on both sides of things," she said simply.

She was above bickering. She had decided.

Her children became for her all there was, so much so that the remark of Jivan's, about loving them, disturbed her. Somehow she found it dangerous.

Her love for them was the love to which she had devoted her life, the only one which would not be consumed or vanish. Their lives would be ascendent when hers was fading, they

171

would carry her devotion within them like a kind of knowledge which swam in the blood. They would always be young to her; they would linger, walk in the sunshine, talk to her to the end. She was reading Alma Mahler. "Viri, listen to this," she said. It was the death of Mahler's daughter who had diphtheria. They had gone to the country and suddenly she became sick. It grew quickly worse. On the last night a tracheotomy was performed; she was choking, she could not breathe. Alma Mahler ran along the edge of the lake, alone, sobbing. Mahler himself, unable to bear the grief, went to the door of his dying child's room again and again, but could not bring himself to go in. He could not even bear to go to the funeral.

"Why are you reading that?" Viri asked.

"It's so terrible," she confessed. She reached over and touched his head. "You're losing your hair."

"I know."

"You're losing it at the office."

"Everywhere," he said.

She was sitting in the armchair covered in white, her favorite chair—his, too; one or the other was always sitting in it, the light was good for reading, the table was piled with new books.

"Oh, God," she sighed, "we're in the grocery store of life. We sit here at night, we eat, we pay bills. I want to go to Europe. I want to go on a tour. I want to see Wren's cathedrals, the great buildings, the squares. I want to see France."

"Italy."

"Yes, Italy. When we're there, we'll see everything."

"We couldn't go until spring," Viri said.

"I want to go this spring."

The thoughts of travel thrilled him too. To wake in London, the sunlight falling, black cabs queued outside the hotels, four seasons in the air.

"I want to read about it first. A good book on architecture," she said.

"Pevsner."

"Who is that?"

"He's a German. He's one of those Europeans who become strangely at home in England—after all, it is *the* civilized country—and live their entire lives there. He's one of the great authorities."

"I'd like to go by boat."

The winter night embraced the house. Hadji, who was growing old, lay against a sofa, his legs stretched out. Nedra was borne by a dream, by the excitement of discovery. "I'm going to have some ouzo," she said.

She poured two glasses from a bottle Jivan had brought at Christmas. She looked like a woman for whom travel to Europe was an ordinary act: her ease, her long neck from which there hung strings of Azuma beads, putty, blue and tan, the bottle in her hand.

"I didn't know we had any ouzo," he said.

"This little bit."

"Do you know how Mahler died?" Viri said. "It was in a thunderstorm. He'd been very sick, he was in a coma. And then at midnight there came a tremendous storm, and he vanished into it, almost literally—his breath, his soul, everything."

"That's fantastic."

"The bells were tolling. Alma lay in bed with his photograph, talking to it."

"That's exactly like her. How did you know all that?"

"I was reading ahead in your book."

As they stood on the corner near Bloomingdale's, the crowd passing, brushing against them, the buses roaring by, she said to Eve, "It's finished," by which she meant everything which had nourished her, most of all the city beyond the far margins of which she had found refuge, still subject to its pull, still beneath a sky one end of which glowed from its light.

Passing through the doors of the store she looked at those going in with her, those leaving, women buying at the handbag counters ahead. The real question, she thought, is, Am I one of these people? Am I going to become one, grotesque, embittered, intent upon their problems, women in strange sunglasses, old men without ties? Would she have stained fingers like her father? Would her teeth turn dark?

They were looking at wineglasses. Everything fine or graceful came from Belgium or France. She read the prices, turning them upside down. Thirty-eight dollars a dozen. Forty-four.

"These are beautiful," Eve said.

"I think these are better."

"Sixty dollars a dozen. What will you use them for?"

"You always need wineglasses."

"Aren't you afraid they'll break?"

"The only thing I'm afraid of are the words 'ordinary life,' " Nedra said.

They were sitting at Eve's when Neil arrived. He had come to visit his son. The room was too small for three people. It had a low ceiling, a little fireplace covered by glass. The whole house was small. It was a house for a writer and a cat, off the street at the end of a private alley, a disciplined writer, probably homosexual, who occasionally had a friend sleep over.

"Too bad about Arnaud," Neil said.

"It's horrible."

"Eve says he . . . may never talk right again," he said to the water glass. He had a thin mouth, the words leaked out.

"They don't know."

"Would you like some tea?" Eve asked.

"Let me make it," Nedra said, rising quickly to her feet. She disappeared into the kitchen.

"Rotten weather, isn't it?" Neil murmured after a pause.

"Yes."

"It's a lot colder than . . . last winter," he said.

"I guess it is."

"Something to do with the . . . earth's orbit . . . I don't know.

174

We're supposed to be entering a new ice age."

"Not another one," she said.

4

THE SEASONS BECAME HER SHELTER, her raiment. She bent to them, she was like the earth, she ripened, grew sere, in the winter she wrapped herself in a long sheepskin coat. She had time to waste, she cooked, made flowers, she saw her daughter stricken by a young man.

His name was Mark. He made beautiful line drawings, without shadow, without flaw, like the Vollards of Picasso. He resembled them; he was lean, his legs were long, his hair faded brown. He came in the afternoons, they sat in her room for hours with the door closed, sometimes he stayed for dinner.

"I like him," Nedra said. "He isn't callow."

Afterwards Franca looked up the word. Destitute of feathers, it said.

"She likes you. She says you're feathered."

"I'm what?"

"Like a bird," she said.

Franca he was in love with, but Nedra he revered. Their world had a mysterious pull. It was more vivid, more passionate than other worlds. To be with them was like being in a boat, they floated along their own course. They invented their life.

The three of them met in the Russian Tea Room. The headwaiter knew Nedra; they were given one of the booths near the bar. It was one she liked. Nureyev had once sat nearby. "At that table there," she said.

"All alone?"

"No. Have you ever seen him?" she said. "He's the most beautiful man on earth. You simply can't believe it. When he

175

got up to leave, he went over to the mirror and buttoned his coat, tied the belt. The waiters were watching, they were standing in adoration, like schoolgirls."

"He comes from a little town, isn't that right?" Franca said.

"They knew he was very talented. They thought he should go to Moscow to school, but he was too poor to ride the train. He waited six years to be able to buy a ticket."

"I don't know if it's true," Nedra said, "but it fits him. How old are you, Mark?"

"Nineteen," he said.

She knew what that meant, what acts were burning within him, what discoveries were ordained. He had been to Italy on a year of exchange and inspired in Franca a desire to do the same. Imagine a boy of eighteen landing in Southampton. He looked at a map and saw that Salisbury was not far. Salisbury, he suddenly thought, the painting of its cathedral by Constable came to his mind, a painting he knew and admired, and here was the name on a map. He was overwhelmed by the coincidence, as if the one word he knew in a foreign language had brought him success. He took the train, he had a compartment all to himself, he was delighted, the countryside was ravishing, he was alone, traveling the world, and then, across a valley, the cathedral appeared. It was late afternoon, the sun was falling upon it. He was so deeply moved he applauded, he said.

Viri arrived and sat down. He was urbane; in that room, at that hour, he seemed the age one longs to be, the age of accomplishments, of acceptance, the age we never achieve. He saw before him his wife and a young couple. Franca was surely a woman, he knew it suddenly. He had somehow missed the moment it had happened, but the fact was clear to him. Her real face had emerged from the young, sympathetic face it had been and in an hour become more passionate, mortal. It was a face he was in awe of. He heard her voice saying, "Yeah, yeah," eagerly in response to Mark, the years of her girlhood

176

vanished before his eyes. She would take off her clothes, live in Mexico, find life.

"Don't you want a drink, Viri?"

"A drink? Yes, what's that you have?"

"It's called White Nights."

"Let me taste it," he said. "What's in it?"

"Vodka and Pernod."

"Is that all?"

"A lot of ice."

"I was coming down in the elevator today, you'll never guess who got on: Philip Johnson."

"Really?"

"He looked fantastic. I said hello to him. He had on a terrific hat."

Mark said, "Is this Philip Johnson, the . . ."

"Architect."

"Why was he wearing the hat?" Franca asked.

"Ah, well. Why does a rooster wear his feathers?"

"You're as talented as he is," Nedra said.

"It didn't seem to worry him."

"I'm going to buy you a marvelous hat."

"A hat isn't going to help that much."

"A big, doe-colored velour hat," she said. "The kind that pimps wear."

"I think I've somehow given you the wrong impression."

"If Philip Johnson has a hat, you can have a hat."

"It's like the joke about the actor who dropped dead on the stage," Viri said. "Do you know that story?" He turned to Mark. It was one of Arnaud's, pungent, homely. "It was in the Yiddish theater. I think he was playing Macbeth."

"They dropped the curtain, but everyone could see there was something wrong," Nedra said. "Finally the manager came out and told them: it was a terrible thing, terrible, he was dead."

"But a woman in the balcony keeps calling, 'Give him some

177

tsicken soup. Give him some tsicken soup!' And the manager is standing there next to the body, and finally he calls out, 'Look, you don't understand. He's dead! Tsicken soup couldn't help him, lady!' 'It couldn't hoit,' she says."

They told it together as fondly as they had once joined lives. No one knew Nedra as well as Viri. They were the owners of a vast, disordered merchandise; together they had faced it all. When he undressed at night, he was like a diplomat or judge. A white body, gentle and powerless, emerged from his clothes, his position in the world lay tumbled on the floor, fallen from his ankles; he was clement, he was froglike, a touch of melancholy in his smile.

He buttoned his pajamas, brushed his hair.

"Do you approve of him?" Nedra asked.

"Mark?"

"I'm sure they've made love."

The coolness of it stung him. "Oh. Why?"

"Wouldn't you?" she asked. "Well, maybe you wouldn't."

"I think it's very important that she knows what to do."

"Oh, she knows. I've given her everything she needs."

"What do you mean, pills?"

"She didn't want to take pills," Nedra said.

"I see."

"I agreed with her. She didn't want chemicals in her body."

His thoughts suddenly rushed to his daughter. She was not far away, she was in her room, the music on softly, her dresses neatly hung. He thought of her innocence, of the prodigality of life as if it had surprised him, like a sudden, unheard wave that catches a stroller on the beach, soaking his pants, his hair. And yet now, struck by that wave, a sense of acceptance, even pleasure, came over him. He had been touched by the sea, that greatest of earthly elements, as a man is touched by the hand of God. The need to fear such things was ended.

That night he dreamed of a seashore silver with wind. Kaya came to him. They were in a vast room, alone, there was a

178

convention going on outside. He did not know how he per-
suaded her, but she said, "Yes, all right." She slipped from her
clothes. "But I like it in the evening too."

Her hips were so real, so dazzling, that he hardly felt shame
when his mother walked by, pretending not to see. She would
tell Nedra, she would not tell Nedra, he could not decide, he
tried not to worry. Then he lost this shining woman in a crowd,
near a theater. She vanished. Empty rooms, corridors in which
old classmates were standing, absorbed in conversation. He
walked past them, conspicuously alone.

In the morning he looked at Franca more closely, concealing
it, trying to be natural. He saw nothing. She seemed the same,
if anything more affectionate, more in harmony with the day,
the air, the invisible stars.

"How are things going at school?" he asked.

"Oh, I love school," she said. "This year is the best."

"That's good. What do you like most?"

"Well, of everything . . ."

"Yes?"

"Biology." She was tapping at the crown of a soft-boiled egg,
dressed neatly, her face clear.

"And next to that?" he said.

"I don't know. I guess French."

"Wouldn't it be nice to spend a year of college there?"

"In Paris?"

"Paris, Grenoble. There are a lot of places."

"Yes. Well, I'm not sure I want to go to college."

"What do you mean?"

"Now, don't get excited," she said. "I only mean I might
want to go to art school or something."

"Well, it's true you paint beautifully," he admitted.

"I haven't decided." She smiled like her mother, mysterious,
assured. "We'll have to see."

"Is Mark going to stay in school?"

"He doesn't know, either," she said. "It depends."

179

"I see."

There was such reason in her voice.

5

IN THE FALL—IT WAS OCTOBER, A windy day—she drove to Jivan's for lunch. The river was a brilliant gray, the sunlight looked like scales.

He had moved. He had bought the small, stone cottage at the end of a rutted drive, a long drive that crossed a brook. The trees were everywhere, the sun spilled through them. She was in a white dress, cool as fruit.

The brightness of Asia Minor filled the room when she opened the door. There was a silver-legged table that bore, like a catalog, perfect unused objects: art books, sculpture, pebbles, bowls of beads. On the walls were paintings. It was she who had been responsible for the decoration; her touch was everywhere. The chairs were filled with cushions of beautiful colors —lemon, magenta, tan.

Jivan came forward. He was polite. "Nedra," he greeted her, extending his arms.

"What a beautiful day."

"How is your family?"

"All well."

There was a man in a business suit sitting quietly whom she had not noticed.

"This is André Orlosky," Jivan said.

A pale face and prominent jawbones. He wore gold-rimmed eyeglasses, also a vest. There was a strange disharmony between his person and his clothes, as if he had dressed for a photograph or borrowed a suit. An impassive face, the face of a fanatic.

"André is a poet."

"I just gave a ride to a poet," Nedra said.

She had seen a white-haired man loping along the road. "Where are you going," she had asked, slowing down. He told her. It was about a mile further on. He was gardening there. And why was he running? He lived in Nanuet; he'd run from there.

"He was old, but he had a wonderful face, all tanned."

"And very strong legs."

"Really, he was interesting. He came from California. He recited one of his poems for me. It was about the astronauts. It wasn't very good," she admitted.

Jivan brought her a glass of wine.

"It was his courage I admired," Nedra said. She smiled that stunning, wide smile. She looked at André. "Do you know what I mean?"

"How have you been?" Jivan asked.

"We're going to Europe," she announced.

"When?" he said, a little weakly.

"We're going to Paris, next spring, I hope."

"Next spring."

"We're going to rent a car and then drive everywhere. I want to see it all."

"How long will you stay?"

"At least three weeks. I want to go to Chartres and Mont-Saint-Michel. After all, this is the first time."

"But Viri has been there."

"So he says."

"André knows Europe."

"Is that right?"

"I went to school there," André said. He had to clear his throat.

"Oh, yes? Where?"

"Near Geneva."

"It's funny," Jivan said, "I don't have any desire to go to Europe. I'd like to go and see my mother, but for me this is the land of marvels. Whatever there is in Europe, there's more here."

"But you've been there," Nedra pointed out.

"You'll see."

She sipped her wine. Jivan had laid out an elaborate cold meal. He was serving as they talked. "Europe . . ." he continued.

"No more," she said.

"No meat?"

"No more about Europe. I don't want you to spoil it." She opened her napkin and accepted a plate. "I love lunch," she said. "It's so good to have it with friends."

"That's true," André said.

"People suspect you for it, though."

He made a vague motion with his head.

"Do you live in the city?" she asked.

"Yes."

In the city and alone. That was very interesting to her, she said, the idea of living alone. What was it like?

"Luxurious," he said.

"You get used to it," Jivan added.

"It depends so much on who you ask, doesn't it?" she said.

"If you don't have a woman you must have some other passion," Jivan said. "One or the other."

"But not both," André muttered.

He said little and said it mildly, almost indifferently. He ate very little. Instead he smoked a cigarette and drank the wine. The aroma of tobacco in the sunlit room was faint and delicious. Jivan brought out small dishes of candied grapes sent to him by his mother, and beside them placed tiny silver spoons. He poured coffee. The cigarette of the poet blued the air.

"What have you written?" Nedra asked.

These bbones in bbed." He spelt it out.

"Is that a poem?"

"It's a poem and a book."

She sipped the coffee. "I'd love to read it," she said. She liked the way he was dressed, like a businessman. The small cup in her hand, the clearness of her voice, the white of her clothing—it was she who was central to the room, her movements, her smiles. Beneath their brilliance women have a power as stars have gravity. In the bottom of her cup lay the warm, rich silt.

"More coffee?" Jivan asked.

"Please."

He poured the black liquid as he had so many times, Turkish, dense, it made no sound. "You know, in all my time in America," he said, "I count it as one long day, I've never been able to like the coffee. And friends. I've made very few friends."

"You've made a lot of them."

"No. I know everyone, but that's not a friend. A friend is someone you can really talk to—cry with, if necessary. I've made very few. One."

"More than that."

"No."

"Well," Nedra said, "I think you find them as you need them."

"You're so American. You believe everything is possible, everything will come. I know differently."

He was like a seller who has lost a deal. There was something resigned in him; his appearance was the same, his gestures, but somehow the energy had gone. Beside him, thoughtful, like a divinity student, a vaulter, she could not characterize him, she would have liked to stare at him and memorize his face, sat a man of—she tried to guess—thirty-two, thirty-four? Their glances met briefly. She was beautiful, she knew it, her neck, her wide mouth, she felt it as one feels strength. She had been swimming aimlessly, resigned to vanishing in the sea, and suddenly she was at a sunlit meal, the light occasionally gleaming on his glasses.

When she left, Jivan walked with her outside.

"It was like the lunches we used to have," she said.

"Yes. Somewhat."

"I like your friend."

"Nedra, I must see you."

"Well, wasn't this very pleasant?"

"I miss you terribly."

She looked at him. His eyes were black, uncertain. She kissed his cheek.

She drove through the autumn sunlight. The horses she passed were at peace, straying, bathed by a day more brilliant than any of the year. The trees were calm, sentient. The sky seemed endlessly deep, teeming with light.

She sat in the white chair reading. Abandoned cities far up the Amazon, cities with opera houses, great European vessels beached in the green. She imagined herself traveling there, a guest at the old hotels. She walked in the early morning when the streets were cool, her heels struck the pavement like the clap of hands. The city was gray and silver, the river dark. At mirrors which had never seen her face she sat before dinner, preparing herself. There were automobiles without tires running on the railroad tracks, mosaic sidewalks, whores like Eve at twenty in the dim cafés. She flew to Brazil as light flies, as the words of a song go to the heart. She was wearing the white dress she had worn to lunch, she had taken off her shoes. The winter of the year was coming, the winter of her life. There it was summer. One crossed an invisible line and everything was reversed. The sun poured down, her arms were tanned. She was a woman from a far country, already part legend, unknown.

She was lost in the fantasies spreading before her; they flooded her with contentment. At four o'clock, muted, like an intermission bell at a concert, the phone rang. She rose to answer it.

"Nedra?"

She recognized the voice instantly. "Yes."
"This is André Orlosky."

6

THE SUN APPEARS, WITHOUT BODY,
without heat, its color is pale, serene. The water lies as if dead.
The moorings are dark on its surface, the pennants hang limp.
The river is English, cool as silver. On the lawn is a body. It
is Mark, asleep. He has arrived before daylight, down from
New Haven, and lies beneath their window, a collection of long
ax-handle limbs within his clothes.

Nedra, risen early, watches him from above. He is sleeping
peacefully, she admires this simple act. Her thoughts pour
down on him, she imagines him stirring beneath them, becoming animate, his eyes opening slowly, seeing her own. He is
young, graceful, filled with abrupt ideas. The seminal overwhelms him, makes him drive long distances, search everywhere. To see him at rest is, for a moment, to be able to weigh
and examine him, otherwise he is unapproachable, he runs,
laughs, vanishes behind the face of youth.

She lay on the floor and began her exercises: first a profound
relaxing, arms, shoulders, knees. She had found a yogi, Vin-
hara, in the city. She went to him four times a week. He was
bald with a long, greasy fringe of black hair. He moved about
in flowing clothes. His voice was confident, commanding.
"Water purify de body," he said. "Truth purify de mind."

He was dark. His nose was broad and pitted, his hands
enormous, his ears hairy as a cat's. Wisdom purify de intellect,
meditation purify de soul.

His apartment smelled of incense. The kitchen was filled

185

with dirty pans. He slept on a mattress on the floor. In one corner was a dented dressmaker's dummy which he sometimes struck with a stick. "Practice," he explained.

For an hour, feeling warmer, more supple, feeling the parts of her body become manifest as if they were pointed out on a chart, she submitted herself to him. Then, tender, awakened, she walked the few blocks to André's apartment. He was waiting for her; he knew almost to the minute when she would be there.

"I sometimes think," she told him, "that if you lived on the West Side, I wouldn't be doing this."

"The West Side?"

"Not just there. Anywhere else."

He had three rooms, clean, carefully furnished, everything in its place. The music was playing: *Petrouchka*, Mahler. The blinds were already drawn.

To her husband she was understanding, even affectionate, though they slept as if there were an agreement between them; not so much as a foot ever touched. There was an agreement, it was marriage.

"We must speak of it like a dead person," she told him.

All about them in the morning, entering at every window, in the very air, was the autumn light. The hard yellow apples were on the table, the sections of the newspaper.

"Nedra, it's obviously not dead."

"Would you like some toast?"

"Yes, thank you."

"It is," she said.

Mark was coming through the door. He had been up in Franca's room; he had washed his hands, his sleeves were rolled. They sat talking of the weather, of the first, faint yellows which were now in the woods. No leaves had fallen yet. It was dry underfoot. The earth was still warm.

"You don't have a chill from sleeping out there?" Viri asked.

"No."

186

"Well, I often take a nap near that spot," Viri admitted. "In the daytime."

"The grass is beautiful," Mark said.

Nedra brought them toast and butter, figs, tea. She sat down. "It's like a burned photograph," she said calmly. "Some portions of it are there. The main part is gone forever."

Viri smiled slightly. He did not reply.

"We're talking about marriage," she said to Mark.

"Marriage . . ."

"Do you ever think about it?"

He hesitated. "Yes," he said finally.

"Probably not very much," she said. "But once you're married, you'll find you think about it a great deal."

"Good morning, Papa," Franca said. She was still a little sleepy as she sat down beside them. They welcomed her; she was doelike, warm, her smile said everything, she sat there comfortably. Her life was her own, but it was deeply entwined with these other lives: her gnomelike father's, with her mother's brilliant smile. She was like a young tree demure in the sunlight, in a clearing, graceful and alone, but the moss on the earth around, the stones, buried roots, the distant groves, the forest—all of these had their influence and spoke to her still.

On the counter was a glass bowl green as the sea, filled with bleached shells like scraps from the summer. Three photographs, each of a different female eye, were pinned one above the other to the wall. Keys hung in an old gilt frame. There were drawings of birds, beautiful onyx eggs, a framed post card from Gaudí to a man named Francisco Aron.

They were talking about the day ahead as if they had only happiness in common. This gentle hour, this comfortable room, this death. For everything, in fact, every plate and object, utensil, bowl, illustrated what did not exist; they were fragments borne forward from the past, shards of a vanished whole.

We live untruth amid evidence of untruth. How does it

accumulate, how does it occur? When Viri mentioned André, whose presence was just beginning to be felt, who did not yet leave telephone messages or sit at their table, Nedra calmly replied that she found him interesting.

They were alone in the kitchen. Autumn filled the air.

"Just how interesting?"

"Oh, Viri, you know."

"As interesting as Jivan?"

"No," she said. "To be honest, no."

"I wish I didn't find it so disturbing."

"It's not that important," she said.

"These things . . . I'm sure you realize these things, done openly . . ."

"Yes?"

". . . can have a profound effect upon children."

"Well, I've thought about that," she admitted.

"You certainly haven't done anything about it."

"I've done quite a lot."

"Is that meant to be funny?" he cried. He got up abruptly, his face white, and went into the next room. She could hear him dialing the telephone.

"Viri," she said through the doorway, "but isn't it better to be someone who follows her true life and is happy and generous, than an embittered woman who is loyal? Isn't that so?"

He did not answer.

"Viri?"

"What?" he said. "I'm afraid it makes me ill."

"It all evens out in the end, really."

"Does it?"

"It doesn't make that much difference," she said.

7

DANNY FELL BY CHANCE, AS A BIRD
to a cat.

It was winter. She was with a friend. They met Juan Prisant
on the street near the Filmore. He wore a rough white sweater,
nothing more. It was cold. The teeth in his bearded mouth
were perfect; they were like the soft hands that betray fleeing
aristocrats. He was twenty-three. From the first instant she was
ready to forget her studies, her dog, her home. He paid no
attention to her in that tribute which the stricken have learned
to expect. She was too young, she knew, too middle-class; she
was not interesting enough for him. She was wearing a coat she
hated. She stared at the sidewalk and from time to time dared
a glance to reaffirm a face that dazed her with its power. No
matter what she did, she could not seem to remember it, she
could not stare at it long, like the sun. He radiated an energy
which terrified her and drove all other thoughts from her mind.

"Who is that?" she asked afterwards.

"A friend of a friend."

"What does he do?" Her questions were helpless, she was
ashamed of them.

He lived on Fulton Street. At the first chance she leafed
feverishly through the telephone book: there was his name. Her
heart was jumping wildly, she could not believe her luck. He
was no closer, but she had not lost him, she knew where he was.

Love must wait; it must break one's bones. She did not see
him, she could not imagine any coincidence by which it would
happen. Finally—there was no other way—on a pretext she
called. His voice was puzzled, cold.

"We met near the Filmore," she said awkwardly.

189

"Oh, yeah. You have a purple coat."

She rushed to denounce it. She wondered, she was going to be in his neighborhood that day, could she . . .

"Yeah, all right."

She had never known a happier moment in her life.

They met at a place on the corner, a long, ancient room such as once existed everywhere in the city, its tile floor worn down, the bar deserted. There was now a kitchen in back. The air smelled of soup. He was sitting at a table.

"Still the same coat," he said.

She nodded. The hateful coat.

"You want anything?" he asked. "Some soup?"

No. She could not eat, like a dog that has been sold.

"So what do you do? You work?" he asked.

"I'm going to school."

"What for?"

"I don't know," she said.

"Come on."

An afternoon in winter, bright and cold. They crossed a wide street, almost a square, with gulls standing in the middle of it. There were gulls on roof peaks white from droppings.

They were walking fast and then running. She tried to keep up. They were passing the dirty fronts of commercial shops, cutting through open lots where he found the timbers for his work, running, he was pulling her across the rubble. The ground was strewn with bricks; she stumbled and fell. The heel of her shoe was broken.

"It's nothing," she said. She held the broken piece in her hand.

He ran on, reaching back for her. She hobbled after him. He took her into an entrance filled with broken glass; the doors were empty, a ruined mattress was lying there, bottles beside it. Limping, she climbed the stairs.

He lived in a huge room, a warehouse, the windows filthy,

190

the floor splintered wood. Someone else was already there, standing near the stove.

She looked around her. In the darkness where the light could not penetrate there were partly assembled structures. It was like a shipyard; there were hammers, shavings of wood on the floor. The bed was mounted on four columns, high up, close to the fleurs-de-lis stamped in the metal ceiling. There were sketches tacked to the wall, announcements, photographs.

She stood quietly while they talked about work, shelves to be built in a gallery on Sixtieth Street. They were to run the length of the room, to be painted white. She did not look at either of them, they were warming their hands. She was afraid to look, the blood was jumping in her arms, her knees, she dared not see his face. He handed her a cup of something dimly colored, aromatic. She sipped it. Tea. His pants were a faded blue, his shoes had cleated soles.

"You want some sugar?" he asked.

She shook her head. He had not bothered to introduce her, but he was standing close as he talked, as if to include her. His limbs were spreading their authority. She tried not to think of them. She was weak as if from illness. She did not know what her face was doing, her body; she was too bewildered to remember them. They would plane the edges of the wood, they were saying, but allow the surfaces to remain rough. The walls were plaster over brick; they could not use ordinary nails. She listened uncomprehending, like a child listening to grownups, she knew them to be wiser, more powerful than herself.

Finally the other man left. She was not nervous, she was not frightened, she simply had no ability to speak.

"Let's get in bed," he said. He took the cup from her hand and helped her climb up. It was a man's bed, unmade, the quilt dirty, the sheets with streaks of gray. She did not know what to do. She knelt there and waited. She thought of the houses

on stilts in Thailand, the Philippines. The ceiling was barely
a foot from her head.

He knelt beside her and stroked her hair. She trembled
beneath his kisses. She had no second person within her wondering what would happen, what he would do next; every part
of her consciousness was willing, compelled. She hardly realized what he was doing. As he lifted the dress from her raised
arms, they wilted as if powerless. The broken shoe fell to the
floor. His hands were slipping gently inside the elastic of her
panties, her body was marked there, printed in red from the
waistband. The marvelous, dumb mound, hair pressed flat, is
revealed to the light. He touches her; it's as if she is killed, she
cannot move. The only thing she can remember is to murmur,
"I haven't done anything."

He did not answer. She managed to repeat it.

"Don't worry," he said.

He was naked, his body was scalding her. She was helpless,
he was parting her knees.

When it was over, she lay beside him dreaming, content.
She could feel the creases in the sheets beneath her, smell their
age. She was wet, afraid to touch herself. His body was hard,
the muscles were embedded within it. The smell of his hair,
like wood smoke, made her dizzy.

She did not move. I have done it, she thought. The light that
came through the windows was wintry. There was a bite to the
air, as of coal. High up, faint, the sound of a jet crossing the
city, en route to Canada, France.

He watched her as she dressed. "Where are you going?"

She could not continue. She sat half-naked, her arms bare,
her breasts heavy, firm. She was calm beneath his stare, almost
lifeless. "I have to go."

"Listen, I want to leave an order with you."

"An order?"

"You deliver, don't you? Three quarts a week. And a pint
of cream."

"I could come on Wednesday," she said.

"Good."

He had turned her life upside down. She wanted to kiss his hands; she wasn't sure she was liked enough to show her feelings. She was embarrassed as she put on her clothes. They seemed childish, artificial.

8

A MORNING IN SUMMER, THE GREEN trees lashing one another, the leaves sighing in the wind, luggage by the door. Breakfast was hasty; they could not settle down to it.

"Do you have your passport, Viri? Do you have the tickets?" They were going to England at last.

Danny said goodbye at the door and again at the car, the windows rolled down. Hadji was unhappy. She was holding him.

"My God, he's heavy!"

His eyes were clouded with age.

"Write to us at the hotel," Nedra reminded.

"I will."

"Come on, Viri, we'll be late," she cried.

The morning, open to light, untouched, lay before them like the sea. They sped into it, Franca with them to drive the car back. She was nineteen. She was going on a trip to Vermont.

"Too bad you're not coming with us," Nedra said. "I suppose it wouldn't be as exciting."

"I wish I could do both."

"Viri, I can't believe it," Nedra said.

"That we're going . . ."

"Finally."

He cleared his throat and searched for Franca's face in the mirror. "Next time we'll go together," he told her.

The car was drifting off the road.

"For God's sake!" Nedra cried.

"Sorry."

The day was like a river that began far off. Slowly, fed by streams and tributaries, it became wider, faster, until it arrived at last in a watershed where the noise and confusion of the crowd rose like mist.

The engines had started; the great cabin, lurching slightly, was borne toward the runway's end. Nedra, already satisfied that nothing of interest was to be seen from the window, was flipping the pages of *Vogue*, while Viri examined a card that illustrated the plane's emergency exits. It was as if they had made this flight a dozen times. They waited a while in a shimmering line of aircraft, then, trailing a roar that even within was prodigious, the seats themselves trembling, they took off.

Nedra wanted champagne. "Will you have some?" she said to her husband.

"Of course."

They spent six days in London and two in Kent in a beautiful house with gardens down to the sea. There was a graveled court and iron gate. The house itself was brick, painted cream and white. It belonged to Thomas Alba, a friend of the Troys'. He had a strong face, wide all the way down, cultured, reassuring. His voice was slow and clear. "We live a quiet life, I'm afraid," he said.

The house was filled with pictures and prints. The windows in the study had shelves across them, and on these a collection of teacups. The views from every room were thrilling, views of remote, ordered country, of English sea. But the best thing was his wife; she was the real thing of value. She'd lived in Bordeaux. She'd been married before—all the best ones have, as Nedra said.

"Doesn't this talk of London make you yearn for it?" Claire asked.

"No," Alba said calmly.

"We haven't been to London for a month."

"Has it been a month?"

"It's at least a month. Tommy hates London," she said.

"Well, I used to like it, I suppose. I prefer this, now."

"Oh, her lamps of night! Her goldsmiths, print-shops, toy-shops, hardware-men, St. Paul's Churchyard, Charing Cross, the Strand!"

"You've got it all muddled."

"It's something like that," she said. She had a wonderful face.

They were at dinner, the sort of dinner Nedra liked to give, not elaborate but over which one could linger for hours. The windows were open to the garden, the cool of the English night had entered the room.

"I like to garden," Alba said. "I go into the garden every day. If I don't, I'm really not happy. I'm bearable, but not happy. Sometimes we travel. We went to Chester, do you remember?" he asked Claire. "I don't mind traveling occasionally."

"Providing it isn't too far."

"I like to visit botanical gardens, actually. Sometimes a nice ruin. They're all right if no one is there. You see, the thing is, I don't drive. Claire does all the driving, and we like to go along slowly. We might go fifty miles in a day."

"In a day!" Nedra said.

"That's all."

"Imagine."

"Well, we like to stop," he explained.

Claire was pouring coffee.

"What's your life like in America?" Alba asked. "What do you do there?"

"Well, I have my family," Nedra said.

"Apart from that."

"Oh, I study things."

"Isn't that strange," he said.

"What?"

"American women always seem to be studying things."

Nedra did not protest. She liked Alba, his candor, his faded hair.

"Actually, we talk frequently about America. We even read your newspapers," he said. "I'm more or less obsessed with the idea of your country which has, after all, meant so much to the entire world. I find it very disturbing now to see what's happening. It's like the sun going out."

"You think America is dying?" Viri asked.

"Darling, could we have a bit of cognac in the coffee?" Alba said. "Is there any?"

He offered the bottle she brought back. "I don't really think nations can die," he said. "A place and a history as vast as America cannot disappear, but it can become dark. And it seems to be slipping toward that. I mean, the utterly blind passions, the lack of moderation—these things are like a fever. Well, it's more than that. Perhaps we're alarmed over something we just hadn't noticed before, something which has always existed, but I don't think so. Do you know the history of the Spanish Civil War? I don't mean the military aspect."

"We're very worried ourselves," Viri said. "Everyone is."

"The thing is, we depend on you so. We're quite small now. It's over for us."

"I don't think so."

"Of course, we have our memories."

They sat together afterwards, talking on. Alba and his wife were side by side. Her arm lay along the back of the sofa, a long, fine arm, well-shaped, white as bone. Their faces too were white, alike, standing out against the density of shadowed books, curtains, windows of night. Their life was calm and well-arranged; there was no passion in it, at least not on the surface, but there was great good-nature, almost laziness, as in beasts that are resting.

"We have our little jokes," Alba said, "don't we, Claire?"

"Occasionally."

They were man and woman. They seemed at that moment like an unimprovable photograph, the pear trees invisible in the garden, the seeping gravel of the drive, the problems with her grown daughter all were held suspended, at peace within the regency of this pair.

Viri sat stunned by the image, one with which he had so often stunned others, of conjugal life in its purest, most generous form. He was suddenly vulnerable, helpless. It seemed he knew nothing, had forgotten all. He tried to see the blemishes in their contentment, but the surface blinded him. Her fingers which bore no rings, their slim nakedness confused him, the shape of her cheeks, her knees. He became terrified, that moment of terror which cannot be confessed when one realizes one's own life is nothing.

Nedra saw it, too, but to her it meant something else: the proof that life demanded selfishness, isolation, and that even in another country a woman utterly unknown to her could confide this so clearly, for the Albas, she was sure, insisted on a certain life and no other, and they had found it—luckily together. On Porto Bello Road, in London, she bought a beautiful Lalique crystal flask, the color of hay. She sent it to Claire as a gift.

It was summer, the blue exhaust from automobiles tinted the airless city. They had cucumber sandwiches at tea. They dined at Italian restaurants. They visited Chelsea and the Tate. In a section of New York that was deserted after five, Danny sat with her god. The streets were empty. The terrible sadness of abandoned days had fallen over everything, but this sadness did not touch them, it was their empty stage. They sat alone at a table, drawing on a paper napkin: inscriptions, an initial, a name. He drew her mouth. She drew his. He made a D that was all leaves and vines, a thicket, and within it she drew the two of them, a sexual Adam and Eve.

"You're flattering me."

"That's how it feels," she murmured.

They made their way past closed warehouses and pathetic figures slumped in doorways, hands filthy, clothes soiled. The sky was exhausted, bled by the heat. At its bottom edge the gulls sat in rows, the roofs beneath their feet white as chalk.

The room was always cool and dark. It smelled brackish, like the hold of a ship. He had built a table, he had painted the wall near the bed. She was a young girl stunned by love. They were the same age, they were nearly the same. You cannot imagine the depth of those summer days, the silence. She came to his room almost daily. He employed her with the greatest pleasure on earth.

Her parents dined in Marlow, a town an hour from London. The restaurant was crowded. The heat of the day was ebbing at last. They had a table in the corner. Beyond the windows the Thames, narrow here, was filled with pleasure boats. They read the long menu. The waitress appeared. Viri looked up at her. She was fresh-faced, even freckled, with large, blue eyes. She did not seem to notice him, she moved with a deep self-involvement, her hand a bit jerky as she carefully placed the spoons before them—she had memorized all her acts—and folded the napkins into cones before their eyes.

"Do you take our order?" Viri asked.

A long pause while she continued to work. She looked at him vacantly. "No," she said.

She left them, the faint smile still on her face. Her legs were shapely, she wore a very brief skirt. Near the hem was a spot of whipped cream.

198

"Did you see that girl?" Nedra asked.

"Yes. This promises to be quite a meal."

In the end it turned out she merely served and poured the wine. The headwaiter, a foreigner whose jaws had a dark sheen, took the order. Every table was filled. There were silent older couples, girls with outrageously painted eyes. The interval between courses was long. They drank the white wine.

"Have you noticed these people?" Viri said. "Look around. Isn't it incredible?"

"How ugly they are?"

"But every one of them. If their noses aren't long, their teeth are bad. If their teeth aren't bad, they have dandruff on their collar. Can you believe they come from the same clay as the Albas? That it's all one race?"

"I was very impressed by Alba," Nedra said. "Did you see his hands? They were very strong."

"It's strange how you feel right away that some people are your friends, isn't it?"

"Yes, very strange."

The waitress, in slow bewilderment, was serving other tables. One could see above her stockings when she leaned forward. At last she brought the fish.

"You know, this has really been the most wonderful trip," Nedra said. "It's just the way I always knew it would be, I've loved every minute. Look at the river. Everything is perfect. And whatever we've seen, it's only been a glimpse. I mean, you realize that England has so much; endless riches. I love that feeling."

"Would you like to try and get tickets for the National Theatre tomorrow night?"

"I don't think you can get them."

"We can try."

"No, I don't think so. Anyway, it's our last night here and I don't want to spend it at the theater."

"I suppose you're right."

"I just want to thank you for a wonderful trip."

"I'm sorry we didn't make it long ago. We always wanted to."

"I'm glad we didn't. Think of how much better it is now. It's like opening a door in your life." She took a sip of wine. "And that can only happen when the time comes. Well, there's one thing I've decided definitely . . ."

"Yes?"

"I don't want to go back to our old life."

She said it casually. The waitress was trying to pour more wine, but the bottle was empty. She looked into the neck for a moment as if uncomprehending and then turned it upside down in the bucket of ice. "Would you like some more wine?" she asked.

"Uh, no, thank you," Viri said.

They ate in silence. The river was flat and unmoving.

"Would you like to see the sweet tray?" the girl recited.

"Nedra?"

"No."

Afterwards they strolled across the bridge into the little market town where Shelley once lived. The whiteness of day still filled the heavens. The shops were closed.

They stood near the church. "The hand of St. James," Viri said, "is reputed to be in the chapel."

"His real hand?"

"Yes. A relic."

He was still disturbed by her words; he had been unprepared for them. In the summer heat, in the silence of the village with its dark houses and curving streets, he suddenly felt frightened.

He was reaching that age, he was at the edge of it, when the world becomes suddenly more beautiful, when it reveals itself in a special way, in every detail, roof and wall, in the leaves of trees fluttering faintly before a rain. The world was opening itself, as if to allow, now that life was shortening, one long,

200

passionate look, and all that had been withheld would finally be given.

At that moment as they stood in the leafy churchyard redolent with the dust of Englishmen, with murmured ceremony, he had a sickening vision of what the years might bring: the too-familiar restaurant, a small apartment, empty evenings. He could not face it. "What do you mean by our old life?" he said.

"Look at this headstone," Nedra said. She was reading a thin, weathered slab dense with words. "Viri, you know what I mean. That's one of the things I like best about you. You know what I mean at every level."

"In this case I'm not certain," he said hesitantly.

"Don't worry about it now," she said reassuringly.

"It was like being hit by something. It was just such a surprise."

"No, it wasn't."

"When you say our old life, I don't know exactly what to imagine. Our life has been changing all the time."

"Do you think so?"

"But you know that, Nedra. As time has gone by, it's always taken a form that more or less satisfies us, that allows us to be content. It isn't the same as when we started."

"No, it isn't."

"So what do you mean?"

She did not answer.

"Nedra."

She turned toward the bridge. "The time will come to talk about it," she said.

They walked back in the dusk. The river slept beneath them. The boats were almost gone.

They slept in Brown's, the midnight cool at last, the city covered only with the sound of an airliner crossing. They bathed and undressed in the comfort of rooms maintained for a race that loves hunting, that knows perfectly the rules of behavior, is laconic in personal talk and triumphant in public. Side by side in separate soft beds they lay, like rulers of different realms.

She wrote to André: *We have never walked in Hyde Park, which is one of the things you said you'd like to do when you showed me London. Of course it hasn't been hard to avoid the park, there's so much to see. It's such a great city that you could never use it up.*

I walk along these marvelous streets, I think of your face and how I love you, of those things you say which are somehow everything. I think of you often and and in ways I leave for you to imagine. For some reason I feel quite close to you here, and I'm really not unhappy because we are apart. No unhappiness can come because of you—that is the sun you've put inside me (the only son, I hope). I miss you, I long for you, I see you everywhere.

We are having a wonderful time. We talk buildings, we travel to see buildings, we track them down. I'm like the wife of a bug collector. We are on this extraordinary island of forests, concerts, restaurants—and everything is bugs. But I've always believed, I know it's true, that any main branch leads you straight to the trunk. If you know one thing completely, it touches everything. But, of course you have to know it.

I love you very much today. I hug you with all my heart.

IV

THEY WERE DIVORCED IN THE
fall. I wish it could have been otherwise. The clarity of those
autumn days affected them both. For Nedra, it was as if her
eyes had been finally opened; she saw everything, she was filled
with a great, unhurried strength. It was still warm enough to
sit outdoors. Viri walked, the old dog wandering behind him.
The fading grass, the trees, the very light made him dizzy, as
if he were an invalid or starving. He caught the aroma of his
own life passing. All during the proceedings, they lived as they
always had, as if nothing were going on.

The judge who gave her the final decree pronounced her
name wrong. He was tall and decaying, the pores visible in his
cheeks. He misread a number of things; no one corrected him.

It was November. Their last night together they sat listening to music—it was Mendelssohn—like a dying composer and his wife. The room was peaceful, filled with beautiful sound. The last logs burned.

"Would you like some ouzo?" she asked.

"I don't think there is any."

"We drank it all?"

"Some time ago."

She was wearing slippers and brown velvet pants. On her wrist were bracelets of silver and bamboo, her hair was loose. She was leaving to achieve a life, even though she was forty. She used the figure forty, in truth she was forty-one. She was miserable. She was content. She would do her yoga, read, calm herself as one calms a cat. *Monkey breed tirty, tirty-two times each minute, monkey lib twenty years. Frog breed two, tree times each minute, go beneat mud in winter, frog lib two hundred years.*

"That's insane," Viri had said. "Frogs don't live two hundred years."

"He's thinking of something else."

"They'd be as big as we are."

She would have difficulties, of course, but she did not fear them. She was confident of what lay beyond. Perhaps—so many thoughts and ideas, most of them brief, came to her—she would even achieve, in the end, a kind of new, more honest understanding with Viri; their friendship would deepen, unfettered at last. In any case, she could imagine it as she could imagine many things. She was turning away from all that was useful no longer; she was turning to face what might come.

The next day she left for Europe. The car stood before the house in the late afternoon. From afar it seemed like any other departure, like one of the thousands that preceded it.

"Well, goodbye," she said.

She started the engine. She turned on the radio and left quickly. The road was empty. The lights of nearby houses were on. In the early darkness, going swiftly, she passed the ghostly

204

white fence of the field where Leslie Dahlander had ridden her pony. The silence of that meadow bade goodbye to her in a way that nothing else had. It was solemn, dark, like the site of a sunken ship. The pony was still alive. It had foundered; it was in a field beyond the house. And now she began to weep, without bowing her head, tears for someone's dead child streaming down her face as the six o'clock news began.

Viri was left in the house. Every object, even those which had been hers, which he never touched, seemed to share his loss. He was suddenly parted from his life. That presence, loving or not, which fills the emptiness of rooms, mildens them, makes them light—that presence was gone. The simple greed that makes one cling to a woman left him suddenly desperate, stunned. A fatal space had opened, like that between a liner and the dock which is suddenly too wide to leap; everything is still present, visible, but it cannot be regained.

"Perhaps we should go out to dinner," he said to Danny.

They hardly spoke. They ate in silence, like travelers. When they returned to the house, it stood lighted and empty like some hotel in the outskirts, open but lost.

"Hello, Hadji," he said. "We got you something good to eat. Poor old Hadji, your mother's gone."

He held the dog in his arms. The gray muzzle lay against his chest, the stiffened legs hung down. Danny was cutting into scraps the steak they had brought back.

"Don't worry, Hadji," Viri said. "We'll take care of you. We'll still have fires. When it snows we'll go down to the river."

"Here, Papa." She handed him the dish. She was crying.

"Poor Danny."

"I'm all right. I'm just not used to it yet."

"No, of course not."

"I'm going upstairs."

"I'll light a fire," he said. "Perhaps you could come down in a while."

"Yes, perhaps," she said. She was like her mother, provisional, discreet. She had a fuller figure than Nedra and a somewhat cruel mouth, the lips soft and self-indulgent, the smile irresistible, sly. Her face had the sullen resignation of girls who are studying subjects they see no use for, girls betrayed by circumstance, forced to work on Sundays, girls in foreign brothels. It was a face one could adore.

2

THAT WINTER NEDRA WAS IN Davos, which she had been mistakenly told she would find an interesting town. It was oppressive even when covered with snow. The sun was dazzling, however. The air, clear as spring water, filled her room.

At lunch one day she was introduced to a man named Harry Pall.

"Where do you live, in Paris?" he asked her.

"I haven't decided yet."

"You look like Paris," he said. He poured wine generously into his glass, then gestured with the bottle toward hers.

"I'd love some," she said.

His hair was curly, his eyes a fading blue. He was fifty, with a large torso and a face coming apart from age like wet paper. He dominated the table with his power and voice, and yet there was something in him that touched her immediately. It was the resemblance to Arnaud. He was like some battered survivor of the same family, the older brother who would die without pain, convivial, still joking, leaving a hundred dollars for the nurse. His hands were paws. He was the last of the bears, or so it seemed. Wine, stories, friends; he was a man lying fully clothed in the stream of days.

206

"I don't want to leave anything," he confessed. To his ex-wife, definitely not. "She has everything, anyway, except my lawyer's home telephone number." To his son, that was different. He would leave his son some mistresses, "Like Dumas did." He laughed. "You're sure you're not from Paris?"

"Why do you say Paris?"

"You're tall, like a Dior model."

"No."

"An ex-Dior model. There's a time in life when everything becomes ex—ex-athlete, ex-president, expatriate, x-ray." The food was spilling from his fork. He found it again. He ate steadily. "Where are you staying?"

She named the hotel.

"In Davos?" he exclaimed. "Terrible town. You know it's the setting for *The Magic Mountain*. What are your plans for dinner? I'll take you to the Chesa, it's my favorite place in Europe. You know the Chesa? I'll come by for you at seven."

He rose abruptly, settling the bill amid cries from friends which he ignored, waved and walked out. She saw him putting on his skis, his face red from the effort. He had an extraordinary face, a face on which everything was written, lined, coarse, like the bark of a tree. The glass he had been drinking from was empty, his napkin was thrown to the floor. When she looked again he was gone.

She returned to her hotel in the late afternoon. There were no letters. A subdued race of people was leafing through the Zurich and south German papers. She asked for tea to be sent to her room. She took a hot bath. The chill of the day which was part of its glory began to leave her in feverish waves, and a sense of well-being, of bodily delight replaced it. Afterwards, as after all deep pleasure, she was a bit undone. It was evening. The last, cold light had gone. A vague disorientation came over her, a feeling of nonexistence. Swallows were screaming over the stained roofs of Rome. The sea was crashing at Amagansett on a beach gray as slate. She was pulled by terrestrial forces to places far away. She could not seem to summon herself into the present, into an hour as empty as that before a storm.

The room had the bareness of tables in closed restaurants. It was an invalid's room, the rugs worn, cold. It was a room in which objects began, in isolation, to radiate an absurdity. A book, a spoon, a toothbrush seemed as strange as a sofa in the snow. She had dressed this barren space with her clothes, with lipsticks, sunglasses, belts, maps of the ski lifts, but nothing had dented the coldness. Only in the first, clear light of early morning did she feel secure, or when it stormed.

She prepared her eyes in the mirror. She examined herself, turning her head slowly from side to side. She did not want to grow old. She was reading Madame de Staël. The courage to live when the best days were past. Yes, it was there, but still she could not think of it without confusion. The rooms in hotels when one is alone, when the telephone is silent and voices from the street are like gusts of music—these were things she had already decided she would not endure. She had her teeth still, she had her eyes. Drink, it's the last of it, she thought.

She stepped back. How to re-create that tall young woman whose laugh turned people's heads, whose dazzling smile fell on gatherings like money on restaurant tables, snow on country houses, morning at sea? She took up her implements, eye pencil, cucumber cream, lipstick the color of isinglass . . . Finally she was satisfied. In a certain light, with the right background, the right clothes, a beautiful coat . . . yes, and she had her smile, it was all that was left from the early days, it was hers, she would have it always, the way one always remembers how to swim.

He arrived at the door unexpectedly with a bottle of champagne. "I've had this on ice for weeks," he said, "waiting for an occasion."

The champagne poured over his hand when he opened it and fell to the floor in long, foaming gouts. He paid no attention. He smelled the glasses in the bathroom, they were clean.

"You're married," he announced.

"No."

"You've been married." He handed her a glass. "I can see it. Women become dry if they live alone. I don't think it needs explaining. It's demonstrable. Even if it's not a good marriage, it keeps them from dehydrating. They're like the fruit flies in Franklin's wine. You know that story? Incredible. One of the great stories of all time—I mean, even if you know it, it's still amazing, it never disappoints you, it's like a trick. And I believe Franklin; he was our last, great, honest man. Well, Walt Whitman, maybe. No, forget about Whitman."

He took a large swallow of champagne.

"This is like youth," he said. "Nothing is sweeter, even though I hardly remember it. Well, I remember some things. Certain houses people lived in. Latin class. I don't think they even have Latin classes any more. It's all like a suit that's been pressed too much, nothing left but the spots.

"The flies—listen to this—the flies had been drowned in the wine, they were at the bottom of the bottle with a little sediment, the dirt that tells you things are real. That's what's missing in American life, the sediment. Anyway, Franklin saw these little drowned flies, they were fruit flies, they're always hovering over peaches and pears, and he put them on a plate in the sunlight to let them dry. You know what happened?"

"No."

"They came back to life."

"How could they?"

"I told you it was incredible. This was wine that had come all the way from France. It was at least a year old. You can say that's the power of French wine, but the story is true. So that's my plan. If it works for flies, why not for primates?"

"Well . . ."

"Well what?"

"That's been tried many times," she said.

At dinner they had a good table, he was clearly at home, there were flowers, the wineglasses were large. The young head-waiter in his high collar and striped pants came over to talk. "How are you, Mr. Pall?" he said.

"Bring us a bottle of Dôle," Pall told him.

A fire crackling. Dry Swiss wine. It disappeared rapidly into the glasses.

"So what are your plans?" he asked. "You're not staying in Davos? You should come here. It's very comfortable. I'll talk to the owner; I'll see if I can get you a room."

"I love the restaurant."

"Consider it done. This is the place for you. Do you like the wine?"

"It's delicious."

"You don't drink very much," he said. "You have a great economy of act. I admire that. Tell me about your life."

"Which one?"

"You have many, eh?"

"Only two," she said.

"Are you going to spend the winter here?"

"I don't know. That depends."

"Naturally," Pall said. He drank some wine. He had ordered dinner for them without looking at the menu. "Naturally. Well, I have friends here you should meet. I used to have a lot of them, but during the divorce you split everything, and my wife took half of them when she left—some of the best ones, unfortunately. They were really hers, anyway. I always liked her friends. That was one of the problems." He laughed. "One or two of them I liked a little too much."

He ordered more wine.

"The best friend I ever had—you never heard of him—was a writer named Gordon Eddy. You know him?"

"No."

"I didn't think so. Wonderful guy."

There were beads of saliva in the corners of his mouth. His

movements were loose, his hands waved freely. Solid, generous, practical, he was all hull; he had no keel. The rudder was small, the compass drifting.

"He was the friend of my life. You know, you only have one friend like that, there can't be two. He had no money—I'm talking about a certain period after the war. He was living with us. I'd give him some money and he'd go right down and lose it at the casino. He'd bring back girls who'd stay for a day or two. Naturally, my wife didn't like him: the girls, and he'd leave cigarette ashes around and come downstairs with his fly open. What she remembers most about France, she says, is Gordon's fly being open. So finally she said either he went or she did. I should have said, All right, you. I knew nothing then."

The dinner was served on large, warm plates: sliced steak and *rosti*, raspberries in cream for dessert. He was emptying the second bottle of wine. Outside it was cold, the small streets dark, the snow creaking underfoot. His eyes were glazed. He was like a beaten boxer waiting in his corner. He could still smile and speak, his embrace of life was not loosened, but he was spent. When people stopped to talk to him, he did not rise, he could not, but he remembered Nedra's name.

"Let's have a brandy," he said. He called to the waitress. "Rémy Martin. *Zwei.* Rémy Martin is good," he advised Nedra. "Martell is good, but I know Martell. I mean personally. He's rich enough as it is."

"You seem to know a lot of people. What do you do?"

"I'm an owner. I used to be in banking, but I retired. Now I'm having a little fun. I don't have any responsibilities. I can do everything by telephone. I've gotten rid of my problems."

"Such as?"

"Such as everything," he said. "I'm thinking of going to India."

"I'd love to go to India. I've studied with Indians."

"I'd be willing to bet you don't know anything about it."

"About India?"

"Have you ever been there?"

"No."

"Well, that's the trouble," he said. "You study, but India is something else."

"There's probably more than one India."

"More than one India . . . no, there's only one. There's only one Chesa, one Nedra, and one Harry Pall. I wish there was another one, with two livers."

"Have you been to Tunisia?"

"Don't ever have anything to do with Arabs."

"Why?"

"Just believe me. Believe me," he murmured. "You don't have to worry, you're not that young, they don't even care how young you are. They're a sick people."

"Desperately poor."

"They're not so poor. *I* was poor. Look, I don't care what you do, they've always been like that, they're not going to change. You can give them schools, teachers, books, but how do you keep them from eating the pages?"

He had the bill brought to him and signed it in a scrawled, illegible hand. "Carlo," he called.

"Yes, Mr. Pall."

"Carlo," he rose to his feet, "will you arrange for Mrs. . . . Berland," he finally remembered, "to be taken to Davos." He turned to her. "We'll meet tomorrow on top," he said, "for lunch. I'm too drunk at the moment to entertain you further."

His eye fell on the glass of brandy. He drank it down as if it were medicine. It seemed to revive him, a sudden, false wave of composure came over him.

"Nedra, good night," he said very clearly and left the room in a firm, deeply preoccupied walk, as if rehearsing. He fell on the entrance steps.

"Shall I call you a taxi?" the headwaiter asked her.

"In a few minutes," she said.

She felt confident, a kind of pagan happiness. She was an elegant being again, alone, admired. She had a drink at the bar with friends of his. She was to meet many others. It was the opening of the triumph to which her bare room in the Bellevue entitled her, as a schoolroom entitles one to dazzling encounters, to nights of love.

3

FRANCA WORKED AT A PUBLISH-er's, it was a summer job. She answered the telephone and said, "Miss Habeeb's office."

She typed and took messages. People came to see her—that is to say, employees, boys in the mail room, young editors passing by. She was the girl for whom, in a sense, the whole house suddenly existed. She was twenty. She had long, dark hair which she parted in the middle and, as is sometimes the case with breath-taking women, certain faintly male characteristics. How often one is stunned by a girl who runs swiftly, a back slim as a farmboy's or a boyish arm. In her case it was straight, dark brows and hands like her mother's—long, useful, pale. Her face was clear, one could almost say radiant. She was not like the others. She smiled, she made friends, in the evening she disappeared. The sacred is always remote.

Outside the streets were burning, the air heavy as planks. A city without a tree, without a green fountain, even the rivers were invisible from within it, even the sky. She found it thrilling, its crowds, its voices, the heads that turned as she passed. She talked to the writers who came to the office and brought them tea. Nile was one of these.

He was wearing the clothes of a man released from prison —of two men, in fact, since nothing matched. His shirt was from a surplus store, his tie was loose. He had the confidence, the cracked lips of someone determined to live without money. He was a man who would fail any interview.

"How did you get this job?" he asked. He had picked up a book and was turning the pages.

"How? Well, I just applied."

"You applied," he said. "Funny, when I apply . . ." His voice trailed off. "They usually ask you a lot of questions. Did you have to go through that?"

"No."

"Of course not."

"I'm sure you can answer all the questions."

"It isn't that easy," he said. "I mean, you never know what they're driving at. They ask you, Do you like music? What kind of music? Well, I like Beethoven, Mozart. Beethoven, uh huh. Mozart. And what about reading, do you like to read? What books do you read? Shakespeare. Ah, he says, Shakespeare. So he writes down—you can't see it, the cover of the folder is up: Talks only about dead people." He turned the pages as if looking for something. "You've heard about the cannibal?"

"No."

"He said to his mother: I don't like missionaries. She said: Darling, then just eat your vegetables." He turned more pages. "Is this one of your books? I mean, did you publish it?"

She looked to see.

"It's meaningless," he continued. "Listen, this is a conversation I had with a friend; this is not a joke. We were talking about a couple who'd had a baby. He said: What are they naming it? I said: Carson. Carson, he said, is it a boy or a girl? A boy, I told him. So, he said, that's interesting, so they named the kid Carson . . . Well, I told you it's not a joke. It's just a . . . What do you suppose is going on?" he interrupted himself. "I'm filled with this great urge to talk to you."

He was clever, he was helpless. At that time they were publishing his stories in the *Transatlantic Review*. He was the son of a woman who worked as a psychologist and who had been divorced since he was three. She had no illusions about her son: the thing he was most afraid of was succeeding, but one would have to know him very well to understand that. The impression he gave was of weakness, a voluntary weakness like certain vague illnesses. But after a time these illnesses cry out to be legitimatized, they insist on being treated as a natural condition, they become one with their host.

He knew everything; his knowledge was vast. He was like the irreverent student who passes any examination. His eyes were dark, the muddy brown of a Negro. His cuffs were soiled. Many of his sentences began with a proper noun.

"Gödel was at Princeton," he said. "He was walking down the hall one day, apparently deep in thought, when a student passed and said: 'Good morning, Dr. Gödel.' Gödel looked up suddenly and said: 'Gödel! That's it!' "

During their first meal together as he questioned her leisurely, he learned of her house in the country. "Ah," he said. "I knew it. I knew you had a house like that."

"What do you mean?"

"I imagined it. It's a large house, yes? Where is it? Is it near the river?"

"Yes."

"Quite near," he guessed.

"Quite."

"As near, in fact, as one would expect such a house to be."

"Yes," she said. "Just that near."

He was elated. "There are trees."

"Bird-thronged," she said.

"This is meaningless," he exclaimed.

"Why?"

"Your life," he said. "Because there is no pain in it. After all, what is life without a little sorrow now and then? Will you show it to me?" he asked. "Will you take me there?"

She thought of her house. Suddenly, though she had grown

up living inside it and knew it in every weather, she longed to go back as one longs to hold a certain book again though knowing every phrase, as one longs for music or friends. In her life, which had become more fortuitous, brushed by other lives like kelp in the ocean, in the city which was the great, inexplicable star toward which her suburb with its roofs and quiet days had always faced—suddenly this well-loved house reentered her thoughts through the words of a stranger. Like ancient churchyards in the heart of commerce, it was suddenly inextirpable.

There had been many changes. Her mother had gone. The house existed without her as clothes exist, photographs, misplaced rings. It was part of these memories, it contained them, gave them breath.

"Yes, I'll take you," she said.

Nile drove. The sun whitened his face. She was able to examine him in profile as he looked ahead.

"Are we on the right road?" he asked.

"Yes."

His skin was pale. His uncombed hair was splitting at the ends. It was also thinning, which pleased her somehow, as if he had been ill and she would see him regain his strength.

A half-mile from the house she was suddenly shocked to see the land dug out. They were erecting apartments, the shape of a huge foundation was clear, the yellow construction machines lay abandoned in late afternoon.

"Oh, my God," she said.

"What?"

"Look what they're doing."

The trees, the few old houses had been swept away, there was only bare, ruined earth. She almost wept. Somehow it could never have happened when Nedra was there—not that she would have prevented it, but her departure, in a sense, was the knell. Events need their invitation, dissolutions their start.

The shadow of change lay across everything. Her first view

216

of the house from a place on the road she knew well—the chimneys above the trees, the line of the roof—brought a feeling of sadness as if it were doomed. It seemed empty, it seemed still. The rabbits that fled before Hadji—had they really been fleeing, they veered so rapidly, they leapt, they vanished into air—all gone.

They parked in the driveway. It was after five. No one was there. Nile stood looking at the house, the trees, the terraced lawn. "This is where you grew up?"

"Yes."

"No wonder," he said.

They walked to the pony shed; bits of straw were still scattered there. They sat in the conservatory with its gravel floor. The sun was setting fire to the glass. She went to get some wine.

"How did you ever manage to rise above all this?" he asked.

"I don't know."

"It's a mystery. What a life you've had. It's so superior. I mean, I could mention a dozen things, but it's manifest." He spoke sincerely. His breath was a little bad.

"Laurence lived here," she said.

"Laurence . . ."

"A rabbit."

The sunlight fell like cymbals through the flats of glass. In the still air, a faint aroma of wine. The distant memory of the rabbit—his blackness, his long, rodent's teeth—seemed to come upon her like a flush.

"Have you ever known any rabbits?" she asked.

"Periodically," he said. "There seems to be no pattern. I worked in a laboratory once. There was this big, Belgian hare, her name was Judy. Could she bite!"

"Yes, they do that."

"I had to wear my overcoat."

"Laurence used to bite."

"Everything does," he said. "What became of Laurence?"

"He died. It was in the winter. It was very sad. You know how it is when animals are sick, you want so much to do something for them. We put him in a bed of straw and covered him, but in the morning he was gone."

"He ran away?"

"He was in a corner, sort of fallen over. His eyes were open, but he was already stiff; it was as if he were made of wire. We buried him in the garden. He was bigger than we thought, we kept having to make a bigger hole. His fur was still warm. I threw the dirt on him with my bare hands. I cried, we were both crying, and I said, Oh, God, accept him, Thy rabbit . . ."

She had wept in the garden, in the cold. They had found a smooth gray stone and started to carve it, but it was never finished; it was there still, hidden in weeds. LAU . . .

"Your sister—what's her name again?"

"She's changed her name."

"What do you mean?"

"Well, her name is Danny, but she's changed it to Karen."

"Karen?"

"It's a long story. She's with someone who thinks that should be her name."

"I see."

"Well . . ." Franca shrugged. "That's not the only thing. That's minor. She pierced her ears for him."

"I see."

"Whatever he says . . ."

Nile nodded as if he understood. He was dazzled by this glimpse of immolation, the acts of this sister stunned him. He could not imagine them, he was bewildered, as if by light. The more powerful the need to know, the more difficult to ask. He wanted to say something. In rooms above his head, hallways, by curtained windows, these girls had passed their adolescence.

Questions about it drenched him; whatever he knew was useless compared to this.

"I see," he murmured.

4

DEAD FLIES ON THE SILLS OF sunny windows, weeds along the pathway, the kitchen empty. The house was melancholy, deceiving; it was like a cathedral where, amid the serenity, something is false, the saints are made of florist's wax, the organ has been gutted.

Viri did not have the spirit to do anything about it. He lived in it helplessly as we live in our bodies when we are older. Alma still came three times a week to clean and dust. He left her forty dollars in an envelope each Friday, but seldom saw her. It was as if something terrible—blindness or the loss of a limb, something without recourse—had happened. No amount of sympathy could overcome it, no distraction make it fade.

At the theater one night he saw a revival of Ibsen's *The Master Builder*. The ceiling lights faded, the stage poured forth its spell. It was like an accusation. Suddenly his life, an architect's life as in the play, seemed exposed. He was ashamed at his smallness, his grayness, his resignation. When on the stage, Solness first talked to his mistress and bookkeeper, when he first whispered to her, Viri felt the blood leave his face, felt people staring as if he had given an involuntary cry.

When Solness, in that first scene alone with her at last, called her fiercely and she answered, frightened, 'Yes?' When he said, 'Come here!' And she came. He said, 'Closer!' And she obeyed, asking, 'What do you want of me?' Viri was devastated; his heart shattered, for a moment it gave way.

And when Solness said—all of this at the beginning before

there was a chance to be prepared for it, there was no way to have been prepared—'I can't be without you, do you understand? I've got to have you close to me every day.' And, trembling, she moaned, 'Oh, God! God!' And sank down murmuring how good he was to her, how unbelievably good. Her name —he could not believe it—lay printed in his lap: Kaja.

That was only the beginning. As it went on, as Viri sat through acts he slowly lost his power to resist, the play became that thing most dangerous of all: an unforgettable example, unforgettable and false. Caught by its strength, by phrases that pierced him like arrows, by a story the end of which was already written, the lines stored in the actors' brains in the exact order in which they were to come forth—and yet he could never dare to try and imagine them—he was like a child, a young boy overhearing behind a door a voice he was not meant to hear, a statement that would crush him for life.

He looked at the other faces, those at an angle in front of him, faces uplifted, lit by the performance. He was so completely helpless, so unable to answer, to argue, to even imagine a world that did not move subject to the energy he saw before him, that it seemed he was free; he could listen, observe, it needed no effort. He traveled endlessly, a hundred times farther than the play, he lived his own life backwards and forwards, he lived their lives, he entered into fantasy with women sitting three rows away.

Afterwards, with everyone leaving, he stood at the entrance, intelligent, composed, as the audience vanished rapidly, fading into the night. It seemed that truth was swimming by in all these people with destinations, these men and women wed to each other, bound up in tedium and ordinary trials. He had always been one of them, though he denied it; now he was one no longer.

He walked along streets half empty, lit by the neon of Chinese restaurants, the doors of cheap hotels. He was thinking of his wife, of where she was. He was not yet free of her, of her approval, her whims. Suddenly, twenty paces ahead of him, he saw his father. For a moment he could not believe it. They were walking in the same direction. He looked more closely: the gait, the shape of the head, yes, they were unmistakable. Reality fell away in slabs, in great segments reaching toward the center. An old man walking along, his mouth a little open, his eye watery and slow. They were coming to a corner, Viri would see him plainly, his heart began to race, he did not want to, he was afraid. It was as if a coffin lid were about to be opened and a man more ill than ever brought forth, the lines black at the corners of his mouth, breath reeking of cigars. He would need medicine and care. He's going to ask me for money, Viri thought desperately. He would have that gray cast to his cheeks, that sadness of old men who have not shaved. Embraces of those who have already parted, unbearable agonies repeated. For God's sake, Papa, he thought. His mind, loosened by the heart cries of Ibsen, was alive but powerless, like an oyster cut from the shell. Come home, he thought, come home and die!

He stared at the stranger beneath the streetlight, a man with a face marked by the city, unhealthy, dark with greed. For a moment they were like men in a railway station, alone on the platform. They examined each other coldly and turned away. He stood on the corner as the old man walked on, glancing back once, suspicious. He looked nothing like Isaac Berland. The empty storefronts devoured him, the roaring buses, the night.

It was late when he reached the house. Hadji was barking in the kitchen, he was so old it sounded like a saw.

The house had changed; he had a sudden sensation of it at the door. He knew this house, it was as if someone were hiding in it, an intruder pressed flat against the wall—no, his imagination was overstimulated. As he went from room to room—his

221

dog losing interest meanwhile and lying down, he himself calm, resigned, accepting the peril—he gradually recognized it was empty.

"Nedra!" he began calling. "Nedra!"

He ran as he shouted, frantically, as if there were an urgent telephone call.

"Nedra!"

He was trembling, undone. He turned on the lights as he ran, and in the hallway unexpectedly came across his sleepy daughter who mumbled in confusion, "What is it, Papa? What's wrong?"

"Oh, God," he cried.

In the kitchen she made him tea. She was barefoot in her robe, her face still thick with sleep. The face, he noticed as he sat gratefully at the table, a bit foolish, a bit ashamed, was not as fine as Franca's. It was more human, not so mysterious; it might have belonged to a serving girl or a young nurse. And without make-up it seemed even more truthful, more revealing, like the palm of a hand. He sat in the kitchen and his daughter made him tea. This simple act that was like love, in which no insincerity could ever be concealed, touched him deeply. In bewilderment he realized it was like some worn piece of furniture in a refuge, it might be nothing to someone else but in these poor times it was everything, it was all he had.

She sat with him. In her womanly gestures, her movements, her clear, direct glances, he constantly saw her mother.

"How was the play?" she asked.

"Apparently it was quite powerful," he said. "It turned me into some kind of maniac, running around the house and baying for your mother."

"Yes, it was strange. For a moment, when I woke, I thought she must be here."

He drank his tea. He heard the clack of his dog's old nails on the floor. Hadji sat at his feet, looking up, hungry like all the aged. His dog that had run in the breathless snow, strong-legged, young, his ears back, his keen glances, his pure smell. A life that passed in an instant.

He looked at his daughter. In the way that a gambler who has lost can easily imagine himself again in possession of his money, thinking how false, how undeserved was the process that took it from him, so he sometimes found himself unwilling to believe what had happened, or certain that his marriage would somehow be found again. So much of it was still in existence.

"How is the missus?" Captain Bonner would ask. He gathered junk up and down the road. Half the time he didn't recognize Viri. Was the question malicious or only dull-witted? Stained, brown suitcoat, a stocking cap, a face old as Punch's, a yellow face, teeth long gone, smiling as he thinks of something, is it food, women? He was carrying a door down the road; he leapt in front of the car as Viri drove toward him, waving, demanding a ride.

"I'm going to town," he announced. He could not get the door into the car. He struggled. "I'll put it on the roof," he said. "I can hold it with my hand."

The skin on his hands was blue, paper-thin, on his dried cheeks a stubble. His shoes were like dirty slippers, the toes curled up.

"Nice weather," he said. He smelled of wine. Then, after a pause, that casual question about Nedra.

"She's fine," Viri answered, "thank you."

"I don't think I've seen her around."

"She's in Europe."

"Europe," the old man said. "Ah. Lot of nice places there."

Viri was watching the door, which overhung the windshield. "Have you been there?" he asked distractedly.

"No. No, not me," Bonner said. "I've seen enough right here." There was a pause. "Too much," he added.

"What do you mean, too much?"

The old man nodded. He smiled vaguely at nothing, at the

223

white sunshine before them. "It's a dream," he said.

The house still smelled of her potpourri, the garden lay neglected. In a drawer of a desk that the sun fell on were children's notebooks from school in years past. Franca, her handwriting so obedient, so neat, had saved every one.

The feast was ended. Like the story he had read to them so many times, of the poor couple who were given three wishes and wasted them, he had not wanted enough. He saw that clearly. When all was said, he had wanted one thing, it was far too small: he had wanted them to grow up in the happiest of homes.

5

ONE OF THE LAST GREAT REALIZA-
tions is that life will not be what you dreamed.

He went to dinner at the Daros'. There were people there he did not know. "How do you do?" they said. Handsome people, quite at ease. The woman wore an emerald floor-length dress with a gold necklace and bracelets of gold mesh. Her name was Candis. Her husband was an art director. He worked on films; he designed the jackets of books.

"Viri, what would you like to drink?" Peter asked.

"Do you know what I think—I haven't had one for a long time . . ."

"Whatever you like."

"I think I'd like a martini," Viri said.

He drank one, icy cold, in a gleaming glass. It was like a change in the weather. The pitcher held another, potent, clear.

"How do you make them so cold?" he asked.

"Well, you happen to have commanded the drink which is, in my opinion, the one true test. You have to have the right

224

ingredients—and also you keep the gin in the freezer."

"Ah."

"I once was going to do an article on the ten greatest bars in the world. I did a lot of research. It just about ruined my health."

"Which is the greatest?" the art director asked.

"I don't think you can pick one. It's really more a question of which of them is nearest at hand. I mean, there's an hour in the day when one's tongue begins to depend, when nothing will avail except to have a drink, and to be close to one of these establishments at that time is like Mohamet's paradise."

"I don't believe you'd find any liquor there," Candis said, "not in a Moslem paradise."

"Right," Peter said. "Which would rule it out for me."

"But women in abundance," the husband said.

"I think," Peter began, "that by the time I am being conducted into paradise . . ." He had risen to go into the kitchen, it was he who cooked the dinners ". . . my connection with women will be entirely historical."

"Never, darling," Catherine corrected, entering.

"Or imaginary," he said.

"You will never lose your interest in women," she said. "Hello, Viri. How are you? My, you look well."

"My interest perhaps not, but my ability, I'm afraid . . ."

"Eternal," she said.

"Well, I don't know what you've been drinking in there," he murmured, "but I'm moved by your confidence in me."

"I think women know these things, don't you?" she asked.

"They are sometimes in a position to," Viri said.

During the laughter his glance caught that of Candis. She had a long nose, an intelligent face. Her eyes were very white and clear.

"Viri, we've missed you," Catherine said.

Another couple arrived. Viri found himself talking freely. He was describing an evening at the theater.

225

"I'm the one in our family who loves the theater," Candis said. "One of the first plays I ever saw—there's a wonderful story about this—was *The Petrified Forest.*"

"Oh, you're not that old," Viri said. He felt immensely warm and at ease.

"I was fourteen at the time."

"It was written before you were born," he said.

"Well, perhaps it was a revival. Anyway—"

"How old are you?"

"Twenty-eight."

"Twenty-eight . . ."

"When I came home afterwards, they said, 'How did you like it?' And I reported it was a very funny play. For example, there was a line in it when he says to the girl, 'How about a roll in the hay?' And the audience laughed, I said, because of course there's no hay in the desert."

The richness, the comfort of this apartment in an unfashionable neighborhood. It was in an old building, an apartment lovely as a park, like a beautiful volume found among the stacks in a secondhand bookstore.

Peter knew history, he knew painting and wines, the second and third Bordeaux growths that were as fine as a first. He knew a small town that was better than Beaune, he knew vineyards by name. He stood in the narrow kitchen, fresh vegetables and plates on every surface, and amid the clutter chopped parsley with a huge knife.

"In our next house," he told Viri, "I'm going to have a kitchen big enough to maneuver in, a kitchen like yours." He was wearing an apron over his suit. As he prepared the dinner he called out periodically, demanding of his wife where something was or whether she had bought it. "I want a kitchen big enough to give a dinner in—or for that matter, even sleep in. You know, I'm slowly going out of business. It's not that I'm failing—in fact, just the opposite—but the trouble is the supply of good prints is drying up. I just can't find them to sell,

226

or if I do find them, I have to pay so much there's no possibility of profit. I mean, if I sell a Vuillard, I can't get another. You used to be able to go to Europe, but not any more. Their prices are higher than ours. There are plenty of buyers, but there's nothing to sell them."

"What will you do?"

"Spend more time in the kitchen. I really want only two things . . ."

"Which are?"

"I want a real kitchen," he said, "and I want to die under the stars."

The guests were deep in talk, the curtains drawn, the wine open on the long buffet. Peter was looking for the anchovies. "They're in a small, thin can," he muttered. "Thin but impregnable. Former battleship builders design them." He had been in the navy. "If the battleships had just been half as strong—ah, here they are."

"What are you going to do with anchovies?"

"I am going to try and open them," he said.

The excellent smells, the disorder which was beautiful, the open pages of a cookbook written by Toulouse-Lautrec, a book filled with the dinners and outings of a lifetime—all these were creating in Viri the warmth of a night of love. There are hours when one literally drinks life.

He found himself beside Catherine. "This fellow you've just met . . ." she whispered.

"Which one?" The remark seemed very funny to him, he could not help laughing.

". . . in the brown suit," she was saying.

"The brown suit." He leaned close to listen to her revelation. His eye, meanwhile, was on the subject of it, a heavy man with eyeglasses. "Tremendously brown," he murmured. "What's his name again?"

"Derek Berns."

"Right," Viri cried.

Berns glanced at them, as if aware. His face was smooth with somewhat large features, like a child who will be ugly, and he held his cigarette between his first and second fingers at its very tip.

"He's a colleague of Peter's, he has a marvelous gallery," Catherine said. "He's very close to one of the Matisse family. He gets all their things."

Viri tried to talk to him later. By that time he had forgotten both his name and that of Matisse, but was afraid of nothing. He had some difficulty in pronouncing, which he overcame by forming carefully all consonants. In the middle of the conversation, he suddenly remembered the name and immediately used it: Kenneth. Berns did not correct him.

His attention was drawn back to Candis. She was sitting near him and was talking about the first thing men look at in a woman. Someone said it was the hands and feet.

"Not quite," she said.

Together they found themselves going through the phonograph records.

"Is there any Neil Young?" she asked.

"I don't know. Look at this."

"Oh, God."

It was a record of Maurice Chevalier. They put it on.

"Now there's a life," Viri said. "Menilmontant, Mistinguett . . ."

"What's that?"

"The thirties. Both wars. He used to say that until he was fifty he lived from the waist down, and after fifty, from the waist up. I wish I could speak French."

"Well, you can, can't you?"

"Oh, just enough to understand these songs."

There was a pause. "He's singing in English," she said.

How enormously funny this was he could not explain. He tried, but could not make it clear.

"Have you ever seen him?" he asked.

"No."

"You've never seen him?"

"No, never."

"Wait," Viri said. "Wait here."

He was gone for five minutes. When he came into the room again he was wearing a straw hat of Peter's, and before the astonished eyes of everyone, with passionate movements, in a hoarse, imitative voice, he did the whole of "Valentine," shrugging, stumbling, forgetting the words, and before dinner was ever served, had staggered through the kitchen to pass out, face down, on a bed in the maid's room.

"Who is that pathetic man?" they asked.

He called Europe the next morning. It was afternoon there. Her voice was husky, as if she'd been asleep, "Hello."

"Hello, Nedra."

"Hello, Viri," she said.

"It's been so long since I've talked to you, I just felt like calling."

"Yes."

"I was at Peter and Catherine's last night. He's really a marvelous man. Of course they asked about you."

"How are they?"

"Well, you know, their life is very curious. Their affection for each other isn't very great, and yet they're devoted." He paused. "I suppose we were something like that."

"Well, everybody is."

"How have you been?"

"Oh, not bad. And you?"

"I've often been tempted, really innumerable times, to fly over."

"Well, Viri, I mean, the idea is lovely, it would be good seeing you, but it wouldn't . . . Well, you know, we're past that."

"It's hard to keep reminding myself."

"It is, I suppose."

She answered his pleas with wisdom, it always stunned him. He wanted to cling to her to hear what she would say.

"You know, you're going to be forty-four in a couple of weeks," she said.

"Yes."

"I'm sorry to miss your birthday."

"Forty-four," he said. "I'm afraid I'm beginning to look it."

"The easy part is over."

"It was easy?"

"We're entering the underground river," she said. "Do you know what I mean?"

"Yes, I know."

"It's ahead of us. All I can tell you is, not even courage will help."

"Are you reading Alma Mahler again?"

"No." Her voice was even and knowing.

The underground river. The ceiling lowers, grows wet, the water rushes into darkness. The air becomes damp and icy, the passage narrows. Light is lost here, sound; the current begins to flow beneath great, impassable slabs.

"What makes you say that courage won't help?"

"Courage, wisdom, none of it."

"Nedra . . ."

"Yes."

"Is everything all right?"

"Of course."

"No, really. Nedra, you know, I always . . . I'm here."

"Viri, I'm fine."

"Are you happy?" he asked.

She laughed. Happiness. She meant to be free.

6

IT WAS MARINA TROY WHOM NE-
dra was drawn to when she came back at last. She even stayed
with them for a while. The saint of the theater at that time
was Philip Kasine. His plays were not announced, the news of
them was passed by word of mouth, one had to search, to find
them like a voodoo ceremony or a cockfight. The man himself
was inaccessible. He had a thin nose, bony as a finger, a city
accent, emanations of myth. He would not talk on the telephone. A sense of self so great that it was taken for selflessness,
the two had merged. He was a source of energy rather than an
individual. He obeyed the laws of Newton, of the greatest of
suns.

The night they went to his theater it was in an old dance
hall. The audience had to wait in line for an hour on the stairs.
Kasine did not appear, though someone said later he had been
the man sweeping the stage while everyone was being seated.
At last there was an announcement; the performance that
evening was named. Silence. An actor walked out. He had the
face of someone not to be trusted, a man who has tried everything, whose hunger is great enough to kill. His movements
had the intensity of a maniac's, but above all Nedra was struck
by his eyes. She recognized their power, their derision; they
belonged to someone who was her brother, the self she envied
but had never been able to create.

"Who is that?" she whispered.

"Richard Brom."

"He's extraordinary."

"Do you want to meet him?"

She did not understand the play, but it did not disappoint

her. Whatever its meaning—it was all repetition, anger, cries —she was won by it, she wanted to see it again. When the lights came up and the audience clapped, she rose almost without realizing it, applauding with her hands held high. In her unashamedness, her fervor, she was clearly a convert.

Backstage was like a grocery that stays open all night. The lights were ancient and fluorescent; a number of badly dressed people who seemed to have no connection with the acting company were wandering back and forth. Brom was not there.

"Come to the party," someone said.

They drove in a cab. The dark streets jolted by. "Did you like it?" Marina asked.

"It's so overpowering. Not the play, but the performances. They don't seem to be acting—at least, that's not the word for it."

"Yes, it's some kind of slow-motion madness."

"There's a fantastic power in the way they seem to just turn themselves inside out. I was simply overcome. Does one man teach this?"

"He has a place in Vermont that was given to him," Marina said. "Everyone goes there, they work, they discuss. Everything is done together."

"But is he the teacher?"

"Oh, yes. He's everything."

They rode in a creaking elevator. Other people were already there. Among them was Brom. He was dressed in ordinary clothes.

"Your performance," Nedra said, "was the greatest I've ever seen."

His dark eyes stared at her. He merely nodded, still lifeless, still spent. She did not know what he thought or felt. Like all great performers, he stood in a kind of unconcealed exhaustion, like a bird that has flown too far. There was nothing to reply.

She was given a drink. Everyone was friendly. They laughed, they talked softly, they were the most congruous people she

232

had ever seen, they accepted her. She listened to stories of Kasine. His gifts were prodigious. He was an extraordinary teacher; he knew instinctively where the difficulty was, like a healer.

"I went to him every day for two months at the same hour. We talked, that was all. I learned everything."

"What did you talk about?" Nedra asked.

"Well, it's not that simple."

"Of course not. But, for example . . ."

"He always asked me the same thing: What did you do today?"

They were content in a way she envied but could not fathom. It was like meeting the members of an orthodox family, all of them different but firmly joined.

"I would like to study with him," she said. She made no apologies, no conditions.

He had once taught an actress how to speak in only four hours. "What do you mean, to speak?"

"To use her voice. To make people listen."

She wanted to meet him. She looked around like St. Joan; she wondered if he might be hiding among them.

"You must come to Vermont," they said.

The hours passed without her noticing. Standing near the window later she realized the night was gone. The fragment of city below was silent and gray. She looked up. The roof of the sky was blue, a blue that was descending, as she watched, to earth. The trees in the street unfolded their leaves. As if in sympathy the lights in the room were turned off. Now it was clearly dawn. Outside were a few birds, the only sounds of nature; beyond that, stillness. She was not tired. She would have liked to stay. Her hands were cool and unused as she pressed in farewell the hands of those near her. She slept; she had never slept so well.

Ten or twelve pupils a year, that was all he took. They lived together, worked together. She wanted to be one of them, to shed all diversion, to study one thing and one thing only.

"Do you think it matters that I'm not an actress?"

"You are," Marina told her.

"They have such strength, all of them. Such naturalness. It's as if you're seeing life for the first time. Come with me," Nedra urged.

"I'd like to. I can't."

"Gerald would let you."

"No, he wouldn't."

She asked Eve. They sat in a booth at dinner, long menus in their hands. "Do you think it's foolish?"

"Everyone I know wants to study with him."

"Really?"

"Did Marina introduce you?"

"Well, I haven't met him," Nedra said.

Eve seemed worn, resigned. Arnaud had gone. He had never been the same, anyway. Whether it was physical or not, no one knew. She was thinking of remarrying her husband.

"Are you serious?" Nedra asked.

"We've talked a lot about it. Perhaps we should try it again. We do have a lot in common."

Nedra did not reply.

"He's gone on a diet," Eve said. "He looks quite well."

"It wasn't his weight that caused trouble."

"He's just showing that he wants to change. You don't think it's a good idea?"

"I don't know. It just seems . . ."

"What?"

"That you've been through so much."

"To be going back to the beginning, you mean?"

"It seems like giving up."

"What can you do?"

"Let's have some wine," Nedra said.

She drove to Vermont for an interview. She was nervous. There were fifteen or twenty others. They waited on benches near the barn. Kasine was receiving applicants in the kitchen. Sometimes half an hour would pass before the door would open, sometimes longer.

She waited through the afternoon and into evening. No one brought them food or anything to drink. They sat in silence. It became dark. It was April; it grew cold. Finally it came her turn. She felt weary. Her legs were stiff. She entered the house through a screen door.

Kasine was sitting at a bare table in dark glasses. He wore a chalky, black suit. She saw him in the village the next day in the same worn suit, a brief case in his hand like an accountant or lecturer. At the end of the table, impassive, sat Richard Brom. During the whole interview he said nothing.

She told them she'd had no experience. She told the truth: that somehow, without knowing, she had been preparing herself. Physically she was supple, strong. She had no responsibilities, no needs, she was free to devote herself completely. She had been reading St. Augustine . . .

"Who?"

"The Confessions," she said.

"Yes, go on."

There was the passage about our backs being turned to the light and our eyes seeing things lit by the light but not the light itself. That was what had overwhelmed her: the things lit by the light. She turned to look at Brom who sat immobile, as if not listening, as if in dreams.

"How old are you?" Kasine asked. He was looking at his hands clasped together on the table.

"Forty-three," she said.

There was silence, as after a final question, the one that will linger. She felt a moment of helplessness, of anger.

"But that means nothing," she assured them.

"We are a theater company," Kasine said simply. If they accepted a young actress, he explained, she would of course grow older . . .

Yes, yes, she wanted to interrupt. She knew what would follow.

"I think for the present," he said, "you should study elsewhere and see what happens. Perhaps it will make clearer whether or not there is a possibility for you here."

This was the man who had written that just as the greatest saints had first been the greatest sinners, so his actors came from the most hopeless, the most desecrated and unlikely material he could find. But it was all the same—a woman asking for a passport, a work permit, anything; no matter what she said, she was no longer young.

"Age is not a true measure," she said. "Surely nothing is so arbitrary here. I have more to learn, yes, but at the same time I know more."

"It's unfortunate," Kasine said.

They were immune to her. She could not see the eyes of the man with whom she was speaking, she hardly dared glance at the other. She had shown them everything, her honesty, her devotion, it was not enough.

"Thank you for coming here," he said.

There were four or five people still waiting. She tried to reveal nothing as she walked past them. She was like a woman leaving a cathedral, descending the steps, unapproachable, her face grave.

At midnight there was a knock on her door. A man was standing there holding something forth. It was Brom.

"Would you like a glass of wine?" he asked.

"Yes," she said. "Come in."

The room was cold. It was a novice's room, bare floor, a small lamp. He did not smile, but neither was he distant. The range of possibilities of his mouth alone seemed infinite, but laid aside.

"Are you finished?" she asked.

"Not quite."

She had washed her face. It was naked, the lines about her

mouth and eyes were faint but eternal. She was a woman who had read, dined in restaurants, a woman to whom nothing need be explained.

He was a man of one talent, he had no minor interests, no flaws. He was like an illiterate, a martyr; there was no possibility for him either to the left or right. The severity of his life, its spareness, could be writ in an epitaph, a single line.

The land beyond the window, the trees, the dark hills were in moonlight. The moon itself was too large, too white. He had a chest like a runner's, flat as boards. His arteries were thick, like a horse that has galloped. She was later to search them for scars. His fingers were strong.

It was as if they were aboard ship: some old, island steamer, clean and uncomfortable, the doors to the cabins thin. They were the only passengers.

"I think you're discouraged," he said. "Don't be. You will find the way. You'll find your new life."

"I feel I'm just beginning to swim," she said.

"I think you know how very well."

"I'm just finding the river."

"Yes," he said. "It's only a question of having water."

That was the first passus. A little later she added, "Except that now I want to fly."

In the morning he gave her a small silver object from around his neck. It was a primitive fish, smooth as a dime. He allowed it no history. It was a kind of pass-safe; it would see her home.

She was living in a studio that Marina kept. It was down among trucks and littered streets. A couple with a child lived on the floor above her, she heard them arguing.

She bought a bedspread that was tan and rose, incense, dried flowers. There were books by the bed, a collection of magnifying glasses, a clock. Her daughters called her every day. She complained of nothing. She was filled with strength.

She wore the glinting fish and that alone beneath her dress

when Brom came. Sometimes they had dinner late, after he had performed. He ate only lean meat then and salad, he drank wine, afterwards a bit of fruit. Scriabin was playing, Purcell. When he slept beside her, he was silent, still. His power did not leave him, it lay coiled. He was not muscular, but he was strong, like rope. They made love slowly. He was motionless, only an invisible flexing, faint as the gills of a fish. Her knees began to jerk. Moans came from her lips. Fifteen minutes, twenty, she was staggering, crying, he held her tightly, her arms against her sides, and began to roll a little one way and the other in a slow, meaningless annunciation. She was jerking like a slaughtered beast, the great, unstinted strokes had started, long, unending, like the felling of a tree. His hand was across her mouth as she tried to cry out, he was reeling, he fell as if shot from a foot away, abrupt, inexplicable.

An exhausted sleep from which she could not wake, a drunk-ard's sleep. The night air poured over them. From the avenue came the sound of trucks.

A breakfast of chocolate and oranges. Reading, falling again into sleep. He said very little. They were deep in contentment; it was full, beyond words. It was like a day of rain.

Sometimes she went to see him perform. She sat in the audience, hidden among them, feasting on the sight of him, nourished by everything that existed between them and was unknown. She went to be able to watch him endlessly, to hoard, to steal his face, his mouth, the power of his thighs. Satisfied at last, she went to have a drink with Eve or dessert and coffee at the Troys'; they did not ask where she had been, they introduced her, she was more welcome than their guests, she was stunning, drunk with life, provocation written all over her. She was a woman both husband and wife liked to see, she excited them, they could talk in her presence, things that would have been unmentioned became easy, and at the same time the sweep of her life assured them somehow of the virtue of their own. She was living on more than she had, it was

238

evident in her face, her every gesture; she would spend it all. They were devoted to her as one is devoted to the idea of life drunk in gulps. Her fall would confirm their good sense, their reason.

"Your life," Marina told her, "is the only real one I know."

Nedra said nothing.

"I'm sorry now that I didn't go with you."

"Well, I wasn't accepted."

"I know, but you're one of them."

The theater was nomadic. One week it was in a rehearsal hall, the next in the ballroom of some rundown hotel. His performances were never the same, whether beneath the lights or during quiet days. They met in cafés. She wore oval, steel-rimmed glasses.

"What are those for?" he asked.

"Very small print."

"No, you have perfect eyes. I can tell from the color, the clearness."

"That doesn't mean anything."

"Of course it does," he said. "Everything speaks through the body. The way someone moves, how they look at you—from that you can tell worlds if you know what to look for. Everything is visible."

"Nothing is."

Their legs were touching beneath the table. "Especially that," he added.

"These are the real hours," she said.

The afternoon is fading. She shows him photographs of her family, Franca, forgotten days.

"This is your daughter?"

"Incredibly."

Later he brings forth, without a word, a picture of his own. It's a clipping of a Van Dongen painting of Picasso's mistress, the famous Fernande. She is naked, displayed like a tapestry. The resemblance to Nedra is startling.

"Where did you find it?"

"I've had it for a long time," he said. "Even if you cannot marry, you must have some idea of a wife. So I've carried her around. She's very convenient."

Nedra felt a spurt of jealousy.

"I don't believe in marriage, and I have no time for it," he said. "It's a concept from another age, another way of living. If you do what you really should do, you will have what you want."

"That's true."

"The Bhagavad-Gita," he said.

In the evening at the hour when, across small gardens, one can see people gathered in lighted rooms, she lies, her legs each pointing to a corner of the bed, her arms spread wide. From the street comes the faint sound of horns. Her eyes are closed; she is caught like a marvelous beast. Her moans, her cries excite him beyond anything. It takes a long time. Afterwards she lies naked, unmoving. She kisses his fingers. They are bathed in silence, in the long, swimming afterdream. She knows quite well—she is absolutely convinced—these are her last days. She will never find them again.

7

DANNY'S WEDDING TOOK PLACE AT the house of a friend. It was in the country, near Ossining, a wedding somehow old-fashioned despite its youth and informality. The day was warm. It was like Sundays in small villages. Her mother and father were there, of course, her sister, her lover, Juan. She was marrying his brother.

Theo Prisant was taller than Juan, younger, not as well-formed. He was still in school, his last year of law. Before he had ever met her he had heard his brother talk . . . the daughter of an architect, nineteen, she was fantastic in bed. An incandescent fragment was struck off in some sort of darkness. A longing and envy flooded through his veins.

"What do you mean, fantastic? What's so fantastic about her?"

"She's incredible."

He was eager to meet her, half afraid. When he saw her for the first time, it was as if her clothes fell away before his eyes. He grew dizzy. He hardly dared show interest; he was ashamed of his knowledge. It was a knowledge which doomed him, singing in his ears from the first moment, whispering to his blood.

Their first time together they went to the Metropolitan, up the steps of which her father had once run. It was afternoon, lingering, serene. In the great guarded halls he could hardly look at her though she was at his side. He was aching to talk, to be able to speak to her as if nothing were at stake. He was conscious only of her limbs, her hair, the things he knew she had done. She seemed beautiful and calm. Everything reflected her, everything suggested love: the torsos, the clean, marble limbs, the roll of muscle that encircled the hips of a Greek boy. He was standing a bit behind her. He saw her gaze pass over the shoulders, the stomach, pause at the genitals and scribed, curling hair. It was as if she were scorning him. They walked on; his mouth was dry, he could not even make a joke. She cared nothing about him, he could feel it.

And now in a suit and a straw hat, the kind farmers wear, a dandelion in his buttonhole, he stood, possessor at last of the woman his brother had found, had prepared for him, brought to him unknowing. His face was young, his hands brown from the sun. He had met Viri a number of times but hardly knew him, and Nedra only once. He was waiting for them to arrive.

They were late. They parked where the road had broken and washed away—there were already eight or ten cars—and

241

walked up a small stone path to the house together. It was a house shaded by huge trees. There were glasses gleaming on a buffet table inside, fruit, flowers, cake. The sunlight poured through large windows. Several cats strolled past their feet.

"I'm glad to see you," Theo told them.

"We're glad to see you."

"What a lovely house," Nedra said.

"Come and meet our host."

She found her daughters upstairs. They wept together, they wept and smiled. They wiped the tears from Danny's face that were running in straight lines down to her mouth. When Viri appeared hesitantly at the door, she began to cry all over again.

"What are you crying for?" he asked.

"Nothing."

"Me too."

A vast, brilliant day, the trees sighing, the rooms a bit warm. The ceremony was brief, a cat was rubbing against Viri's leg. The wedding march was played as the bridal couple entered the reception room. In that moment as he saw his daughter in sun-struck white, near now to another, departing, already gone, he felt a sudden pang of bitterness and loss, as if he had somehow been proved a failure, as if his whole life could be dismissed in a word.

They drank red wine and opened the presents. They turned to Viri for a toast.

"Theo and Danny," he began. He raised his glass and looked at it. "Come what may, you are entering the true happiness, the greatest that one ever knows."

They all drank. There was a telegram from Chicago. MAY YOUR LIFE BE STREWN WITH FLOWERS NOW AND FOREVER. SEND PHOTOGRAPHS. ARNAUD. They talked about him; perhaps he knew they would. They told adoring stories. These stories had become his true existence, he was like a character in a play one imitates and admires. He could not fail or disappear. He was like a marvelous guest who leaves early, the memory of him

242

lingering, made stronger by being cut off at just the right moment.

The marriage car departed, abruptly it seemed, suddenly there were waves, farewell cries, it was starting down the road, a Labrador running beside it.

"Well, there they go," someone said.

"Yes," Viri agreed.

Far off the black dog was running in the dust of the car, running and falling behind. Finally he abandoned the chase and stood in the road alone at the edge of some trees.

That was spring. Franca spent that summer with her mother at the sea. They had a small house faded by the weather on the edge of potato fields. Parked in front was the car, an English Morris they'd bought from the garage man, its paint gone to chalk in the sun. There was a garden, a bathroom in which water came, crippled, from the faucets, a view of the vanishing dunes.

They had long lunches. They drove to the sea. They read Proust. In the house they went barelegged and without shoes, their limbs tan, their eyes the same gray, their lips smooth and pale. The calm days, companionship, the sun leached all care from them, left them content. One passed them in the morning. They were in the garden, a beautiful woman watering flowers, her daughter standing near her holding along her forearm and stroking slowly a long white cat. Or the house when they were gone: the windows silent, brief bathing suits spread on the woodbox, the robins with their dark heads and weathered bodies hurrying across the lawn.

There was a wooden table outside at which they sat in the sun. Small yellow bees were eating the cheese rinds. Nedra's palms lay flat on the smooth, hot boards. It was the beginning of August. The sea was singing. Above it was borne a silver mist risen that morning in which, in the empty hours just after lunch, a few children shouted and played.

They visited Peter and Catherine. Dinner beneath the great trees. Afterwards they sat and talked of Viri. Nedra had partly unbuttoned her dress and was rubbing her stomach. It aided digestion, she said. Overhead, the airliners crossed in darkness with a faint, lingering sound, their lights passing among the stars.

"I had lunch with him last month," she said. "He's a little tired from . . . you know, life. It hasn't been easy for him, I don't know exactly why."

"Oh, I think there's quite a simple reason," Peter said.

"One is so often wrong . . ."

"Yes, but you and Viri—any two people when they separate, it's like splitting a log. The pieces aren't even. One of them contains the core."

"Viri has his work."

"But it's you who's carried off the sacred part. You can live and be happy; he can't."

"He's really better now," Franca said.

"We haven't seen him for a long time."

"He's much better," she assured them.

"He's still living in the house?" Catherine asked.

"Oh, yes."

They had talked about food and old friends, Europe, shops in town, the sea. Like a businessman who keeps important matters till the end, Peter asked, "What about you, Nedra?"

"Me?"

"Yes."

"Well, I've had such a good dinner, and I have such a comfortable bed . . ."

"Yes . . ."

"I'm thinking. I suppose I'm not used to giving an answer to that kind of question, especially to someone who will understand me." She paused. "How do I seem?"

"Peter," Catherine explained, "Nedra doesn't want to talk about it."

244

"The fact is," Peter said, "I don't want to disappoint you, but you seem wonderful; you seem the same as ever."

"The same as ever . . . No. We're none of us the same. We're moving on. The story continues, but we're no longer the main characters. And then . . . I had a strange vision a few days ago. The end isn't like those woodcuts of a skeleton in a black cloak. The end is a fat Jewish man in a Cadillac, one of those men smoking a cigar, you see him every day. The car is new, the windows are rolled up. He has nothing to say, he's too busy. You go with him. That's all. Into the dark. Why am I talking so much?" she asked. "It's the brandy. We must go."

During the days, though, she was utterly at peace. Her life was like a single, well-spent hour. Its secret was her lack of remorse, of self-pity. She felt herself purified. The days were cut from a quarry that would never be emptied. Into them there came books, errands, the seashore, occasional pieces of mail. She read them slowly and carefully, sitting in the sunshine, as if they were newspapers from abroad.

"I feel very sorry for her," Catherine said.

"Sorry? Why sorry?"

"She's an unhappy woman."

"She's happier than ever, Catherine."

"You think so?"

"Yes, because she doesn't depend on a man, she doesn't depend on anybody."

"I don't know what you mean by depend. She's always had one."

"Well, that's not depending, is it?"

"She's a woman bound to be unhappy."

"Isn't it funny?" Peter said. "I feel just the opposite."

"You don't know that much about women."

"I saw her arranging flowers the other day."

"Arranging flowers?"

"Yes."

"What does that mean?"

"Nothing, except that I don't think she's unhappy."

"Peter, I don't know anything about what you may have seen, but a woman who leaves her home is bound to be unhappy, now, isn't she?"

"Well, Nora Helmer left home."

"I'm talking about real life."

"So am I."

"What you're saying simply doesn't make sense."

"Catherine, you know perfectly well that in great works of art there is a truth that transcends mere facts."

"If you're talking about Nora . . . you mean Ibsen's Nora?"

"Yes."

"One doesn't know what happened to her. You can form your own conclusions. Isn't that so?"

"I like what Nedra represents," he said.

"Of course you do."

"I don't mean that. You know exactly what I mean."

"Yes, I think I do."

"Damn it!" he shouted.

"What?"

"I'm talking about something else, don't you understand? A certain courage, a kind of life."

"I think it's something you imagine."

"A woman's realm."

"Why this sudden interest in women?"

"It's not sudden."

"It seems to be."

"Men's lives bore me," he said.

8

PETER DARO HAD ONCE, AS A YOUNG man, lived in the Hotel Alsace in Paris where Oscar Wilde had died. In the very room, in fact; he had slept in the very bed. All that had disappeared.

He was a man of habit and a single comic expression: his mouth turned steeply down in mock dismay. It served all purposes, confusion, disbelief. He came from the city by train on Friday evenings, the axles creaking on the worn, disintegrating cars. Voices at the stations as they stopped in the mist, the exuberance and crudeness as policemen, steamfitters got off at their towns. Then the long, jolting ride through the flatlands, the fields at last appearing, restaurants he recognized, shops. Catherine sat waiting in the car; they drove home beneath the heavy, summer trees.

Their house was open, barnlike, unprotected. Its awkwardness was appealing, like a traveler stranded without money. The dirt road widened before it to form an island in which there was a cemetery of leaning stones, names that had faded, men drowned at sea. The car turned in to a drive of smooth pebbles. The lights were on inside, fires burning in the grates, the pale retrievers barking.

A creature of habit and, yes, eccentricity. He cooked the dinner, his children playing in their rooms upstairs. His wife was in the front room talking to Nedra. The platforms of the small stations were empty now, darkness was falling, the little houses everywhere were alight.

He moved about confidently; fresh scallops and cold, white Graves. He knew how to make things—a drink, a fire, dinner, what kind of stove to have. From his house one looked out on

247

long, empty fields in which gulls sometimes stood.

His great love was fishing. He had fished in Ireland, the Restigouche, he had fished the Frying Pan and the Esopus. "That's where I won Catherine," he recalled. "A miraculous day. We went down to the river and she sat on the bank and read while I fished. Finally she said, 'I'm hungry.' And exactly at that moment, as if on cue, I pulled out two beautiful trout.

"But the best fishing story I know," he said, "happened to a friend of mine who lives in France. His father-in-law has a big country house with a pond, and in this pond lived a huge pike. Very cunning fish, very old. The gardener had been after him for years, he had sworn his death. One day Dix was fishing there, he had nothing serious in mind, and he just cast out and accidently hooked the pike in the tail. Unusual, but it sometimes happens. Enormous struggle. The pike was three feet long. Dix was fighting and shouting for help. The gardener ran to the house and came racing back with a shotgun, and before they could do anything to stop him, was blazing away at the pike. There was blood all over, great confusion. The fish was stunned but alive. They put it in a bathtub where it was floating around, wounded. That night it died. There was some question of exactly how it died because there was evidence of stabbing, but anyway there was nothing to do, they froze it in a block of water—this happened in winter—and later it was sent to Paris to make a fish soup for an important dinner the father-in-law was giving. Dix was there, everyone, including the Minister of Education, who took a bite of fish and reached up to his mouth in bewilderment to take out pieces of buckshot. The father-in-law looked at Dix, who . . . what could he say? He just shrugged.

"Women don't like fishing," he decided, "do they?"

"Of course we do, darling," his wife said.

"They don't like to get up early in the morning. Actually, neither do I."

248

He liked brandy, crystal glasses, vermouth cassis at the Century. His life was solid, well-made, perhaps not happy but comfortable; there were feasts of comfort like nights in sleeping-trains with their clean sheets and cities floating in the dark. The first anachronisms were appearing in his clothes, the first blotches of age on the back of his hands. There was seldom music in his house. Books and conversation, reminiscences. He wore blue-checked shirts, faded from many launderings. English shoes a little out of style. In his face a marvelous alertness, in the iris of one eye a small dark key like a holy stain. He had traveled, he had dined, he discussed hotels with the affection one usually reserves for women or beasts. He knew exactly in which museum a painting was hung. His French was a rickety structure based on a vocabulary of food and drink. He spoke it grandly.

The hours passed quickly. The mist was forming, the brandy gone.

"My God," Nedra said, "what time is it?"

Peter looked at his wrist watch. After a moment of consideration, he answered, "One o'clock."

"I've had too much brandy," she said. "I can't drink it any more."

"Well, it's all gone."

"It goes to my legs."

Silence. He nodded in agreement. "Nedra . . ." he said finally.

"What?"

"It's not doing them any harm," he said.

A last image of him standing in the lighted doorway, the fog obliterating all else, the house, even the windows, the dogs crowding behind him.

"Let me drive you home," he suddenly decided. "The fog is awful. You can get your car in the morning."

"No, that's all right."

"I know the roads," he said. He was earnest, his speech slurred. "Damn it, dogs! Wait a minute!" he shouted. "You shouldn't drive alone," he decreed.

They got only as far as the end of the driveway where he hit a post.

"I was right. You'd never have made it," he said.

That fall, in November, his legs began to swell. It was something inexplicable. It affected his knees and ankles. He went to the hospital, they made tests, they did everything but nothing helped, until finally, as if by itself, the fluid disappeared and in its wake, like a mortal drought, a terrible change began. His legs began to stiffen and grow hard.

The doctors now knew what it was.

"It's the gout," he told people calmly, lying in bed. "I've always had it. It flares up every now and then."

It was richness of living, he said, the fate of Sun Kings. He was in pain, though one could not see it. This pain would grow greater. It would spread. The skin and subcutaneous tissue would harden. He was turning to wood.

"What is it?" their friends asked Catherine.

It was innominate.

"We don't know," she would say.

9

NEDRA DID NOT SEE HIM UNTIL THE spring. It was a Sunday. When she rang the bell, Catherine came to the door.

"He'll be glad to see you," she said.

"How is he?"

"Not any better," Catherine said. "He's in the next room."

"Shall I go in?"

"Yes, go in. We're having drinks."

She could hear voices. Through the doorway she could see a fat-cheeked man she did not recognize. As she entered the room and came closer she suddenly realized that this swollen face was Peter's. She had not even known him! In six months what a giant step he had taken toward death. His eyes were deeper, his nose seemed small. Even his hair—could he be wearing a wig?

"Hello, Peter," she said.

He turned and looked at her blankly like some dissolute stranger propped in a chair. She could have wept.

"How are you?"

"Nedra," he finally said. "Well, considering everything, not bad."

Beneath the sleeves of his coat lay the wasted arms of a paralytic. His body had hardened everywhere, it was like the lid of a chest, he could barely move.

"Feel it," he told her. He made her touch his leg. Her heart grew faint. It was a statue's leg, the limb of a tree. The flesh that enclosed him had become a box. Within it, like a prisoner, was the man.

"This is Sally and Brook Alexis," he said.

A young, red-haired woman. Her husband was thin, folded like a mantis in nondescript clothes. Their children were playing with the Daros' in the back of the apartment.

The conversation was innocuous. Other people came, a cousin of Peter's and an old woman who had a glass eye. She was the Baroness Krinsky.

"The doctors," she said, "my dear, the doctors know nothing. When I was a child I was sick and they took me to the doctor. I was terribly sick. I had a fever, my tongue was black. Well, he said, it's one of two things: either you have been eating a lot of blackberry jam or it's cholera. Of course it was neither."

Nedra found the chance to talk to Catherine alone. "But what is it?" she asked.

"Scleroderma."

"I've never heard of it. Is it only the arms and legs?"

"No, it can spread. It can go anywhere."

"What can they do for it?"

"Not very much, I'm afraid," Catherine said.

"Surely there are medicines."

"Well, they're trying cortisone, but look at his face. Really, there's nothing. They all say the same thing: they can promise nothing."

"Is he in pain?"

"Almost constantly."

"You poor woman."

"Oh, not me. Poor man. He wakes up three or four times a night. He never really sleeps."

"Catherine!" he was calling. "Can you open some champagne?"

"Of course," she replied. She went to get it.

"What have you been doing?" the cousin was asking.

"Thinking," Peter said.

"Things in general?"

"I've been thinking of what my last words will be," he said. "Do you know the death of Voltaire?"

He was interrupted by Catherine returning with a tray and glasses. She opened the bottle and began to pour.

"No," Peter said as soon as he had tasted it, "something's wrong."

"What?"

"This isn't the good champagne."

"Yes it is, darling."

"It's not."

"Darling," she protested, "it's what we always drink."

It was in a silver bucket. She withdrew it to show him the label.

252

"Why does it taste so strange?" He turned to the Baroness. "How does it seem to you?"

"Quite good."

"I see. Don't tell me my sense of taste is going. That would be serious." He smiled at Nedra, a strange, imitation figure, florid and corrupt.

His voice was the only thing unchanged, his voice and his character, but the structure that held them was dissolving. All the old and interconnected knowledge—architecture joined to zoology and Persian myth, recipes for hare, the acquaintance with painters, museums, inland rivers dark with trout—all would vanish when the great inner chambers failed, when in one final hour the rooms of his life dropped away like a building being wrecked. His body had turned against him; the harmony that once reigned within it had disappeared.

"The great specialists for this are in England," he said. "Dr. Bywaters. What's the other man's name, Catherine? In Westminster Hospital. I forget. I thought of going to England, but why undertake such a long trip when I know the answer? The time to go to England was when you and Viri went. We should have done that, I really regret that we didn't. I love England."

"We stayed at Brown's," Nedra said.

"Brown's," he said. "I was having tea there one day. You know how rigorous their afternoon tea is—the fires burning in the fireplaces, cakes. Well, at the next table there was an Englishwoman and her son. He was in his forties and she was one of those county women who ride until they're eighty. They'd been to a matinée, and for an hour they sat there discussing the play they'd seen, it was *The Cherry Orchard.* Of course I was listening, and in that hour they exchanged about four sentences. It was a wonderful conversation. She started by saying, after a long silence, 'Quite a good play.' Nothing for about fifteen minutes. Finally he said, 'Um, yes, it was.' Long, long pause. Then she said, 'Those marvelous silences . . .' About ten minutes more passed. 'Yes, quite effective,' he said.

'So typical of the Slave temperament,' she said. You know, the English have an absolutely unbending attitude toward pronunciation. Slave, that's exactly the way she said it." He fell silent, as if having said something he regretted.

"I'd love to go back to England," Nedra said.

"Oh, yes. Well, you will." His voice trailed off.

At the end his wife led him from the room. Small, shuffling steps, as if bearing what remained of his existence.

"He was so pleased to see you," Catherine said at the door.

We cannot imagine these diseases, they are called idiopathic, spontaneous in origin, but we know instinctively there must be something more, some invisible weakness they are exploiting. It is impossible to think they fall at random, it is unbearable to think it.

Nedra reached the street. She was uneasy, as if the air she had been breathing, the glass from which she drank, had been contaminated. What do we really know of all this, she thought? She had touched his leg. Her throat seemed a bit sore. She must watch herself to see if there were any unusual signs. Foolish, she thought, unworthy. After all, his children lived in the same apartment, his wife slept in the same room. She passed cluttered drugstores in the rear of which pharmacists worked. Cosmetics, medicines, asthma inhalers—she saw her image reflected among them, the sacred objects which could heal, bring happiness. And somewhere above them all, perhaps sleeping now or lying in what passed for sleep, was the victim for whom all cures and benefices were in vain.

Is illness an accident, or is it a kind of choice, the way love is a choice—hidden, involuntary, but sure as a fingerprint? Do we die of some kind of volition, even if it cannot be understood?

"Come and see him again," Catherine had said.

A month later he was worse, back in the hospital. His family had given up hope; they were waiting for the end. It was already hot. Death in the summer, in a haggard city from

254

which everyone wanted to flee, death without meaning, without air.

He lingered six weeks. He was too strong to die.

The doctor came as part of his routine. "Well, how are you today?" he asked.

"They say I'm fine," Peter managed.

"But what do you say?"

"I can't be against the whole world, can I?"

The doctor felt his abdomen, his legs. "Are you very uncomfortable?"

"No."

"But it hurts?"

"It hurts like hell."

"You're a tough fellow, Peter."

"Yes."

He wanted to leave the hospital and go to his ocean house. His life was now a series of small incidents; it had lost all scope. He had one ambition, he said, one goal. He could hardly move, he could not bend his arms or legs, the joints were swollen like Tutunkhamen's. He had sworn to walk to the sea.

"Darling, you will," his wife said.

"I mean it," he told her.

"I know you do."

He turned his face to the wall.

In September he was driven to Amagansett. There is no more beautiful time there. The days pour down their warmth, in the morning the smell of fall. The house was a summer house; in the winter it was always closed. The walls were thin. It was like going to sea in a fragile boat; the first cold, the first storms would end it.

He lay in bed upstairs. The room faced east to the broad Atlantic. Under his windows, on the lawn, in her white uniform a nurse was taking the sun.

There were many arguments now; every hour of the day brought its quarrel. Beneath these difficulties lay deeper grievances. He accused his wife of wanting to leave him, of giving him up for dead.

"She's been magnificent," he confessed to Nedra, "an angel, there are very few women who could have done it, but now she wants to go, she wants to go to the city for a few days and rest —now, when I need her. And a few days . . . I know what that means. How is Viri?"

He hardly listened to the answer. He was reading biographies, there were three or four on the table beside him— Tolstoy, Cocteau, George Sand.

"How is Franca?" he asked. "How is Danny?"

He told her stories of his family, things he had never mentioned before, the first wife to whom he still occasionally wrote, his sister, his plans for the winter.

They had dinner in his room. His friend John Veroet, with whom he often fished, had cooked it. They ate on rose-colored cloth. Gleaming glasses, stiff napkins, a wood fire burning, the chill of evening at the windows. Peter lay in bed with his hair combed, his shirt open at the neck. A beautiful dinner, festive, perverse, like a New Year's dinner in St. Moritz where the host had, unhappily, broken a leg.

He ate nothing himself. For almost a week he had been unable to eat; it would not go down. Only a bit of yogurt, some tea. Propped up on pillows, he talked to them. "What are the good plays, John?" he asked.

Veroet was eating the new peas mixed with mushrooms that he had made himself. He was a heavy man with a bitter tongue. He wrote on the theater. He owned a small house. His wife and his mistress were friends.

"There aren't any," he said finally.

"Oh, come now. Surely there's something good."

"Good? Well, what do you mean by good? There are all sorts of terrible plays people think are good. My God, it's an absolute disgrace. Every year they publish the plays of people like John Whiting, Bullins, Leonard Melfi—plays that absolutely no-

256

body went to see, that the critics unanimously condemned, it's criminal to put them between hard covers, but they do it and people begin to call them masterpieces, modern classics. The next thing you know, they're being performed in repertory at the University of Montana or someplace, or adapted for television." He spoke to the plate. He seldom looked at anyone directly.

"John, you're always saying the same thing," his wife said.

"Keep out of it," he told her.

"The plays you like, nobody goes to see either," she said.

"People went to see *Marat-Sade*, didn't they?"

"You didn't like that."

"I didn't like it, but I didn't dislike it." He drank some wine. His upper lip was damp.

Had he heard of Richard Brom, Nedra asked.

"Brom?"

"What do you think of him?" she said.

"Well, I have nothing much against him. I've never seen him."

"I think he's the most astonishing actor of our time."

"You're lucky. Most of the time you go to see his plays and end up on some street of used furniture stores and dry cleaners, all closed. We're all interested in the invisible, but in his case it's carried a little far."

"He believes in a committed audience."

"By all means, by all means," Veroet cried. "He's tired of the old audience, and I'm tired of being part of it. But there's really no such thing as unseen theater, that's contrary to the whole idea. Eventually it must come out into the light. If it doesn't, it's not theater, it's something else, it's just recited lives."

"Who is this man?" Peter asked.

Nedra began to describe him. She told about his performances, the strength in his body, the inexhaustible energy. Veroet had toppled over sideways and was asleep on the window seat. "He always does that," his wife explained.

"John, wake up, listen to this," Peter was calling. "No wonder you never find anything interesting in the theater. Wake up, John! Nedra, don't mind him, he's hopeless, go on . . ."

The Veroets drove her home. It was past eleven. What did they think, she asked.

"About Peter?"

"Yes."

"He could live a month," Veroet said. "Or he could live five years. There's a woman in Sag Harbor who's had it as long as I can remember—not as bad, of course. It depends if it attacks a vital organ. He was feeling very well tonight."

"He was marvelous."

"It was like old times," Veroet said.

Peter Daro never walked to the sea. He died in November. At his funeral, in the coffin, was a face colored with cosmetics, like an invincible old woman or some kind of clown.

V

 WHERE DOES IT GO, SHE
thought, where has it gone?

She was struck by the distances of life, by all that was lost
in them. She could not even remember—she kept no journal
—what she had said to Jivan the day of their first lunch together. She remembered only the sunlight that made her amor-
ous, the certainty she felt, the emptiness of the restaurant as
they talked. All the rest had eroded, it existed no more.

Things she had known imperishably—images, smells, the
way in which he put on his clothes, the profane acts which had
staggered her—all of them were fading now, becoming false.
She seldom wrote letters, she kept almost none.

"You think it's there, but it isn't. You can't even remember feelings," she said to Eve. "Try to remember Neil and how you felt about him."

"It's hard to believe, but I was crazy about him."

"Yes, you can say that, but you can't feel it. Can you even remember what he looked like?"

"Only from photographs."

"The strange thing is, after a while you don't even believe them."

"Everything has changed so."

"I always just assumed the important things would stay somehow," Nedra said. "But they don't."

"I remember my wedding," Eve said.

"I don't think so."

"Oh, yes. My mother was there."

"What did she say to you?"

"She just kept saying, 'My poor baby.' "

"I was seventeen the first time I came to New York." She had never told this to Eve. "It was with a forty-year-old man. He was a concert pianist, he'd passed through Altoona. When he wrote to invite me, there was a rose in the letter. We stayed at his house in Long Island. He lived with his mother, and he came to my room late at night. You know, I don't even remember his face."

It was all leaving her in slow, imperceptible movements, like the tide when one's back is turned: everyone, everything she had known. So all of grief and happiness, far from being buried with one, vanished beforehand except for scattered pieces. She lived among forgotten episodes, unknown faces bereft of names, closed off from the very world she had created; that was how it came to be. But I must show nothing of that, she thought. Her children—she must not reveal it to them.

She formed her life day by day, taking as its materials the emptiness and panic as well as the rushes, like fever, of contentment. I am beyond fear of solitude, she thought, I am past it. The idea thrilled her. I am beyond it and I will not sink.

260

This submission, this triumph made her stronger. It was as if finally, after having passed through inferior stages, her life had found a form worthy of it. Artificiality was gone, together with foolish hopes and expectations. There were times when she was happier than she had ever been, and it seemed that this happiness was not bestowed on her but was something she had herself achieved, had searched for, not knowing its form, had given up everything lesser—even things that were irreplaceable —to gain.

Her life was her own. It was no longer there to be taken by anyone.

2

WHEN VIRI SOLD THE HOUSE, SHE was startled. It was something she assumed would never happen, for which she was unprepared. She was disturbed by the act. It was either sickness or great strength on Viri's part; she did not know which she feared most. There were many things there that belonged to her, she had never bothered to take them, she was always free to. Now, when she suddenly saw them about to vanish, it did not matter. She told her daughters to take what they liked; the rest she would attend to.

Viri was going away, they told her.

"Where?"

"His desk is covered with travel folders. He has some of them marked."

She called him. "I was so sorry to hear about the house."

"It was falling apart," he said. "Not really, but I couldn't take care of it. It's a whole life, you know?"

"I know."

"I got a hundred and ten thousand for it."

261

"That much?"

"Half is yours. Less the mortgage and all that."

"I think you got a very good price. It isn't worth that. I'm sure they didn't look in the cellar."

"It's not the cellar, it's the roof."

"Yes, the roof. But in another way, it's worth much more than a hundred and ten thousand."

"Not really."

"Viri, I'm very pleased with the price. It's just . . . well, we can't sell it again, can we?"

He sailed on the *France* in the noisy, sad afternoon. Nedra came to see him off, like a sister, an old friend. There was a huge crowd, a crowd that would stand at the end of the pier finally, jammed together, waving, a crowd of the twenties, of revolutions in Mexico, threats of war.

They sat in the cabin with a bottle of champagne. "Would you like to see the bathroom?" he said. "It's very nice."

"How long will you stay, Viri?" she asked as they examined the fixtures, the details that had been designed for rough sea.

"I'm not sure."

"A year?"

"Oh, yes. At least a year."

Franca came at last. "What traffic!" she said.

"Would you like some champagne?"

"Please. I had to get out of the taxi three blocks away."

Viri took them on a tour. Glasses in hand, he showed them the salons, the dining room, the empty theater. The stairways were crowded, the passages redolent with Gauloise smoke.

"All these people aren't going?" Franca asked.

"They're either going or someone they know is."

"It's incredible."

"It's completely booked," he said.

The announcements had begun for passengers to go ashore. They made their way toward the gangplank. He kissed his

262

daughter and embraced her, and Nedra as well.

"Goodbye, Viri," she said.

They stood on the pier. They could see him at the rail on the deck where they had parted, his face very white and small. He waved; they waved back. The ship was enormous, there were passengers at every level, the vastness of its black, stained side overwhelmed them. It was like waving farewell to a library, a hotel. At last it began to move. "Goodbye," they called out. "Goodbye." The great moans of the whistle were flooding the air.

At dinner that night, Nedra found herself thinking of things that had gone with the house—or rather, despite herself, they were somehow washed up to her like traces of a wreck far out at sea. Nevertheless, much remained. She and her daughter sat now in a house—it was really just some rooms—left over from the one that was gone. They drank wine, they told stories. All that was missing was a fire.

Viri dined at the second sitting. He had a drink at the bar, where people entered with cries of greeting to the bartender. In the corridor were women of fifty, dressed for dinner, their cheeks rouged. Two of them sat near him. While one talked, the other ate long, triangular bread and butter pieces, two bites to each. He read the menu and a poem of Verlaine's on the back. The consommé arrived. It was nine-thirty. He was sailing to Europe. Beneath him as he lifted his spoon, fish were gliding black as ice in a midnight sea. The keel crossed over them like a comb of thunder.

Franca had become an editor. She had manuscripts to think about now, to coax into being. She worked in a cubicle that was piled with new books, pictures, clippings, distractions of every sort. She went to meetings, lunches. In the spring she was going to Greece. She was serene, her smile was winning, she did not know the way to happiness but she knew she would arrive there.

263

"Are you still seeing Nile?" Nedra asked.

"Poor Nile," Franca said.

Nedra was smoking a cigar, it provided a dash of authority, of strength. She turned on music, as a man might do for a woman, and drew her feet beneath her on the couch.

"This afternoon, on the boat, I was thinking how backward it all was. We should have been seeing you off," she said.

"I'm going to fly."

"You must go further than I did," Nedra said. "You know that."

"Further?"

"With your life. You must become free."

She did not explain it; she could not. It was not a matter of living alone, though in her own case this had been necessary. The freedom she meant was self-conquest. It was not a natural state. It was meant only for those who would risk everything for it, who were aware that without it life is only appetites until the teeth are gone.

3

NEDRA'S APARTMENT WAS NEAR the Metropolitan. It was on street level, an annex to a building. It had only two rooms, but there was a garden, more than that, a wall entirely of windows like a greenhouse. The garden had died; it was dry, the vines were brittle, the stone urns empty. But the sun fell into it all day long, and within, behind the bank of glass, she had many plants, protected, cared for. They bathed in the light; they gave off a richness and calm. The door to the garden, like that of a house in France, was of painted iron with glass in its upper half. There was a fireplace in her bedroom and a narrow, decaying bath. At a small table, in the mornings, barefoot, alone, she sat, and set her imagination free. The silence, the sunlight enclosed her. She began—not seriously she told herself—she was too proud to risk early failure —to write a few stories for children. Viri had been wonderful at making them up. Often she thought of him as would the widow of a famous man; she saw him again drinking tea in the morning, smoking a little awkwardly, his slightly bad breath, his thinning hair only adding to the memory. He was so dependent, so foolish. In a time of hardship or upheaval he would have quickly vanished, but he had been fortunate, he had found himself always in sheltered times, the years had been calm. She saw him with his small hands, his blue-striped shirt, his ineffectiveness, his vagaries. When it came to stories, though, he was like a man who knew railroad schedules, he was exact, assured. He would begin in wonderful, faintly witty sentences. His stories were light but not frivolous; they had a strange clarity, they were like a part of the ocean where one could see the bottom.

She saw herself in the mirror. The light was mild. A mole near her jaw had darkened. The lines in her face were tentative no longer. There was no question, she looked older, the age of one who is admired but not loved. She had made the pilgrimage through vanity, the pages of magazines, through envy itself to a vaster, more tranquil world. Like a traveler, there was much she could tell, there was much that could never be told.

Young women liked to talk to her, to be in her presence. They were able to confess to her. She was at ease. There was one who worked with Franca, Mati, whose husband had left her, who acted as if she had already drowned herself. One afternoon Nedra showed her how to paint her eyes. In an hour, just as Kasine was said to have changed an actress, she transformed a plain, defeated face into a kind of Nefertiti able to smile.

She could see the lives of such young women clearly, things invisible to them or hidden. And one day there came to her a

Japanese girl, small-boned, mysterious, a girl born in St. Louis but indelibly foreign, completely of another place. It was like watching an exotic animal that eats in its own way, that has its own stride. Her name was Nichi. She came often, sometimes she stayed for two or three days. Her *s*'s were soft, with an Oriental secrecy. She was graceful, like a cat, she could walk on plates without making a sound. She had lived with a doctor for five years.

"But that's over," she said. "A psychiatrist, he had no practice, he was in research. A very intelligent man, brilliant."

"But you never married."

"No. I slowly realized that . . . the answer isn't in psychiatry. You know, they're strange, they have very strange ideas. I don't even want to tell you. He'll be a famous man," she said. "He's writing a book. He's worked on it for a long time. It's about unconventional healing. Of course, it has to do with the mind, the power of thought. You know, there are men who can perform what we think of as miracles. There was a famous one in Brazil; we went to see him. He was a clerk in a hospital, but after work he saw patients, they came from all over, from hundreds of miles away. He even operated on them without anesthetic. They didn't even bleed. It's the truth. We made a film of it."

"I've never heard of him."

"Oh, the government suppresses everything," she said. She was intense, certain. "The doctors try to deny him."

"But how does he work? What does he say to a patient?"

"Well, I don't speak Spanish, but he asks them: What's wrong? Where does it hurt? He touches them, like a blind man touches all over, and then he stops and he says: It's here."

"Incredible."

"Then he cuts, with an ordinary knife."

"He sterilizes it?"

"A kitchen knife. I've seen it."

They hypnotized one another with talk and admiration. The

266

hours passed slowly, hours when the city sank into afternoon, hours that were theirs alone. Nedra had a taste for the East given to her, perhaps, by Jivan, and now, in the presence of this slim girl who spoke of having nine senses, who complained that she had no breasts, she found herself drawn to it once more. Nichi had small teeth, terrible teeth, she swore, she had just paid her dentist two hundred dollars and even that was a special price.

"I told him that when I was under the gas, he could do what he liked."

"And?"

"I'm not sure."

She was perfectly shaped. She was, as they say so often, like a doll. Her fingers were thin, her toes bony as the feet of a sparrow. In her own apartment she burned incense; her clothes had a faint scent of it. She had a master's degree in psychology, but aside from her studies had read nothing. Nedra mentioned Ouspensky. No, she had never heard of him. She had never read Proust, Pavese, Lawrence Durrell.

"What did they write?" she said.

"And Tolstoy?"

"Tolstoy. I think I've read some Tolstoy."

They met in the garden of the Modern Art, the city muted beyond its walls. They had lunch, they talked. Beneath the gleaming black hair burning in the sun, behind the intense eyes, for a moment Nedra saw something which touched her deeply—that rare thing, the idea of a friend one makes when the heart has already begun to close.

She was like a fruit tree, she thought to herself, past bearing but still strong, like the trees in the sloping orchard of Marcel-Maas long ago. His name had been in the paper recently. He had had an important show, there were articles about him. He was being conceded at last, all he had dreamed and wanted, the things he could not say, the friends he had never had, the acclaim—all of it was laid now at the foot of canvases he had painted. He was safe at last. He existed, he could not disappear. Even his ex-wife was saved by this. She was part of it, she had made her exit before the final act, but she would have it to talk about for as long as she lived—at dinners, in restaurants, in the great, empty rooms of the barn, if she lived there still.

The young women came to her. Telephone calls, conversations with friends, an occasional letter from Viri. She realized that life consisted of these pebbles. One has to submit to them, she told Nichi. ". . . walk on them," she said, "bruise one's feet."

"What do you mean by pebbles? I think I know."

". . . lie on them, exhausted. Do you know the way your cheek is warmed by the sun they have gathered?"

"Yes."

"Let me read your palm," Nedra said.

The hand was narrow, the lines surprisingly deep. It seemed naked, this palm, like that of an older woman. She traced the chief lines. She felt those flat eyes glancing up at her own face with its leanness, its intelligence, its immobility, in fascination and belief, but she acknowledged nothing.

"Your hand is halfway between emotion and intellect," she said, "divided between them. You are able to see yourself coldly, even in periods when you are ruled by emotion, but at the same time you are a romantic, you would like to give yourself completely, without thinking. Your intellect is strong."

"It's the emotion I'm worried about."

"That there isn't enough?"

"Yes."

"There's enough. There's more than enough. Oh, yes."

They were both looking in the small, bare palm.

"But you know that already," Nedra murmured. She was creating truth, devising it. The brightness of plants and sunlight was behind her, the air was filled with panels of light in which floated a luminous dust. She did not answer, as she

268

might have, "No, the truth is, you are a woman who will never be satisfied. You will search, but you will never find it."

She was close to things which were too powerful. She sensed an ascendancy over this willing girl; she could easily go too far. Suddenly she understood how the prick of a pin in a doll could kill.

She told this to Eve later as if it were an accident that had been averted.

"Well, what did you do?"

"I took her to lunch at L'Étoile."

"L'Étoile?"

"I felt guilty," Nedra said. "Of course, I didn't feel quite so guilty when I got the bill. It was thirty dollars."

"What did you eat?"

"I don't know what makes me spend money like that. I've struggled against it."

"Occasionally."

Nedra smiled. Her teeth were still white, the teeth of a woman well cared for. "No, I've tried. For some reason, it's difficult for me. I know I'm going to die in poverty . . ."

"Never."

". . . without a cent. Having sold everything—jewels, clothes. They'll be coming to take away the last bits of furniture."

"It's impossible to imagine."

"Not for me," Nedra said.

4

VIRI WAS IN ROME, HAVING COME to it slowly, as a scrap of paper comes down to the street. He was living in the Inghilterra. His clothes were pressed, the maids brought his laundry, his shirts folded neatly on top. The maids were named Angela, Luciana, names of fabulous heroines. The room was small, the bathroom large, a strip of heavy darkened brass at its threshold. There was a narrow tub, a white tile floor, a red dot for hot water, blue for cold. In the hallway Angela called to Luciana. Doors were slamming. A porter sighed.

He had unpacked his things. His shoes were arranged beneath the bed, there were photos on the glass-topped table that served as a desk, the glass amplified the ticking of his watch where it lay. He was in exile in this country of waiters and lame serving girls. He had no real work. He pretended to be visiting, seeing at last all the things he had neglected. He was reading a life of Montaigne. Once or twice he talked of writing a book.

Dawn. The traffic had started. Already the day was filled with a flat, Italian light like the doors of a theater opened in the morning. He was alone. With the solemnity of a peasant, he broke the five-part rolls, faintly pale and dusted on the bottom, that came with breakfast. In silence he spread the soft curls of butter and drank the tea. The distant city was snarling with cars and the faint insistent tapping of workmen's hammers on stone.

In the narrow, neglected streets that he liked to walk along, he looked in antique shop windows filled with reflections of passers-by. In the cool of the interiors, among huge chairs, the dealers sat talking as the morning passed, gesturing with their hands occasionally, unaware of his curious glance.

He was forty-seven. His hair was thin as he walked in the Roman sunlight. He was lost in the cities of Europe, pigeons huddled in every niche, asleep on the knees of saints. He was a man who waited for the *Tribune* to be delivered to the kiosks, who ate by himself. When he saw his face in windows, struck by light, he was shocked. It was the face of ancient politicians, of pensioners, the wrinkles looked black as ink. Don't despise me for being old, he begged.

He had lunch in a restaurant, sitting near the window. Cold noon, a cold light. Outside the trees had already lost their leaves. It was in the Villa Borghese; the air of the great park was damp and still, the sound of things far off came through it like distant icefalls. Before him was a piece of paper on which he was writing, during the long intervals between courses, a list of those things which could even for a short while, save him, that is to say, pleasures which remained. *Wood fires*, he had written, *The London Times, dinners with friends* . . .

Time had spoiled for Viri. It reeked in his pockets. He had projects, somewhat vague, appointments, but nothing to do. His eye would not fix on things, it slipped off them like a dying insect. He was staggering, swaying between those times when he had no strength at all, no reason, no urge to struggle, when he felt, ah, if only he could run to death like a fanatic, a believer, delirious, dazed, on those quickened feet that run to love—and then, in the quiet of the early afternoon, seated somewhere, opening the newspaper, he was completely different.

He stood in the bathroom amid the white chair, the sill of gray marble, the huge frosted windows which seemed to intensify the light. The inward curve of the bidet's edge, the smoothness of it gave him for a moment a sensation of deepest longing. The curve complemented the portion of the body meant to fit against it, and he weakened as one does at the sight of an empty garment or the underclothes, fresh and minimal, of a loved woman, tossed aside.

He could not see himself clearly, that was the thing. He knew he had talent, intelligence, that he was not going to perish like a mollusk washed up on shore. All the past, he told himself, all that had been so difficult, that he had struggled with like a traveler with too many bags—idealism, loyalty, all

271

your virtues, your decency—they will be needed when you are old, they will preserve you, keep you alive; that is, they will interest someone. And then, a day later, the disease would strike; it was something he did not recognize or understand. Suddenly he had never been so nervous, frightened, depressed. He had a flash of realizing what a breakdown was: the act of life going out of control. His chest ached, his legs were cold, he kept swallowing, his mind raced foolishly. He looked out on the back courts in the winter afternoon, courts with glassed-in balconies and landings. His only contact with the world, beyond the faint sound of traffic, the voices in the hallway that never ceased, was the black telephone, a frightening instrument shrill as a nightmare and over which abrupt voices came, voices whose mood he could hardly guess. He had no strength, no desire to go out. The thought of people terrified him. He did not want to speak Italian; it was not his language, not his sensibility. He wanted to see his children again, only once, before the end.

The next day, in the sunshine, everything was better. The sky was mild, people were smiling and friendly. It was as if they could see he was an invalid, the survivor of a wreck.

He went to the office of two architects with whom he had corresponded. They were young and serious. One of them he had met in New York. The reception room was calm and luxurious, the luxury that is formed of infallible choices. It spoke of order, understanding, he felt immediately at home. The fever had passed.

The secretary looked up. *"Buon giorno."*

"I'm Mr. Berland."

"Good morning, Mr. Berland." Her face was turned upwards, a small, intelligent face, short hair, black, like the wing of a bird. "We were expecting you," she said. "Mr. Cagli has someone in his office; it will just be a few minutes."

"That's all right."

They looked at one another. It seemed she nodded slightly, in the way of the East. "Have you been in Rome long?" she asked.

"Several weeks."

"Do you like it?"

"It's strange; I think I'm not quite accustomed to it yet."

"Do you speak Italian?"

"Well, I've started."

"Bene," she said simply.

"I'm a disgrace to it."

"No, I don't think so. *Trova quale più facile, parlare o capire?"*

"Capire."

"Sì," she agreed.

She smiled. Her mouth was small as a child's. Her name was Lia Cavalieri. She was thirty-three. She lived near the Protestant Cemetery. Had he been there? she asked. He was slow in replying. He recognized her. "No," he murmured.

"Keats is buried there."

"Is he? Here in Rome?"

"Then you haven't seen his grave? It's very moving. It's off in a corner by itself. It has no name on it, you know."

"No name?"

"A beautiful inscription, but no name."

She was about to say, "I'll take you there if you like," but restrained herself. She said it on his second visit.

They walked toward the grave on a soft, winter day. The ground was dry underfoot. Far off, near a tree, he could see the two stones. Afterwards they went to lunch.

Like Montaigne whose life he was reading, he had met an Italian woman during a journey there and fallen in love. All that was missing was the baths of Lucca. Montaigne had been forty-eight. A freshet thought dead had burst forth.

5

LIA WAS FROM THE NORTH. HER
father had been born in Genoa with its steep necropolis; her
mother, more romantically, in Nice. She told him all this. He
loved the details of her life, they electrified him. He had entered the period when everything in his own seemed to be
repetition, occurring for the second or third time, a performance for which he knew every possibility. She made that
forgotten.

"Nice. Didn't that once belong to Italy?"

"Everything did once," she said.

The names she told him, the history, the incidents of her
childhood—all of it was new, all of it glinted like the energy
in the black of her hair. She had a resigned intelligence, she
was fastidious, she was shy. The great unhappiness of her life
was that she had never married.

From the moment he had seen her sitting confident and
small behind her desk, when he saw her type or use the telephone, he realized how capable she was. But she had ventured
nothing, she was merely waiting, all these years she was waiting
for a man. She was a kind of brilliant cripple; she could imagine
anything, but she could not walk. And he was only slightly
better. Though from the first he felt enormously drawn to her,
he was uncertain; he had not hunted in so long and had been
poor at it even then.

They went to dinner in a restaurant named for the baker's
daughter, La Fornarina, who had been a mistress of Raffaello.
It was winter, the garden was closed. She had wanted to talk
to him as soon as she saw him, she said. She had formed an
idea of him from having heard him talked about and from

274

letters, but no expectation could explain the closeness and recognition she felt when he entered the reception room for the first time.

"You are one in a thousand," she told him. "Yes, you are very special."

A warmth flooded through him, a dizziness as if he had fought an enemy. With a word, a glance she embraced him; she had opened the dull sky, the light poured down. It is always an accident that saves us. It is someone we have never seen.

She knew Rome as a lifelong prisoner knows it. She knew its shops, its sun flats, its streets with a special view. She would show him some of that. His hungers returned to him, his yearnings, his capacity for joy.

She filled his glass with wine but took only a little for herself which she did not drink. She told him, without the slightest urgency, that she had no power to resist him.

"I think you know that," she said. Her hand slid beneath his. The touch of her fingers took his breath away.

She had a small car, many pairs of shoes, she said wistfully, some money in Switzerland; she was like a meal all prepared.

"And you have come to sit down to it," she said. "Yes, it's a marvelous dinner, it's the meal of a lifetime."

Zuppa, carne, verdura, formaggi. The procession of worn, white plates upon the tablecloth, the coarse, simple bread, the waiters in their jackets, slightly soiled. The wine had no effect on him, he was too stimulated for it. When she leaned across to help him with the menu, he could feel the warmth of her face. She ate very little, she smoked a few cigarettes, she talked. Her father was a grain dealer. He was conservative, small, bitterly disappointed in her brother. His daughter he had loved perhaps too much; it had sometimes been too heavy, too carnal. He kissed her always on the mouth, deep, unflinching kisses. When her mother died, he used to say, he was going to marry Lia. He was joking, of course, but he once touched her breast on the bus, she had felt revulsion.

"Am I boring you?"

"Of course not," he said.

"You're sure?"

"I'm marveling at you. You have such an astonishing vocabulary. How did you learn to speak English so well?"

"I've spoken it for a long time," she said.

"Why is that?"

"I suppose I was waiting for you, *amore.*"

Should one describe the act of love which united them, it may have been this night? She had the key to an apartment that belonged to a friend. She unlocked the bolt three times; a narrow, varnished door, one of two, fell open. There were no rugs, the floor was cold. He felt no hesitation, no fear. It was as if he had never seen a woman before; the sight of her nakedness, the darkness of its core overwhelmed him, his mind mumbled devotions, his ears were filled with whispers. The city opened like a garden, the streets received him and poured forth their names. He saw Rome like one of God's angels, from above, from afar, its lights, its poorest rooms. He blessed it, he fell into its heart. He became its apostle, he believed in its grace.

She left him at the entrance to his hotel, and her car, noisy, plain, sped off. Every detail of going up to his room—the face of the *portiere*, the heavy key, the coming together of polished doors, the rising, his slow walk down vaulted corridors—everything affirmed his feeling of triumph. He lay in bed content to be alone at so solemn a moment, to be able to savor it. In the streets of the sleeping city, along its bare, new avenues, across its empty squares her car still dashed, its headlights jumping nervously on the roughness of the road, his thoughts enclosing it, sheltering it as it went.

In the morning, the telephone rang. *"Ciao, amore,"* she said.

"Ciao."

"I wanted to hear your voice."

"I was sleeping," he confessed.

"Yes, of course. The sleep of the blessed. I too . . ."

Her words stirred him. The maids were dropping brooms in the hall.

"I imagine you lying there . . ." At last she was free to speak. She had so many things to say, so much that had waited. "I picture you taking a bath. The water is pouring into the tub, filling the room with a luxurious sound."

"Are you at home?" he asked.

"*Sì*. At home, in my bed. It's only a small bed, it's not like yours."

"Like mine?"

"You have a big one, don't you? At least, I imagine it so."

She was calling from her room in a voice that was slightly guarded, even though, as she said, her mother spoke no English. He was in Italy. The girls on the street, the mechanics, the boys in the outskirts driving motorbikes home from work on winter evenings with newspaper wrapped around their hands—suddenly he felt he might share their lives.

They went again to the apartment with its wooden doors. In the daylight it seemed abandoned. The floor had a vague pattern of flowers, the walls were tan. The owner's English clothes, pushed to one side, were hanging in a wardrobe. The sun, as if by chance, fell in one window. It was bare and chilly, but visit by visit it became theirs.

They went on Saturdays. He sat sketching the ruins opposite. There were stacks of torn magazines near his elbow: *Oggi*, *Paris-Match*. In the street the sound of occasional footsteps, the racketing cars. He seemed calm but he was terrified. I will never learn it, he thought, the language, the hours, the life. He concentrated on the drawing, searching for the right colors.

She appeared at his side. "Does music bother you?"

"Not at all."

She put on a record. She watched him work. In the afternoon they went to a film. They parked three blocks away.

Approaching the theater he felt like a boy who has not studied his lessons and is entering class. He mingled uneasily with the others. They sat in the audience and she whispered important lines to him in the dark.

The radio was playing softly. It was cold in the evening; they were chilled. The light, even in these southern latitudes, was fading. She had put the kettle on and was arranging the cups and spoons—faint, homely sounds that struck him like voices from afar. He felt the first touch of panic at her kindness. It was not kindness he needed. His life was being washed away, it was coming to pieces, floating like paper on the tide; he needed hours that were useful, work, responsibility. He smiled wanly as she brought the cups to his chair and knelt beside it. Silence. In the manner of a servant girl she began to remove his shoes and socks. His feet were bare. She drew them to her.

"You are cold," she said. She held them in her hands. "I will warm you." She spoke to them as if they were children. "There, that's better, isn't it? *Sí.* Yes, you are not used to winter, not these winters. These are something new. They can be cold, more cold than you imagine. In your nice English shoes everyone thinks you are warm and content. Look, how nice your shoes are, they say, such fine shoes. Yes, they think you are warm because you look nice; they think you are happy. But happiness is not so easy to find, is it? It's very difficult to find. It's like money. It comes only once. If you are lucky, it comes once, and the worst part is there's nothing you can do. You can hope, you can search, anger, prayers. Nothing. How frightening to be without it, to wait for happiness, to be patient, to be ready, to have your face upturned and luminous like girls at communion. Yes, you are saying to yourself, me, me, I am ready."

Her cheek was pressed to his naked feet. She seemed very small.

"And nothing happens," she said. "It happens to all the others. Yes, you think, it will happen to me. And every year you have more to give, nothing is spent, nothing is taken away, you are richer, you are laden, and every year the same: nothing. Until finally there are almost no others, you are left alone like one flower in a great meadow, and it is autumn, yes, the days are growing shorter, the grass bends beneath the wind. And the sun comes and shines on you still, alone in that great field, the last flower, beautiful, yes, because of that, and there you are in the long, endless afternoons, waiting, waiting . . ."

She was a woman of great strength. She was slight, but she possessed will and also a terrifying loneliness. The city echoed it. The great, steel shutters closed at night, the streets became empty, the people disappeared. There were lights in occasional restaurants and empty cafés, the rest was darkness, void. The monuments were sleeping, the cats were crouched beneath parked cars. It was a city built on matrimony and law, even if ridiculed, even if despised; all else was fugitive, all in vain.

"You will find happiness," he told her. They were at lunch. The winter held days of sunshine, noons of infinite calm. He broke a piece of bread to cover his confusion, dismayed at the tense of his verb.

"Do you think so?" she said coolly. Nothing escaped her.

"Yes."

"That's encouraging." She examined his face. She was cautious, warned.

He regretted what he had said, it was as if he had tried to release himself from involvement in her life. His guilt and the healthy faces of those at tables nearby created turmoil and shame in him. The long, dark hair of the Italian women, their passionate faces—faces all the more poignant because they were soft and would not last a decade—the talk of couples, of families, their intense interest in one another, their laughter, all of it seemed to celebrate connubial life, the many facets of it richer than his own, and richer too than any possibilities of his. He was frightened to realize that he had already passed with Lia into the silence of dutiful meals, their attention straying to others, to people being seated, as they waited for dishes to be placed before them.

"You are silent," she said.

"Am I?"

He did not know what else to reply. He could see across from him, as if it were already accomplished, the woman he had married, with whom he was destined to sit at table for all the remaining years of his life. He envied everyone about him who had married someone different and was engaged in easy conversation; in the long run, what is more important than that? It is the bread of sexual life.

At the same time, he saw that it was a kind of panic which was making him mute, that he was not himself, he was unsure. There were deep, almost invincible yearnings and hungers in this woman. They would not reveal themselves in a day, they had been too long steeping. She was like a convict, an outcast in whom one must believe or she would be lost, who needed someone to save her. And that man she would astonish, the man who committed his life. Thoughts of the underground river passed through his mind, the voyage few men dared take, in which one risked everything.

"You know what I'd like to do, Lia . . ."

"Tell me."

"I'd like to take a trip. I'd like to go somewhere with you, away from Rome, the two of us. Would you like that?"

"Sì, amore."

"For a week or so."

"Sì. Can you wait just a little? My parents are planning to go away. That would be a good time."

"Where are they going?"

"To Sicily."

"We'll go north."

"Don't worry, they won't find us."

He could not hold his thoughts intact long enough to understand what was happening. He was in turmoil; was he being tested? Was anything more than this swooping from a semblance of happiness to boredom and fear still possible for him? Or perhaps, in the way of someone blind to his own weaknesses, he was about to enact again a hopeless domesticity, to repeat those things which had already brought him here, to a strange country far from home.

Sometimes he slept in the apartment, uneasy, alone. She came to him in the morning. She had oranges in her handbag, flowers, pictures of her childhood, of the father who adored her too frankly, photos taken on Mikonos, in London when she weighed fifty-five kilos—horrible, she turned them over quickly, she was ashamed of them but she wanted to show him everything—the homely English girl friend at whose country house she spent an icy Christmas. She wanted him to share her life. In her white underpants she sat kneeling on the bed and prepared an orange. She was solemn, she did not speak. The shutters were open, the sunlight poured in.

She showed him her city, the keyhole in the Piazza dei Cavalieri di Malta through which one saw a hidden garden, and beyond it, floating in air, vast as the sun, the dome of St. Peter's. She showed him museums and the ruins at Ostia, San Giovanni at Porta Latina with the tree struck by lightning, St. Agnese where the barbers of Rome shaved the beggars, small restaurants, graves. In the faded red stucco of a wall where a madman lived beneath the sidewalk when she was a child—they used to listen to him and run when he howled—an inscription was scratched. Viri stood reading it. YOUNG MAN, GOOD-LOOKING, INDUSTRIOUS. OBJECT: MATRIMONY. SEEKS SERIOUS AND *CARINA* GIRL. Beneath was a telephone number and certain irreverent comments.

"Yes," Lia said dryly. "Matrimony."

"But doesn't he mean it?"

"Who knows?"

It was a mild day. The winter was almost past.

6

THEY WENT TO THE ARGENTARIO in April. The roads were empty. They drove for hours and in the warmth of the sun through the windshield, the gentle swaying of the car, he felt at peace. The country they were passing through was not what he had expected; it was bare, industrial seacoast. There were no quiet towns, no farms.

Lia was driving. As he looked at her, talked, watched her small hands, he realized that he was somehow holding something back despite it all: it was his opinion of her. Instead, he was wondering vaguely what Nedra would think; he was almost nervous, he imagined everything, even a curt dismissal, he was preparing to argue with her—those arguments that were always infuriating, that he never won.

"What are you thinking of, *amore?*"

"What am I thinking of? Somehow I'm never able to answer that question."

"Are they secret thoughts?"

"No, not exactly."

"Tell me."

"Nothing is secret. It's just that certain things can't be said very well."

"You make me curious."

"I'll tell you at dinner tonight," he said.

She smiled.

"You don't believe me?"

"I don't want to pry."

The hotel she had chosen was on the side of a hill. It was isolated and expensive. They signed their names in a small reception building before a young man dressed in striped trou-

282

sers and a morning coat. Their luggage was carried down to one
of the wings below, the door to their room was opened. Like
a prisoner who is taken from an administrative office, along
corridors, and finally hears the steel bolts close his cell, Viri, the
moment they were alone, felt depressed beyond words. The
floor he stood upon was tile. The room was chilly, dark, the
window lay in the shadow of other walls. There was a wide bed,
composed in a practical manner: two smaller beds put together.
Given the bed, not much additional space existed.

"I'm sorry," he said to her. "Do you like this room?"

She looked about briefly and shrugged.

He climbed the steps to the office, where, after much consul-
tation of ledger pages though the hotel was almost empty, and
several discussions between someone invisible in the back room
and the clerk, it was arranged that they should have another
room—a suite, in fact.

Viri could not bring himself to speak in Italian. "Will it be
the same price?"

"Yes, the same price," the clerk said, not bothering to look
up.

"Thank you."

"Certainly, sir."

They walked down to the *cala* after lunch. The sun was
warm. The descent wound past villa after villa, all new, all with
freshly sodded lawns. Lia was talking about where one could
live in Rome, in what kind of apartment. His mind was wandering. The roofs of the villas, the little driveways, were all identical. From time to time, he offered a sound of agreement. He
tried to seem at ease.

They lay on the pebbled beach. The bar of bamboo and
palm fronds was closed, it was still too early in the season.

"Talk to me," she said. "You talk so little about yourself. I
am fascinated by your name. How did you come to be named
Vladimir?"

"It's a Russian name. My family came from Russia."

"From which part?"

"I don't know. From the south."

He lay there silent. A lone attendant was raking up seaweed. The water was too cold for them to swim. Looking down, he suddenly saw beneath him the thin, white legs of his father. He wrapped the towel around himself. Lia's flesh, always a faint brown, exotic, strange, was faintly goose-pimpled from the wind.

"Do you want a towel?"

"I prefer the sun," she said.

"What is it like in Sicily?"

"I've never been to Sicily."

They walked up slowly. It was very long, he had tried not to think of it on the way down. Twice she stopped to rest and he stood waiting, once above a trash heap. "They throw it anywhere," she said. "You know, there's a strike, *amore*. They don't collect it any more."

He began to notice the green plastic bags stuffed in the underbrush along the road.

"We should have driven down," he said.

"*Sì.*"

In the late afternoon the room had a smell of dampness. He noticed a mosquito gliding along the upper wall. He lay on a small daybed near the terrace doors, Lia beside him. Her robe was open—he had untied it—her eyes concealed in shadow. The black print of her navel, the even blacker cuneal hair shone up at him like dark stones at the bottom of a pond. She was thin, her flesh was soft, easily bruised. There he was, between her legs, she was uncovered, sprawled among her clothing. The mosquito had slipped from sight, vanished. They were clasped in each other's arms, disinterested, naked, soiling the rumpled bedspread that covered a mattress.

The act was somehow shameful, an act of boredom and desperation, entered into because everything else had failed. It ended quickly. He lay by her side and put his arm beneath her

284

head, drawing the robe over her at the same time as if she were a shop and he were closing her for the night—a shop one had to talk to. She said nothing. She lay unmoving in the dark.

In Porto Santo Stefano they found a restaurant and sat down for dinner. Only one other table was occupied. "I suppose it's a little early," he commented.

"*Sì.*"

He was counting on the meal to replenish some of the joy that had fled from him, as one counts on medicines or amusements. He read the menu, he read it again like a man looking for something which is inexplicably missing. The waiter stood near his elbow.

She was not hungry, Lia confessed. The announcement disheartened him. He began to suggest things she might like. "*Bollito misto.*"

"No."

"They have some fish."

"Nothing, *amore.*"

The restaurant was empty; even the street outside was quiet. He sprinkled salt from the small glass dish by dipping into it with the tip of his knife and then tapping. He tried to drink the wine. He had ordered too much.

She watched him eat and said little. She was like a stranger he had encountered on a journey, suddenly he did not know if he could trust her. He was certain she could sense his nervousness. The waiter was sitting near the door to the kitchen; the owner seemed half asleep.

"It feels as if we were in exile," Viri said. "The *tagliatelle* is good. Have a taste."

She accepted. His hand held forth the fork in the deserted room, like a room where an assassination is to take place.

"Do you want to go back to Rome?" she asked.

He felt guilty. He felt he was spoiling everything. "I don't know. Let's decide tomorrow," he said. "I'm a little nervous, I don't know why. I'm sure I'll get over it. And the hotel

. . . Perhaps it's the barometer or something. Give me a day or two, it will be all right."

And later, in bed, he saw her approach, raise her arms and take off her nightgown. Even this act frightened him. She slipped in beside him, naked, unhurried. *"Amore,* of course I'll wait," she said. "You know that. I am yours," she said in a voice without hope. "Do what you like to me."

7

THE TERRORS OF BANISHMENT, OF a new world. What in the beginning was novel, curious, slowly hardens to intractable life, the laughter fades, it is like a difficult school, one which will never end. He did not recognize the holidays. Even Sundays were meaningless, feared, with everything closed like a book.

Adorato, she whispered, *amore dolce.* Forgive this relentless courtship. She had little restraint left, she said. She had hungers only an orphan could know. She had begun to lose hope. Somehow it strengthened her. The terror of desperate longing which she had unfurled before him she now withdrew. In its place was a kind of aristocratic submission. She went to Milan with her parents. They saw the opera. She had her hair cut. *The proprietor of the hotel wants his daughter to cut hers like mine,* she wrote. They went to exhibitions, shopped. *Even that does not quite kill the loneliness. I am wistful for you. I smoke a cigar in the evenings. They call me Cigarello, brown and thin.* She came back witty and beautiful. Her eyes were cool. She wanted him, she said. She was living a d'Annunzian passion, one of acceptance, despair. *I would like to fit your hand like a favorite soap.* They were sitting on a bench in the Villa Borghese, eating milk chocolate from a bed of foil. The color of her nipples, she said later. She had to go home for dinner. *Ciao*, my swan, she smiled.

They were married on a Sunday. Lia's mother gave Viri an enameled French ring that had been in her family. She believed in him. She was gay at the bridal supper, the greatest of her dreads had vanished. Even the brother was cordial.

They began a second life. They lived on Via Giulia in an apartment on the third floor. One ascended an oval stairway at the end of the hall. It was not large, but it had a study. There was morning sun, a small kitchen, a bath. Lia was very happy. An intellectual apartment, she said.

They were calm, they were at peace in Vecchia Roma, the part of the city he liked. He began to walk among its shops and streets, routes to the Piazza Navona, to Sant'Eustachio. He slept well. He was slim. He worked with Cagli and Rova. He seemed younger, there were fewer lines in his face or, having been deep from uncertainty, they were fading now. Perhaps it was only the light.

The door had two locks. "Rome is filled with thieves," Lia said.

He stood beside her as she turned the key two, three, four times, driving the bolt ever deeper. There was also a key for downstairs, and two for the car. He remembered how once they had never locked anything except when they went to the city. He remembered the river, the dry lawns of autumn warmed by the sun. He longed for home.

He recognized the state he was in. Was I only free for that brief time, he thought? Looking back it seemed deceptively sweet. His life was closed in by ancient walls, families he was unrelated to, customs that would never change. In the small rooms of the flat, in the narrow streets, all Lia's faults seemed to leap forth, to present themselves for recognition: her nervousness, lack of independence, her insistence on being loved. He learned that she could not amuse herself, that she was desperate without him.

287

"I love you," she explained. "I want to be near you, *amore*. Don't deprive me, don't keep me hungry."

He could not discourage it. He saw in her eyes how much she meant it. Her devotion was too strong, it had a pathetic quality.

They drove to the country for lunch, to a simple place called Montarozzo. It was a mild day, like the first day of a convalescence. She was wearing a navy skirt and a sleeveless blouse. In the fields little girls were playing in communion dresses, white in the sunshine, while their families dined. There were train tracks beyond. Occasionally, drawing glances, there passed a great express.

As usual she ate little, he was used to it. He had finally come to a deep vein of understanding. He was not on a journey, he was to spend his life here, to have this life and this only. Patience, he thought to himself; it will open. The bread was delicious. He dipped morsels of it into his wine like a peasant. This was her sea, this sunlight which fell upon them through the vine leaves. She shined in it. Her hair was short and gleaming, her shyness fell away. The faint circles under her eyes, blue, enduring, made her seem sensual. She was like a refugee, a woman who had seen armies pass, destruction, absurdity. She had survived all this, she had come through alive.

"You are a very good architect. You know, they respect you greatly."

"Really?"

"They like you very much."

He smiled vaguely, but he was pleased. "It would be strange, wouldn't it, having failed in America, if I achieved something here?"

"No. You were meant to come here."

"I suppose."

"To discover me," she said.

"Discover you . . ."

"Yes, like a mushroom. You pushed aside the leaves and there I was." She seemed calm, submissive. "You have the nose of a truffling pig, *amore.*"

"Do you think so?"

"You have intuition," she said. "It's very strong, well developed. I'm interested in these things, you know, I study them. I will become a mystic in the end," she confessed. "When the time comes. When the last hungers of the flesh have left me," she added with a slight smile.

There was a clairvoyant, a woman who lived among animals, she often went to see. Viri accompanied her. It was in a residential neighborhood, a building like any other, modern, cold. The apartment was filled with plants, birds, bizarre paintings, tanks of fish. There were other visitors: couples desiring children, women with sickly sons. Signora Clara touched them. She spoke to them with the voice of someone struggling, distant. The soft bubbling of the air pumps rose behind her. To Viri she said, "Come, look at this. Do you speak Italian?"

They stood before the dim water through which a pearly stream of bubbles rose. She was wearing carpet slippers and an unbuttoned sweater.

"These are my children," she said.

The fish hung in luminous shadow, their movements curiously abrupt. She tapped the glass lightly.

"Come, children, come," she said, and reaching into the tank slowly, affectionately, she took one in her palm and withdrew it. It lay quietly in a bit of water in her hand. "All life is one," she said.

She lived with her maid. She had a husband and family, Lia said, but she had left them to devote herself to her work.

Within you are two seeds, the woman told Viri: one live and one dead. You love the dead one best. He did not know what she meant.

"She can heal," Lia said. "She knows everything."

"She seems cold to me," Viri said. "Very distant."

"Yes, she is cold. To understand everything is to love nothing," Lia quoted.

She made tea for him, she kept his clothing in order, she drew the water for his bath. The shelves of the medicine cabinet were dense with her creams and lotions. In the courtyard the bathroom windows gave on, there was never any change. It was evening. When he came out she was lying there, olive skin naked, slim as a line. He brushed his teeth with Italian toothpaste, he ate Italian meat, he was vanishing day by day into the aged streets, the dark-faced crowds. He boarded the great green buses with their silver numbers and passed, noticing them less and less, the worn columns, the statues weeping black. He was lost among them, the passengers, audiences, crowds, condemned just as they to the humblest of daily acts. He turned corners in sunlight, disappeared in the shade of awnings announcing TRATTORIA, lingered before bookshops.

There were hours between afternoon and evening when he desperately wept for his children. He wrote to them feverishly, letters he could barely finish, their faces appeared before him, days they had spent. His hand was like a sick man's. *Be generous*, he wrote, *know the meaning of joy, carry my love with you all through life.*

He was gentle, composed. They went from meal to meal and from place to place, meals that fell silent over empty cups.

"Kari kiri?" she suggested solemnly, taking up the knife.

He managed to smile. "Have patience with me," he told her. He could think of nothing else.

And late at night she talked to him. She woke him if necessary, and he lay listening.

"Yes," she said, "you are frightened, I know you are frightened. I know your habits, I know your thoughts. You have married me for my sake, but not for your own—not yet. That will come. Oh, yes. It will come because I will wait. I am a cornucopia, I am overflowing. I am not sweet—no, not in the way one tastes at first. But sweet things are forgotten quickly, sweet things are weak. I have the patience to wait, yes, as long as necessary. I will wait a month, a year, five years, I will sit like a widow, playing a kind of *napoleone*, because slowly, slowly I will enslave you. I will do it when the moment comes, when I know it is time, that I can succeed. Until then I will sit at your table, I will lie beside you like a concubine—yes, I will give myself to you in whatever way you like, I will raid your fantasies, I will pillage them and keep the pieces to hypnotize you with. I will say, 'Those things you are dreaming of, I will make them real.' I will be your Arab girl, I will serve you naked, yes, I will hold food between my teeth for you, I will be your daughter, I will be your whore. You cannot believe what I know —no, never—what I have imagined. *Amore*, the secret is to have the courage to live. If you have that, everything will sooner or later change."

He rose and went into the bathroom to find refuge. Her intensity, the loneliness of her voice overpowered him. In the mirror he saw a man with the paleness of someone who has just been awakened. He seemed mortal, weak. He saw clearly that something unthinkable was already expressing itself: he was going to become an old man. He did not believe it, he must prevent it, he could not permit it to be—and yet at the same time it was the meaning of his entire life.

She was tapping at the door. "Are you all right, *amore?*"

"Yes." He opened the door. She had put on her robe. "Yes, I'm all right."

"Come," she said. "I'll make you some tea."

His progress was slow, like the passage of days, but in time he no longer noticed the coldness of terrazzo floors, the shrill ring of the telephone, the taps from which water came without force, as if in the midst of a drought. After endless depression, nights without sleep, realization that the life he had entered was calamitous, without hope, he slowly became lucid, even calm. He was able to read and think. The days dawned quietly.

I am through it, he thought. Like the survivor of a wreck, he took stock of himself. He touched his limbs, his face, he began the essential process of forgetting what had passed.

He was in a period of contentment with daily life, of peace. He looked about himself gratefully. It was still not completely real to him, it was a kind of scenery he watched like someone on a train, some of it vivid, going by, some of it bare.

8

IN THE LETTER BOX WAS AN EN-velope addressed in the clear hand he recognized instantly. He opened it in the hallway and began to read, his heart thudding. *Dearest Viri . . .* How instantly she spoke to him across the miles, across everything. His eye fled through the lines. He expected always to hear her say she had been mistaken, she had changed her mind. There was not a day, not an hour, that his immediate, undefended response would not have been to surrender. He was like those veterans, long retired, to whom one day there comes the call to arms; nothing can keep them, their hearts come alive, they lay down their tools, leave their houses, their land, and go forth.

She wanted to borrow ten thousand dollars; she needed it, she said—*you know how life is.* She promised to pay it back.

Ten thousand dollars. He did not dare tell Lia; he knew what she would say. The venality of Italian life, the rigidity of it informed everything. The woman who came to clean received twenty thousand lire a week, the price of a pair of shoes on the Via Veneto, not even the price. How could he tell her? Rome was a southern city, a capital laid out on the iron axes of money and wealth, the banks were like mortuaries. They bared their teeth over money, the Italians, they showed them like dogs.

292

Lia read the letter. She was silent, cold. "No," she said, "you cannot. Why does she need money?"

"She's never asked for anything."

"She will milk you. She cares nothing for money, you told me that yourself, she throws it away. If you give her money now, six months later she will want more."

"She's not like that."

He could not explain it, he knew that, not to this woman suddenly suspicious, alert. She was slight, she was certain, she knew the language, the machinery of this world.

At dinner that night she opened the subject again. The desolate sound of forks hung in the air.

"*Amore*, I want to ask you something."

He knew what she was about to say.

"Yes, of course, you know," she agreed.

She seemed despondent, subdued, as if she accepted the presence of this other woman.

"Don't send it," she pleaded.

"Lia, why?"

"Don't send it."

"All right," he said.

"*Amore*, believe me. I know." She was the guardian of a bitter knowledge.

"But the fact is," he said evenly, "you don't."

There was silence. She took the dishes to the kitchen. She returned. "Have you ever heard of Paul Malex?" she asked.

"No."

"Paul Malex is a writer, he is *the* intelligence of Europe. You've never heard of him?"

"I don't think so."

"Then believe me, his knowledge is rich, his insight; there is no one to approach him. He reads fluently in Greek and Arabic. He passes freely in the most elevated groups in Europe."

"What does this have to do with—"

"Malex has gone below the plankton. He has gone below a level in the mind, like the level in the sea where the whales feed. Beneath it is the blackness, the cold, creatures with huge teeth that devour each other, death. He has penetrated that. He does it at will. He perceives structures there, the basic structures of life."

He had lost the thread. "What are you saying?" he asked.

"I am saying that in Europe one knows certain things. They have been proved again and again. This city is almost three thousand years old. You will see."

The letter lay on the brown marble surface of a bureau in their bedroom, its words invisible in the dark. They had been written quickly, as Nedra always wrote, in long sentences, without pausing, words which, like an insult or exact judgment, had to be reread, one could never recall them exactly, they were like their author, instinctive, glinting, like a glimpse of fish in the sea.

. . . you know how I hate to go over things that are past, but how I wish we'd bought a little house somewhere near Amagansett. Either a house or ten acres of land. Marina told me what they wanted for land now and I couldn't believe it. I suppose the reason we didn't was the same as always: we had no money. I'm doing some interesting things now, things I always wanted to do. I'm working part-time for a florist, it's ideal for me, it's like going to a house I'm especially fond of. Very few flowers, actually. Mostly plants. It doesn't sound too glorious as I write it—a florist—but I may not continue, I may do something else. Viri, there is one great favor you could do for me, and I want to ask it without a lot of explanation . . .

All night these words lay folded. They had arrived in Rome like so many other appeals, now they were waiting, they had joined that world of everything attendant, timeless, in despair. Still, they were dangerous. They lay amid crystal bottles, tattered lire notes, a comb, a gold pen. They were there at dawn.

Naked, Lia knelt near his waist. The morning light filled the

294

room, he was still half-asleep. She was unbuttoning the worn, white buttons of his pajamas, her cool fingers did not hesitate, she was calm, assured, the Arab woman she had sworn. His head was rolled to one side, his eyes closed.

"Look at me," she commanded.

She was dark, like a girl of the streets, struck along one side by the bright morning sun.

"Look at me," she said. She was the blade of an angelic light; her arms were lean, her breasts like a sixteen-year-old's.

She hesitated. Her movements were slow and dreamlike, her hands supporting her near her thighs. The letter was her audience, she was performing for it as if it had eyes, as if it were a poor, ineffectual child before whom she would demonstrate her shamelessness, her power. Her voice was uneven as she bent.

"Yes," she whispered, "I will be your whore."

His head lay back, as if severed, among the pillows. His thoughts were tumbling.

"Everything," she swore.

Afterwards she stepped from the bed. She was deliberate, unhurried, her act was not ended. The door to the bathroom closed. He lay with the room growing still, the walls fading, the ceiling, like silver water after the leap of a great fish. He was witness to this setting which remained, this world of memory as against the one of flesh, and his thoughts turned irresistibly to all he had been entreated to forget: to Nedra who was living on despite the letter, whose life still blazed strength, in whose wake—even before they had been husband and wife, before, during, after—he had always traveled. And then to her rival of whom he was afraid. These women with their needs and assurance, their dazzling selfishness, their smiles—he would never conquer them, he was too timid, too consenting. He was helpless with them; he was close to them, yes, enormously close, even kindred, but at the same time completely different and alone, like a lame recruit in barracks.

Alone, he lay in the sheets of the still-warm bed. He had drawn the covers to his waist, he could feel a wetness, dense and chill beneath one leg; alone in this city, alone on this sea. The days were strewn about him, he was a drunkard of days. He had achieved nothing. He had his life—it was not worth much—not like a life that, though ended, had truly been something. If I had had courage, he thought, if I had had faith. We preserve ourselves as if that were important, and always at the expense of others. We hoard ourselves. We succeed if they fail, we are wise if they are foolish, and we go onward, clutching, until there is no one—we are left with no companion save God. In whom we do not believe. Who we know does not exist.

9

DEATH TAKES THE LAST STEPS quickly, in a rush.

Nedra was ill. She did not admit it except to feel uncomfortable suddenly in the city. She wanted the open air, she wanted the invisible. Like those anadromous creatures that start without knowing it to their final sites, that somehow, across incredible distances, find their way home, she went—it was the beginning of spring—to Amagansett and took a small house that had once been the shed on a farm. There were some apple trees, long past bearing. The boards of the floor were worn smooth. The village and fields, everything was empty and still. Here she made her ashram, beneath the open skies, by occasional fires, near the continent's fingery edge.

She was forty-seven. Her hair was rich and beautiful, her hands strong. It seemed that all she had known and read, her children, her friends, things which had at one time been disparate, contending, were quiet at last and had found their place within her. A sense of harvest, of abundance, filled her. She had nothing to do and she waited.

She woke in the silence of a bedroom still cool and dark. She was not sleepy, she was aware the night had passed. The small, gnarled branches of the apple trees were stirring in a soundless wind. The sun was not yet up. The sky to the west was the deepest blue, with clouds almost too brilliant, too dense. In the east it was almost white. Her body and mind were rested, they were at peace. They were being readied for a final transformation she only guessed.

In Rome the old woman who cleaned for Lia sat crying. She was eighty. She was slow but still able to work. Her hands were blunt with age.

"What is it?" Lia asked. "What's wrong?"

The woman only went on weeping helplessly. Her body sobbed.

"Ma come, Assunta?"

"Signora," she moaned, "I don't want to die." She was sitting on a chair in the kitchen, grief-stricken.

"To die? Are you sick?"

"No, no." Her face was worn and pleading, the face of an ancient child. "I'm not sick."

"Well, what are you talking about?"

"It's just that I'm afraid."

"Oh, dear," Lia said gently. "Now, don't be upset. Don't be foolish." She took the old woman's hand. "Everything will be all right, don't worry."

"Signora . . ."

"Yes."

"Do you think there's anything after?"

"Assunta, don't cry." How touching old people are, she thought. How honest they are, how emptied of deception and pride.

"I'm afraid."

"I'll tell you what it's like," Lia said, calming her. "It's like being tired, very, very tired and just falling asleep."

"Do you think so?"

"A beautiful sleep," she said. "A sleep which only those who have worked a long time deserve, which does not end."

She was warm, she was comforting with the strength of those who have nothing to lose. She could not even begin to imagine an end to life. She had decades before her, trips to Paris in December with her husband, dinners in small hotels near the Place Vendôme, the lights and Christmas decorations outside, oysters—her first—in the cold afternoon, the half-lemons beside them, the small squares of bread.

"A lovely sleep," she said.

The old woman wiped her eyes. She was quieter now. "Yes," she agreed. "Yes, that's it."

"Of course."

"Still . . ." she said, "how beautiful to wake in the morning and have fresh coffee . . ."

"Yes."

"The smell is so good."

"Poor woman," Viri commented later.

"I gave her some wine," Lia said.

"She has no family?"

"No, her family is gone."

That summer Franca came to visit her mother once more. They sat beneath the trees. Nedra had money, she had bought some good wine. "Do you remember Ursula?" she asked.

"Our pony? Yes."

"She was so impossible. I wanted to sell her, your father wouldn't permit it."

"I know. He really loved her."

"He loved her at certain times. Do you remember Leslie? Leslie Dahlander?"

"Poor Leslie."

"It's strange. I've been thinking of her lately," Nedra said.

"But you didn't know her very well."

"No, but I knew those years."

She looked at her daughter, a feeling of envy and happiness swept her, a gust of it thick as air. They talked of the house, of days long past, the hours lay beside them like a stream that barely moved. All around stretched the wide farmland made thrilling by hidden sea. Rabbits were feeding in the dusty fields, there were sea birds on the shore. All this would vanish, it would belong to poodle owners, Arnaud had said. Its remoteness had saved it, but now the farms were melting like ice in the spring; they were breaking, drifting off forever. All this vast endland, this barren province would disappear. We live too long, Nedra thought.

"Do you remember Kate?" Franca asked.

"Yes. What's become of her?"

"She has three children now."

"She was so thin. She was almost a boy—a beautiful, wicked boy."

"She lives in Poughkeepsie."

"Exile."

"Her father's famous," Franca said. "Did you see the article?" She went inside to find the issue of *Bazaar*.

"I read something," Nedra recalled.

Franca was flipping the pages. "Here," she said. She offered it. It was a long essay. "He had a show at the Whitney."

"Yes, I remember."

A large, gray face, pores visible in its nose and chin, stared at her. It was as if she were looking at a kind of passport, the only kind which mattered.

"He's really a very good painter," Franca said.

"He must be. He's right in here with the French countesses."

"You're making fun of him."

"No, I'm not. Well, goodbye, Robert." She turned the page

to vivid, green pictures of the Bahamas, green and blue, long, tanned girls in caftans and white hats. "It's just that it's hard to believe in greatness," she said. "Especially in friends."

They lay in the holy sun which clothed them, the birds floating over their heads, the sand warm on their ankles, the backs of their legs. She too, like Marcel-Maas, had arrived. She had arrived at last. A voice of illness had spoken to her. Like the voice of God, she did not know its source, she only knew what she was bidden, which was to taste everything, to see everything with one long, final glance. A calm had come over her, the calm of a great journey ended.

"Read to me," she would ask.

In the tall brown grass of the dunes, a pagan couch that overlooked the sea, she sat clasping her knees and listening while Franca read, as Viri had so often, to his daughters, to them all. It was Troyat's life of Tolstoy, a book like the Bible, so rich in events, in sorrow, in partings, so filled with struggle that strength welled up on every page. The chapters became one's flesh, one's own being; the trials washed one clean. Warm, sheltered from the wind, she listened as Franca's clear voice described the landscape of Russia, on and on, grew weary at last and stopped. They lay in silence, like lionesses in the dry grass, powerful, sated.

"It's good, isn't it?" her daughter asked.

"How I love you, Franca," Nedra said.

Of them all, it was the true love. Of them all, it was the best. That other, that sumptuous love which made one drunk, which one longed for, envied, believed in, that was not life. It was what life was seeking; it was a suspension of life. But to be close to a child, for whom one spent everything, whose life was protected and nourished by one's own, to have that child beside one, at peace, was the real, the deepest, the only joy.

Barefoot along the hissing shore, sometimes touching, hip to hip, in the shadowy interior of cars, entering shops, were couples lost in obsession with each other, heavy with the satisfac-

300

tion of possessing, laden with it, brimming. She saw them, they passed before her blandly, as ordinary souls appear to a pilgrim. She had no interest in them. They were limp, translucent, like petals. Their time had not yet come. Gone from her completely was the knowledge she once was sure she would keep forever: the taste, the exaltation of days made luminous by love—with it, one had everything. "That's an illusion," she said.

Her thoughts reached backwards, deeply forgiving, fond. There were things she had nearly forgotten, she had never told. They came to her unexpectedly for perhaps the last time.

"Your grandfather," she said, "my father—he was in the navy, did you know that? He was boxing champion of his ship. He used to tell stories about it. When I was a little girl, I can remember him doing it all, reenacting it. He'd put up his hands, you know. The admiral was there, and all the men. And across the ring, with his face shining and his teeth gold, the Cuban . . ."

"You never told me that."

"I used to love those stories. I suppose he wanted a son. When I was about twelve, when it was quite clear I was a girl, that's when he stopped. He was a difficult fellow. Not easy to know. You know, the strangest thing, I learned it by chance: Eve's mother and mine are buried in the same little cemetery in Maryland. I mean, it's a very small place. In the country.

"She came from there. She met my father at a picnic. It was so long ago. And now they're dead. Her family were storekeepers. They came from Virginia. She had two sisters and a brother, but the brother died when he was a little boy. He was the favorite. His name was Waddy."

"I wish I'd known her."

"She had beautiful hands. I think she pined for Maryland. She wasn't very strong."

"What was her maiden name again?"

"McRae."

301

"Yes, McRae."

"Not one of them with money." Nedra said. "That's the pity of it. Honest, yes, but you can't pass on honor."

"So I have Scotch blood."

"Mostly Russian, I think. You're a lot like your father."

"Do you really think so?"

"Yes, it's good."

"Why?"

"Let me look at you. Well," she said, "because there is something unfathomable there." She reached out to touch Franca's cheek. "Yes," she said. "Unfathomable and divine."

Franca took the hand and kissed it.

"Mama . . ." she began. She was close to tears.

"You know, I'm so glad you could come this year," Nedra said. "I keep thinking we won't be coming here much longer, we'll have to find someplace else. We should really go out to dinner once or twice. Catherine tells me there's a Greek place run by two brothers, that isn't bad. We can have *moussaka*. I had it in London. There's a wonderful Greek restaurant there. We'll go sometime."

"Yes."

She was stroking her daughter's hair.

"I'd like that," Franca said.

10

SHE DIED LIKE HER FATHER, SUD-denly, in the fall of the year. As if leaving a concert during a passage she loved, as if giving up an hour before the light. Or so it seemed. She loved the autumn, she was a creature of blue, flawless days, the sun of their noons hot as the African coast, the chill of the nights immense and clear. As if smiling and

302

acting quickly, as if off to a country, a room, an evening finer than ours.

She died like her father. She felt ill. Abdominal pains. For a while they could diagnose nothing. The x-rays showed nothing, the many tests of blood.

The leaves had come down, it seemed, in a single night. The prodigious arcade of trees in the village gave them up quickly; they fell like rain. They lay like runs of water along the melancholy road. In the turning of seasons they would be green again, these great trees. Their dead branches would be snapped away, their limbs would quicken and fill. They would again, in addition to their beauty, to the roof they made beneath the sky, to their whispering, their slow, inarticulate sounds, the riches they poured down, they would, besides all this, give scale to everything, a true scale, reassuring, wise. We do not live as long, we do not know as much.

They had given up their leaves as if to mourn her, as if weeping for an arboreal queen.

Among those few at the funeral, Franca stood alone. She had no husband. Her face and hands seemed bare as if washed clean. She was numinous, pale, her face the very face of the dead woman but more beautiful, far more than her mother could ever have been. The present is powerful. Memories fade.

Danny had her children with her, little girls of two and four who had hardly known their grandmother. Grandmother! It seemed incredible. They had pure features and a serene nature, though the older talked aloud during the service as if no one else were there. Two daughters, one on each side, who, though they were unaware of it, would know another century, the millennium. Perhaps they would read aloud as Viri had done on those long winter evenings, those idle summers when, in a house by the sea, it seemed the family he had created would always endure. Certainly they would be passionate and tall and one day give to their children—there is no assurance of this, we imagine it, we cannot do otherwise—marvelous birthdays, huge candle-rich cakes, contests, guessing games, not many young guests, six or eight, a room that leads to a garden, from afar one can hear the laughing, the doors open suddenly, out they run into the long, sweet afternoon.

There were so many things one wanted to ask her. The answers were gone. The small cemetery that lay in the road near the Daros' was where they wanted her to lie. She may have even spoken about it at night when she'd been drinking, but it could not be arranged. Nedra herself might have managed it, but Franca tried in vain. There were very few plots, they told her, there was a board of trustees that decided such things; did the family live in town? The more difficult it became to gain entry, the more it became the only course. They wanted her to be apart from the ordinary dead. They did not want equality; she had never believed in it, not even for a moment.

Eve stood near them. Beneath the sleeves of her coat the bones of her wrists showed, they made her seem gaunt. Her lean fingers and long hands were like a woman's on a foreclosed farm. The coat was cloth, the hat dark straw. As always, there was something thrillingly vulgar about her. She was the kind of woman who could say calmly, "What do you really know about it?" and in her face one could see that, yes, compared to her, one knew nothing. She stood impassively. As the casket was lowered, she suddenly seemed to cough, to bend her head as if choking. Her face was wet with tears.

"Your children are beautiful, Danny," she said when it was over. She was introduced to them. She took a ring from her finger and the bracelet from her wrist and held them out. "Here. I didn't give you anything when you were christened. But you probably weren't christened, were you?"

"No," Danny answered.

"It doesn't matter. You should have something. It's a very nice ring," she said to the larger child. "You won't lose it, will you? At one time I'd have given anything in the world for that ring."

304

Artis, who was the younger, had dropped the bracelet. Danny picked it up. "Hold it tightly," she instructed.

"It's antique gold," Eve said.

There was a brief reception at Catherine Daro's. They said goodbye to everyone, they accepted the murmured regrets, they lingered and started back to the city finally in a hired car. The little girls were sleeping. The sun seemed very warm. At first there was nothing to say. They drove through the vacant countryside in silence, the last, unnatural heat of the year drifting from arm to lap.

"There's the store that's shaped like a duck," Franca said. "Remember?"

They saw it ahead where the road curved, the round, somewhat primitive shape, a door in its breast. A relic of childhood love, how often they had passed it at dusk with light spilling from the door.

"Papa hated it," Danny said.

"Remember?"

"It was because we loved it so much. We wanted to live in a house shaped like an enormous chicken. I was going to have a room in the beak. All right, he said. But covered with real feathers, we insisted. And then we'd begin to cry. We'd howl and hear each other and then howl even louder."

Franca nodded. "Why aren't we doing it now?" she murmured.

"Because it isn't pretending."

"No."

Eve sat silent, as if by herself, the tears rolling down her flat cheeks.

The car, which had tinted windows, fled along the highways, the bare, unplanted earth on either side, the fruit stalls with their hand-painted signs, the plain homes. An hour and it was into the thickness of buildings, still in hot afternoon, apartments, stores, speeding over trash-strewn roads into the center of life, into the swarm.

11

IT WAS A SPRING WHEN VIRI RE-
turned. He drove up from New York on a warm day. He had
come alone. The still, silent air, the light, filled him with a kind
of dread, the fear of seeing again things too powerful for him.
He stopped at a place on the cliffs above the river and stood
looking out. The height made him strangely dizzy. He glanced
down. Hundreds of feet below lay glacial rubble at the foot of
the vertical walls. The great, soiled river gleamed in the sun.
On the far shore, the endless houses; he could almost smell
their still rooms, the warmth of cooking in them, of bedclothes,
rugs. The radios were playing softly, the dogs lay in squares of
sun. He had severed himself from all this, he looked at it with
a kind of indifference, even hatred. Why should he be so stung
by what he had rejected? Why should he offer it even disdain?

He looked down once more, his thoughts spilling slowly. The
idea of falling was terrible to him, yet at that moment it seemed
that everything that had gone before, all of his life, was no
larger somehow than the time it would take to pass through the
air.

There were only two other cars parked, both empty, as he
left. He could not see where their occupants had gone. He was
afraid of meeting someone, even of being smiled at by a
stranger. The rubbish cans were empty, the refreshment stand
closed.

Everything unchanged seemed terrible to him, a gas station
with its wooden buildings, the very land. His mind grew numb.
He tried not to think of things, not to see them. Everything
was a confirmation of days that had continued, of requited life.
His own was cast into vagrancy, despair.

306

He walked in the greening woods beyond his house. He could see it briefly through the trees, silent, strange. The leaves about him were pale and sun-filled. Fallen vines tugged at his feet.

He was wearing a gray suit bought in Rome. He walked slowly. The soles of his shoes grew dark with moisture. The trees were huge and without lower branches. They had died and fallen while the crown sought the light. Damp, buried, they broke beneath his feet. He saw the faded flag of a surveyor's stake; further on, forgotten, a children's fort. Nearby was a hammer, rusted, its handle eaten by worms. Every step he took bristled with the sound of twigs and branches, the debris of years. He tried the hammer, the handle snapped. In the silence birds were calling. There were tiny flies in the air. Above, in the far sunlight, the roar of airliners bound for Europe.

The fort had fallen, the children were gone. They had hidden in these woods, had lain among the small wild flowers. Hadji had rolled in the snow, bathing in it, squirming on his back and pausing, fragrant beast, eyes dark as coffee, smiling mouth. Those afternoons that would never vanish, all ended. He, resettled. His daughters, gone.

An old man in the woods, his thoughts flashed forward as quickly as they had gone back. He walked with slow, careful steps, his gaze to the ground. He saw something then, domed and wondrous. He stopped in disbelief. How it had escaped the cars, the keen eyes of children, of dogs, he could not understand, but somehow it had. It was the tortoise. It had not seen him, he watched it going its way, rustling the leaves as it walked. He bent and picked it up. The reptilian face, impassive, wise, acknowledged nothing; the pale eye, clear as a bead, seemed anxious to look away. The powerful legs were curving their strokes at his fingers, but in vain. Finally it withdrew into its shell on which, faint as weathered writing on a board, the initials were scratched. He could barely make them out. He wet

307

a finger and rubbed; miraculously they became plain. He put the tortoise down, he was reluctant to. He watched it for a while. It did not move.

It seemed the woods were breathing, that they had recognized him, made him their own. He sensed the change. He was moved as if deeply grateful. The blood sprang within him, rushed from his head.

He walks toward the river, placing his feet carefully. His suit is too warm and tight. He reaches the water's edge. There is the dock, unused now, with its flaking paint and rotten boards, its underpilings drenched in green. Here at the great, dark river, here on the bank.

It happens in an instant. It is all one long day, one endless afternoon, friends leave, we stand on the shore.

Yes, he thought, I am ready, I have always been ready, I am ready at last.

ABOUT THE AUTHOR

JAMES SALTER was born in New York,
and now lives in Aspen, Colorado,
with his wife and four children.
He has written three previous novels,
including *A Sport and a Pastime*,
as well as several plays.